FICTION   Jedren, Susan.
JEDREN
           Let 'em eat cake.

WITHDRAWN

DATE			

LET 'EM
EAT CAKE

LET 'EM EAT CAKE

A NOVEL

SUSAN JEDREN

PANTHEON BOOKS
NEW YORK

Grateful acknowledgment is made to the following for permission to reprint previously published material: Harcourt Brace & Company and Faber and Faber Limited: Excerpt from "The Hollow Men" from *Collected Poems 1909–1962* by T.S. Eliot, copyright © 1936 by Harcourt Brace & Company, copyright © 1963, 1964 by T.S. Eliot. Rights outside the U.S. administered by Faber and Faber Limited, London. Reprinted by permission of Harcourt Brace & Company and Faber and Faber, Ltd. · *Harry Wayne Casey:* Excerpt from "(Shake, shake, shake) Shake Your Booty" by Harry Casey and Richard Finch. Reprinted by permission of Harry Wayne Casey. · *Music Sales Corporation:* Excerpt from "The Name Game" by Lincoln Chase and Shirley Elliston, copyright © 1964 (renewed) by Embassy Music Corporation (EMI) and Al Gallico Music, c/o EMI Music Publishing. International copyright secured. All rights reserved. Reprinted by permission of Music Sales Corporation. · *Shapiro, Bernstein & Co., Inc.:* Excerpt from "Too Fat Polka (She's Too Fat For Me)" by Ross MacLean and Arthur Richardson, copyright © 1947 by Shapiro, Bernstein & Co., Inc., New York, NY. Copyright renewed. All rights reserved. International copyright secured. Reprinted by permission of Shapiro, Bernstein & Co., Inc.

Library of Congress Cataloging-in-Publication Data

Jedren, Susan.
    Let 'em eat cake : a novel / Susan Jedren.
      p. cm.
    ISBN 0-679-43361-9
    1. Women truck drivers—New York (N.Y.)—Fiction.
2. City and town life—New York (N.Y.)—Fiction. 3. Single mothers—New York (N.Y.)—Fiction. I. Title.
PS3560.E3L48 1994
813'.54—dc20   94-4033
                                              CIP

Book design by M. Kristen Bearse

Manufactured in the United States of America

First Edition
9 8 7 6 5 4 3 2 1

Acknowledgments

THERE'S FIVE PEOPLE I would like to dedicate this book to and more that I would like to mention. I worked nine to five and wrote this book nights and weekends with the help of a lot of people. Some were there for me as friends. Others even helped me on my job when I most needed it.

Last year when I was writing this book, Aline Wolff, a best friend and remarkable editor, worked closely with me day and night. Her ideas, suggestions, and changes made each chapter brighter, funnier, more real. And her daughter Kate devotedly put up with both of us.

My agent Eric Simonoff laughed when I busted into his world with my fists flying and begged him to look at my book. And he stayed at my side throughout, giving me the confidence and hope I needed to reach the end.

My sons Aram and Noah, Nick and Joey as you know them, two of the nicest people I know and love, let me back in their lives again with all their hearts.

This was no small thing for me, going after my dream of a lifetime. And these people were there for me:

Erroll McDonald, my editor and friend. Zoe Graves and Joan Abelove, who've stood by me for years. Joanie's husband, Steven Hoffman, and my godson, Andy Hoffman. My boyfriend Tomas who was loving and a pain in the ass all in one. Lynn Nesbit and Mort Janklow, both wonderful to me at every turn.

I would also like to include: Edith Klemm; Anne Sikora; Marge Anderson; Susan Norton; Judy Costa; Clara Campos; my brother Jerry; my nephews Nick, Danny, and Sam; my nieces Julie, Amy, and Juniper; Danielle Kim; Linda Marks; Andrea Zitman; Carmela Inghilterra; Marita Finsie; Marion Blanchard; Louis Musano; Alberta Middleton; Miguel Ortiz; Rose Katz Ortiz; Fred Merritt; Joe Garamella; MaryJo Schnatter; Anne Canadeo; Gary Barnett; Rob Miller; Keith Becker; Lisa and Luke Harrison; Hope White; Carol Tucker, Darlene Mackey, Sal Burdi; Patrick Rigney; Miriam Pabon; Barbara Silverman; Phil Marraffini; Mike Henry; Donna Budall; Jackie Adamkiewicz; Jill Pincus; Danny Mack; Allison Postman; and Tanya Le Bras.

Contents

Author's Note

LET 'EM EAT CAKE

Anna and Rudy

"WHEN THE HEAT HITS the city, it's the worst place to be," Joanie, who was the cashier and my best friend at the depot, said. We both worked for HomeMade Cakes out of the old Knickerbocker Avenue depot in Brooklyn. "It must be over a hundred degrees out there," she added. "That makes three days in a row, or is it four?"

Over one hundred degrees three days in a row meant it was at least a hundred and twenty in the trucks. And my truck didn't even have a fan. Times like these, even though us drivers worked twice as hard, our salaries went down, because money was deducted from our paycheck for the heavy returns. When it's this hot, people stop eating snack cake and it just sits there on the store shelves growing old. And then, just when we should be slashing our orders, HomeMade Cakes decides to do a big promotion and runs a special on pies for the next two weeks. So every morning we drive out to our routes carrying hundreds of extra pies.

"Nothing worse than HomeMade pies warming up in those old trucks in the heat of summer," Mario the Mole said as he loaded at least ten extra trays of pies off the racks and onto the back of his truck. "The crusts get softer and mushier as the day wears on," he warned. "By noon those pies are nothing but dripping cherries, apples, and blueberries that no customer would ever buy. If we had any sense we'd save ourselves a lot

of work by smashing half those pies and getting Home-
Made where it hurts, in their pockets.''

On the fourth day of the pie special, the temperature
rose to a hundred and five degrees and Mario the Mole
passed out at the wheel, driving straight into the back wall
of the BestMart parking lot. And I was so nauseous that
I bought ice wherever I could and put it under my tongue
to keep me from throwing up. Days like this, most drivers
wore shorts even though it was against the rules. But being
a woman, I could never get away with shorts. So I wore
the usual HomeMade summer uniform, which wasn't
much lighter than the winter one. A black short-sleeved
shirt and long pants, both made of polyester that was way
too thick to let any air through. The shirt and pants stuck
to me like an extra skin. I had what looked like a diaper
rash across my thighs and ass and along my shoulders to my
breasts.

Midday, the sun was blazing and I was feeling too sick
to finish the route. I decided to just do Rudy's, an Italian
deli at Avenue K and Flatbush, and skip my other two
stops. I always put off doing Rudy's until last, but I
couldn't miss him all together. He was the kind of storekeeper that'd report me to Jed, my depot manager, for the
least little thing, and get a kick out of doing it. I'd already
been fired and rehired twice this year and didn't need any
more trouble. Anyway, even though he was a tough customer, Rudy was like a goomba to me, which is why I
didn't take to heart things that would make me mad in
another store owner. He even looked like family, a big
bear of a man, like my Uncle Carmine, with the same full
head of wooly brown curls.

Avenue K and Flatbush was in a nice section of Brooklyn, and I liked driving the fifteen blocks to Rudy's, past

the pretty houses, clean and nicely painted with flowers, and hedges in all the front yards. I pulled up in front of Rudy's spotless, polished delicatessen thinking that at least the day was almost over and I'd soon be out of the heat. I hurried in and said hello without looking around and headed straight for the glass case where the HomeMade Cakes were kept. As I rested the tray on the counter, I caught a glimpse of Rudy bent over a sink in the back, scrubbing his hands with a small wooden brush. He stood up, seeming not to have heard me come in and examined himself in the mirror over the sink, adjusting his white smock and patting down the mass of hair above his ears. I had to turn away when he stuck his finger in his ear, held it out, and then wiped it on his smock. There were two squashed pies and a box of coffee cake was facing backwards, so I picked up the pies and straightened the shelf up before I headed out.

"My, my, look who's here. Hey, paesana!" Rudy called from the back and I glanced up as he grabbed a pickle out of a huge jar and stuffed it into his soft, loose lips, heading toward me. The best thing about Rudy's deli was the smell, and I stood there smelling the lasagna, roasted peppers, creamy polenta, things you never smelled in other delis, while I waited.

"Hi there," I said and removed two Chocos with slightly torn wrappers. "Two pies and two Chocos going out." I held them up as I headed for the door.

"What? Wait a second, signorina, come back. I didn't see what you got there." I held them up higher but kept walking as I repeated what I was taking out. But he moved quickly and was standing in front of me before I reached the door, his pale brown eyes narrowing.

"Didn't you hear me, dear?" He looked hard at me

and nodded for me to come back in. "I said I want to see what you got there."

I walked over to the counter and he grabbed my wrist and reached for the Chocos. "Now what is wrong with these?" he asked. He took the Chocos from me, smiling by lifting only one side of his mouth, and held them up to the light. He moved his face close to mine so that his cheek lightly touched my cheek. For just a moment I remembered when I was a little girl, my father holding tight to my wrist as he pressed his dripping, drunken face against my cheek. "My kiss, don't you have a kiss for Daddy?"

"Are they old?" Rudy wanted to know. "Did you leave old Chocos out for my customers the last time you came in?" He dropped my wrist as he turned the Chocos over to read the date.

"No, the packages are ripped. I was going to bring in new ones." I leaned over to take the Chocos but he moved them out of my reach.

"How did they get ripped. Do you think one of these teenage hoodlums, or—"

"I don't know." I didn't want him to go on and on like he always did about the teenagers, or about blacks and Jews taking over the neighborhood. "I'm in a hurry today," I said, and I headed for the door saying I'd pick up the two Chocos when I returned.

"You're always in a hurry. When will you have a little time to stay and chat with old Rudy?" he called after me, following me out to the street. "Don't you like bachelors, huh, a nice friendly man like me? A country-man?" As hot as it was on my truck, I slid the door closed tight in case he tried to follow me.

The deli's usual order was a coffee cake and three boxes of doughnuts since its customers were mostly old people. But I always added snack cake for the school kids. Today I only gave him a box of doughnuts and a few pies since he had plenty of cake left on the shelf. While I figured out his bill, I saw a tall, blond, well-dressed lady enter the store and I waited a few moments before I followed her in.

Rudy was in front of the counter talking to the blond woman, spraying polish on a paper towel and shining up the chrome trim of the glass case as they talked. They were both smiling and Rudy seemed to be charming her the way he sometimes did with me when he was in a good mood. Those times he'd describe all the small towns that he'd visited on his trips to Italy every summer and what the weather was like and the roads he drove along.

Rudy looked up and introduced me to the blond woman as I came in. "Mrs. Borson, you've met our HomeMade girl, haven't you?"

"Yes, I've seen her before." The blond lady barely moved her head as she spoke.

"Hello," I nodded to her and held the door of the case as I reached for the doughnuts in my tray, lining the boxes up on their sides so the doughnuts faced out.

"Hard little worker, isn't she?" Rudy said to the blond lady. "Have you ever seen her delivering to the big supermarket down the street? She carries more than the men do. The last driver I had found the work too hard. Wore a brace for ten years and then quit. Our own little superwoman, isn't that right, Miss HomeMade?" And he gave me that half-smile again.

I shrugged.

Rudy came over to where I was working and took hold of my bare arm, feeling for the muscle. "She doesn't look strong, does she?" The blond lady studied me as he waved his hand up and down the length of my body.

"You'd swear she was a skinny little thing, no?" The woman agreed with her eyes, though the rest of her face was still. "It's the men's clothes she wears. They hide everything. But I'm sure she's strong. Has to be to do the job. There's no fooling me, I can tell there's a strong little body in there."

I handed him the bill.

"Wait a second," he hissed, "don't you see I'm still waiting on Mrs. Borson?"

So I moved away and leaned against the refrigerator case with the juice and milk, trying to feel the cool against my back while I added up the bill again to make sure it was right, hoping Rudy wouldn't start his stories about Italy and that the woman would finish shopping and leave.

"Actually, Rudy, I think I should take this milk home to Alex before it gets warm." Mrs. Borson reached carefully for her bag so as not to break her red fingernails, which were nearly an inch longer than her fingers. Rudy put down the paper towels, took her hand in both of his, and walked her to the door.

"Goodbye, dear," she called to me over her shoulder.

"It's good to see you again, Mrs. Borson," Rudy said as he opened the door. "Go right home to your nice cool house, my dear. And don't be such a stranger. Come again soon, and next time bring Alex. Tell him Rudy was asking for him. That I said he was a good little Schnauzer, and there's a treat waiting for him when he gets better. And I have some nice stories about Milano for you."

"We'll stop by sometime next week, Rudy, if the heat lifts. Alex isn't fond of the heat."

Rudy closed the door slowly and leaned against it, saying nothing until he seemed to remember me and held out his hand. "All right, missy, let me pay you so you can get out of here." I handed him the bill again. He looked it over, his head and lips moving as he went over the figures.

"Looks all right to me, young lady." He walked behind the counter, opened the drawer of the register, and slowly counted out the money, licking his fingers as he separated the bills. Instead of passing the money over the counter, he came back around to the front and stood smiling, holding the money out, flicking through the bills with his fingernail. As I reached for the money, he took his hand and closed it around mine, bringing it down to his crotch, forcing my fingers around his penis, which was pushing against the cloth of his pants, five- and ten-dollar bills slipping out and scattering across the floor.

"Oh no," I whispered and pulled on my hand but he held it tight, squeezing my fingers together so they hurt. My body shook and a sour taste filled my mouth. I started to gag.

"Like it, huh?" he asked and rubbed my hand up and down against the front of his pants. It was warm and wet there with sweat, mushy like the pies. My teeth bit into a cut on my lip as I tried again to pull my hand away but his fingers dug in even harder, so that my fingers felt sore where he held them. I could feel his penis, puffy like his body, getting bigger and bigger and I was sure he never washed there, that it smelled foul and dirty.

I drew back my left hand and swung, but he was fast and he grabbed that hand too, bringing it down to the other one. "Mmmm, nice. Feels nice, doesn't it?" he asked.

"Lousy son of a bitch," I said, trying to wrench my hand away, "ugly lousy son of a bitch."

I pulled hard, but as fat and sloppy as he was, he was

as strong as an ox. He held my fingers there, squeezing them one last time until it sounded like something cracked, then threw my hands away laughing. "Stupid girl," he said and stood there watching with a big smile on his face, his eyes narrowed to little slits.

All my life I'd heard about how much it hurts to hit a man in the balls but I'd never done it. My right hand was still sore so I grabbed a bottle of seltzer from the case with my left and swung it from below, straight up, right between his legs as hard as I could, whack. He moved and the blow landed on his thigh. I pulled back my arm and hit him again, aiming for where he had held my hand against his warm, puffy bulge. I felt the bottle thud against the cloth of his pants and he let out a long loud kind of howl and collapsed, holding his hand to his crotch. I wouldn't look at his face as I whacked him one last time across the shins. "I'm no kid," I said quietly. "I don't take that kind of shit."

I grabbed another bottle and threw it at the glass case hearing the sound of breaking glass as I ran to the door. My hands were sweaty, so the door handle slipped out of my hand. I got it open and glanced back to see Rudy slumped down on the floor, his head on his chest, hands between his legs. I kept going and jumped into my truck. It was about ten blocks before I stopped on a deserted street and threw up everything that was in my stomach.

I pulled into my spot in the depot but didn't unpack the truck except for the pies. I took out all those pies, tray after tray of blueberry, apple, and lemon, all the flavors, and arranged them in rows along the ground. There were over two hundred pies spread out there. I lined them up right outside my truck. It looked like one long carpet of pies. As usual, Ramon, the packer, had his radio playing Latin music as he worked. I went over and asked him to turn up the volume until the music was blasting through the garage. I clapped my hands and began to move my feet to the beat.

"Hey, Anna, what's up?" Jimmy, one of the other HomeMade drivers, called out as he headed into the office. "You putting on a show or something? You wanna teach me how to cha-cha-cha?"

I raised my hands over my head and started to sway and move my feet to the beat. Then I danced over to the pies, carefully stepping onto the trays, one after the other. "Olé!" I yelled as I stamped and twirled and danced on every one of the pies, jumping from tray to tray until the strawberry, blueberry, and lemon pies all blended into one. I could feel them being squashed flat under my feet, turning into one mushy, oozing, gooey mass, sticking tight to the bottom of my shoes. Somebody, probably Jimmy, called from the office, "Come, everybody look, Anna's gone crazy. She's fucking dancing on the pies." But I kept on dancing and never looked up. A hand reached out to grab me but then quickly disappeared as Jed, our depot manager, drove in on one of the last trucks. Jed was covering Mario the Mole's route while Mario was in the hospital. He pulled his truck up right next to mine, got out, and fired me on the spot.

Pudgy, Nick, and Joey

"YOU CAN NEVER be too paranoid," a police-man said to me the year before I got the job with Home-Made Cakes. It was right after me and Tom split up, when Tom was treating me like a tramp, never setting foot in our apartment, as if I was dirty, even though it was him that had been sleeping around all those years. When he first left, everything felt hard and I could barely get out of bed in the morning. But after a few months, I started to put myself together again. Instead of the big T-shirts and baggy sweats that I wore as a park mother, I went back to skimpy tops and tight jeans and skirts. I began to walk like I used to walk years ago, like I was something worth looking at. I was not a nobody just because I wasn't what Tom wanted.

So it was me and the kids living on what I earned from two part-time jobs as a teacher's helper and a HoJo's waitress—eighteen thousand a year. We paid very little rent in one of those old rent-controlled buildings in Washington Heights just a few blocks from the George Washington Bridge. And child care cost next to nothing, since Joey was in a city day care and Nick was already in first grade. Two evenings a week and sometimes on the weekend, my next-door neighbor, Mrs. Mahoney, or her older son, Sean, took the boys, but they hardly charged me anything at all. Even so, we barely made it from paycheck to paycheck.

Early one morning, I realized we had no food in the house, not even enough for breakfast. I got the kids dressed and took them shopping at the Red Apple on Broadway, where I bought milk, cold cereal, and fruit. On the way back, when we passed the entrance to the subway, some guy followed us home. I never noticed him. Maybe because I was getting mad at Nick, my older boy, who kept complaining about how hungry he was. I was trying not to slap out at him like I wanted to. And Joey, the little one, started saying his stomach was growling too. In my mind, I was yelling at their dad, cursing him and telling him, "Tom, these are your damn kids too. I birthed them but you helped make them. You owe them something!" I tried not to, but sometimes I'd hit the kids to get back at Tom.

When I unlocked the front door of our building, the guy stuck a knife to my neck and asked for money. I had two dollars left, which I would've given him, but I couldn't think straight. All I could think of was for him not to hurt the kids. I moved Nick and Joey in front of me so I was in the middle, between them and the guy with the knife. "Somebody help us," I screamed silently.

Joey started to cry and I covered his mouth with my hand. He must've understood because he stopped real fast. "Please," I cried inside, "they're little and they don't understand a person hurting someone with a knife." I wanted to beg the guy to not hurt the kids, to do anything to me but let Nick and Joey go. I didn't say anything. I didn't even mention them, thinking that maybe he'd keep thinking about the money and not notice them at all. I pushed Nick and Joey forward, shoved them through the door, hoping they'd know to run up the stairs. But they just stood by the door and watched me.

Just then, an old man came into the building pulling a small dog on a leash. The old man and the dog looked familiar, I think they lived on the first floor in the back. But the old man was stooped over and didn't look like he could help. So I said nothing and moved aside to let him pass. The robber moved the knife farther down so the old man wouldn't see it. "Hurry," the guy hissed in my ear, "the money." He had sliced my arm with the knife to show he was serious. I couldn't believe the old man didn't see the blood dripping down my arm. As the old man opened the door wide, I threw the two dollars at the robber, picked Joey up, and grabbed Nick's arm. "Run," I screamed at the old man and my kids. "Keep running and don't look back!"

"Please God please God please God," I kept repeating as we ran up the back stairs. I could hear the dog barking the whole time we were climbing. We lived six flights up. By the second flight, Nick was moving too slow, so I picked him up and carried him. Halfway up, I felt a sharp pain in the back of my right leg, but I never stopped. I knew when I got to our door that the guy hadn't followed us. He would have caught us long before if he had.

When the police showed up, that's when I was told I could never be too paranoid. The cops spent maybe ten minutes asking questions and taking notes, but I knew nothing would come of it. They didn't even check the streets or the subway station. They said the guy would be long gone by now.

I tried to make the rest of the day seem like any other day. I was too afraid to take Nick and Joey out, so we stayed inside and played with clay and trains, whatever I could remember that we usually did. My mind was fuzzy. I put on a long-sleeved blouse to hide the cut. I must have still been worried, though, because it was four o'clock before Nick said to me that I hadn't given them lunch. So we had lunch and dinner in one meal and I explained that that's what they did in other countries, ate only two meals a day. But to add to everything else, while I was cooking dinner, Joey got a splinter in his finger. He stood there screaming, "I can't be brave, I can't be brave," while I got it out with a needle and Nicky sat next to us covering his ears with his hands. I gave Joey a few uncooked tortellini, which was one of his favorite snacks, to calm him down. There were no bedtime stories that night and when I was sure they were asleep, I lay down and covered my face with a pillow so they wouldn't hear me sobbing. I couldn't think of anyone to call, to tell how bad I felt.

Right before Tom moved out, it was clear that everyone in the neighborhood—Mrs. Mahoney, Adeline, Sean, Pudgy, and Lily—thought we were a nice, young, close-knit family. Tom still wore his wedding band, I stayed home to clean house and watch the kids, and Nick and Joey were handsome, well-behaved boys. Anyone would've said that we'd make it through our twenty-fifth wedding anniversary for sure. It was easy for them to think that. I believed it myself. I had to, in order to have things go on as usual, because I didn't know where else to go with my life.

But then things changed between Tom and me, not a little but a lot. And it was like, out of nowhere, all the tension, the coldness, the straight-out anger that had been inside, blew up in our faces. I started having war dreams, like when I was little, with machine guns, and hand grenades, and soldiers running. I woke myself out of the dreams feeling like I was a kid again, trapped in my mother's house, my body tired and achy from the fighting.

It was Saturday morning and I hadn't spoken to Tom for almost two days, not since late Thursday when Tom's brother, Peter, came over to talk about his wife, Connie. I was surprised that Tom was home that night. He usually stayed in the library until eleven or twelve o'clock. But when I came out to the kitchen after I had put the boys to sleep, there he was, making a chicken sandwich from the night's leftovers. Then Peter showed up, saying he needed to talk and we all went into the living room. Peter sat at the edge of the seat in the comfortable chair and I thought how different he was from Tom. Though Peter worked for the Sanitation Department, he looked like a college professor, tall and thin with horn-rimmed glasses and long, delicate fingers. He never finished high school but he always carried some kind of book in his hand, a paperback, a date book, an address book. He even had a birthday book, where he wrote down birthdays he wanted to remember. Tom was a head shorter than Peter, a flashy dresser, and looked like a hairstylist in a fancy salon. And even though Tom was in school all the years I knew him, I'd never see him reading a book.

Tom was sitting next to me on the couch, relaxing against the back cushions while I only half-listened as I browsed through the paper wondering what I wanted to do for my birthday, which was only a few weeks away.

Peter leaned forward in the comfortable chair and began by saying, "Tom, this is embarrassing for me," his voice flat and so low you could barely hear him. "But I've been wanting to tell someone and I couldn't think who to tell. I finally decided the best one to tell is my brother."

He was almost stuttering. "It's terribly awkward. I mean, I'm not sure how to say it. It's about Connie."

He was quiet for a minute, but then said quickly, "Connie confessed last week that she's sleeping with her boss. It's been going on for some time. As soon as I find a place of my own, I'm moving out." Peter sat back and closed his eyes while he caught his breath.

Tom pulled his fingers, one by one, and the sound of his knuckles cracking was the only noise in the room. Then he began speaking slowly and carefully. "Peter, I'm certainly surprised, shocked I guess. I didn't think Connie was that type of woman." He got up and stood by Peter's chair, resting his hand on Peter's shoulder. "I'm sorry to hear it, for your sake, but if that's the way she is, I guess it's better not to have to live with it." He patted Peter's shoulder two or three times and then said, "But, you know, Peter, my life with Anna has been going downhill too. The last few months have been really bad, and I'm seriously thinking about leaving her and the kids."

I thought I couldn't be hearing right. This was the first time he ever said he wasn't happy with our marriage, and I couldn't believe he was saying it to his brother and not to me. I didn't get it. We hadn't even been arguing or fighting or anything. We never did. Whenever he was home, we were a regular family. I looked from Tom to Peter but it was as if neither of them knew I was in the room. Tom wasn't smiling, so I knew it wasn't a joke. I got up and left without a sound. I spent Friday with the kids as if nothing had happened.

That Saturday morning it took me only a few minutes to scramble some eggs and put on an English muffin and a few strips of bacon. While the bacon was cooking, I washed up and brushed my hair. I needed makeup, I thought. It would make me look more awake. Twice I poked myself in the eye with the eyeliner, rubbed it off, and started again. The smell of burnt bacon drifted back.

"Joey, Nicky, breakfast's ready. Now!"

"We were right in the middle of a game," Nick said as he took his seat at the table, Joey trailing behind, his favorite Matchbox fire truck in his mouth.

"It's stopped raining. We're going out to the park." I stood by the window at the sink, scrubbing the burnt pan. "Look outside," I pointed with my sponge, "the first sunny day in almost a week."

"But we were in the middle of a game," Nick repeated. "We need to finish."

"Nick wins everything," Joey said. Joey was almost four, two years younger than Nick, and he still pronounced his *r*'s like *w*'s, like Elmer Fudd, so it sounded like "Nick wins evweething."

"You can finish the game when we get back." I unplugged the toaster and opened the bottom to shake the crumbs into the sink. Then I wiped the toaster down with a sponge, cleaned the counter, and put water up for coffee. The boys were mashing at their eggs with a fork and neither of them had tasted the bacon. Only the English muffins had bites taken off the sides.

"Hey, guys," I said, "what's up? You can do better than that. Finish your breakfast."

"I'm done," Nick got up.

"Me too," Joey stood next to him.

"C'mon, fellas, you didn't touch the eggs." I went over to the table and looked from one to the other, pointing to their plates. "Each of you take two more bites."

"We did," Nick said, "it was great. You make great bacon and eggs."

"But you love bacon and you didn't finish it."

"We're not hungry."

"Not hungry? Give me a break! You've been up for hours, you must be starving. Sit down, both of you!" They sat back down. I put Ajax on the sponge, climbed up on a stool, and starting rubbing the rust stains off the top of the refrigerator. I tried not to look their way. After a few minutes I glanced over. Nick was sitting perfectly still and Joey was wiggling on his seat. Neither of them were eating.

"Daddy doesn't eat burnt bacon," Nick said softly.

"Who gives a shit what Daddy eats," I screamed and threw the sponge at Nick and missed. "Your daddy looks through the garbage every day to see what else I burnt, and that means your daddy's a pig, nothing else." The sponge had hit the wall and bounced off into Joey's eggs. "I don't care what you eat, do you hear me?" I jumped from the stool and grabbed first Nick's and then Joey's arm, pulling them toward the hall. "Get out," I said, "it wasn't burnt that bad. You could've eaten some of it." Nick stood there with his eyes closed and Joey started to cry. "Get dressed, both of you. I want to get out of here before Daddy wakes up."

While I was cleaning their plates, I stopped being mad. I went back to their room and found Joey and Nick facing each other on the floor playing cards. Joey, as usual, was holding his cards upside down, "I'm sorry," I said softly. "You have lots of time to finish your game while I clean up, okay?"

"Okay."

It was 7:30 A.M., still too chilly to go without sweat-shirts, but sunny enough for a nice morning in the park.

We were the only ones at the swings, in the whole park actually, except for the park attendant. While Joey was figuring out how to pump his legs, he asked me to read the graffiti on the wall that ran the length of the park, from Fort Washington Avenue to the side that faced the river. Some of it I skipped, like who should suck what and the name "Jew Park." Tom had said the park got that name from the Puerto Ricans and Dominicans who moved into the neighborhood and named it for the old Jews who lined the park benches. He swore the park had a real name too but could never remember it. A lot of the graffiti I made up, like "Dinosaurs Live Here" and "Bobo Eats Worms." Nick asked if I remembered the time Joey ate worms from Tom's tackle box and I told him that I tried not to, remembering that he'd finished the whole can.

We walked from the playground, past the old people's benches, to the grassy part by the handball courts. On the way, Nick tried to teach Joey how to spit.

"Move your mouth in and out until you get it all together." Nick showed him how and then watched as Joey simply leaned over and let it roll out of his mouth and down his chest. Nick was a head taller than Joey and had blond hair and big blue eyes. Joey was olive-skinned, with brown eyes and dark brown hair topped by a crown of red from the sun. Neither of them looked like me or Tom, but something about the shape of their faces and their smiles made you know they were brothers.

"Don't let it fall, shoot it," Nick coached, wiping Joey's face with his sleeve. Joey squinted hard as Nick demonstrated by shooting a wad onto his sneakers. "See?" Nick said. By the time we reached the handball courts, Joey's round face and Yogi Bear sweatshirt were wet and bubbly, the ties of the hood sopping wet.

"Cut it out," I finally said.

"Why? What's wrong with Joey learning how to spit?"

"It's not a great idea."

"But it doesn't hurt anyone."

"Hurt? I didn't say hurt, I just said stop it. Do you like walking on a sidewalk covered with spit?" I asked. "Well, I don't. Look, it's all over him. Teach him something else."

My fingers curled around a ball at the bottom of my bag and I threw it with all my might against the handball court. It hit the wall, then rolled to a stop in the dirt by the bushes. "Man running to first and one on second!" I yelled. "Nick, Joey, what are you waiting for? The man is running toward third."

Nicky was fast, picking it up as he ran to the wall, calling over his shoulder to Joey, "Out! I'm up first." But Joey had flopped down in the dirt and was taking aim at an overflowing garbage can with one of the rocks that he carried in his rock bag. "Come on, get up." Nick insisted, pulling Joey to his feet. "It's almost your turn, this is a game."

"This is a game," Joey repeated and ran alongside Nick as Nick threw the ball at the wall yelling, "Go, blue team, go!" even though neither of them was wearing blue.

"I'm going to the other side to practice some handball," I told them.

I took another ball from my bag and squeezed through the opening between the wall and the fence to the other court. I hadn't played handball since before Joey was born and had only started again about a month ago. Next to chess and boxing, my father loved handball and taught me all three with the same fierceness. He began my training when I was only a little older than Joey. "Keep moving! Up on your toes! That's it, left foot forward, serve. Get in there! What are you waiting for?" he'd yell. "Now kill it, you idiot. Don't slap at it, kill it!" By the time I was ten, I'd played in every tournament in the city. "Remember," my father would say before the game, "aim for the corner or right at their face. They'll never return it."

"Hi, Anna, hi," a voice called down from the ramp overlooking the courts that led into the park. I couldn't see who it was, but it was a man's voice and I stopped playing, waiting to see if he'd come around to my side of the wall. A minute later I could hear his sneakers scraping on the pebbles as he headed toward my court.

"Hi, it's me, Pudgy," he said as he squeezed past the fence, smiling and reaching out to shake my hand. "You couldn't have forgotten me so soon."

Pudgy and I had been partners a few weeks ago and had beaten the guys we played against two games in a row. He had a nice way about him, soft-spoken and shy, almost gentle. He was thin but tall, slightly over six feet, and at first I thought he was a teenager, but the lines around his eyes made me realize he was more like twenty-four or -five. With drooping eyes on either side of a long nose that stopped at a reddish mustache which you could barely see, Pudgy wasn't good-looking. But he definitely wasn't bad-looking either.

We volleyed at first, hitting the ball lightly back and forth. Pudgy had a neat way of hitting, snapping his wrist and whipping the ball off his fingertips, but mostly he used his left hand. He moved easily, almost slowly, but he always got there before the ball did. Every once in a while I'd stop to check on Nick and Joey, who had started a game of skully on the other side, crawling around the court on their hands and knees as they shot bottle caps from one place to another.

Me and Pudgy started playing hard and were a good match, but I was still out of shape for one on one. I was glad when he finally said, "Enough! That's plenty for our first game of singles." He leaned back against the fence, sliding down until he was sitting in the dirt at the side of the court. From a ripped pocket in his dungaree jacket he pulled out a beer. "C'mon," he patted the ground next to him. My mouth was dry, so I slid down next to him and said yes even though I hated beer. He pried the bottle open on the fence, and I covered my face with my hands as the beer sprayed over both of us.

"How'd you get the name Pudgy," I asked, passing the bottle back to him and taking off my glasses to dry them on my T-shirt, "since you're obviously not?"

"I was fat when I was little and by the time I thinned out, the name stuck. Besides which, my real name is Erasmus Kasourakas."

If he were dark instead of fair, it would've been easier to tell that he was Greek, but even when I knew him better, his red hair and blue eyes always threw me off.

Nick and Joey came over from the other court and squeezed in next to Pudgy, who remembered their names from the last time he met them. After a few more sips of beer, Pudgy stood up and scouted through the trash lying around the court, rounding up six empty beer cans. He showed Joey and Nick how to stamp on the cans so they wrapped around the soles of their sneakers. The three of them banged and clanked around the court in their beer-can shoes until Joey's feet got caught on each other and he fell over, scraping his hands on some pebbles when he hit the ground. Pudgy swooped him in the air before Joey had a chance to cry. He wiped off Joey's hands, then lifted him onto his shoulders. "I'm thirsty," Joey called out to me.

"You're thirsty 'cause you've been spitting all day and you're dried out," I told him. "Okay, let's go home."

"Are you coming home with us?" Nick asked Pudgy as we walked up the ramp together.

"No, but I'll see you guys soon." Joey was still riding on Pudgy's shoulders.

I stood on my toes and softly smacked Joey's arm, "Cut it out," I said. He was practicing again and had formed a ball of spit that was about to roll onto Pudgy's head. Pudgy was smiling and bouncing along, singing, "Shake shake shake, shake shake shake, shake your bootie," as Nicky ran alongside. I joined in, singing "Shake your bootie," and started shaking and twisting my whole body, and Nicky laughed and started wiggling too.

We said goodbye, everybody shook hands, and we made plans to meet the following week in the park. But Nick got the flu that week, and Joey got sick just as Nick was getting better, so it was more than a month before I saw Pudgy again. And in between, so much happened.

Lily and El Jefe

WE GOT BACK from the park around 9:30 A.M., just as Tom was waking up. I could hear his grunting, grumbling noises coming from the bedroom and a few minutes later saw him padding groggily toward the bathroom, naked except for a towel wrapped around his waist. The bathroom door slammed, followed by the sound of the shower. His showers usually lasted half an hour, which gave me time to straighten up. Ever since the night that Peter came over, I'd been dreading seeing Tom again. All morning I was hoping he'd have left for the library by the time we got back from the park. As I cleaned, I thought about Pudgy. Joey had asked him if he fixed cars like his daddy and Pudgy had said no, he drove a truck for Home-Made Cakes and that next time he saw Nick and Joey he'd bring them some Chocos.

"Guess what?" Tom called cheerily from the bathroom as he was shaving. Nick and Joey were in their room building a sugar trap to catch ants and I was making beds and emptying trash. I'd been dumping the kids' trash into a big garbage bag when Tom's voice broke into my thoughts. I stood still and waited for him to go on, nervously ripping a hole in the bag and then watching litter from the guinea pig's cage scatter across the floor.

Tom came and stood in the doorway with his face half lathered, his head tipped up as he scraped away at the beard under his chin.

"I don't have time for guessing games," I said, bending to clean up the mess I made. "Lily's coming at eleven and I still have work to do."

"Relax a minute," Tom said, "I have something to tell you. C'mere." He put his arm around my shoulders and guided me to the bathroom. I waited while he lowered his face into the sink and splashed at the shaving cream that still remained.

"What?" I asked, picking up his wet towel from the floor and wiping at the little black specs that were scattered around the sink from his shaving. He grabbed my hand and held it.

"What?" I almost shouted again. I wished he would look in the mirror and clean out the lather that was still in his ears and nostrils.

"Well," he said turning to face me, his hands on his hips, "I'm starting my vacation today, right this minute. From now on, I'm going to be all yours. Yours and Nick and Joey's."

"Vacation from what?" I asked. "You took three weeks off in the spring to study for your finals."

"Not from work, from college, from getting my degree." Tom turned back to the mirror and examined himself closely, picking up the small scissors I used to cut Nick and Joey's nails and snipping at the long hairs coming out of his nostrils.

"For how long? For what?" I asked. For as long as I knew him, Tom had been going to college at night. He'd started out working as a mechanic ten years ago and was promoted to service manager in a car dealership. He put in his forty hours a week but never liked the job. His dream had always been to get a degree and become a mechanical engineer.

"I decided to take a few months off to be with you and the kids."

Did this mean he'd changed his mind and decided to stay? I was too afraid to ask. My left eye was twitching and I put my hand over it to get it to stop. "But why now?" I wanted to know. "You should finish school. Why would you stop at this point?" I tried to smile at him but ended up just turning up my lips. "Honestly, we're okay, we don't mind waiting a little longer."

"Actually, it wasn't my idea," he said. "My advisor suggested that I take a leave of absence."

"But it'll take even longer to get a degree and find the kind of job you want. It's a crazy idea." I could hear my voice rising, getting shriller. "Does he know how many years you've been working on this? Did you tell him that you don't have the rest of your life to do this, that you have kids?"

Tom rocked back and forth on his heels, smiling as if it all made perfect sense to him. I went on, "Why would you drop out six months before you're supposed to graduate? If you ask me, it's not just crazy, it's downright stupid." I grabbed the white bag from the trash can and stormed out of the bathroom.

His voice followed me down the long hall as I headed toward the kitchen. "They threw me out," he called after me and I stopped in my tracks. "I failed so many courses they kicked me out." I went back to where he was standing. He wasn't smiling and was actually shaking as he stumbled over his words, trying to explain. "I guess I didn't study enough. I just kept failing. I still can't believe that I blew it." Tears rolled down the rough skin of his cheek to his mustache.

"Oh," I said softly reaching out to pat his arm, "I'm

sorry." But I didn't feel sorry. Mostly I was angry. I thought about all the times he said he was in the library, coming home every night after we were asleep, barely seeing me or the kids. I wondered again if instead of studying he'd been sleeping around.

"So that's that!" he said, wiping his face with a towel and staring at me hard. "You'll have a husband again and I'll be a real dad to the boys." He smiled at me expectantly and all I could think about was how he'd told his brother he was thinking of leaving me. I was glad when the doorbell rang and he quickly pulled on his pants and a shirt and went to answer it.

"Liliana!" His voice was loud and friendly-sounding. "I'm a new man, Liliana, and you and I are going to get to know each other better now. Maybe play some soccer, or go for bike rides together. Even Spanish lessons. How does that sound to you, huh?" I couldn't hear Lily's response, but then Tom called, "Aaaaanna! Anna, Liliana's here!"

I stepped out into the hall. "I'm in the bedroom," I said and went back to making the bed. Before I saw Lily, I smelled her, a strong lemon scent that was always with her. I didn't have to look to know she was wearing dungarees and a clean, nicely pressed white shirt. Summer or winter, she never wore anything else. She had the look of a neighborhood tomboy, her curly hair pulled straight back into a braid, no makeup or jewelry, not even earrings. She didn't need them. She was beautiful with her dark skin, heart-shaped face, and intense, almost black eyes. I shook the bedspread out and Lily moved to the other side of the bed, pulling on the corner of the blanket to straighten it out with me.

"Hey, chica," she said softly, putting her hand on my

shoulder, "are you okay? What's happening here? Why is el jefe home?"

"The chief got himself thrown out of school," I said, keeping my voice low. "He's going to be around a lot from now on."

Tom came into the room and grabbed his brown bomber jacket from the closet. "I'm taking the kids to the lighthouse down by the river," he said, reaching over and patting me on the ass, which was more awkward than anything else.

"But I told them this morning that we were going for pizza with Lily."

"I know, don't worry. They already know there's been a change of plans. We'll pick up sandwiches at the deli. See you gals later," he said and called out to Nick and Joey that it was time to leave.

When I heard the door slam, I went to our room, fell backwards on the bed, and pulled a pillow over my head. "Thank God," I yelled, though it was muffled in the pillow. "The first time he's taken the boys out in almost a year."

Lily had followed me back into the room. She tugged on the pillow. "Hey, chica," she said, "get dressed. It's a day for las muchachas!"

Lily'd brought her bike, a ten-speed, black, man's bike that was almost identical to mine. The difference was that mine had a seat on the back for Nicky and another seat that I'd rigged up for Joey on the front.

That's how Lily and I met, on our bikes. We rode past each other so many times that one day I just stopped her and introduced myself. "My name's Anna," I said. "I always see you riding on your bike and I thought I'd just say hi." She looked surprised but pleased and smiled directly into my face, tugging lightly on the dark strands that had come loose from her thick, long braid.

"Liliana Maria," she said, "but my father calls me Negra, and my friends call me Lily." We stood with our bikes balanced between our legs as I put out my hand.

"Anna," I said again and she shook my hand holding it an extra second or two.

"I've seen you with los muchachos," she said.

"Yeah, they're my kids." We talked about where we liked to ride and then checked out each other's bikes. After that, we rode together once or twice a week, sometimes just me and her but often with Nick and Joey strapped on the front and back.

That morning, after Tom left with the kids, me and Lily rode to the Cloisters, up and down the hills and then back, along the streets, to a Cuban-Chinese restaurant for lunch. I got home about five and lay down, hoping to get a half-hour nap. I was startled by the kids leaning on the bell at seven o'clock. Tom had forgotten his keys.

"We had a great day! What's for supper?" Tom asked as I opened the door.

"I'm sorry, I fell asleep."

"You mean I spent the whole day with the kids and you don't have dinner ready!"

"Yes, I mean no, I don't. I just told you, I fell asleep."

Tom looked at his watch. "You slept all day?" he asked.

"No, not all day, but I wasn't going to cook all day. I was going to cook when I woke up from my nap."

The boys looked exhausted, so I made some spaghetti and hurried them to bed. I sang "A hundred bottles of beer on the wall, a hundred bottles of beer," to them until we were down to about fifty bottles and I heard Nick's heavy breathing and Joey's gentle snoring. It was late when I left their room and I still had the kitchen to clean, but I went and took a bath instead.

After my bath, I found Tom asleep at the kitchen table, his head resting on his arms between the dirty plates. Melted cheese stuck to his mustache, which fluttered as he snored. I washed the dishes in just a trickle of hot water so as not to wake him. He awoke suddenly as I brushed against his pants with the broom as I swept the floor.

"Time for bed," he mumbled. I turned out the light, picking up his shoes and socks and following as he padded barefoot down the hall to the bedroom. He stood by the foot of the bed, taking off his clothes and dropping them at his feet, before crawling naked under the sheets. "So tired," he murmured as his head reached the pillow, and within seconds he was asleep again.

I read through my magazines, checking the horoscopes and fashions. Finally I got tired and went to sleep at about twelve. Sometime in the night Tom got up and I heard him peeing and flushing as I fell back asleep. It was probably not long after, that I woke up with Tom clumsily unbuttoning my pajama top. One of the buttons came loose and I heard it hit the wall and then roll along the floor. Tom sat up and grabbed the legs of my pajama bottoms and tugged at them. They slipped past my hips and inched slowly along my thighs to my knees. I said nothing as I lay there feeling groggy and cold. Then he raised me up, holding me with one hand while with the other he pulled my pants off completely. I opened my eyes to see Tom kneeling above me with his penis in his hand, kneading it between his fingers, squeezing it to get it ready to stick into me. He poked with it at my opening.

"What are you doing?" I asked. He didn't say anything as he touched himself to get it harder, pulling and tugging on it, and then poked again.

"That's great," I said. "Would you stop, please?" He just kept rubbing himself and trying to push it in. "Do you hear me? Stop it!" I said louder. He gave one last try and then I shoved him so hard that he toppled against the wall. He sat there like a rag doll, looking only partly awake, his penis limp and small against his thigh.

"Look," I said, and the words came pouring out, "I'm sick of this. It wouldn't take much for you to make me want you. But you won't kiss me or touch me or be tender. That's how it's been for as long as I can remember." I stopped, realizing that what I was saying was true and that I hadn't wanted to think about it before. "But no more, do you hear me? From now on, if you want sex, you have to make love to me. You've got to get me to want it too." It took me a second to catch my breath and then I went on. "If not, put it someplace else, I'm not interested."

The only sound in the room was the sound of him cracking his knuckles. I counted a different crack in the wall every time he cracked his knuckles. Finally Tom turned toward the wall and lay there breathing hard, his body tensed and stiff. I couldn't think of anything else to say, so I started singing softly to myself, "A hundred bottles of beer on the wall, a hundred bottles of beer," until, like Nicky, Tom's breathing got heavier and I knew he was asleep. It felt like hours before I could stop all the thoughts going round and round in my head and then, finally, I dozed off too.

.   .   .

A week later, Tom telephoned from the street saying he was out bike riding with a friend and that they wanted to make a seven o'clock concert in the park. Could I have dinner ready by six? I said sure, even though it was already twenty after five. The lamb chops were thawed and the kids were playing quietly in their room. I used linen napkins, which we still had from our wedding, and made some Pepperidge Farm rolls, which I covered with paper napkins and served in a pretty woven bread basket. I sprinkled the chops with rosemary and checked that we had mint jelly. When I had a few minutes free, I combed my hair and put on a little lipstick and blush. Nick and Joey let me wash their faces and change their shirts because, like me, they thought it was a big deal when Tom invited someone home.

At six-thirty I went into Nick and Joey's room and sat with my hands in my lap, watching them play. Finally Joey must've heard Tom's key in the lock 'cause he jumped up excitedly. "Daddy's home, they're here."

"Just washing up," Tom called out and I remembered the wine which I had put in a small trash can filled with ice an hour ago.

I was surprised when Joey came in holding Lily's hand. In her other hand was a bag of grapes. I looked behind her for our guest. "Where did you come from?" I asked her.

At that moment, Tom came in telling everybody to sit down. "We're in a hurry. Here, sit!" he said, pulling out a chair for Lily, and then I realized that she was his guest. He took the grapes from her and put them in a bowl on the table.

I was ready to kill Tom, only I didn't want to make a fuss on account of the kids. But no way was I going to sit at the table with them. So I said I was nauseous and wanted to stay by the window for air.

I sat on the window ledge, looking out at the dark street, wishing they would eat quickly and go to the concert. I noticed that yesterday's rain had washed our chalk games from the sidewalk.

I looked over at Joey who was licking each of the grapes before eating them.

"Lily," I asked, "did you wash the grapes?"

"Yes, of course."

"Joey, stop licking those grapes," I yelled at him. "They're clean, Lily washed them."

Lily came over holding out a glass of wine to me but I shook my head no. "He called me this morning," she said quietly. "Tom called my house and said you wanted me to come to dinner. The bike ride and concert idea came later, but I didn't see any harm. I wouldn't do anything on purpose to make you mad, chica. You know you're my compañera," she said.

"It's okay, just sit down," I told her.

"Don't you like your trees?" Tom asked Joey, stabbing a few green beans and holding them in front of Joey's face.

"They're not trees," Nick corrected him. "Broccoli are trees. Those are green beans, and Joey hates green beans."

"Just a taste." Tom kept the fork in front of Joey's face. "You've got to learn to taste things." Joey turned away and Tom accidentally stabbed Joey in the head.

"That's enough," I said, jumping off the windowsill and clearing the string beans from Joey's plate into the trash. "They don't have to taste everything, they're not guinea pigs," I snapped.

Tom turned to Lily, who kept her head down, looking at her plate. "Who said anything about guinea pigs? Lily, did you hear me say anything about guinea pigs?"

"We tasted them already at Grandma's house, and I have to pee," Nick said. He jumped out of his seat and ran down the hall. Joey slipped out of his seat and followed. "To pee," he echoed. The three of us waited, listening to the noise of the toilet flushing over and over again.

"Joey loves to flush," I said to no one in particular.

A few minutes later Tom said to Lily, "You don't have to eat it if you don't want to. It's overcooked."

Lily had a piece of lamb chop on her fork. "It's fine," she said, "it's perfect. Really, it's delicious."

Tom reached over and moved Lily's plate away. "Everything is overdone," he said. "It always is."

"That's not fair," I said. "Dinner was ready at six. The lamb chops got dried out 'cause you were late."

Tom went over and picked up the heavy frying pan, waving it in front of my face. "See?" he said and then brought it over to Lily, turning it on its side and pointing. "Look," he said, like a teacher explaining to his slowest students, "this is the problem. It's almost black on the bottom." He turned to me. "You let it stick to the pan and that's why the lamb chops are hard." He put down the pan and picked up the muffin tin. "The biscuits are dark brown. You leave everything in too long."

"I don't always do that," I said.

"It certainly happens often enough. The meatloaf last week, burnt grilled cheese, soft pasta. You don't understand the concept of tender or al dente. Everything ends up either too soft or hard as a board." He turned to Lily and grinned, "I think she believes she's doing it for our health, isn't that wild? She's afraid we'll get trichinosis

from string beans. She has no idea of the principles involved.''

"Shut up!" I said.

"What?"

"Shut the fuck up and go to your stupid concert," I
yelled.

"C'mon, Anna, that's not nice. Besides, I think it
might be too late for the concert," he said.

"Not nice?" I asked, clearing the table and bringing
a pile of dishes to the sink. "Okay, smartass, so now
you're an expert on what is and isn't nice." I raised a dish
and threw it at the cabinet near his head. It smashed and
fell to the floor. "Is that nice?" I asked.

"Are you crazy?" he said and bent to gather the
broken pieces.

"No," I said, picking up another dish, "maybe this
is nicer," and I threw it at his feet. It hit his shoe and
bounced off.

"You're crazy," he said, moving backwards out of
the kitchen.

"Get out," I screamed after him, "you and your
lousy fucking guest!" and I threw a bowl and a few dishes
at him. He edged over to the front door and stood there,
just staring at me. I ran back to the kitchen and returned
with the frying pan. "I want you both out now," I yelled
as I swung the pan at his head. It crashed against the door
with a loud bang. He went flying through the door with
Lily after him. "And stay out!" I yelled at the closed door.

I walked slowly down the hall to the kids' room. Nick
and Joey had put on their pajamas and were sitting on their
beds waiting. I gave each of them a huge pile of books to
read and kissed them goodnight. I didn't even turn Joey's
book right side up like I usually did.

I went and lay on my bed, terrified, wondering if Tom would really leave. How would we live? Where would I get money for the rent? Who would want me if Tom didn't?

Tom called two days later. I was ready to ask him to come back. I couldn't imagine a life alone with just me and the kids.

"Hello, Anna? It's Tom."

"I know."

"I want to come home."

"Where've you been?"

"At Lily's."

"Did you sleep with her?"

"No, no, of course not."

I didn't say anything so he said, "Anna, Anna are you there?"

I wouldn't answer. We sat there silently and I just waited. Then he said, "Well yes, yes, I guess I did. She'd probably tell you anyway if I didn't. But Anna, what did you expect? You told me not to come home, didn't you? And that other night when I was touching you, you said I should put it someplace else. So that's what I did. Look, you may not want me, but women like Lily can't keep their hands off me. As far as I knew, that was fine with you. I'm right, aren't I? Look, it's not Lily's fault. Don't go making a big deal out of this."

"I'm not, it's just another sign that things are wrong between us."

"I want to come home."

"Please, not yet," I told him, "I need time to think."

"Listen," Tom said, "it's my home and I'm coming back anytime I want to. Don't pretend that you think this is the first time I've messed around. Lily's probably not even the ninth or tenth woman I've been with. So don't play innocent with me. As if what I get from you would satisfy me."

I barely listened while he talked, trying to remember what I liked about him. When I first met Tom I was seventeen, and I remembered thinking that with his black hair and eyes and handsome face he'd make beautiful kids. But that was all I could remember while he ranted on.

"Tom, I had the locks changed. I'll finish packing your stuff by the end of the weekend. Call and tell me when you want to pick up your bags. I'll leave them in the hall."

I hung up and called the locksmith. I said I had an emergency and needed the locks changed immediately. The kids had gone next door to Mrs. Mahoney's, so I scrubbed the house until they came back. In the morning when I woke, the house was spotless and I felt really scared.

Lily called at ten that morning.

"I don't want to talk to you," I told her, "not ever." I was about to hang up.

"Please, chica, give me a chance. Listen, I didn't think that letting him stay would hurt you. He didn't want to tell his family or anybody that you weren't together, so that's why he stayed with me. But I should've called and explained."

I was furious. "Really? Well, how do you explain that you slept with my husband?"

"You're kidding, chica, right? You must be kidding."

"That's what he said."

"He couldn't have told you that."

"He did."

"I don't understand why he did or how you could think that," she said and there was no sound from her side for a while. I could almost hear her thinking while I waited. "He never touched me," she said, "you're both loco." She let out a funny kind of noise, like a giggle. "I thought it was written all over me, chica, why I keep to myself and don't want nobody in my business. Except for my brothers, I don't have anything to do with men. I like women, chica, not men. I'm gay and if you weren't so stupida, you would have realized it a long time ago."

"What? Oh, I'm sorry," I said. "I mean, I'm not sorry that you're gay, I'm sorry I didn't get it. I guess I *am* stupida, or crazy, like you said."

"No problema, chica. But I'm sorry too that I didn't send him away. I should have told him go to his own friends."

"Do you know what he said about you?" I asked. "He made it seem like you couldn't keep your hands off him, that he was irresistible."

"Yup, that's me, I was all over him. I hate to say this, but that man is a terrible liar."

"And he makes a mess in the bathroom," I laughed as I began to cry.

"He does, a big mess! Hey, chica, will I see you again? Can I stop by Tuesday afternoon to go bike riding with you and los muchachos?"

"Yes, I'd like that. I'd like that a lot." I hung up and found it hard to stop crying. Tom, you lying son of a bitch, I screamed silently, you were never around for me and the kids, not ever.

About eleven there was a loud knock on the door and

then the bell rang. I was surprised to see Pudgy standing there. He explained that he had met the kids the day before playing in front of the house with Eddie and his big brother, Sean, and they had asked him to stop by today.

"You guys want to come out to play?" Pudgy asked and he reminded me of Joey as he stood there with his toes turned in, looking embarrassed. I said no, I wasn't up for it but then realized it would be good to get out of the house with the kids.

"Nick, Joey, look who's here," I yelled. Nick and Joey were thrilled to see Pudgy, and each took one of his hands as we left the house. The three of them walked ahead, laughing and whispering all the way to the park. I didn't join in or ask what was going on. When we got to the courts, we squeezed past the wall to the side where I'd played singles with Pudgy a few weeks ago.

There were about ten people standing around smiling—my next door neighbor, Mrs. Mahoney, Adeline from across the street, their kids, and some of the guys from the courts. At first I didn't understand what was going on, but Adeline was holding a cake with candles on it while a few others surrounded it with newspapers to protect it from the wind. Everyone was singing "Happy Birthday."

Pudgy told me later that when he met Nick and Joey on the street the day before, they were excited because they had just bought birthday presents for me. It was then that the three of them came up with the idea of making a party on the courts the next day.

Pudgy handed out Chocos while Adeline cut the cake and there were six-packs of soda and beer sitting by the fence. Everybody sang, "For she's a jolly good fella," and Mrs. Mahoney pinned a small corsage with two pink carnations on the front of my T-shirt. Mrs. Mahoney was a big, heavy woman and had trouble working the pin with her thick fingers. She accidentally stuck me twice and kept apologizing while Nick and Joey sang real loud—*"jolly good fellaaaaa, that nobody can deny."*

Then we played catch and Monkey in the Middle and ran races. I got drunk on two beers and told Pudgy that I totally loved him and he said that was great news. I called Nick and Joey my special dummyheads and sweethearts and kissed them whenever I could grab them. And I thanked whoever I was standing next to. Then I sat down in the dirt and opened my presents, which included a nightgown from Mrs. Mahoney and Adeline, two hand-balls, a white T-shirt, and a canteen half-filled with water from Pudgy and the boys.

Pat, Roger, Lenny, and the Flatbed Truck

T O M S H O W E D U P every few weeks to take Nick and Joey out and give me some cash that covered less than half the rent. I was working hard but the money didn't go far. Nick and Joey spent a lot of time with Eddie next door, because Eddie's mom, Mrs. Mahoney, was real nice and never made me feel bad for asking favors from her. I called her Mrs. Mahoney rather than Edith out of respect, because she was older.

One evening, I was on my way to get Nick and Joey from Mrs. Mahoney's when Pudgy called. "I want to stop by and talk to you," he said.

"I got to get Nick and Joey from next door," I told him. "Tell me over the phone."

"It's too important, Anna. C'mon, say yes. Tell me to hurry over."

The way he said it made me laugh. "Okay, hurryover," I said in one breath.

I'd just finished polishing my waitressing shoes when the doorbell rang. "That was fast," I said as he stood at the door trying to catch his breath. "I didn't mean for you to kill yourself getting here."

"I didn't want to keep you waiting." He was excited and kept laughing as he threw his jacket on the couch and blurted out, "I got a job for you."

"What are you talking about? I already have a job. In fact, I got two."

"That's the point," Pudgy said, bending over and grabbing my face between his hands so I was looking in his eyes. "This would be one job, not two, and you'd be making maybe three times the money. It's for HomeMade Cakes. They're hiring women," he said. "My boss said they have to meet some kind of federal regulation. So far one woman applied, but she quit after orientation. Home-Made is desperate. They'll take any woman who wants it. You'd be perfect for it, Anna. So what do you think? Want me to recommend you?"

"What would I be doing?"

"You'd be delivering HomeMade Cakes, working out of a depot, like me. They call it a salesperson but that's just a fancy name for a delivery person. You seen the guys in the morning bringing bread and cake and milk to the stores? You'd be doing the same thing. I started out as a packer, worked my way up to a salesperson, and I just been made supervisor. You could work your way up too. It's not hard. All you do is go to the stores on the route and give them Chocos and Bonzos and doughnuts and then collect the money. That's the job."

"But I can't drive a truck."

"These aren't big trucks, and HomeMade doesn't care. They'd take you no matter what. They don't have a choice anymore."

"I don't know," I said.

But a part of me did know. And when Pudgy, on his way next door to get Nick and Joey, said I should think about it and we could talk more over the weekend, my thoughts went back to when I was a kid and how much I loved trucks. I remembered a time right after my ninth birthday when me and Carmela and Georgie were hanging out on our block, University Avenue, which is not far from

Yankee Stadium, and a flatbed truck pulled up right in front of the Blue Eagle Supermarket. Me and Carmela and Georgie watched out of the corner of our eyes as the driver came out of the supermarket drinking a Yoo-Hoo soda and climbed into the cab of his truck. As soon as we heard the engine start up, without a word, we went running and one by one took a flying jump onto the flat board on the back.

We kept quiet as the truck slowly made its way down the hill toward the highway. We lay flat on our bellies, out of sight of his rearview mirror, smiling at each other and making the thumbs-up sign. The truck picked up speed and I could've ridden around all day like that, watching nothing but parts of trees and buildings go whizzing by. We didn't come to any traffic lights but I knew we were getting near the highway, so when I felt the truck slowing down, I crouched at the side of the truck, ready to jump.

"I'm Supergirl," I said softly into the wind.

Behind me, Georgie whispered, "Then fly, Supergirl, fly," and I felt his hand in the middle of my back when he pushed me over the side. But I wasn't ready. I went straight down. My arms went shooting out and I tried to tuck my head in, thinking that my mother would kill me if I got another hole in my head. But as soon as I hit the street, my arms bent in and my head crashed into the concrete.

My mother was waiting in the emergency room when the ambulance pulled up. "Not again," she said when she saw me. She went outside for a cigarette while the doctor stitched me up. She said she was sick of seeing me get sewed back together. She was still mad when we got home that night because there was blood over everything and she was sure I had ruined her dress; it was orange and green checked, and it was one of her favorites. But that didn't stop me from loving trucks the way I did.

Pudgy came back with Nick and Joey and wrestled with them until it was time for bed, and then he went home.

I didn't even realize I was thinking about the job with HomeMade until something happened at HoJo's that Friday night. I waitressed there two nights a week, and I was late getting to work that Friday because the trains were backed up at Times Square. And then everything else went wrong, ending with a fight between two of my tables over a bottle of ketchup. All of a sudden, arms shot out, dishes were flying and people shouting as some guy knocked into me. He thought I was trying to block him from leaving so he turned and punched me in the face. Everything got straightened out by the end of the night, except by then my eye was closed shut and my glasses taped together with Band-Aids. When I got home that night, I called Pudgy and asked him how to apply for the job. I never went back to HoJo's.

I went in and filled out an application for a HomeMade Cakes salesperson, and they sent me for a series of tests, starting with a urine test, which is the one I did best on. Pudgy had told me to stay away from poppyseed bagels for a few days, because they show up as opium.

I didn't do so well on the road test. I had time for only one practice session with Pudgy before the actual test. Pudgy showed me how to work the clutch and shift gears, and we drove once around the block at five miles an hour with him yelling for me to let the clutch out slowly and not keep letting go of the wheel.

I was lucky, because the guy who gave me the road test was nice. He didn't get scared or mad when I couldn't stop the truck from weaving from side to side, and he didn't say a thing when I jumped the curb and hit the NO PARKING sign. I kept saying how nervous I was, but he just patted my hand and told me not to worry.

"Relax, honey, you're doing fine, just fine." Toward the end, I told him I had enough for one day and he said that I showed great promise. He swore that with a little practice I'd be one of the best.

The lie-detector test started out fine. I had never had a lie-detector test and I was scared, even though I didn't think I had anything to hide. But when I was living with Tom, I started lying all the time. Like I'd lie about how much money I needed for food and then spend some on little things for me and the kids. Or I'd make muffins from a mix and tell him it was from a recipe, because he only liked homemade. So now I was afraid that I had gotten so used to lying that maybe I lied without knowing it.

I waited in a small room for over twenty minutes, wondering how a machine can figure out that you're lying. By the time the guy got there, I had bitten my nails so bad that my pinky had started to bleed. There weren't any magazines to read and the walls were covered with mirrors, so there was nothing to look at. He was so late that I was sure I was waiting in the wrong place. Twice I got up to read the sign on the outside of the door but it said STANDARD SECURITY, which is what was stamped on my application. He had no jacket or coat when he came in, and I wondered if he'd been somewhere in the building the whole time. Probably in the john, I thought.

The guy was a little taller than me, had on twenty-year-old brown bell-bottom pants and was mostly bald except for a few strands of very greasy brown hair that hung straight down the sides. Off and on through the interview he chewed at his nails. His nails were so badly bitten, they looked mangled. I thought, if that's what I look like biting my nails, I'd better stop right now.

"There are hidden electrodes in the chair," the guy began, "therefore every response you give, whether it's verbal or physical, is being registered and evaluated."

"Terrific," I said to myself. I smiled at him but he wouldn't smile back. The lines in his face all curved down, which made his face one big frown.

"We'll start with the easy questions," he said and asked my name, age, address, where I worked.

"Now that we've established what you're like when you tell the truth, we'll go into the more shady parts of your life. We'll begin with drugs. How many times have you smoked marijuana in the last year?"

"None."

"Now, that's not true, is it?" he asked me, smiling into my face. I didn't answer. I just waited for the next question.

"What other drugs have you done?"

"None."

"Now, come on, you can do better than that. Aspirin? Tylenol? Something for PMS?"

"You said, what drugs have I done. I don't do drugs. And I don't get headaches, so I don't take aspirin. I never had PMS. I've never been exactly sure what it is."

"Let's go on. How many car accidents have you had? Now think hard about this one. Tell me about any big accidents, but don't forget those little ones, the ones you thought you could get away with." He took a handkerchief from his pocket and blew his nose but continued talking through the handkerchief. It made it hard to understand him. "Maybe you swiped someone's fender or smashed a headlight backing up." When he finished blowing his nose he put the handkerchief in his shirt pocket.

I almost told him about the driving test and hitting the NO PARKING sign but I didn't like him, so I didn't want to give him even that much. I just said none again.

"Now, you don't expect me to believe that, do you Mrs. Ferrara?" he asked.

"It's Miss or Ms."

"What?"

"I'm not married anymore, so it's either Ms Ferrara"—I spelled out the *Ms*—"or Miss. Take your choice."

Sweat was dripping down his forehead and he took out that same handkerchief and wiped his face saying, "Excuse me for a minute," and left the room. By this time I had decided that he was the liar and that there were no electrodes anywhere. I got up and checked the chair. It looked like any old overstuffed chair, no wires running underneath, no metal buttons. I took off the cushions and still found nothing, then sat down again to wait.

After maybe ten minutes, he came back. "We don't seem to be getting anywhere. I would like you to be a little more truthful on this next part. We'll start with your stealing. When was the last time you stole something?"

"Never."

"Never, Mrs. Ferrara? Wouldn't you rather say hardly ever, or once? Or 'I can't remember,' or 'I refuse to say'? Do you think I am totally naïve? Never?" He chuckled but it was just a strange little noise, not a real laugh.

This time when I answered, I stood up and put my coat on. "Yes, never."

"Mrs. Ferrara, sit down, I'm not finished with you yet."

"Mister," I said as I headed for the door, "I want this job and I want it bad. But not bad enough to sit here while you tell me I'm lying, cheating, and stealing. You ask questions but you don't listen to the answers. You already decided everything I say is a lie, so why ask? How can you go around treating people like shit? Well, not me, I'm not shit." I tried not to slam the door when I left.

HomeMade hired me anyway, saying the lie-detector man suggested I was highly emotional and at times irrational, but that they were going to take a chance on me.

"Previously our girls worked in the thrift stores and offices. Last week we brought two into the bakery. But you'll be our first female salespersons," Dick Moran, HomeMade's head of personnel, said to me and Audrey, the other woman at the orientation.

I was so nervous I was almost shaking. It'd started the night before when I couldn't decide what to wear. I went back and forth three times to Mrs. Mahoney's apartment until I finally settled on a white blouse and a black skirt that was a little tight but didn't look terrible. "Dress it up with this, honey," she said, holding up a pretty black and pink scarf. "You look too serious with those clothes and your glasses." She wrapped the scarf once around, tying a loose knot with the ends hanging down. I watched carefully so

I could do it myself in the morning. Mrs. Mahoney said okay to my hoop earrings but she couldn't believe I didn't own a watch. Watches had always been bad luck for me. "Every professional woman needs a watch," she insisted. She gave me an old but pretty black watch with an oval face. "This is on long-term loan," she explained. "I have another one that's my favorite." I loved the watch but was afraid that if I wore it I wouldn't get the job, or I'd lose it right away. I wore it anyway.

I'd only been asleep a few hours when I woke up screaming. Then I lay in bed waiting to fall back to sleep. I tried not to drift back into the dream I'd had where a guy took my newborn baby, put it on the ground, and tarred over it, making it part of a road driven on by lots of cars and trucks. At five-thirty I was still wide awake, so I got up and made lunch for Nick and Joey and then washed the kitchen floor. By the time I got to orientation, I felt like I'd been up for days. I hated wanting something this bad.

At the start of orientation, we were given little baker's hats to wear on our tour of the bakery. The bakery smelled of Chocos, doughnuts, and cookies and pies. I loved the smell of bread baking, and here it was mixed with the sweetness of the cakes. When I was a kid, my Aunt DeeDee, my father's sister, lived with my grandmother in the back of their store, which was right down the street from a cake factory. DeeDee never got out of bed, not even to go to the bathroom. They kept her in diapers. My grandmother said DeeDee was retarded. Once a month, me and my brothers dressed in our best clothes and went and visited DeeDee. I was scared as we walked round and round her dark room listening to the noises she made like a little squealing puppy. But the smell of baking cake coming through the windows from the factory almost made up for it.

The bakery was so hot that Audrey came close to fainting. Audrey and I thought they were joking when they announced that the tour would be followed by a short film called *Choco World*, but they weren't. I could barely keep my eyes open as I watched fifteen minutes of people baking and eating Chocos. Then there were speeches by what Dick called "assorted HomeMade personnel." We sat around a large conference table, under a huge red, white, and blue sign that said HOMEMADE TASTES SOOO GOOD. The first talk was given by a chief mechanic on how to care for your truck. Next, a branch manager described how best to display HomeMade products in your average neighborhood supermarket. I was fine until a sales expert began tracking the Choco's rise over the past twenty years to one of America's favorite snack cakes. I didn't know if it was because I hadn't slept well or because I was nervous, but I was just too tired and finally I gave up. My eyes closed and my face landed flat on the table. It must've been at least five minutes before they got me to sit up, forcing Chocos and Honeybelles into my mouth, gently calling to me, "Anna, Anna Ferrara, are you okay? When was the last time you ate? Do you think you need a doctor?" I was so groggy I don't know what I answered. When I got home I realized it must have been nervousness that made me so sleepy, because just a little while later, me and Lily and the kids went on a two-hour bike ride and I wasn't tired at all.

HomeMade made me go through an unusually long physical exam before I was certified as healthy and allowed to begin working as a delivery person for HomeMade Cakes.

. . .

Audrey started working for HomeMade the same day I did. She was sent to the Merrick depot on Long Island, which everyone called the "country club" because it was big and clean and had fine-looking trucks. Pudgy said that when he pulled a route out there it was like being on vacation, compared to other depots. Fancy stores, easy pace, and no robberies.

Maybe it was because they never expected me to last as a driver that I ended up in Knickerbocker Avenue, HomeMade's dumping ground. Drivers, mechanics, and supervisors who were "trouble" or on probation were sent there. It was a small, old, converted warehouse located in the burnt-out section of Bushwick, in Brooklyn. To get to the depot from the train station, every morning at 5:00 A.M. I'd walk past six blocks of empty buildings, some of them half standing, others piles of ash and broken concrete. The smell of old fires would follow me as I kept a sharp watch for the packs of wild dogs that roamed the streets. After the morning when the dogs chased and attacked a new driver, I ran the whole way from the station to the depot and only felt safe when the garage door closed behind me. And inside the depot wasn't much better. The floors were filthy, wet, and slimy, and if I got there too early, before the other guys showed up, I'd end up chasing mice or a rat off my truck.

But that first day on the job, and for a long time afterward, I felt like I had been given the chance of a lifetime. No more begging Tom for money to get through the month or worrying that we'd have to move back to the housing project where we lived until Joey was born, to save money on rent. Nick could have the easel and paints he'd been asking for since Christmas, and I'd buy Joey a red scooter like Eddie's to take to the park. I'd buy them snow boots and we'd get rid of Joey's hand-me-down mittens and let him pick out gloves like Nick's. It was hard to believe that we'd be able to afford everything we needed.

Pudgy had been working out of Knickerbocker Avenue, but the week before I got there he was transferred to the Woodhaven depot in Queens, where the bakery was. I was glad, because I liked having a new beginning all my own. The only thing I still hadn't figured out was what to do with the kids since I left so early in the morning. For the time being, Sean Mahoney was sleeping in what used to be Tom's workroom. He took care of Nick and Joey in the mornings. He gave them cold cereal for breakfast and dropped them off at school. Sean swore he didn't mind and that he was glad to be making money of his own and to be out of his house, even if it was only next door. He'd pad around our apartment barefoot, dressed in gym shorts and a muscle shirt. Nick and Joey loved it that Sean painted his pinkies and his toenails black and that he shaved partway down the side of his head. And I could finally pay Sean a real salary. But this was only temporary. I still had to find some other way.

That first day on the job, none of the other drivers seemed glad to see me. They didn't bother looking up or nodding, much less say hello or shake my hand. The only friendly face was Joanie. She was the cashier at Knickerbocker Avenue.

"Finally, another woman, thank God," she said, and she sounded like she meant it. "I've seen only men's faces in this barn since the day I started. That's over five years now, but it feels like twenty. Don't expect none of them to like it, though,'' she said, pointing with her head toward the garage. ''You'd think they'd be glad to see a pretty face for a change, but no, they're mad as hell. It's all they been talking about for days. They heard that orders came down to pass you no matter how you did on your tests. Unless you hit a nun or destroyed a truck, you got the job.'' Joanie's reddish-blond curls bounced up and down as she went into an imitation of some of the guys running their mouths about me. ''What right do she have to take a man's job?'' she asked in a deep voice. ''A guy has to put bread on the table, and along comes a woman who steals the opportunity right out from under his nose.'' She went on: ''There are jobs for women and jobs for men, so why does she have to take a man's job? Because of her, some young guy is gonna be out on the street with no other way to support his family.'' In her own voice she said, ''Those guys are fighting mad.'' But then she must've looked at my face and realized how bad I was feeling, because she said, ''Look, I'm only telling you this so you don't take it personal. Give it time, honey, they'll warm up to you. You're so sweet looking, it would be hard not to.''

I went out to wait for Patrick, the supervisor Joanie said was going to show me the ropes for the next few weeks. Our depot manager, Jed, who everyone called the Cowboy, was on vacation, so it would be a while before I got to meet him.

Patrick arrived at a quarter to six, to the sound of the trucks starting up and rolling out onto the streets. We shook hands. ''Patrick Hurley—everyone calls me Pat,'' he said, speaking with a slight Irish accent. He looked me up and down, shaking his head. ''No, no, missus, where's your uniform? And work boots? Those nice clean pants and lovely shirt will be rags before the day's over. They'll end up in the trash. And I'd hate for you to twist an ankle your first day out wearing them fancy shoes.''

I was wearing beige slacks and a white shirt of Tom's that he'd left behind. My shoes were my white waitressing shoes, which I had covered with black liquid polish the night before. ''I didn't know about the work boots,'' I said, ''and Joanie said they got no uniforms small enough to fit me. She said they ordered some but they won't come in for a while. Maybe in two or three weeks.''

Pat started talking about the job and what each day would be like and never stopped until we broke for lunch.

''I'm going to tell you all I know,'' he said that first morning when we started out, ''slowly and carefully, because there's a lot to learn. So don't think you can pick it all up in one day.'' I could feel my eye twitching from time to time as I tried to remember everything he said. ''Stop worrying,'' he said. ''I'm a good coach, and I'll be with you for four weeks. Everything I say, I'll say over and over again. You'll be sick of hearing the same thing and soon you'll be telling me to shut up.''

''I don't think so,'' I said with a laugh, but I meant it. I was sure I couldn't hear it too often. There were so many things to learn. He showed me how to read the route book, to use the directions in the book to follow the streets and find what stores were where. I tried to memorize the price of each piece of snack cake and the larger boxes of Chocos, doughnuts, and coffee cake as he counted them out and added them up. Six times forty-five and a quarter cents, five times a dollar ninety-eight. And he yelled out driving tips all day long as he drove. ''See, ya just pull out the choke, then step on the clutch and give it enough gas.

Nice and easy now. Right signal here, and for the time being, use hand signals just to be safe." He taught me how to bully. "Because the truck is big, it has the right of way. If you want to switch lanes, you nose your way in slowly and then just go. Everything smaller will give way. Cars and taxis won't bother you. But don't try it with anything bigger than that, like one of those city buses. They'll plow right into you."

In the beginning, I never noticed that my truck was old or dirty, I was so glad that it was mine. One of the regular drivers, Little Dominic, had slipped on some garbage on Flatbush Avenue one rainy day and put his back out. So my first job was to pull Little Dominic's route for the two weeks he was laid up. The stores were in a nice neighborhood around Brooklyn College. Pat held the route book between us while he counted how many stores Little Dominic did each day. There were twenty-one stores three days a week and another eighteen on Tuesdays and Thursdays.

"This is a joke, isn't it?" I asked. "There's no way someone can finish that many stores in one day. Is he crazy? How does he do it? They can't expect me to do that much."

"Calm down," Pat said, "I'm helping you with it. Actually, I'm doing it for you, so there's no problem. You don't have to worry about how fast you are in the beginning. Your job is just to learn. You'll pick it up as you go along. You'll get faster once you know your way around the stores and streets."

Pat swore that his method of packing out cake was the best. "You can do it your way, it's your choice. But I'm a veteran of HomeMade Cakes for over thirty years.

HomeMade was a small two-by-nothing company back then, before JayCee took it over and it became part of a huge multinational giant. But I can tell you, my method's the fastest. And most important, you won't have crushed cake. Be smart," he said, "use my method now, choose your own later." He packed it in HomeMade's metal trays from left to right in order of size. "Pies on top," he said. "Never forget, pies on top."

Pat treated me to lasagna at a small Italian restaurant hidden on a little side street under some trees. We ate in a garden in the back. Even then his mouth kept running, but the conversation got more personal and he told me a lot about himself. "Three years ago," he said between bites, "I was a miserable lonely old man. I had a nervous rash and a stomach condition." He pulled up his sleeve and held out his arm. "See, it was all the way from my wrist to the elbow." He pulled down his sleeve and smiled, remembering, "Then I met Katie, my wife, at my cousin's wedding. We were both newly divorced and neither of us had kids. I'd been married twice before and she was married to a guy for twenty years. None of them happy marriages." Pat sat poking at his lasagna with a fork. Whenever he found a piece of something that looked green, like spinach, he pushed it to the side and went on eating. "I must say I can't understand God's ways. Why he arranged for me and Katie to meet so late in life. We had to wait all those years for a little happiness. But boy, was it worth it! I'm fifty-six years old, Katie's forty-three, and we're madly in love for the first time. Can you imagine that?" He laughed quietly, almost to himself. "To top it off, Katie's pregnant, due any day now. We don't care if it's a boy or girl. Either way, it's a blessing." He smiled a big, soft smile as he ran his hands through his thick gray hair. "Yup, either way, boy or girl, it's his way of saying he's happy for us."

By the end of the day, I felt like I couldn't see straight. When we reached the depot, Pat showed me how to settle up. Count the cash, the checks, what you took out, make sure it equals what you bring back plus the money and the stale. I passed out on the train ride home.

Pudgy showed up as I was leaving to get Nick and Joey from the after-school center. He took us out for pizza, and when we got home, it was Pudgy who made brownies with the boys for their bake sale in school the next day. I walked in on Joey with three brownies in his hand telling Pudgy he wasn't going to eat all three, he just wanted to taste each of them to make sure they were okay for people to buy. Then, when he saw me, he said, "Pudgy says him and me and Nicky are so skinny we could eat a million brownies and never get fat."

"Don't try it," I said.

Pudgy came by the next night, and the next, every night until the weekend, taking us to the restaurant of our choice each time.

The next two days on the route with Pat were slightly different versions of the first day, the only changes being that the stores were different and a few of the guys at the depot were starting to nod or say hello.

But on Thursday, everything changed. "Bad news," Joanie called out as I came through the office door. It was a quarter to five and I wondered what could have happened so early in the morning. "Well," she said, "actually there's good news and bad news. First, the good news.

Katie, Pat's wife, had a baby girl at five in the morning. They named her Elizabeth, after Pat's mom, but they're going to call her Beth.''

I waited but Joanie didn't say anything more. "And the bad news? Didn't you say there was bad news too?''

"Yeah, well, I wish I didn't have to give the bad news. I'll say it fast. Pat had a heart attack.''

"What?" I couldn't believe it. "When did it happen? He seemed so healthy when he was working on the truck.'' Driving, carrying heavy trays, running in and out of the stores. "And he was happy and excited about the baby coming,'' I said, half to myself.

"It happened at the hospital, while Katie was giving birth, which was damn lucky.''

"What does it mean? Did he get to see the baby? Is he dead?''

"No, he's not dead. The attack was a small one. It was his first, which is good, but they're going to keep him there for observation, and then he has to stay home for a few weeks. So that's the news.''

I wondered what that meant for me. Who would supervise me on the route? I didn't want to ask, because it seemed selfish to worry about that with Pat in the hospital. But Joanie said right off, "For today, they're sending Roger from Douglaston. He's young, twenty-four years old, but he's smart. They made him manager of the Douglaston depot a few months ago. And he's cheap. If he tries to get you to buy him lunch, say no.''

Roger from Douglaston was the picture of the New Jersey boy next door—that's where he drove in from every day. He was cute, with a lopsided smile showing a slightly chipped tooth, big blue eyes with long lashes, and a strong jaw with a deep cleft in the center. Handsome, funny, and outgoing, the kind of guy that made you wish you were his girl. Be careful, I told myself, he's not your type and you're not his, but he'll let you think you are. And by the end of our day, I hate to admit it, he'd sweet-talked me, just like he did every other woman on the route, and, like them, I would have done almost anything to get him to like me.

The truth is, we had a lousy day together. Roger wasn't interested in teaching me a thing, and he was pigheaded as well. He'd get us lost, swearing he knew all the shortcuts and refusing to even look at the directions in the route book. He insisted I use his method of packing the cake in order of price into Entenmann's boxes which he brought from Douglaston. "Chocolate on top," he said. "That's the one thing I insist on, chocolate on top." Roger's idea of a good day was to get through the stores as fast as possible, to figure out which ones we could skip, and to get me to buy him lunch. Which I did, even with Joanie's warning, but I swear I didn't have a choice. We'd stopped at a deli, ordered huge hero sandwiches with potato salad, cole slaw, and sodas to go, and when it came time to pay, Roger disappeared. I had no idea where he went. I checked outside but he wasn't anywhere in sight. Finally, after I paid for the food and went out to wait in the truck, I spotted him in the rearview mirror having a cigarette.

After that I got smarter. In the afternoon, when he asked me for a date, I thought about it hard, and even though I wanted to say yes, I didn't. He reminded me of Tom, in that neither of them thought I was pretty or really liked me but for some reason they wanted me to like them. And once they knew I liked them, they'd started looking past me to the next girl they could hit on. At the last three stores, Roger had his arm around the waist of every cute cashier that checked him in. Joanie laughed when I nick-named him Stingray.

That night when I got home, I was too tired to change and went to pick up Nick and Joey wearing the clothes I wore at work. I didn't have a uniform yet but my new black HomeMade jacket had come in and I was wearing that. Pudgy was waiting at the school gate with the boys.

Nick and Joey looked tired as they leaned against Pudgy's legs, but they ran up to meet me and gave me a bunch of big sloppy kisses and a lot of hugs. We started laughing and teasing each other and one after the other they tapped me softly and ran away saying, "Gotcha last." I chased them down the block until I caught them. Then they chased me until I realized that for some reason, they had stopped. When I turned around, they were pointing to me and hitting each other and laughing. "HomeMade Choco!" Nick yelled out, and Joey joined in, "Mommy is a Home-Made Choco!" I had no idea why they were yelling that until Pudgy came over and started pulling stickers off the back of my jacket. The guys at the depot had covered my jacket with stickers that said "HomeMade Choco" and "HomeMade Chocos—Chock Full of Chocolate," some of which also said I was on sale for ninety-nine cents. But I was glad that the other drivers had found a way to break the ice. I peeled off one of the stickers, grabbed hold of Nick, and plastered it across his forehead. "Who's a HomeMade Choco?" I asked, tickling him under the arms. He screamed and laughed and hid behind Pudgy. Mean-while, Joey ran away, yelling, "No, Mommy, no," but I ran after him and stuck one on his fanny.

On the way home, Pudgy came up with an idea that everyone but me loved. Pudgy's idea was that he should move in with us. There was the little room off the kitchen, the one that used to be Tom's workroom and which Sean had been using. Pudgy said it would be perfect for him. It even had its own bathroom. At first it sounded like he was joking, but the kids didn't take it that way, and Joey said, "That would be great, really great." When I didn't say anything, Nick said, "C'mon, Ma, why not? It's a good idea. Then me and Joey would have two people to look after us." It was too outrageous for me to even consider right then, and I was too tired anyway.

"It needs a paint job," was all I could think to say, remembering how the year before, Tom had taken Joey into his workroom and yelled at him for writing on the bathroom wall with Magic Markers. But Tom didn't notice that he was getting Joey so nervous that Joey's hand was going around faster and faster with an open marker. In the end, Joey completely covered the wall with blue circles and scribbles while Tom talked. Tom always bitched about the ruined wall, but he never got around to repainting it.

"I know," Pudgy said, "but painting the room would be the fun part, and the boys could help. I'm sorry. I guess I've been thinking about the idea for so long that it just slipped out."

"It's a good idea," I said, nodding at Nick and Joey, "but it's a new idea and we got to think about it more."

"It's a good idea," Joey agreed, "and I already thinked about it a lot."

The boys took forever to go to sleep that night. All they could talk about was Pudgy moving in. "You guys think about something else nice," I told them, "like what kind of fish we should get next week for our new fish tank. Else you'll be up all night.''

Pudgy stayed for a few hours after Nick and Joey went to sleep. He apologized over and over again for bringing up the idea in front of them without giving me a chance to think about it first.

"Yeah," I told him, "it's hard, 'cause I want to say yes just 'cause Nick and Joey want it so bad. Tom was never around very much for them, so I know it'd be great for them to have a guy in their lives. But I don't really know you and I need to think about what I want for me too.''

We didn't get much of a chance to talk more about it that week, but I did mention it to Mrs. Mahoney and Lily. Mrs. Mahoney didn't say anything about it being a sin to live with a guy I wasn't married to, which is what I thought she was going to say. She just mentioned that she knew Pudgy's grandmother when the old lady lived across the street and that they used to do laundry together Saturday mornings at the laundromat. "A lovely lady," Mrs. Mahoney called her. "Nice, quiet, good manners. The whole family's like that.''

Lily, who usually never gave her opinion about anything, agreed with Joey that it was a great idea. "He'll help with los muchachos," is what she said.

When I got to work the next day, the news was that a supervisor was coming over from Merrick who would take Pat's place as my trainer for the next few weeks. Wally, a route rider who covered vacations for our depot and theirs, was the one who told me, but he hadn't heard which supervisor they were sending.

When a guy walked in and called out to Joanie, "Hey beautiful, long time no see," Joanie's mouth closed tight and her eyes narrowed as she turned her back on him without saying a word. He just shrugged and came toward me with his hand outstretched.

"Lenny Boyd. You must be Anna Ferrara. I'm your supervisor for the next three weeks."

He looked nice. But it wasn't like Joanie to walk away from somebody, and she seemed really mad. He was young and almost handsome with dark, close-cut curly hair and real soft-looking baby skin with rosy cheeks. I was about to tell him that he looked like the shoe salesman that used to take care of Nick and Joey in a store on Fort Washington Avenue, but I stopped myself just in time. Later I realized that if I'd said it, he'd have had one more thing to hold against me.

We didn't get started until seven o'clock, because Lenny had to wait for a call from his wife. Every morning, she'd do a check of their food and supplies and phone in a list of things for him to pick up. He explained that she didn't go out much, so he did their food shopping on the route.

"We've been married two months," he said, taking out a picture of him standing with his arm around a very short, very fat woman. "Doesn't she have a pretty face? A pretty face and great boobs," he said, smiling, running his eyes from my face down to my breasts.

"Excuse me?"

"Nothing, just kidding. By the way, as a supervisor I consider my job to be that of an observer. The best way to learn is to do it yourself. So it's your route and your day. It's up to you to make the mark and me to make sure you do it." Lenny waved the *Daily News* and *New York Post* in my face. "Getting through the papers is my work for the day."

I felt sick to my stomach, which happened whenever I was really nervous, because I knew I wasn't ready to run the route myself. For the last few days, I'd done nothing but watch Pat and Roger do all the work. Sometimes I helped carry trays, that was it. Since Pat and Roger wanted to finish early every day, they did the driving, loaded the truck, packed out the cake in the stores, and took care of the accounting. They were always in a hurry to get back to the office to finish their paperwork. The only time I'd sat behind the wheel was once when I moved the truck across the street on Flatbush Avenue. And to add to all this, we were going out on a new route. Little Dominic was back, so for the next two weeks we were pulling Jimmy's route while Jimmy was on vacation.

That day with Lenny turned out to be the hardest and longest day I'd ever have on that job. The directions in Jimmy's route book were impossible to understand, and it took me three quarters of an hour to get to the first stop, which was fifteen minutes from the depot. I started out by stalling twice before Lenny hissed at me, "Let out the choke and then the clutch. And for the rest of the day, let's not forget those little facts. Choke, clutch, choke, clutch because you'll be stopping and starting all day long." And it wasn't as if I didn't stall five or six more times.

Two blocks later it was my right signal. "Turn that damn signal off!" he yelled. I must've left it on since I made a right turn out of the garage. But there were too many things for me to remember and I couldn't keep track of everything. I kept mixing up the prices of Chocos and the pies, the variety packs and the sugar doughnuts. And then I'd try to remember if it should be pies or chocolate

on top. I'd already forgotten that the one piece of direction
Lenny gave me was to put the cupcakes on top. And did
the BestMart cashier give me a ten or a twenty?

I'd carry three or four trays in at once but sometimes
the load would be too heavy and I'd have to put one back.
Each time I came to another store, I'd wander up and
down the aisles looking for the HomeMade rack. It was
easier than trying to find someone to ask, but it took a lot
of time. Then I'd look the merchandise over to see what
the store needed, check the dates, and take out any old
cake. I'd have to go to the office to show the manager the
stale and return to my truck. Bringing the fresh cake in
followed pretty much the same routine. Meanwhile, Lenny
sat in my seat, reading the paper, only stepping off the
truck to shop for his wife or when we broke for lunch.

"What do you do in the stores? What takes you so
long?" Lenny asked after my first two stops. "I hope it's
good for you," he said, making an up-and-down motion
with his hand, like he was jerking off. What a pig! But I
ignored it and instead tried to explain what happened each
time. He put his head down while I was talking and continued to read the newspaper. I walked to the back of the
truck and pulled out tray after tray of cake, trying to
remember what I had to bring in. I was getting even more
mixed up, because I was getting mad.

Later that morning, Lenny looked up from his paper
to say, "The only reasonable explanation for how long it
takes you to serve a store is that you're giving head to
every manager at every stop we come to." By lunchtime,
Lenny's face was beet red and he wouldn't talk to me
except to mumble under his breath, "HomeMade must be
desperate." He wrote pages and pages of notes in a large

black ledger-type book. HomeMade Cakes was going to have an enormous list of my fuck-ups for their files.

It was almost five o'clock when I ended up on a deserted street by the river. There were no stores or buildings in either direction, only vacant lots surrounded by fences. I had been following directions penciled in at the top of Jimmy's route book. "What now?" Lenny growled at me. I handed Lenny the route book, saying, "Look at it, it's not my fault." But he chucked it over his shoulder and told me to head back to the depot. While we were waiting for the garage door to roll up, he got out of the truck, went to his car, and drove off.

Joanie was still in the office. "I waited for you," she said softly, and I burst into tears. She came out and put her hand on my shoulder. "I wanted someone to be here for you. That Lenny is a bigger rat than the ones running around the depot eating cake off the trucks," she said. "Nobody likes him. He was manager of the thrift store but they got rid of him because he hated everybody, the workers and customers too. HomeMade was ready to fire him but he begged them not to, because he had to pay for his honeymoon. They kept him on but made him the lowest-paid supervisor. It was a big pay cut and everybody knew it, and he knew everybody knew it. So now he's even worse than ever and takes it out on 'the grunts'—that's what he calls the drivers who work for him."

She stayed with me while I settled up my accounts, and I would've felt better by the time I was finished if I hadn't come up almost fifty dollars short.

"That's usual for a new driver," Joanie said. "It happens to the best of them. You have to pay it out of your own pocket, so try not to make mistakes anymore, or steal from someplace else to cover your losses when you come up short. That's how all the guys do it." That was before I'd heard of tips or clipping and I must have looked shocked.

"Just kidding," Joanie said. "Okay, baby, time to go home and get some rest."

The next day, things got worse. Again we didn't leave until very late. This time Lenny's wife didn't get up until seven-thirty, which was an hour and a half after all the other drivers pulled out. Instead of twenty stores, like yesterday, there were twenty-five on this side of the route. And one long stretch was mostly supermarkets, with only a few mom-and-pop stores in between. So by lunchtime, I still had seventeen stores left to serve. At one o'clock I came to a big Foodcity and parked in the back lot. I stopped to check my book and when I looked up, Lenny was blocking the door. "Sit down," he said. I sat back down. "This is the biggest joke HomeMade ever pulled," Lenny said, shaking his head back and forth, "but I don't know why I don't find it funny. You don't do one thing right."

I noticed that even though he was young, he had two long hairs growing out of his nostrils.

"I'm a trainee, not an experienced driver," I said, half under my breath.

"No, the point is not that you're new, it's that you're lousy at this job. You can't follow directions and you multiply on your fingers. I can see why your husband left you. I bet you're not even good in bed." He looked me over and kept shaking his head. "It's a shame. Okay, I'm going to give you one more chance and then I'm going to throw in the towel. Foodcity will be your testing ground. Now, go!''

''Good morning, HomeMade here,'' I said to the wrong guy, mistaking a dark navy-blue cleaner's uniform for a manager's. I rushed up and down the aisles two times before I found the HomeMade Cakes on the three lowest shelves in aisle number six. I made a note to myself of what they needed and took out a ripped box of Bonzos. ''One ninety-five going out,'' I told the cleaner. He pointed to a little bald guy in shirtsleeves dusting the shelves. ''Manager's over there,'' he said.

''Thanks.'' I introduced myself to the manager, who said it was nice to see a new driver, especially one with a face that had less than two days' growth on it. When I got back to the truck, Lenny had his sleeve rolled up and was tapping on his watch.

''Not good enough,'' he announced, ''too slow. It's a little unbelievable, but I think you're actually getting worse, if that's possible. This is your last chance, and I'm timing you. Three minutes to go in and out or you're out of a job. I'll write you off as a lost cause. I don't know why I waited this long.''

I went back inside, the manager checked me in, I put up the new cake and ran back to the manager to get paid. The manager was standing outside his office talking to two cops. ''I don't know how they got in,'' he said. ''Yeah, the lady down the street said there were three of them. I have her address. You can stop by any time and she'll talk to you. Home all day, and she always loves a good chat.''

I tapped the manager gently on the shoulder. ''Excuse me, could you please pay me.''

''Look, young lady, you wait a minute,'' the manager

said, "this is important." He turned back to the cops. "About seven this morning, said she was walking her dog, actually walks itself, that dog does, when she saw three men coming out carrying sacks. Thought they were the night help leaving." One of the cops mumbled something. I couldn't hear what, but the manager said, "No, couldn't see if they were black or white but knew they were young by the way they were dressed."

"Please, just a minute," I said quietly at his side, "I'm in a hurry. I need to get paid."

"We're almost finished, miss," the mumbling cop said to me, "just a few more minutes." I put down my trays and told myself to relax, there was nothing I could do about it. I would explain to Lenny what happened and he could time me at the next stop instead.

"The door slams shut by itself," the manager went on, "so you can't accidentally leave it open."

After maybe five more minutes, the manager turned to me. "Just one second, please," he said to the cops, "let me take care of this patient young lady." He checked my bill and counted out my money.

I walked slowly to my truck, knowing what was coming.

Lenny was smiling. "Well, well," he said. This time he held his watch in his hand like a stopwatch. "You beat the record. Did you take a nap in there or spend the time in the john? I don't even want an explanation. You're finished. We're going back."

"There is one—an explanation, I mean."

"Too late."

"Please, give me a chance. Just listen for a minute."

"Don't beg. The office will decide what to do with you. Maybe you can get a cashier's job in the thrift store.

You didn't really think you could handle this kind of work, did you?''

My eyes started to blur like they sometimes did when I got really angry. I shook my head to clear it but it wouldn't go away. I was too mad. "You son of a bitch," I said, "get the fuck off."

"What did you say?"

"I said get off my truck! Now!"

He laughed and went to sit down in the driver's seat. I could see better now and I grabbed two of the metal trays.

"Calm down, let's not have things get out of hand," he said, keeping his eyes on the trays.

"Get off the truck or I'll slam your head between these trays."

"You're kidding?"

"I'm serious and I'm ready," I said.

He stood up and slowly stepped down to the pavement. "Okay, lady, but it's your ass. You'll have a lawsuit on your hands when you get back to the depot."

"Now!" I yelled. He walked away but kept his eyes on my truck as I drove off.

"Well, this is it!" I thought. "I'm on my own." I started to laugh. "Go get it, baby. HomeMade needs women and this might be your only chance to prove yourself."

I had a great day. I took my time, tried not to get too crazy about what was waiting for me back at the depot, and did every store on that side of the route. All twenty-five of them. It was a blast. I loved driving through the streets in that old truck, looking at the world from so high up. I started singing a song I remembered from when I was a kid, with all these instruments playing a piece of the song. I was every one of those instruments, singing each part at the top of my lungs. My voice bounced off the walls of the truck as I rode along, and I took in the sweet smell of cake and the beautiful day. I was having the time of my life. All the storekeepers along the route were glad to see me. I explained that I was new and that it would take a little time for me to remember each store and what they needed, but that one day soon I'd be one of HomeMade's best deliverers. They smiled and wished me luck and helped direct me to my next store. The work wasn't easy but I wasn't scared anymore.

It was dark when I rolled into Knickerbocker Avenue that night followed by two cop cars that had been searching the streets for a HomeMade truck driven by a female driver. I was told that two other trucks, one driven by a supervisor and the other by a mechanic, were still out there looking for me.

Frank Williams, the branch manager, and Roger from Douglaston were waiting for me in the office. They were cheery and well-mannered. "Nice to see you, young lady," Frank said.

"Thanks, nice to see you."

"Did you have a good day?" Frank asked.

"The best."

"I can see that. You look a little tired, I must say, but none the worse for wear."

"Nah, I'm fine. Really fine."

"That was some chance you took today," Frank said. "You could have gotten into big trouble."

"I know."

"Do you have anything to say for yourself?"

"Yeah. I guess I need to know what happens next. Do I get to keep my job?"

Frank laughed. "Well, anyone who spends from morning until night on the route and still wants the job"—he laughed again and put his arm around my shoulder—"can definitely keep it."

"Thanks. But one more thing. No more supervisors, okay?"

"Not a chance," he said. "I value their lives."

"I did a good job," I said.

"I'm sure."

For the next few weeks, I worked a twelve-hour day, getting in late every night as I found my way around the route and learned everything there was to know about the job. And I don't remember even being tired.

During those weeks I never forgot about Pudgy's idea about moving in. He came by more and more often, and me and Nick and Joey were getting used to having him around and were feeling real comfortable with him. He played with the boys and held them in ways Tom never did. Tom rarely came by these days, and sometimes I completely forgot that he was their father. It felt more like he was just some guy we used to know. If I asked Tom which one of the boys was crazy about pets and which one loved anything with wheels, I don't think he'd have known. Pudgy could've told you after the first two days he spent with us.

Night after night I went over the pros and cons of Pudgy moving in. There were good reasons, like him helping with the rent and being company for me and the kids. He was also a good cook, and I knew that, unlike Tom, Pudgy would fix things and help with the cleaning.

But I didn't know what it would be like living with a guy that wasn't my husband. We were becoming good friends, but would he want more from me or start treating me like a girlfriend. And what about sex? That could become a big problem. Could we live together and could I walk around in my nightgown and skimpy clothes in the summer and not worry about whether I was turning him on? When I was ten years old, before I even had breasts, my mother cursed me out for walking from my bedroom to the bathroom in a full slip. Said I was acting like a street whore in front of my father and brothers. I wouldn't want to tease Pudgy like that. Right now I wasn't interested in sex with him. Maybe that would change someday, maybe not, but I didn't want it to become an issue between us.

One night when Pudgy was over, we talked, just me and him, for a long time about what we would want from living together. I told him straight out what my worries were, and that I thought sex could be a real problem. He said he had the same thoughts but that he decided that we had more good things going for us than not, and that we should give it a try. Then he said something that made me think I couldn't say no anymore. Pudgy's schedule had been changed. Now his workday was going to start at nine-thirty in the morning and end in late afternoon or early evening. Which meant that if he moved in, he could be home when I left for work and bring the boys to school every morning. It was the answer to the one problem I hadn't yet figured out in this new life of mine.

Later, I always wondered if he hadn't asked Home-Made to change his schedule, saying there were family reasons or something, just so he could help out by taking care of Nick and Joey in the mornings. But the truth was,

I was starting to like him being a part of us and was kind of looking forward to living with him.

So I said yes, he should move in, and we found an old half-full bottle of Tom's vodka, mixed it with orange juice, and got totally smashed. Pudgy fell asleep on the little bed in what was soon going to be his new room.

The Cowboy, Joanie, and Little Dominic

I GAVE PUDGY A KEY and he came by to fix up the little room and carry over boxes of his clothes and belongings. He scrubbed and hammered and painted whenever he got the chance. By Sunday night, Pudgy was all moved in. Everything was in place, even his books. I teased him when I saw that he'd arranged his books in alphabetical order by author on Tom's bookshelves. But I stopped laughing when he said that ever since he was a kid he had alphabetized his books like they did in the library, but that maybe it was a stupid idea and he should mix them up again.

Pudgy made pizza eggs for dinner. It was Nick and Joey's favorite dish. Sunny-side ups sitting in tomato sauce on an English muffin, topped by whatever cheese we had in the fridge. After dinner, I put Nick and Joey in the bath.

Except for the big talk I had with them when Tom first left, explaining why Tom wasn't going to live with us anymore, I never talked about Tom with the boys and they never asked. I was afraid that if I even mentioned Tom, they'd see how much I hated him, and I didn't think they needed to live with that. That was why Nick's question took me by surprise in the middle of my shampooing his and Joey's hair.

"Mommy, where does Daddy live?"

"A small apartment on Amsterdam Avenue."

"Is it pretty?"

"Nicky, doesn't he take you there when you spend time with him?"

"No." Nick thought for a minute and then asked, "Mommy, does he take you there?"

"No, Nicky, Mommy never goes to Daddy's house. I've never seen it either, but I'm sure it's pretty." While they poured cups of water over each other's heads to get the soap off, I wrote a note to remind myself to call Tom and ask him to show them his new apartment.

I left them splashing and playing in the water and went to clean up the kitchen, but everything was already done, the dishes dried and put away, and even the pots were scoured. I usually washed the kitchen floor every night after dinner, but I decided to skip it as long as Pudgy had done everything else. Pudgy was bent over, his head out the kitchen window, his elbows on the ledge, just leaning on the windowsill, looking out. I stuck my head out too, my arms pressed up against his, and we talked as we looked down at the street.

I remembered how, years before, when I was little, I'd hide in my room on summer nights with the lights off and look through a tear in the shade. Mothers would be out on the street with their kids, getting in an extra hour of play before it got too dark. I'd follow men walking up from the train station to their front doors and check out how the teenagers in the neighborhood flirted and danced to their radios.

Pudgy said he loved living in a real neighborhood and that there was a time in his life when he thought he'd never get to come home again. "I was on a nuclear submarine in the navy," he said, "and there was a radiation leak in the area where I was working. They closed off our part of the ship, with me and another guy still down there to try and stop the leak. We were there for eight days.'' Pudgy fidgeted with his hair, pulling on the ends. ''When we were let out of there, they put us in the hospital for observation. But I freaked out so bad that they kept me in a mental ward, and it was six months before they finally let me go home.''

Some guy walked by with his radio blasting. ''Can you turn it up a bit,'' Pudgy called down to the street, ''our stereo's broken.'' The guy didn't hear, but we laughed together.

I asked Pudgy to tell me about Jed, my depot manager. I was nervous because Jed was coming back from vacation this week. ''Do you think I'll like him and he'll like me?'' I asked.

''I'm not sure if you'll like him,'' Pudgy said. ''I wish I could say yes.'' Pudgy kept tugging on his hair, pulling the ends piece by piece. ''The Cowboy's a tough sort of guy, kind of hard to like. He came up through the ranks like me,'' Pudgy explained, ''from packer to driver, then supervisor to manager, without ever finishing high school. Somehow along the way he got himself a white Anglo-Saxon princess with a law degree, three spoiled-rotten kids, and a house in Westchester. I don't know how he did it, 'cause the guy's no class act.''

Nick and Joey were hollering that they wanted to get out of the bath, and Pudgy offered to put them to bed while I lay down and watched TV. The last thing I heard was Nick and Joey trying to sing a Greek song that Pudgy was teaching them. When I left for work, not too many hours later, Pudgy and the boys were still asleep.

. . .

I heard him before I saw him. I was loading my truck when a loud voice came booming out of the office. "Yup, a little visit with my momma this time. Just the way I remembered it. Kids all over the place, all the food money spent on drink, my best friends' wives copping a feel in the kitchen. Home sweet home!" Then it was quiet for a moment until I heard him bellow, "Are you nuts? My wife wasn't there. She ain't never met my family, and she ain't gonna."

Joanie had said I'd know the minute Jed was back. "You won't have to be introduced, he makes himself known. The Cowboy ain't an easy man except with the ones he likes, and even them he gives a hard time. You might get lucky and be one of his favorites. Then again, you might not. Just go slow with him and don't say nothing that you don't want thrown back in your face."

I was dying to get a look at him, so I headed for the office. About five guys were standing around talking, but they stopped when I walked in. "Hi," I said, and no one answered. I could feel my smile getting stiff on my face and wished I could turn around and walk back out again.

Jed's was the only face I didn't recognize. The others I'd seen around the depot, though I'd never actually been introduced to any of them. Jed wasn't at all like I pictured him. I thought he'd look like Eddie's dad, Mr. Mahoney, big and tall with fair hair and a round red face. Except for the red face, he didn't look like that at all. His hair had probably been black at one time, 'cause his mustache was dark, but the front of his head was rounded and he was totally bald. Because of that, and because of his narrow, dark eyes and beaklike nose, he reminded me of a parrot or an eagle. He was the tallest man there and not very heavy, but he stooped over so badly that his belly pushed against his shirt, making his buttons look ready to pop.

"I'm Anna Ferrara," I said, looking at Jed. "I was wondering if I'm pulling Jimmy's route again this week." Jed let out a loud howl and the others joined in laughing.

"Why is that funny?" I asked.

"We all know who you are but obviously you don't know none of us." Jed tugged his shirt over his belly and tucked it into his pants. "For your information, that's Jimmy standing next to you. He's got some Oriental name, but Jimmy's good enough for us."

"Jin Ho Lee," Jimmy said, with a slight bow. "It's Korean, but Jimmy's easier to remember."

Jed continued. "The big ape attached to him is Ernesto. Red is the one with the blue hair"—Jed laughed at his own joke—"but he's transferring, so you can forget him. And last but definitely least is Little Dominic." Little Dominic shook his fist at Jed and disappeared into the men's room.

"They call me the Cowboy," Jed went on, "'cause I don't follow nobody's rules but my own. I run this depot the way I want to run it. Those little guys in the big Mercedes that run this company give me my paycheck but nobody gives me my orders. And, lady, I heard about you already, which is not good news. I'm hoping not to hear about you for the rest of the year. Anything else?"

"I don't know which route I'm pulling this week," I said.

"Next week we start you on your own route. This week you got Mario's. His mother died, so he'll only be out for a week. Here's his route book." He held out an old torn book, and as I took it, Jed turned to Little Dominic, who was coming back out of the men's room. "C'mere, Dom." Little Dominic came and stood at Jed's side. Jed bent over and rested his arm across Little Dominic's shoulders, which were low, because Dominic was a lot shorter even than me.

"Dominic, sir! Call up your Uncle Guido and tell him I need a good stereo for my boy's birthday. Willing to go as high as five dollars." He laughed and coughed at the same time, and Little Dominic stood there but he wasn't smiling. I knew right then I'd never be one of Jed's favorites.

The men emptied out of the office, and as Ernesto, the one Jed called a big ape, passed my truck, he winked at me. I smiled back. I liked the way he looked. Big, muscular, long dark hair pulled back into a ponytail, and a little friendlier than the other guys. Joanie had already told me a lot about him the other day after someone tried to hold him up on the route. She never said his name was Ernesto, just that he was Cuban and that everybody called him Baby Huey. She said a guy pulled a foot-long knife on him outside one of his stops and threatened to slit his throat if he didn't hand over his money. So Baby Huey grabbed the knife out of the guy's hands and threw it on the truck. Then he picked the guy up by his neck, and after smashing his head against the side of the truck, he dragged him to a phone booth across the street, where he called the cops. He stuffed the guy in the booth and held his foot against the door until the cops came.

The guy with the knife must have been either crazy or desperate, because as I watched Baby Huey walk to his truck, I thought he definitely deserved his nickname. It wasn't how tall he was that made you think of the Baby Huey cartoon, but he was massive, with huge shoulders, arms twice the size of a normal man's, and hands that could easily palm a basketball.

Two minutes later I heard Baby Huey yelling from

inside his truck, which was parked only one spot away from mine. "What the fuck are these fucking cookies doing on my truck? Who the fuck put 'em here? On Friday the moron loads us up with cookies, and he knows we never take cookies out over the weekend. And today you expect us to get rid of another two boxes. You guys are loco. You can take these cookies and stuff 'em." He rode past my truck with his back door still open. We never closed our back doors until we left the depot, so we could see what was happening behind us. Baby Huey drove just a few feet, to the middle of the floor, where he stopped. Then he walked from his seat to the back of his truck. Raising one of the heavy cases of cookies above his head, he heaved it across the garage floor and followed it with a second case. Then he sat back down and started to drive off.

Jed came running out of the office and picked up a case of the cookies. Staggering after Huey's truck, he tossed one and then the other onto the back of the truck, yelling, "If you don't want to do your job, don't. Take the day off and I'll pull your route. I'll get you a nice suspension to go with it too. It's your own choice, ya big ape." The truck came to a screeching stop. Jed stood to the side, his fists up, while Baby Huey walked very slowly past him, not even looking his way, and came over to my truck.

"I got tickets to the Knicks game tonight and don't have time to put out these damn cookies," he said softly. "Take 'em out for me, will ya, honey?"

I nodded. There'd be no problem for me to get rid of the cookies along Mario's route. Baby Huey loaded the cookies from his truck onto mine, threw me a kiss, and drove off. All the other trucks were waiting by the garage door and they followed him out like a caravan.

. . .

The first side of Mario's route was easy, only twenty-one stops and I was finished by two in the afternoon. Even though his book was old, his directions were clear and I didn't have far to drive. Mario was called Mario the Mole, not only by the truckers but by the storekeepers too. He looked like a mole, short and round with a wide face and a snoutlike nose. He had a thick head of brown hair and hair covering his neck and arms. But he didn't get the nickname Mario the Mole just because he looked like one. It was more because of how he worked, like a mole, or a pack rat actually. For the past twenty years he drove the same truck and delivered his cake packed in big cardboard boxes to the same neighborhood stores. Jed swore that Mario brought the boxes down from his attic and used the same ones year after year. "They're a home for roaches is what those damn boxes are," Jed said. But Mario had a bad back and claimed that the boxes were easy to carry, that they were lighter than the trays. I tried his boxes when I did his route, but I found the trays easier to use. It wasn't until a year later, when I visited Jimmy in the hospital after a storekeeper caught him stealing and hurt him bad, that I found out the truth about Mario. Mario used those boxes to rob his stores blind. They were like mock-ups, those boxes. Only the top two layers contained boxes of Chocos. The two bottom layers had empty Choco boxes. If someone checked and lifted the top ones they all looked the same. On the way out the bottom boxes were hidden by the carton. Mario counted out four boxes on top times four deep and charged the stores for sixteen boxes of Chocos, though he only gave them eight.

When I got back that afternoon, Joanie said that Baby

Huey had written me a note before he left and that he kept reminding her not to forget to give it to me. She pulled a piece of paper out of her pocket and put it in my hands. It was written on a sheet from one of the accounting pads and said, "Thanks, little one. I won't forget."

"I got another friend," I said to Joanie. "I hope that's what the note means. I been worried about being alone here when you go on vacation." Joanie was starting her vacation the next day and I'd been nervous all week about her leaving.

"Nothing to worry about," Joanie said. "You'll do fine without me. And if Baby Huey decides he likes you, then you got Jimmy too. They're best friends, more like brothers actually."

Joanie was planning to go out west on her own for two weeks, which I didn't understand at all. She was thirty-eight years old, had never been married, and sort of admitted that she was still a virgin. The only guy who'd ever touched her was a guy selling vacuums who liked her breasts. Joanie lived at home with her parents and had never taken a vacation without them. And now she was going to rent a car and drive through the Rockies, to Yellowstone Park and the Grand Canyon. She planned the whole thing out with Little Dominic. Every day when he came off the route, he sat with her for an hour or so and mapped out every step of her trip, including where she should stop for gas. I'd come in to settle up and find them bent over a map of the United States with markers in their hands. Dominic's beefy arm would be pressed against Joanie's pale thin one as they pointed and wrote, talking in very quiet but excited voices. By the time she was ready to leave, she had the name of every hotel, restaurant, and attraction that she was going to see and how long each stop or visit would take.

"What about one of those Club Meds or something for singles like you hear about on the radio?" I'd asked her. "That way you won't be alone day and night. They got ones for people over thirty. And you might meet someone you like."

"I'm too shy," she said.

I never thought of Joanie as shy, seeing as how good she got along with me and the guys. And with her soft curls, ski-jump nose, and full lips, she was kinda pretty. She was a full head taller than me, and even though she dressed and talked like one of the guys, aside from that, she was feminine.

But she was so excited about her trip that after a while I had the sense to shut up and just let her enjoy it. "I think I'll ask for a convertible so I can be part of the great outdoors," was the last thing she said about it. But Joanie had one more thing to add about Baby Huey that afternoon before we said goodbye. "Anna," she said, "I don't want you to take this wrong, 'cause I know you just met him. But remember we were talking about how Baby Huey would make a great friend?" I nodded, so she went on. "Well, I think that's true, but on the other hand, I think he'd make a lousy boyfriend."

"What does that have to do with me?" I asked, feeling uncomfortable. "Why're you saying that to me? What do I care what kinda boyfriend he'd make? Boyfriends are the last thing on my mind. I just want to make good on this job, not spend my time thinking about guys and things like that." I looked at her face and she smiled, but it didn't look like she was listening to me. "Anyway,

I'd never mess around with someone at work." After a minute or so I said, "But now I'm curious. Why do you think Baby Huey wouldn't make a good boyfriend?"

"I'm not sure, but it's been on my mind and I wanted to say something to you. I know Baby Huey likes you. I seen him sneaking looks at you when you walk by. Half the time, he can't take his eyes off you. And he's a nice guy, everyone likes him, even Jed. But he's not all there, is what. I don't mean he's crazy or anything like that, but something's not right. Like I can't picture him caring for anyone, not really. He's got a good heart, but I think something's missing."

The next morning at work I already felt lonely knowing Joanie wasn't there. But as I was loading my truck, Baby Huey came over. He stubbed out his cigarette and tossed it under my truck, brushing the ashes off his HomeMade emblem as he said, "This here guy's my best friend that I wanted you to meet—mi hermanito Jimmy." Jimmy was standing next to him looking down at his work boots.

"I think we already met," I said and smiled.

"That other day don't count," Baby Huey said. "Jed was telling you our names but he wasn't introducing you nice, like a gentleman."

"I'm glad to meet you," I told Jimmy.

"Me too. Good to see ya," he said.

Baby Huey grabbed at Jimmy's cap but Jimmy moved away fast. "Take off the hat," Baby Huey said, "where's your manners?" Jimmy looked at me and tipped his cap. I could see as he raised it that he used it to hide his hair, which was prematurely gray. He was probably not even thirty. We smiled at each other and then they turned and

left saying, "Have a nice day." I stood there for a minute
or two, still smiling, watching them walk to their trucks,
glad that even with Joanie gone, I wouldn't be alone in the
depot anymore.

The other side of Mario's route wasn't hard either.
An extra store or two but no real heavy work or bad
traffic. And most of his stores were bright and clean. The
only thing unusual about this side of the route was that he
had Creedmore, the mental institution, as one of his customers. In grammar school, when we were bad, our
teacher threatened to send us to Creedmore to live with
the crazies.

Mario's directions were carefully written at the top of
each page of the route book with perfect lettering in red
ink. They were easy to follow and I made it without any
problem to a street where a tall concrete gate circled what
looked like a huge estate. A long metal sign engraved with
the name Creedmore stood in front. The entranceway was
somewhat hidden by thick, green trees that hung low to
the ground.

It reminded me of a mansion in Englewood, New
Jersey, that I visited when I was a kid, and I started
remembering how in nice weather we went there sometimes to play. We were five best friends until Fredericka's
mother got a job as caretaker of the mansion. So Fredericka, who was one of the five, and her brother Tim moved
to Englewood. But when they got lonely out there, all us
neighborhood kids were invited to visit. Fredericka's dad
came and got us every weekend in the spring and summer.
Most of us had never been in the country before. There
was a small swimming pool, ducks and geese, and a huge
dining room table. But the two things I remember most
was me and Carmela and Fredericka trying on hundreds of

dresses that "the lady of the house," as Fredericka's mom called her, left behind. The family that owned the mansion went abroad for a year but ended up never returning to the States. And my second-favorite thing was me and Carmela washing our feet in their strange potties, what Fredericka's mom told us were bidets. We counted them when we hid in the bathrooms at the end of the weekend—there were fifty-three. It always took them a while to go through all those bathrooms to find us. We were usually soaking our feet somewhere between the twenty-third and fortieth bathrooms, because we liked the ones on the second floor best. Those bathrooms faced out over a small garden and a pond. And every time when Fredericka's mom or dad found us, they didn't yell or hit us, they just told us real nice that it was time to go home.

It made me nervous driving through those big gates into a mental institution. And I didn't feel much better when I was inside the gates and realized that most of the people walking around the grounds were inmates. They were wearing hospital gowns and some of them looked real crazy. I would've been more scared but I thought there shouldn't be anything to worry about, because HomeMade wouldn't send us anywhere really dangerous.

Creedmore's grounds were beautiful, but you could definitely tell it was an institution. It was missing the personal touch that private houses had. When I visited my cousin Vicky at college it looked like this, tall trees, perfectly cut grass, and clean white buildings. The problem for me was that all of it looked the same. I had no idea where I was supposed to bring the cake, because there were no signs directing me to a store or a food stand. There wasn't even something that said Office or Main Building.

I drove all around Creedmore until I finally saw a nicely dressed woman in a tailored pants outfit. Her dark hair was neatly tied back with a long velvet ribbon, and I was sure she was a social worker or a doctor, so I parked and called out to her. She started to run but I was faster and caught up to her. I grabbed her arm, "Excuse me, miss, I didn't mean to scare you, but could you please help me. I'm trying to find which one of these buildings . . ." I stopped. She wouldn't look at me, just stood there shaking. "I'm sorry," I said. I let her go and watched her run off through the grass. I waited and stopped two more people passing by. But when I asked if they knew of a hospital store or snack stand on the grounds, they smiled and looked right through me. Then they walked away. I wanted to leave, drive right out of there and go to my next stop, let Mario take care of this one when he came back. But I was afraid to do that after what Jed said about not wanting to hear nothing more about me for the rest of the year.

So I drove even slower and kept my eyes peeled, trying not to miss a thing. Finally there was a small building that had a door open in the back. In front of the door was a hand-painted wooden sign with a picture of a big ice cream soda and two small cupcakes. I knew this had to be the place. I walked down two steps and found myself in a tiny store that was crammed full of everything from magazines to candy to gardening gloves. It looked like a sort of camp canteen, a place where the inmates got to use their spending money. I had no idea what to do next and didn't see any HomeMade Cake when I looked along the shelves. Two guys wearing gray uniform-type jackets were dusting the cans and boxes. I approached the one wearing a tag that said MANAGER. "Hi, I'm from HomeMade Cakes," I said to him. "I'm taking over Mario's job this week and I need your help. I have no idea what I'm supposed to bring in."

The guy was twenty-five, maybe thirty years old, short and thin, with bald patches throughout his dark hair and one tooth missing in front. While I was talking to him, he removed the manager's tag and stuck it on the pocket of the other guy in the gray jacket. The second guy had all his hair and teeth. He stepped right up to me and studied my face. He stood there tugging on his ear with one hand and scratching his back using the wooden duster with the other. "Can you help me?" I asked. He shrugged his shoulders and his eyes moved over my body. I decided to figure it out myself, without their help. There was an empty space near the candy that I thought I could fill with snack cake, so that's what I decided to do.

I came back in with a few pies, Chocos, Honeybelles, and Bonzos. I handed the tall guy my receipt and gave him my pen, showing him where to sign. He scribbled something that didn't look like a name, more like an apple with a smile. I hoped that there was a standing account with Creedmore so that I could get paid somehow. I wasn't going to see any money from these two guys.

I'd left the door of my truck open since I was running in with a such a small load. But when I got outside again, a big fat guy was standing on the top step of my truck. He had two Chocos in his hand and one or two in his mouth. There was a stick lying in the grass, so I grabbed it and ran up the steps. "What are you doing in here?" I yelled. He tried to talk as he moved back against the steering wheel, but his mouth was too full. His eyes opened wide and he kept pointing to his mouth. "Get out of here," I shouted and I held the stick up. He kept his eyes on the stick and tried to squeeze into my seat. I shook the stick at him and he pushed farther back into the seat and growled, showing his teeth and a mouth full of Chocos. I raised the stick again and he growled louder and waved his hands in the air. I decided to back off and go easy with him, so I said softly, "Look, this is my truck. Please go." He kind of wagged his head back and forth and slowly made his way down the steps, tripping on the last step and landing in the grass on all fours. He reared back and sat looking at the two Chocos that were squashed in his hand.

I put my truck in gear and found my way out of there without any more problems.

At the end of the day, I went into Jed's office to ask about the Creedmore account. Baby Huey was standing by Jed's desk, waiting for Jed to get off the phone. As I walked in, I overheard Jed say what a pain in the ass I was and thank God HomeMade had only one woman driver. "If we had any more," he said to the person on the phone, "it'd be murder. It's bad enough having to face one of them when you get home at night, much less have to take their bitching and moaning all day long on the job."

To hell with you, I thought. I wanted to push the button down on the phone, but instead I cleared my throat as loud as I could until Jed looked up. He grinned and held up his hand, gesturing for me to wait next to Baby Huey until he got off the phone.

I could tell by what Jed said next that the person on the other end was asking about Audrey, the woman they hired over at the Long Island depot the same day as me.

"That one? What a waste!" the Cowboy said. "Just 'cause she was Dick Moran's brother's wife we hire her, put her in the best depot with a route where she can make big money and get home early, and what happens?'' He stared straight at me and kept grinning as he continued. ''After hearing about Anna and that meathead Lenny, Audrey decides that she can be as high and mighty as Little Miss Anna here and that she don't need a supervisor neither. So now Audrey goes driving around out there all on her own as well. But then Merrick gets a call from a store saying that a HomeMade truck's been sitting across the street for over five hours, what's up? Seems Audrey was having trouble on the job and never let anyone know. She went home and never come back. Just like that! Didn't even have the courtesy to call the depot and quit.''

He went on for a while more, but I stopped listening and just watched Baby Huey, who was whistling real quietly and tapping on his belt buckle, moving his head up and down in time to the beat. I was standing so close to him that I could smell his aftershave, or maybe his hairspray, and it smelled so good that it was the first time that I missed having a husband or boyfriend since Tom left. The second Jed hung up, Baby Huey started to talk, and Huey was loud.

''You dumb Cowboy, you're such a liar, you know that?'' Baby Huey said. Instead of getting embarrassed, Jed grinned. Baby Huey went on. ''Why didn't you tell the truth to whoever you was talking to on that phone about what happened to Audrey? You're acting as if it's all a mystery.''

''That's private information you're referring to,'' Jed said as he leaned way back in his chair, pushing out his belly and smiling as he tucked his fingers under his belt like it was a holster.

''How private can it be if you told me and Jimmy and Little Dominic and everybody else at Knickerbocker Ave-

nue? Everyone except maybe Anna here.'' Baby Huey
turned to me and said, ''Never mind him. Do you know
why that woman gave up? I'll tell you why. A few days
before she quit, two guys jumped her truck, held a gun to
her head, and made her drive to a deserted area.'' Baby
Huey shook his head like he was picturing it and it was not
good. ''Then they tied her up and pried out her safe. No
one knows for sure what else they did to her, but her
clothes were pretty badly ripped when they found her. The
holdup guys threatened to return when their money ran
low. And the day Audrey left,'' Baby Huey said, giving Jed
a long hard look, ''her truck was stopped at a light when
she saw them again in her rearview mirror. She pulled up
across from one of her stores, locked the door, and ran.''
He looked straight at Jed and said more loudly, ''She called
Dick that night when she finally calmed down.''

I stayed long enough to get the information I needed
about Creedmore, said thanks to Baby Huey, and went
home.

Thursday was the day I had to do the side of the route with
Creedmore again. I was feeling good about the job because
I was getting to be a better driver and deliverer, finishing
about the same time as the rest of the guys. But this day
seemed to be dragging, I guess since I was putting off
delivering to Creedmore. I wasn't exactly dreading going
back there, but I definitely wasn't looking forward to it. At
least I would know my way around this time and wouldn't
have to spend all afternoon driving back and forth across
the hospital grounds.

Creedmore looked pretty much the same as the first
time I was there and I circled the place only twice before

I remembered where the small, round building was. The soda sign was there but the shop door was closed. I knocked a few times before two women answered and, after looking me over carefully, let me in. They were wearing the same gray uniform jackets as the two guys from last time, and they didn't look any more like managers than those guys. One woman looked pretty old, seventy or eighty at least. She was the only one who spoke. "Well, young lady," she said to me. She stopped and looked me over from head to foot, "You are a lady, aren't you?" she asked, pointing at my black HomeMade shirt and pants and adding, "though you don't appear to dress like one." My uniform had finally arrived, and even though it didn't fit, it was better than wearing my own clothes. I had already trashed two sets of shirts and pants in those first few weeks.

I laughed and shook my head yes. "Yup, I'm a lady," I said.

"Well, you just take care of your business and we won't bother you."

"That'll be fine," I said. I went about my work more comfortably this time, particularly since Jed gave me a list of Creedmore's standing order and explained that the account was settled through the office. I was whistling to myself as I walked back to my truck, glad that I had gotten in and out of there without a problem.

I had a soda on the truck that I'd bought at a burger stand a half hour before. There was still ice in the cup, so when I got outside the gates, I parked my truck in front of the Creedmore sign and sat in the grass drinking my soda. I needed a break. I ate half a Choco and closed my eyes for a few minutes. The sun was hot but there was a slight breeze blowing. It was a beautiful day. When I was ready to go, I brushed myself off, and as I got closer to the truck, I heard a soft buzzing coming from inside. I looked in, then tripped as I stepped back, trying to move out of the way as fast as I could. The truck was filled with bees or yellow jackets—I wasn't sure what they were. They were everywhere, swarming around my seat, on the steps, and up and down the aisle. I had no idea where they came from, and as I stood there in the grass, not knowing what to do, I burst into tears.

After a minute or two I stopped crying. Someone at the depot would know how to get the bees out of my truck. There was a phone booth across the way, so I walked over there and dialed the main depot. Jed answered.

"Knickerbocker Avenue."

"Jed?"

"Yes'm."

"This is Anna."

"Yes'm."

"I got a problem."

"Yes'm."

"There are bees in my truck."

"Yes'm."

"Not just one or two bees, Jed, but at least a hundred bees. Only, I think they're yellow jackets, which means they sting bad."

"Yes'm."

"What should I do?"

"What are you calling me for? It's your damn truck, not mine. What do you mean what should you do? What every red-blooded man in the depot would do. Get back on your truck and drive away. What else would you do?"

"You mean I just walk into a truck full of yellow jackets?"

"Listen, Miss High and Mighty. You had the balls to take a man's job but then you start complaining the minute it gets a little rough. Well, if you want to keep the job, you better get off your ass and do the job like a man. And I mean now! Those little bees are just like every other red-blooded American. They love them Chocos, they smell the sweetness right through the wrapping. Now if you don't got nothing else to say, I got work to do. I got double the work with my cashier gallivanting all over the Old West these days." He hung up.

I didn't feel like going back to the truck, so I sat down right there on the curb. As I sat there, I thought about how scared I was of bugs when I was little. Around the time when I was four to about six years old, my mom and dad would go out and leave me alone with my brothers at night. On the hot summer days, my brothers would play what they called the "Flying Bug Game" with me. We all hated bugs, but at that time I was so much littler and easier to scare that I was the best one to play it on. So as soon as my parents walked out the door, my brothers would open the windows and turn on all the lights to attract the bugs. The room would fill with every kind of flying bug. I would sit on a chair in the middle of the room, tears rolling down my face, trying to keep my eyes on the closest ones that crawled or flew toward me. I'd sit there swinging my arms as fast as I could to keep them away, but I'd feel them on my body and in my hair no matter what I did. When I got older, I was still afraid of bugs but I learned not to show it.

I stood up, wiped my face on my sleeve, and

walked to the truck. The inside of the truck was still filled with bees. Just do it, I said aloud, just climb back on. So I stepped up to my seat, sat down, put the truck in gear, and drove off. I kept my eyes on the road and tried not to look at the bees or get startled when they flew at me. It's okay, I kept saying to myself, you're going to be okay. If you don't hurt them, they won't hurt you. And it was true. The bees flew around but they actually didn't bother me. And after a few blocks, I stopped being afraid of them. For some reason, they disappeared on the shady streets and then reappeared on the sunnier ones. I got stung once but it was kind of my own fault. I was careless. A bee was sitting on the steering wheel and when I was ready to drive off, I grabbed hold of the wheel and it stung me in the palm of my hand. It was the first time I'd ever been stung and it wasn't as bad as I thought it would be. I had no problem after that. But I couldn't forgive Jed for the way he handled it.

I drove into the depot and was suprised that most of the guys were still there. Then I remembered that Thursday was everybody's late day and a lot of the guys hung around the depot or hit the bars together after work.

This time when I pulled in, quite a few of them said hi and waved, calling out for me to join them. But I still had to clean out my stale, settle in, and count up my money. So I said thanks, that I'd join them some other time, and started putting my truck in order. Later, when I went inside to settle up, Baby Huey was hanging around talking to Little Dominic.

After I finished my paperwork, I stopped by Jed's office on the way out. He was looking through a thick black manual with the HomeMade emblem across the top.

"I brought you something off my route," I told him. He sat there pulling on his mustache with one hand while he turned the pages of the manual with the other. "I got you something special." I held out my plastic soda cup, which still had the lid on and the straw sticking out the top. Jed wouldn't take the cup, he never even lifted his eyes from the manual. I put the cup down on his desk and took the top off. Three bees came flying out. I guess the rest were still in the cup. I had squashed a part of a Choco in the bottom of the cup and used it to catch five or six bees the last time they invaded my truck. Jed stood up and started hollering.

"You motherfucking maniac," Jed yelled. "I'm giving you a suspension. What if I was allergic to bees?" he shouted as he backed away, his hands moving back and forth in front of his face. Baby Huey and Little Dominic came to the door of the office.

"What if *I* was?" I answered softly. "Besides which, you can't suspend me for bringing you a gift. I wanted to show my appreciation for all the help you gave me this afternoon."

"I can damn well suspend anyone I want for whatever I want," Jed said.

With a newspaper in hand, Baby Huey walked over to Jed's desk, smashed two bees sitting on the manual, and brushed them to the floor. Then he whacked another one sitting on Jed's desk calendar. "I'm ready for a suspension, old man," Baby Huey said so quietly I almost couldn't hear him. "If there's any trouble about these little buggers, I'm going to swear that I gave you the cup. Only everybody will know that ain't true, 'cause if I gave them to ya, I woulda made you drink them." He stopped and looked at Jed. "I think it's time to call it even."

"Just get these damn yeller jackets outta here," Jed said and turned away. I walked off thinking it would be best for me to get out of there quickly, to let Baby Huey settle things with Jed.

On my way to the train, a car pulled up beside me. Soft music was coming from the car. "Hey, lady, want a ride?" It was Baby Huey, his arm hanging over the door, a cigarette dangling from his fingers.

"Nah, I can walk. By the way, thanks for helping me in there."

"C'mon, get in," he said but I shook my head no. Baby Huey drove down the street a bit, stopped the car, and got out. He came over and got in step beside me. "It's my birthday and I need some company," he whispered softly in my ear. I shook my head no again but he took hold of my arm and guided me around to the passenger side of the car. I laughed and said okay. When we were both seated, he said, "I got a message for you."

"Happy Birthday," I said. I leaned over and kissed his cheek. His skin felt warm and soft against my lips. "So what's this message?"

"Another kiss first," he said. So I took his face in my hands, turned it to the side, and kissed him on the other cheek.

"Don't you have any plans for your birthday?" I asked.

"What kinda plans would I have? Me and Jimmy woulda gone out for drinks but his littlest kid got sick and his wife can't take off from work to watch 'em."

"What about your family, your wife?" I remembered seeing a wedding band on his finger my first week at Knickerbocker Avenue, but I hadn't seen it since then.

"What about them?" he asked, frowning.

"Wouldn't they want to celebrate with you?"

"Nah. My family's all in Chicago, and I was married for three weeks and then it went kaput. Why'd you think I was married, 'cause I wear a band sometimes?" I nodded. "I wear a band when I'm working so I don't give girls the wrong idea. What about you? I see you don't wear a band," he said.

"I'm not married anymore, but I got two kids."

"Oh."

"Don't look like it's such bad news. I'm glad I got two nice kids," I said. "They're the only good thing I got out of my marriage." He wouldn't look up, so I changed the subject. "So what's this message you got for me?"

"First, can I get another birthday kiss?" he asked with a big smile, facing forward this time. I leaned over and kissed him softly on the lips. A long, nice kiss, not sexy or nothing, just sweet. Then he leaned back against the seat and said, "Thanks. That was nice."

"The message?" I asked again.

"It's from Joanie. She called the depot yesterday hoping to talk to you but she just missed you. She asked Jed to give you a message, but he never remembers messages. Anyway, she said to tell you she's having the best vacation ever."

"Are you kidding? Driving around out west by herself? Visiting the wonders of the world alone? I don't believe it."

"It's true. You just don't see it, honey," Baby Huey said gently. "Joanie's not alone, not exactly, anyway."

"You mean she's with someone and she's hiding it? Why would she do that?" I couldn't see Joanie sneaking around out west with some guy and not telling people, unless he was married or something.

"No, nothing like that. It's different than you think. She's with Little Dominic."

"Are you crazy? Wasn't Little Dominic at the depot two minutes ago?" I was trying to think. Maybe I had Little Dominic mixed up with someone else. "Wasn't that Little Dominic in the office with us when I was fighting with Jed?" Baby Huey nodded. "Then what are you talking about?"

"He's in her heart. Her and Little Dominic planned out every inch of her trip together. He knows where she is almost every minute of the day. And each time she stops for lunch or dinner or stays at a hotel, he calls her. If she's not exactly on time, he leaves a message. I know, 'cause he told me. He's madly in love with her, and from what I understand, she's botz about him. They never admitted it when she was on the job, even to themselves. And then she goes on this crazy trip and it's like fireworks. He's with her more than if he was actually on the trip. But he says he's definitely gonna take action when she gets back. Anyway, she sends her love."

Joanie and Little Dominic. I couldn't believe it. It was the nicest thing I'd heard in a long time.

When we got to the train station, Baby Huey turned off the engine but left the music on and asked could we sit for a while. I said sure. We sat for a few minutes listening to the music and then he asked, "Can I touch you?" He pointed to my breasts. "There, I mean?"

"Another birthday present?" I teased. "I already gave you one."

"Most people get lots of birthday presents."

I didn't think about it for long. Something about this long, lousy day and being tired and Baby Huey asking so nicely and smelling so good made me glad he wanted to touch me. I shook my head yes. "Okay," I said.

He moved out from under the steering wheel, lifting me up and placing me against the door. Very gently he reached out with both hands and drew them across the front of my shirt. "You got nice breasts," he said softly.

"Thanks." I felt like a sexy woman. Not a trucker, not a mom, just a woman with breasts that this big strong-looking guy wanted to touch. I looked down at his hands, nice big hands. I liked that. I was only five foot four but I had big hands and was always glad when someone had hands bigger than mine.

Baby Huey and I were squashed against each other, my leg over his, his arms over mine. He bent his head and rested it against the window as he ran his hands across my breasts, then all the way down to my thighs and between, then up to my breasts again. "You feel good," he said. He rubbed his hand back and forth over my nipples until they stood out against the shirt. I got embarrassed and covered them with my hands.

"Do you like me?" he asked.

"I think so. I don't know you."

"Do you like what you see?" Baby Huey sat up straight as if to give me a better look.

"Yes, I do. I like what I see." I looked at his dark eyes, his Cuban nose, big but not too big, and with a mole halfway down the side. I ran my hands through his thick hair, combing through it with my fingers, and said again, "Yes, I like what I see."

"Can we go out together?"

"I don't know. I think we got to get to know each other better first."

"Would you like to get to know me?"

I shook my head no and he pulled away fast and wouldn't look at me. "Just kidding," I said, "just kidding.

C'mere." I pulled on his arm and grabbed hold of his face again, making him look in my eyes. I smiled and nodded my head up and down real fast. "Yes, I would like to get to know you."

"Can I have one more kiss?" We kissed again. And this time it was deeper and longer. He rubbed his hands harder along my body, massaging, pulling gently, squeezing.

Finally I pulled away. "Wow," I said, letting out my breath.

Baby Huey took my hand and put it on his crotch. "Feel this," he said, "see what you do to me?" It was hard along the whole front of his pants.

"Hmmm, it feels nice," I murmured and rubbed him very gently. "Yeah, very nice."

"Feels nice to me too," he said. "It wants you."

"What about its owner?"

"Him too."

"We'll see." I moved away and put my back against the door.

Baby Huey lit up a cigarette and sat for a minute just looking at me. Then he said, "You know, you're not really my type. I go for more feminine girls."

"What? Are you saying I'm not feminine? Do you think I look like a guy?"

He laughed. "Of course not. You're sexy, you definitely are. But most of the time I like them kind of petite and dainty-looking."

"Oh, great. Maybe you should keep looking until you find the right size."

"Nah, I didn't mean that, I'm having fun with you."

"Having fun, is that what this is?" I didn't know what to do next. I would've liked to stay there for hours, having him touch and kiss me, and if he had kept saying sweet things, I probably would have. But after him telling me I wasn't his type, I thought maybe all he wanted was to mess around with me and that was it. And I didn't know what I thought about him either. So before it went any further, I said it was getting late and I had to head home. I kissed his cheek, straightened my clothes, and left.

"Happy Birthday!" I called out as he drove away. I took the steps down to the train two at a time, all the time thinking about Baby Huey and Joanie and Little Dominic.

When I opened the door to the apartment, the place smelled of rice and beans and a lot of spices. I found Lily in the kitchen cooking dinner. For the last few weeks she'd been picking Nick and Joey up for me when she had the time and leaving me a message at work that she was doing it. Little by little, the lower shelf in my kitchen had gotten filled with cans of Goya beans. Mama Goya is what Lily started calling herself, and we all loved her dinners.

"They're down in the park with Pudgy watching a basketball game. Let me take this off," she said, untying the only apron I had in the house, one Tom had brought back from New Orleans. It had a picture of a big fat chef on the front. "We can go together to get them."

"Ma, look! Isn't that black guy great?" Joey said excitedly. "He's almost as tall as the basket." Joey and Nick and Pudgy were sitting on a bench right behind the handball courts about a quarter of a block from the basketball game.

"They're all black, Joey, which one do you mean?" All the guys were black and three of them were really tall.

"No they're not, there's only one, see, there he goes," Joey said, pointing to a tall, very thin guy in a black T-shirt and black shorts. "I like the green guy too," he said about a shorter guy in a green T-shirt.

We played a ten-point game of basketball ourselves before we headed home—me and Lily against Pudgy and the boys. The sides were Joey's choice and he always set them up so that he was on the side he thought would win. But Lily and I were good. I'd played in high school and Lily was good at everything. So we scared the shit out of them, only letting them win by a single basket at the last moment.

At dinner Nick told us that for show and tell Joey's class did "What's New in Your House Today" and Joey's new thing had been that he found a baby roach.

"How did you hear about it?" I asked Nick. "Did Joey tell you?" Nick said no, that all the kids in school were talking about it.

"Momma, that was a good 'What's New' thing, wasn't it?" Joey asked and I said yes while Pudgy went into his room to howl. Lily simply smiled behind her hands.

I looked around the table at Nick and Joey and Lily and her nice dinner while listening to Pudgy laughing and hooting in his room and thought that things were definitely looking up.

Jake and Izzy's Superette on Avenue U

WHEN I WAS SEVEN years old, my father said we should take over the vacuuming from my mother. It was enough that she worked from nine to five and then came home and cooked dinner. From that day on, along with the dishes, shopping, and the rest of the cleaning, me and my brothers did the vacuuming too. To make sure we didn't sneak off every Saturday morning before we did the vacuuming, somewhere between 6:00 and 7:00 A.M., my dad would start the vacuum and leave it by the head of our beds. All three of us shared a small room, so it didn't matter whose bed he put it by. I'd go flying across the room to turn it off. After the first few weeks, I began waking through the night to make sure it wasn't light out yet. I wanted to be up and ready to beat the sound of the vacuum. So when people asked, did I mind the hours of my new job, I shook my head no. I was always up long before the alarm clock went off at 4:00 A.M.

The radio said clear skies and sunny, fifty-three degrees, going up to sixty-two. Beautiful weather for my first day on my own route. I dressed carefully, deciding that my HomeMade jacket would be too heavy, and instead threw a light black sweater on over my shirt.

Monday mornings at 4:30 A.M., the trains had very

few passengers, and this morning they were almost empty. At that hour most of the people on the trains were cleaners in big office buildings, but on Mondays the offices were finished long before 4:30 A.M. and the trains didn't have their usual riders. I brought a book to read so I wouldn't be sitting for over an hour doing nothing but waiting for the day to begin. This felt even more like my first day than the first day when I went out with Pat.

The ride down on the A train to Fulton Street was never bad, but I hated taking the M train into Brooklyn. No matter how many passengers it had, I never felt safe. Today it was even quieter than usual, just a woman sitting to one side of me and a man way down toward the door.

Two girls got on at Canal Street. They were only about sixteen, seventeen years old, but for some reason they looked mean. Hair straightened and greased down into man-styled cuts, shirts open low, tight pants ripped at the knees and ass, black leather jackets. But it wasn't the way they were dressed that made me think they were trouble, it was something about their attitude. They took seats on the opposite side, between me and the other woman, and looked over at us with big grins on their faces. I put my head down and stared hard at my book. Slowly I inched down toward the man, who looked half asleep. He reminded me of Baby Huey, tall, dark, and well-built, though he was thin where Baby Huey was broad. My thoughts drifted off to Baby Huey and what it would be like seeing him after what happened last week in his car.

I glanced up once or twice and saw that the two girls were getting into each other, licking, biting ears, working their way into each other's mouths. After a while, when nothing bad happened, I started to relax. They were doing whatever they were doing and I was minding my own business. So I put my head back down and decided not to look up until I got to my stop.

I turned the pages of my book but mostly I was thinking about Knickerbocker Avenue. I wondered what was going to happen between Joanie and Little Dominic when she came back. I could picture him coming to her house carrying flowers, his thick black hair slicked down with gel and his shoes shined like he was going to a prom.

"What're you looking at?" I hear one of the girls say, real slow and hard. Oh shit, I thought, here it comes, but I knew she couldn't be talking to me, since I had my head down low and hadn't checked them out for about ten minutes. "Yeah, you, honey," she said, "in the black sweater." I looked over and saw that the other woman was wearing a tan blazer and the man had on a green uniform. I checked the rest of the car thinking, please don't let it be me, knowing there was nobody else on the train, much less someone wearing a black sweater. "Yeah, you, lady, we're talkin' to you."

I looked up and both of them were staring directly at me. I was hoping the man would hear and come over to help, but he didn't move. I started chewing my nails but then put my hands in my lap so I wouldn't look scared. I'm supposed to be starting my new route this morning, I thought, and instead I'm going to be found dead on the lousy M train. If the doors opened, I could've made a run for it, but we were crossing into Brooklyn and it'd be a while before we stopped. I shifted in my seat, moving toward the door. "Listen, white shit," one of them said. I took a quick look at the shorter, heavier one, who was about as white as me. She was the one doing the talking. "You think your shit's better'n mine?" she asked. I raised my head real slow as the two of them stood up and moved in my direction. I looked from one to the other and back again. I got up and started to walk away, moving backwards, watching them as I went, but they followed me.

They smiled and the shorter one started to laugh and said, "Tag. And Black Sweater is it."

"I like that," the taller one said, and all I could see was her red lipstick smeared across her lips and chin.

This is it, I said to myself. I checked behind me for the other woman but her seat was empty. She must've made it to another car. Then I realized that the man was wide awake. He was looking straight ahead, not at us, but at least his eyes were open. With him awake, I didn't feel as afraid. But all of a sudden he threw his head back, stamped his foot a few times, and neighed. The two girls looked startled. He got up, shook his head, and snorted and neighed again and this time stamped his way into the next car. The two girls laughed and the shorter one said, "And then there were three."

I stopped and faced them, swallowed hard, and said, real soft but clear, "Yeah, I was looking at you two ugly motherfuckers and I'm ready." I planted my feet slightly apart and stood my ground. Joanie had told me to buy Mace but I'd never gotten around to it, so I held up the tiny can of hairspray that I started carrying my first week on the job, making sure my fingers covered the label, and I said, "I'm gonna fucking Mace the shit out of you, and when you're lying on the floor, I'm gonna rip out your ugly little eyes." I started walking toward them.

They backed away, not smiling anymore, keeping their eyes on me with their hands in front of their faces. I kept crowding them. They went through the doors, and the other doors after that. I stopped where I was and followed them with my eyes. I could barely make out their shapes but I'd swear that they took seats two cars down and were getting into each other again, kissing and sucking away. "To hell with you," I yelled, knowing they were too far away to hear. "And your mother and father and anyone who had anything to do with bringing you into this lousy world." I got off at Knickerbocker Avenue feeling shook up and pissed and edgy.

"Flatbush and Sheepshead Bay," I told Baby Huey, Jimmy, and Little Dominic. "My route's mostly in Flatbush but I have some stores in Sheepshead Bay. How does that sound? What do you think about that route for me?"

"Flatbush, huh?" Baby Huey repeated. "That's a good neighborhood, and Sheepshead won't be no problem neither. The storekeepers'll keep an eye on you and if any nasty customers are hanging around your truck, you'll know it. The kind that rob and mug ya don't live in Flatbush or Sheepshead Bay. Check your load before you go out. Make sure you go heavy on the doughnuts, coffee cake, and everything chocolate, 'cause Flatbush got Germans, Jews, and Italians. Don't give 'em no Bonzos unless they ask. Blacks and Puerto Ricans love Bonzos, but they don't go over big nowhere else. Put Bonzos in Flatbush and they'll sit there till ya take them out again a week later."

I couldn't get the two girls on the train out of my mind and every once in a while chills would run through my body when I thought of them. But once my truck was loaded, I started feeling better. I looked over the order carefully but I knew I wouldn't be able to tell how things would sell until I was out on the route and could see for myself. It made me smile to see only five Bonzos side by side in the top tray and I figured that they went into the mom-and-pop stores, where the owners probably ate them themselves.

Those first days driving up onto the BQE were nerve-racking. There was one long stretch along a high elevated ramp over the lower part of Brooklyn. Maybe it was because I was driving too fast or just that the truck was so tall and narrow. But when the wind blew hard, I was blown back and forth on the highway, and once or twice, before I could even check if there was a car beside me, I was thrown right out of my lane and into the next one over. The fact that the steering on my truck was loose made it worse and I had to jiggle the wheel back and forth to keep the truck in line.

The Flatbush and Sheepshead Bay areas were a good route for a beginner. Each day I went out with a pretty small load, which meant that the work was much easier than it had been on Little Dominic's, though not as light as Mario's route. And the neighborhood was safe, no matter what street I drove on. I found myself liking that part of Brooklyn. Everything was neat and pretty. No litter or people sleeping on the streets. Mostly private houses with family life going on behind closed doors. I had a friend named Laura who I met at camp one summer who lived in Flatbush. It was a lousy summer except for Laura. When we got back home in the fall, I started spending weekends with her and her family in a house where we slept up in the attic in a room with a high-pointed ceiling. I loved that house in Flatbush.

This Flatbush–Sheepshead route also had its drawbacks. One thing was that the stores were spread over too large an area, so it took a long time to cover the route from one end to the other. Too much of the day was spent driving around rather than delivering. Another problem was that these storekeepers thought they could take advantage of me, maybe because I wasn't a guy. They cheated me left and right, and if I complained, they called Home-Made Cakes and said the service was lousy.

For instance, the Superette on Avenue U, which was run by two brothers, Jake and Izzy. I was always in a hurry, and whenever I delivered to their store they'd grab hold of me and want to carry on a ten-minute-long conversation. By the time I left I was always short something or other. Even the first day that I met them.

"Nice to meet you," someone had said behind me as I walked through the door and looked around for a manager.

"What?" I said, turning to see a tall man with dark glasses and salt-and-pepper hair, actually more gray than anything else, coming down the stairs from an elevated office built up against the wall. He held out his hand and we shook but he never let go of mine as he talked.

"I said, nice to meet you." Then he turned and called over his shoulder, "Look what we got here, Izzy. Come out of that box and see what's delivering HomeMade Cakes these days, our own little Rican."

"Excuse me? What did you say?"

A stooped, older version of the tall man came down the stairs, his glasses sitting on the end of a long, hooked nose, so that he had to tip his head way back to get a good look at me. "What are you talking about, Jake?" he asked.

"A Puerto Rican. We have a Puerto Rican Home-Made driver," Jake explained. "I could tell the minute I set eyes on her."

Izzy chuckled. "He always was a smart one," he said.

"Uh-huh. What if I said I was Italian and Jewish?"

"We'd know you were joking," Izzy chuckled again.

"Puerto Rican, huh?" I said. "What makes you think that?"

Jake still hadn't let go of my hand, even though I'd tried once or twice to pull it back. We played a quiet tug of war as we talked. He looked me over carefully before answering. "Your hair, your eyes, the way you walk and talk. It's written all over you."

"Yes, we sure do know a Rican when we see one," Izzy said. "We've worked with your people for years."

"What's your name?" Jake asked, bending down the way you would when you talk to a little girl. "Let me guess," he said before I had a chance to answer. "Carmen, or Elena, or maybe Miranda."

"Miranda, that's pretty. I like that!" I said.

"Ha, ha, I told you so," Izzy said. "Miranda, that's muy bonito, very pretty," he said slowly, like I didn't speak English or I wasn't too bright. "A HomeMade girl named Miranda." And from that day on, that's what everyone at the Superette called me, Miranda.

The best thing about it was that the first time Jake called the depot to complain about me, Jed didn't know who he was talking about. When I walked into the depot, Jed asked, "Ya know some woman out there named Miranda?"

"Of course, everyone knows Miranda. She delivers for Hearthland."

"Oh," Jed said, "I didn't know they had another gal out there. The Superette on Avenue U called this afternoon to complain about her. I told the guy, sure, sure, I'd take care of it, but I knew it wasn't no business of ours."

That first day, after I finally got my hand back from Jake, he pointed the way to the HomeMade Cakes rack. I took out a few pies and two boxes of chocolate doughnuts and wrote down what I thought the store needed, knowing I wouldn't keep it in my head. Get the whole picture, the whole picture, was what they'd told us at orientation. I had no idea what the whole picture was. I just tried to remember what Baby Huey said about chocolate and doughnuts and no Bonzos.

I wrote out a slip and handed it to Jake, who hadn't moved from where I'd left him. Izzy was nowhere to be seen. "Five thirty-three going out," I told him. As I walked past, he put his hand on my shoulder. "Let me see. My, my, what is this? What happened to the doughnuts?" The doughnut boxes were torn at the edges, but I'd been in too much of a hurry to realize that each box had one doughnut missing. "Somebody was hungry, I see," Jake went on. "Sarah," he called, and the old woman on the first register turned her head. "Are you putting a little weight on your fanny? Have you been at the chocolate doughnuts again?"

She frowned and waved her hand like she was swatting a fly and went back to working the register. I heard him chuckling as I left.

Jake checked me in when I returned and I went back down the aisle and packed out the cake. Pies on top, snack cake and doughnuts on the bottom. I gave them only one box of chocolate doughnuts even though the usual order was three. Let them eat Tastee's doughnuts this week, I thought. When I finished, I went to see Jake about getting paid.

"Let me get my reading glasses," he said as he walked up the office steps with the bill. From where I was standing, I could see him searching through his desk, scattering papers everywhere until he pulled out a pair of light tortoiseshell glasses with a lanyard attached.

"Ready," he said, bill in hand, and changed glasses.

"Did you take the stale off the bill?" he asked as he examined it.

"Sure," I told him, looking over his shoulder and pointing, "right there on the bottom."

"Oh yes, there it is. But it says here you took five dollars and thirty-three cents out," he said. "I thought you said four thirty-three before."

"No, I said five thirty-three. Where's the slip I gave you?" I asked. "I wrote it down on the slip."

"I put it somewhere. I'll never find it now. Okay, I'll trust you." He stopped and looked at me carefully. "I don't have to worry about you cheating me, do I?" I shook my head no. "So I owe you twenty-three twenty." He took out a pile of money, counted out four bills, folded them up, and put them in my hand. "You come again tomorrow, no?" he asked.

"I guess so," I said, though I thought the store was served only twice a week. Never mind, I thought, I'll check the route book when I get back to the truck. As I walked to the truck, I counted the money in my hand and there were four singles and twenty cents. I went running back into the Superette.

"Excuse me, sir," I said, standing on my tippy toes, trying to look into the office.

"Try aisle number three," Sarah, the old woman on the register, called out. "He said something about the new Pepsi stand." So I hurried down aisle three and found Jake looking over a Pepsi display.

I held out my hand with the money in it. "You made a mistake," I told him. "You gave me four singles instead of a twenty and three singles."

"I paid you," he said and walked down the aisle toward the front of the store.

"Excuse me," I said following right behind him, "you paid me but it was the wrong amount. I'll give you back a single and you owe me a twenty."

"I have no more money for you," he said. "I gave it to you already." He walked up into the office and let the wooden door swing closed.

"You didn't pay me correctly," I called up to him. "I want my money."

"No money. Enough is enough."

"Look," I stopped and took a deep breath, "I don't know if it was a mistake or you're an out-and-out liar. Either way, you owe me twenty dollars." He didn't say a word. I waited a minute or two, and when he didn't come back down I picked up a metal milk case lying by the wall and went up the steps and kicked the door hard. It flew open and I held it ajar with my foot. Jake was sitting there counting his money and I threw a dollar at him. "This is yours," I said softly, like we were having an ordinary conversation. "Now, I want a twenty-dollar bill from you or this milk crate"—and I held it up high—"goes right through your big picture window. I don't joke about things like this. And if you report me to HomeMade, I'll say you put your hands on me."

He looked at me and smiled. "Here it is, shiksa," and he lifted a twenty-dollar bill off the pile. "I probably just made a mistake, don't get yourself so worked up. Go ahead, take it, it's yours." I took it and left as he said, "Tomorrow, right? We see you tomorrow." When I checked the book, I saw that I was right. The store was only done on Mondays and Thursdays.

Jake and Izzy were no different from my other store-keepers, testing me to see what they could get away with, trying to get me to deliver more often, no matter how little business their store did. There was a lot of trial and error those first few weeks, but it didn't take long for me to get used to the route and for the route to get used to me. There were certain rules to be followed on every route, and once I had those down I did okay.

A few weeks after I'd been on my route, I broke an important rule. When the cake isn't moving—meaning, when it's sitting on the shelves and not selling—there are three things a driver can do to get rid of the cake. You can leave the old cake out until it sells and remove it only when it goes green. This is done mostly in neighborhoods where store owners don't check the dates, or don't care. The other two choices are "tripping" or "rolling" the cake. Tripping just means that even though the date on the cake is the fifteenth, and today is the fifteenth, you leave it an extra day before you take it out. Often, in that one day the cake is sold and there's nothing to take out. Or, when cake is not selling in one store, you roll it into another where it might sell better. The date on the cake is still good, but that second store isn't getting fresh cake. Rolling is what I got caught doing. Sometimes the supervisors go around and check dates on a driver's route, but it's usually done only if they're looking to fire or suspend someone. Leaving old cake out is considered reason enough to fire you. Rolling is not.

My mistake was that I was rolling cake without really knowing how or where to do it, and one of my Arab storekeepers caught me. I never listened to all the bad stories about Arab storekeepers, because I had two Arab stores and they always treated me nice. Even when the owner caught me rolling the cake. He grabbed me by the arm and pulled me over to his office.

"We treat you nice here," he said, "just like we treat

the man. But we want you to treat us nice. This means"—
and he shook my arm to make his point—"don't bring
nobody else's garbage in my store. You understand what
I'm saying, woman?" he asked. I said I was sorry and he
let me go. Neither of us ever mentioned it again, and I kept
his store clean after that, never leaving or giving him old
cake. And I was more careful in my other stores.

I was glad when Joanie finally came back from vacation. It had only been two weeks, but to me it felt like
she'd been gone for months. She was so happy and cheerful
when she returned that I realized how wrong I had been
about her taking the trip. Me, Little Dominic, Mario, and
Baby Huey passed around five packs of pictures of the
Grand Canyon, Yellowstone Park, hundreds of wildflow-
ers, and every restaurant and hotel Joanie ate or slept at.
After what Baby Huey told me, I kept watching when
Joanie and Little Dominic were together. But I saw no
signs that they were anything more than friends until the
morning she came in wearing a beautiful silk scarf. Nobody
wore silk scarves in the depot, and this scarf didn't even
match the blouse or jeans she was wearing. When it slipped
down, I could swear I saw teeth marks in a big red spot that
covered the middle of her neck. A few weeks later she
pulled me aside to say that she was pregnant but that she
and Dominic were keeping it a secret until they were
engaged.

"When is that going to be?" I asked.

"October third."

"What! You're kidding, aren't you?"

"No, not at all, we're totally serious." She smiled a
big smile. "We're so very, very happy."

"But are you guys nuts? Why wait that long to get
engaged?" I stood there and counted on my fingers.

"That's a long time from now. By that time you'll be out to here." I held my hands over my stomach in the shape of a huge basketball.

"Dominic wants to propose on his mother's birthday," Joanie explained. "His mother died last year."

Joanie was so happy about the idea that I decided to keep my mouth shut the same way I did about her trip. It didn't seem to bother her that she wouldn't be able to keep it a secret very long.

"Well," I said, "I wish you both the best. You definitely deserve it."

I filled Joanie in on everything that happened while she was away. Everything except about me and Baby Huey in his car. I shook all over again when I told her about the two girls on the train that first day and all the new storekeepers and getting caught by the Arab. I think I talked nonstop for the first few days that she was back.

During the early months of her pregnancy, I found myself watching her belly, trying to imagine what the baby would look like. I pictured a baby with a big-barreled chest, tiny, chubby hands, Joanie's long neck, and a ski-jump nose. And also a head of thick, dark curls, just like Little Dominic's.

As I started to settle into the job and get used to the HomeMade way of life, I began noticing little things at home that made me think that something was not right with Nick and Joey. Everything had felt so much better with Pudgy moving in and Lily coming around more often that I assumed we were doing fine. But now Lily was in Puerto Rico on vacation and Pudgy had gone to Connecticut to take care of his father, who had had a stroke. So it was just me and Nick and Joey, and it didn't feel right. Nick seemed to be talking less and less, and I felt that Joey was hiding from me, finding things to do so we were always in different rooms when we were home at night. Sean was sleeping in Pudgy's room again so he could take the boys to school in the mornings, but mostly me and Nick and Joey were on our own. I tried to make time for us to talk and play and laugh together but it didn't go over big with them. Something was wrong and I couldn't help worrying about it. Things didn't actually get better until after the haircut.

The front of my hair had gotten so long that it hung down and covered my eyes when I worked. "I would say you had beautiful eyes," Joanie said to me, "if I could see them." So after months of putting it off, I went and got my hair cut.

When I got home that afternoon, Joey, as usual, was the first to notice. "You look so pretty with your hairs cut, Mommy," he said as soon as he walked through the door. He kept coming over and asking me to kneel down so he could touch it.

I was in the kitchen cleaning up that night when Nick came in to complain that Joey was drawing on every page in their new pad. He pulled a chair up by the window and sat there with his arms crossed and his head down saying he wasn't going to move until I stopped Joey from ruining the pad. I went in to check on Joey and found him sitting at his little table, lifting the pages of the pad and marking every page with a slash of his purple marker. I noticed that his hair was sticking straight up in the back, so I asked him, "Joey, what'd you do to your hair. You been using my gel again?"

"No, Mommy, I been drawing little, tiny baby fish with my purple crayon," he said.

"That's great," I said, "but save some pages for Nick." I took the pad and tore off the back of it, went into the kitchen, and handed the sheets to Nick.

The next night, we stopped for pizza and then went home and played one-eyed jacks, go fish, and war. I was still feeling like Nick and Joey were miles away from me and that I had to do something about it. I put them in the bath, but instead of letting them wash themselves, I stayed and played submarines with them and washed their hair and toweled them dry. Something was definitely different about Joey's hair. "Honey, did you do something to your hair?" I asked again. I took his hairbrush and ran it through. It used to be that I'd wet a brush, run it once through Joey's hair, and he'd look perfect. Now when I did that it wouldn't stay down. I tried brushing it flat and then brushed it over to the side. But either way, it was still sticking straight up in some places. Maybe it was getting thicker as he got older, or the change in weather made it do weird things. It didn't look the way it used to.

That Friday night, I could barely stand up I was so tired, and I was glad when Nick and Joey offered to make peanut butter sandwiches for dinner. They even cleared the table, and then Joey went next door to play with Eddie while Nick stayed home to wash dishes with me. Nick loved to wash dishes and I was glad to have his company. Even back when he was in diapers, Nick would strip down naked, put his plastic apron on, and I'd put him on a chair, fill the sink with suds, and let him wash. He left rings and marks and food on the plates, but I wouldn't rewash them until after he was asleep. While he washed, Nick liked to talk about all kinds of things. But he'd been so quiet the last few weeks, I wasn't sure he'd talk to me tonight. But he did. He told me about Joey.

"Joey cuts his hair every night," Nick said.

"What are you talking about?" I said. "I hid the scissors from Joey when he cut up the couch. You know that. They're too high for Joey to find. He's not cutting his hair."

"His elephant scissors. He uses his elephant scissors and cuts his hair."

"The elephant scissors are for paper. He can't cut his hair with them," I said. I decided to check Joey out later, but Joey's hair wasn't what was really bothering Nick and that's what I wanted to figure out now. I went over to the sink and hugged Nick while he washed, trying to get him to talk about other things. I told him that I thought it was time to get another tank for the baby fish, since they might not last in the salad bowl, which is where they'd been living all week. He made me promise that he and Joey could pick out the new tank and all the stuff that goes in it.

After that, we were quiet for a long time, and the only sound was that of the running water. I was trying to think how to ask Nick what was bothering him, but instead I blurted out, "Nicky, are you missing Daddy?" Nick's eyes blinked fast, and then faster and faster, and tears came pouring out while he nodded his head up and down, meaning yes. I turned off the water and tried to hug him but he pushed me away and took my hand, pulling me down the hall to his room. He left me in the middle of the room and went to his bed, then reached under his pillow and pulled out two envelopes. He handed them to me. I sat on his bed and opened each one carefully while he stood there crying.

In the first one someone had written the word *DADDY* in big letters across the top of the paper. Underneath was a drawing of a house and a sun and maybe a car with Joey's name crayoned in the corner on the bottom.

The other was a letter written by Nick. Nick said, so low I almost couldn't hear him, that his teacher helped him write it but he didn't have Tom's address and was waiting for Tom to call so he could send it. It looked like he had been waiting for a long time, because the letter was badly wrinkled. I read the letter aloud.

> DEAR DADDY I LOVE YOU. ME AND JOEY ARE GETTING BIGGER. SOMETIMES JOEY CRIES FOR YOU AT NIGHT. ME AND JOEY WANT TO SEE YOUR NEW HOUSE. DO YOU HAVE A BIG BED FOR ME AND JOEY TO SLEEP IN? I LOVE YOU DADDY. PLEASE COME SOON NICK

It had been over a month since they had seen Tom, and he had never gotten around to taking them to his house like I'd asked him to. He kept putting off visiting them and I hadn't realized that it had been so long. And Tom didn't like to speak on the phone either. I tried to hold back the tears when Nicky let me hug him this time. "You'll see Daddy real soon, I promise you," I said.

Later, when Joey came in, I ran my hand through Joey's hair. It was definitely cut, and it looked like it had to be his elephant scissors. I couldn't believe that I hadn't noticed what a mess he'd made of his hair.

I took Joey's hand and brought him into the living room. "Who's my big sweet guy?" I asked and gave him a hug.

"Nick," Joey said.

"Yup," I picked Joey up and sat down in the comfortable chair with him in my lap, "Nick's my big sweet guy, and you are too, Joey. You're my big sweet guy and I love you. Do you like Mommy's new haircut?"

"I love it."

"Joey, ya want Mommy to cut your hair like I always do? Do you think it's time for a haircut?" I cut Nick and Joey's hair myself. When I was a kid, I used to cut my brother's hair, and after I got married, I did Tom's and the boys'.

"No."

"You don't want Mommy to give you a haircut?"

"No."

"Are you sure? It might make your head feel nice."

"No." He sat in my lap shaking his head back and forth, saying no.

"But you like Mommy's haircut?"

He nodded.

"You know who cut Mommy's hair, Joey? A nice man named Eugene cut my hair. He washed my hair and rubbed my head real nice. And then I closed my eyes and he went snip snip snip. And when I opened my eyes, my hair was all cut. And who said I looked beautiful?"

"Joey."

"Do you want to sit in a big chair and have Eugene cut your hair?"

"And Nick."

"Uh-huh. Nick's hair too. We'll go to the haircut place and have Eugene cut your hair, and if Nick wants his hair cut, we'll do his too. Would you like that?"

Joey pushed my head down until I was bent over with my head in my lap. I watched him in the mirror as he buried his face in my curls. Then he lifted my head and ran his little hands over my face, closing my eyes with his fingers and then gently tugging on my ear like he used to do when he was a baby. "I love you," he said.

"I love you, little muffin."

When I tucked them in, I whispered in Nick's ear, "It *was* the elephant scissors."

In the morning, me and Nick and Joey mailed the letters to Tom. Joey wanted to sit on the steps in front of our apartment building to wait for the mailman. It was hard to get him to understand that it would take a few days for his dad's return letter to get to our house.

I must've fallen asleep while I was waiting for Nick and Joey to go to bed so I could call Tom.

I dreamt I was in the Union Army in the Civil War. I led my troops down a hill to a town. A man with a machine gun was waiting for us. I looked into his eyes. He was going to kill all of us! He raised his gun and fired directly at me. I woke myself out of the dream, afraid that I was dead.

I grabbed my pink bathrobe from the edge of the bed, wrapped it around me, and headed for the kitchen. I put up water and dialed Tom's number. It rang a long time before he answered. It was only nine o'clock but his voice was heavy, the way it was when he was first waking up.

"Yes?"

"Hi, Tom, it's Anna."

"What happened? Something happen to the boys?"

"No, nothing's wrong. I mean, nothing happened, I just wanted to talk to you." I had a pain in my side, so I pushed my fingers into my side and poked hard at the spot.

"Go ahead."

I took the phone away from my ear while I gave myself a second to breathe. "Sorry, I dropped something and had to pick it up. That's better," I lied.

"How are they doing?"

"They're fine, just fine." The water boiled and I poured myself a cup of tea.

"So what is it, Anna? Why did you call?"

"It's just that Nick and Joey are missing you. They wrote you letters and they're waiting for your answer."

"Well, I never got them."

"I know. I didn't mean that. They mailed them only yesterday. I just wanted to make sure you answered them as soon as possible." I looked around for sugar and found the box behind a jar of ketchup.

"Of course I will. Is that all?"

"There's something else, actually. I think they need to see you."

"They do see me. I come by and take them out whenever I have time. And I will again, soon."

"No. I think they need to see you now. It's been over a month and they miss you. And they need to have more time with you. I think they want to sleep over and spend a day or two with you. Maybe you could take them for a weekend."

"I have no room for them here." He paused and then kind of chuckled and went on, "But c'mon, Anna, is it them or you? Do they want it or are you using them as an excuse 'cause you're sick of them?"

"Listen, you selfish son of a bitch," I said. "I don't need an excuse to ask the father of my four- and six-year-old sons to spend some time with them." My arm jerked as I was pouring the sugar, and sugar spilled all over the counter and the floor. "If I had my way, they'd never see you again. It'd be easier if you were dead and they could mourn for you and get you out of their heads. It's harder with a father that's alive and just doesn't give a shit. They badly want to see you and there's nothing I can do about it except beg you to spend some time with them. And I don't mean your usual hour or two."

"I'll see what I can do," he said and hung up.

Tom never did answer their letters but he called a week later and told them he was taking them to his mother's for the weekend and that their Uncle Peter was coming too. Nick and Joey had their suitcases packed and ready to go ten minutes after he called. Tom ended up putting it off for two weeks and Nick and Joey kept mixing up which weekend he was taking them, but even though it turned out that Peter got sick and couldn't go, in the end they did go.

I saw Baby Huey every morning and sometimes in the afternoon if I got back early enough. Mostly we just nodded to each other and once in a while stopped to talk about the weather or to joke around—like one morning when he was sitting on Wally, the route rider, who pulled the routes of drivers that were sick or on vacation. Baby Huey was drawing a mustache and a bull's-eye around his navel and asked me if I wanted to do the nose. We never spoke about that time in the car. Sometimes I'd catch him looking at me when he thought I wouldn't notice, but he'd quickly turn away when I caught his eye.

One morning I couldn't sleep, so I got dressed and went to work even earlier than usual. It was only 5:00 A.M. when I walked into the depot. I was nervous when I looked in my truck, thinking I might find a mouse or rat running around, because no one else was there yet. But then I heard the banging of metal trays being loaded from the racks to a truck. I climbed on my truck, feeling more comfortable knowing that another person was in the garage at that hour.

"Why did the monkey fall out of the tree?"

When I looked up, Baby Huey was standing at the back of my truck, watching me through the open door.

"How long have you been there?" I asked.

"A minute or two. Having fun watching you bend and lift."

"Get out of here. I probably looked stupid."

"Why did the monkey fall out of the tree?"

I laughed and shrugged. "I have no idea."

" 'Cause he was dead."

"Is that supposed to be funny?" I said.

"You had to be there," he said.

"Very funny."

"I've missed you," he said and I nodded. "I came in early hoping to see you before the other guys got here." I just waited, not knowing what to say.

"I'd like to see you again," he said.

"Me too."

"Want to meet me for lunch?"

I thought about it and said, "I can't. Lunch is right in the middle of my day. And I'm still so slow. I'd hate to take time out."

"I know. But we could bring sandwiches and have lunch by the water. It would only take half an hour."

"I don't know," I said, "that means I'd be getting back even later than usual. I'm already the last one in. And Mario told me that the union says we have to be off the road by three o'clock, four on Fridays. Someone should have told me that when I first started at HomeMade and was driving in after dark each night.''

''Nobody tells nobody nothing in this place. You have to find out for yourself. Look, we could try it once, and if it doesn't work out, we'll have had a good lunch. I have a great deli on my route that makes heros on fresh Italian bread and the meat is this thick.'' He held his hands wide apart and we laughed.

I thought about how all my days were starting to feel the same so that I couldn't tell one day from the next. ''I like turkey heros,'' I said and he grinned.

It was Wednesday, my lightest day, and I was driving through a part of Brooklyn that I had never seen before. I had no idea what this section of Brooklyn was even called. In my left hand I held a little map that Baby Huey had drawn and with my right hand, I steered the truck. The map reminded me of the treasure maps I drew for Nick and Joey. At the bottom of the map was the word *END,* and Baby Huey had drawn two stick figures standing near two rectangles with wheels which were obviously our trucks.

A half hour for lunch, I thought. What a joke! Obviously Baby Huey hadn't figured for driving time. At this point I was sure I had already taken a wrong turn until I came to a building with a gold gate that I remembered Baby Huey saying was two blocks from the water.

He was standing in front of his truck.

''We got to watch for supervisors, just to make sure,'' was the first thing Baby Huey said as I stepped off my truck.

''What for?''

''I just like to be careful,'' he said. ''Ever since they caught Jimmy with his truck parked outside a private house.''

"Why was his trucked parked outside a private house? I don't get it. And what's wrong with that?"

"Jimmy's got so many girlfriends on the route, he can't keep track of them. Women say they like the quiet type, and they like his eyes. Bedroom eyes, they call them. No matter where we go, by the time we leave, Jimmy's got some girl holding on to his arm, looking into his eyes. And one time, he must've really been going at it, 'cause he was inside this lady's house for three hours and when he came out, Jed was waiting there with a three-day suspension for him."

"*Now* you tell me. You mean a supervisor might follow us out here."

"It won't happen to us, but you can never be too careful."

"Great, another thing to worry about."

Baby Huey even brought a blanket, a green army blanket full of moth holes, but it was nice to have something to sit on. The sandwiches were delicious. Mine was fresh roasted turkey with lettuce, tomatoes, and Russian dressing. We didn't say a word as we sat there munching, except every once in a while when one of us would say "Mmmmmm" because the sandwiches were so good.

When we were done eating, we sat looking out at the water, holding hands as we finished our sodas. Baby Huey leaned over for a kiss. I looked around and then gave him a quick kiss on the lips. "I'm nervous," I said, "after what you said about the supervisors."

"Then come on the truck and give me a kiss there," he said.

We climbed up the steps to his truck and I heard the click of a lock. At least his lock works, I thought, not like my truck, which had two broken locks. Standing there between the racks, he kissed me long and hard, pressing me up against the back door. He held me to him real tight and I could feel him getting big as he rubbed and moved against me. His breathing got heavy as he pushed and ground himself into my crotch. I heard the sound of his zipper as he opened his fly and took it out.

"Please touch it," he begged. He opened a button on my blouse and reached under my bra for my breast, squeezing my nipple as he pleaded again, "Please, Anna, I need you to touch it."

It was all too fast for me. I didn't know why I got myself into this, but I didn't want to just be a tease either. I glanced down and his cock looked so thick and red and fleshy. I remembered watching TV with my brother one time when we were teenagers and my parents weren't home. My brother sat in front of me and took out his penis, standing it up in his hand. Then he played with it, rubbing it hard with both hands until it was big and red and ugly-looking. I told my brother I had to go to the bathroom and locked myself in there until my parents came home. "No, please," I told Baby Huey, "I don't want to."

"Just once, touch it once. Please, Anna, it would feel so good if you touched it."

I reached down and took it in my hand. He moaned and I moved my hand gently around the head. "More, please, more, oh yes," he whispered and I did, but it didn't feel right doing it here on the truck. I wrapped my fingers around the shaft and slid my hand up and down while pleading, "Not here, I can't, please." Baby Huey moaned again, murmuring, "So good, so very good," and reached down into my pants, and under my panties. I tried to push his hand away but he rubbed my clit hard and then forced a finger inside me even though I was dry. He moved his finger in and out and I kept saying no but he wouldn't stop. I started to like it and got all wet but it made me feel so dirty. I grabbed his hand and pulled it out of my pants. Then I pushed him away. "I'm sorry," I said, "I just can't do this here on the truck." I moved away so he'd know I meant it. I buttoned my blouse and tucked it back in my pants. "I just can't. It doesn't feel right to me." He stood there looking hot and sweaty, his cock hanging out. "I've got to go." I kissed him and turned away, then walked back to my truck and drove off.

That afternoon, when I came off the route, Baby Huey was waiting for me. When I finished settling in, he asked if he could drive me to the train and I said sure.

"Are you mad at me?" he asked.

"No."

"Will you go out with me?" he asked and kept looking straight ahead. He looked so shy and uncomfortable that I smiled.

"I guess."

"Yes or no?"

"Yes."

"When?"

"Next Saturday night is good," I said. I heard him let out his breath. "Do you want to come to the house?"

"No, not if your kids are there."

"They're going away with their dad for the weekend."

"I still don't want to be in their house," he said. "It don't seem right. But I'll ring the bell and pick you up downstairs."

"That'd be great. I'm looking forward to it."

Carlos from Bay Ridge
and Grandma Vera of Rhinebeck

"GODDAMN YOU, WALLY!" Baby Huey was coming off the back of Wally's truck, which was parked straight across from mine. "Next time Jed wants to give you something, he can give it to you himself. Why do I have to bring you your paycheck every week? You can go to the office and collect it like everybody else. I'm no mailman—and, *man,* I hate going near you, 'cause you smell something awful." Baby Huey stood at the side of the truck mouthing off while Jimmy tried to quiet him down.

I was running late. Pudgy had been away almost three weeks and we'd had a few glasses of wine the night before to celebrate his coming home. I woke up with a splitting headache and had the worst time getting out of bed this morning. But Jimmy and Baby Huey were late too. Most of the other trucks were already long gone, and those two were usually the first to pull out. Jimmy had said something about his car having a flat on the way in this morning.

"I don't care who hears me," Baby Huey said to Jimmy, and his voice got even louder. "He's the one should be embarrassed, not me. He smells like a pig's asshole. The whole truck smells." By this time Baby Huey was yelling.

"C'mon, Ernesto"—Jimmy was the only one who called Baby Huey by his real name—"leave him alone.

What's it to you what he smells like?'' Jimmy reached up to put his arm around Baby Huey's shoulders but Baby Huey was too tall, so Jimmy patted his shoulder instead.

Wally backed his truck out, yelling, ''Fuck you, Mr. Clean,'' to Baby Huey as he passed.

Baby Huey raised his fist to him. ''The guy don't have no self-respect walking around like that,'' Baby Huey said to Jimmy, ''no respect for us, either, 'cause we got to smell him.'' Baby Huey had seen me watching him and came over to my truck with Jimmy right behind him. ''And the worse part is, that even when I'm not near him, I *remember* how bad he smells. I don't even remember my mom's perfume that good.''

He stopped talking for a minute and just looked at me, his face softening, and he said, ''Aren't I right, Anna?'' I smiled at him but didn't say anything and went on loading my truck.

''Lemme tell you both something,'' Baby Huey said, ''in the three years I was in Nam, none of the guys were as bad as that.'' I remembered hearing Jed telling Joanie that Nam made Baby Huey so crazy that the supervisors were afraid he might get mad sometime and pull out a gun and blow them away without thinking twice about it. ''There were times we weren't even near water,'' Baby Huey went on, his voice getting quieter as he remembered, ''but we kept clean. We didn't go around smelling, stinking like that pig Wally.

''You know, once me and these three other guys got separated from the rest of our unit. We got cut off and trapped, stuck in a trench for days, down there maybe three, four days, I don't know. No water, no food, no nothing. But we washed, damn it, we fucking washed.

Figure that. None of us near water, scared shit, sweating like cornered rats, and not one of us smelled as bad as Wally. We used pee to do it. Splashed it under our arms and all over ourselves and we got clean. I mean, you don't have to pee on yourself to keep clean, but I can't see how a guy wouldn't wash if he got the chance. Stuck down a hole never knowing exactly where we were was enough to drive us crazy. But we kept our heads and we kept clean.''

Finally Baby Huey stopped talking and stood there shaking his head and shoulders like he had a chill. Then he looked around the depot, probably noticing for the first time that the garage was empty and how late it was. All of a sudden he was gone and so was Jimmy. A minute later their trucks rolled by. I stood at the back of my truck and waved but neither of them looked my way as they drove past.

I jumped when I saw someone in the shadow of my truck. It was Joanie, standing there watching me.

''What are you doing here?'' I asked. I had never seen her out of the office before.

''Nothing. We heard Baby Huey yelling and Jed sent me out to see what was wrong.''

''What are you going to tell him?''

''Nothing. That Baby Huey was upset about Wally smelling so bad. That's all. Maybe Jed can talk Wally into taking more showers. Tell him it's bad for business to smell so dirty. At least he can give it a try.'' She didn't say anything else but she didn't go away either.

''Yes?'' I said.

''I'm starting to worry about you.'' I didn't ask about what, because we both knew. ''It's not good to mix your job and your love life, especially here.''

"Look who's talking," I said. "What about you?"

"That's different. Me and Dominic have known each other for a long time and we're getting married."

"Eventually—at least I hope so," I said, looking at her belly, which already looked pretty big to me. "I'm sorry," I said, "that wasn't nice."

She looked down and patted her belly. "That's okay, I don't care what people say, and the baby seems to be sleeping, didn't hear a thing."

"I just don't know what to say about Baby Huey, is what. I don't feel like I have a crush on him, but then I find myself thinking about him all the time."

"I know, it's written all over you."

"But, you know, up until a few months ago, nothing was going right for me. I was worried about every little thing and I was blaming Tom and God and everybody for making my life so miserable and so hard. Then I got the job and Pudgy moved in and Baby Huey started coming after me and things felt better. But now with this Baby Huey thing, I'm feeling all mixed up again and I can't tell which end is up."

"Yeah, and I don't mean to say you're not doing great." She smiled a big, warm smile and nodded her head.

"Well, I'm doing better, I wouldn't say great," I said.

"I think you're doing great, I really do. But it seems to me you want someone or something so bad that you're making Baby Huey into something he's not. What you're looking for and what he is might be two different things."

"I know," I told her. "I don't think he's a prince or nothing. I just like the way he makes me feel."

She came close to me and brushed at my bangs with her fingers, smiling at me again. "I got some good news too," she said. "Look." Joanie held out her left hand, which had a thin gold band with a small diamond on her third finger.

"Congratulations." I gave her a hug. "I thought you guys were going to wait until October, for Dominic's mother's birthday."

"Yeah, well, I had a little trouble last week, so we thought it was better to do it sooner rather than later. We're getting married in the next month or two. You'll get an invitation in the mail when we know for sure."

"What kind of trouble? How come you didn't say anything?"

"I didn't want everyone to worry. It was nothing much. Some of my water leaked over the weekend. They thought there was a hole in the sac, but it seems to have healed itself. The doctor says I'm fine, but Dominic wants to get married right away, just in case."

I laughed. "That's great!" I said. "Not about the water, but the marriage. My water broke when I was pregnant with Nicky," I told her. "Six weeks before he was due. I was only eighteen and didn't know anything about water, so I called the doctor and told him the baby kicked a hole in my bladder."

We both laughed. "Well, that's good to know," Joanie said, " 'cause I was afraid it happened 'cause I was older." We heard Jed calling Joanie from the office, so she gave me a hug and walked back inside.

Later that afternoon, I drove my truck up to the big sliding door of the depot, then sat there blowing my horn until the door slid open. The new mechanic, who spoke mostly Spanish, stood there smiling. I tooted my horn and he waved. Then I drove straight to my spot and headed for the bathroom because I still had a headache from the morning and wanted to take some aspirin. I kept forgetting to do it when I was out on the route.

On my way to the office, Baby Huey and Jimmy snuck up behind me and before I got to the door I was hanging upside down by my feet. I wasn't in the mood for fooling but there wasn't much I could do while I was in Baby Huey's hands. He had me by the ankles and was gently swinging me back and forth, saying, "You looked like you were storming the barricade," he said. "I didn't want you to go in there looking so mad and get yourself into trouble again."

"Let me down," I said. "I'm not mad and I'm not in any trouble." My work boots were resting on his shoulders as I swung back and forth and I was glad to be close to him even in that way, as ridiculous as it was.

"I know, I know. I just want to make sure you calm down before anything happens."

"Put me down. I have a headache and you're making it worse," I said.

Baby Huey bent over and looked carefully at my face. My head was pounding and I must've looked like I was going to cry, because he started calling me "sweetie" and saying he was sorry, he could see I was having a hard time and he hadn't meant to make it worse. He held out his hand and I grabbed it as he swung me right side up and stood me back on my feet. I lost my balance and when he reached out to steady me, just for the moment, I felt warm all over and wanted him so bad.

"Don't worry, I'm fine," I said, "I'm really fine."

"Take it slow. Do you want me to come in with you?" he asked, still holding on to my hand. I laughed and shook my head no. "Then I'll call tonight so we can plan something for the weekend, okay?"

He started to walk away, then came back and gave me a kiss on the cheek, mumbling, "I can't wait," before going out the door to the street with Jimmy at his side.

Friday night when I went home, I made dinner and packed the boys' clothes and toys for the weekend, then folded and sorted laundry. The kids were ready. They had been ready for the last few days. All they could talk about was visiting Grandma Vera in Rhinebeck. And I had to admit, I was looking forward to their going, to being on my own. When it was time to leave, Nick and Joey grabbed hold of me and hugged and kissed me like they weren't going to see me for months and then kept waving until they got on the elevator.

I watched from the window as they ran down the street to Tom's car, ready to begin their first full weekend away since me and Tom split up. Pudgy was at Sally's, a girl from the Bronx he was dating, and I was alone for the first time in years. As I cleaned the boys' room and put away their toys, I was sure I heard their voices out on the street. But when I ran to the window, Tom's car was nowhere in sight. Later, I thought I heard Joey calling me from down the hall. I was glad when the phone rang and it was Baby Huey asking was Saturday night still okay, around seven o'clock? I said seven o'-clock would be great, I was looking forward to it. I tried to think of something else to say but I got tongue-tied and hung up.

Saturday I slept late and woke up feeling great. I found a murder mystery in Pudgy's room and spent the day reading until it was time to shower and dress for my date.

Baby Huey arrived exactly at seven. He rang the bell

but wouldn't come upstairs, saying it was a nice night and he'd rather sit in the car and smoke. I found him parked in front with the window rolled down, music blasting and a cigarette hanging from his lip. I could tell by the way he was dressed that tonight was as big a deal for him as it was for me. He had on soft gray gabardine slacks and a beautiful Italian silk shirt with a really classy design running across the chest and the sleeves. He even polished and cleaned out his car. There weren't the usual paper bags, napkins, and soda bottles that were there the other times I rode with him.

We drove downtown and went to dinner at a steak house. The meat, potatoes, and veggies were good, but I was so nervous that I spent most of the time looking at the side of my knife to see if I had food stuck in my teeth. We went to a movie in Times Square and the place gave me the creeps, but the movie was funny and we both laughed hard. At about eleven we were back on the street and Baby Huey asked if I would go to a hotel with him.

"A hotel?" I said. "Why a hotel? I'm not sure I want to sleep with you or what I want. And anyway, why not just come home with me and see what happens? The boys are away and Pudgy went to stay with a girlfriend."

"It don't seem right, I couldn't," Baby Huey said. I didn't exactly understand why, but if he didn't feel right being in my house, I wasn't going to push him.

"Okay. Then what about your house? It's on Long Island, right? It would be fun to drive out there, like taking a ride in the country."

He shook his head hard. "Nah, I don't bring girls home."

"Well, I'm not exactly a girl, and anyway, what do you think I'd do, take a dump on the lawn?"

"That's not a nice way to talk," he said. "No, it's not that. It's just that I'm saving the house for my wife."

"What wife? I thought you were divorced."

"Yeah. But for when I get married again."

"You mean I can't sleep on your clean sheets 'cause some time in the next twenty years you're going to get married again?"

He nodded.

"Wonderful, but I'm not paying for no hotel when we can sleep free in my house or yours."

"I'll pay." Which I guess was something, because Joanie said that even though Baby Huey wasn't exactly cheap, he wasn't generous either. The hotel idea didn't seem right to me, but I went along with it anyway.

We drove all the way to Brooklyn, to an old hotel on Baby Huey's route, since neither of us knew where else to go and he said the hotels in Manhattan were too expensive. An old man in a red suit and cap took down all the information, then brought us up in a creaking elevator and led us down a narrow hallway with a frayed red carpet to room number seventeen. Seventeen is one of my lucky numbers, so I hoped it meant we were going to have a good night. But even with the lights on, the room was dark. The paint was peeling off the ceiling and there was a smell like the exterminator had just left.

"We're paying ninety-five dollars for this?" I whispered to Baby Huey. "No way. Let's go to my house. I swear, anything's better than this." The old man was busy blowing his nose into what looked like a large linen dinner napkin.

"Look, I'm paying, not you," Baby Huey whispered back, "and I'm not going back to your house. So let's just tip the guy and do what we came here for, okay?"

Baby Huey put some money in the old man's hand and he left. I felt a little better with the old guy gone and the door locked.

"It ain't Miami," Baby Huey said and lay down with all his clothes on, looking up at the ceiling. I climbed on top of him.

"It's okay," I said. "The bellboy's as old as the people in Miami, and we just have to steal the towels to know we're on vacation."

"Very funny."

I kissed him softly but he seemed more interested in looking at the paint strips hanging from the ceiling. "I think I see a whale up there," he said, pointing to a spot near the window. "Over there in the corner."

I got off and lay down next to him and looked up. "Where?" He showed me again and this time I saw it too. "You're right. See? It really is Miami."

"I got a favor to ask you," Baby Huey said as we lay there.

"Yes?"

"It's kind of a special favor."

"What is it?"

"I want you to pierce my ear."

"What?" I yelled, thinking it was some weird joke and sat right up. "You're kidding, right? This is a joke? Did you say pierce your ear?" I looked at him and he had this big grin on his face. "C'mon," I said, "tell me this is one big joke."

He looked at me with that big grin and shook his head from side to side. "Uh-uh," he said, "it's something I've been wanting for a long time."

"Well, that's great. I mean, it's fine for you to want it, but what's it got to do with me? Look," I said, "I take lots of chances and do some wild things, but I'm no doctor or nurse. I don't know how to pierce an ear.''

''My sister's friend's a nurse.''

''Then ask her.''

''I did. But she lives in Chicago, so she's out of the question. But she told me how to do it and what to buy. Please, Anna, I've been thinking about it for years but there was no one I could trust.''

''What about your doctor? You can go to a nice big clean office where they got everything sterile already. You can even draw a dot on your ear exactly where you want him to put it. One, two, three, and it's done.''

''They're butchers, all of them.''

''Excuse me. Those butchers have years of medical experience and I have none. Zero. Nada. Please, say you're kidding. I am not piercing your ear.''

He was already off the bed and going through his bag. ''Look, I got everything she said to get.'' He held up a tiny gold stud earring and a small block of wood. ''See, this goes behind my ear. And here's the needle.'' He had a huge thick needle, like ones I'd seen my mother use to fix upholstery. ''Look at all this.'' He took out a bottle of peroxide and a tube of Bacitracin. ''I even have matches so all we need is ice. I'm sure they have an ice machine down the hall.'' Before I could say anything, he was out the door.

I ran to the door and called down the hall, ''I won't do it. Don't bother. Come back, I refuse.'' I had no idea which way he went but he definitely wasn't listening to me, because my voice bounced off the walls and then there was silence. I hid in the closet and closed the door.

When he returned, he called to me and I heard him go into the bathroom. ''Where'd she go?'' he said aloud, and then the closet door slid open.

"Didn't you hear me?" I said. "I refuse. I will not chop up your ear."

"Of course you won't," he said, and he took my hand and spoke in a gentle voice, like he was talking to a child. "My sister's friend said it will barely bleed, and it's all cartilage, so I'm not gonna feel a thing. Come on, be a big girl and do me this little favor."

I thought, I am not going to have any peace until I do this crazy thing. He's dead set on doing it, and most of all he's dead set on me being the one to do it. If I don't try it, we'll be fighting all night. "Okay, sit down," I said as coldly as I could. He was grinning again and already had the ice pressed against his ear.

"Relax," he said. "She told me to hold the ice for as long as I could stand it. I'll tell you when."

"Relax! Easy for you to say," I told him.

He walked into the bathroom holding the ice to his ear. He came back without his fancy clothes, dressed only in a T-shirt and a towel wrapped around his waist. After a few more minutes, he screeched, "Yikes, it's cold! Now! Do it now!"

I had been standing there sterilizing the needle with a match and practicing holding the block of wood and aiming the needle at it. I put the wood behind his left ear, pulled my hand back, and was about to drive the needle through when I couldn't decide where the hole should go. "Hold it," I said. I made him get up and look in the mirror and point to where he wanted it, and then I drew a tiny dot with a pen. He sat down, iced it a little more, and then told me to try again. I drew my hand back, but I must've been scared, because I only poked lightly at his ear with the needle. It went through the front part and started to bleed, which got me so shook up that I pulled out the needle and ran for a towel. "Is it done?" he called after me.

I came running back and covered his shoulder with the towel. "No, not yet. I'll need at least one more shot at it," I said. He sat there as if he hadn't felt a thing. I decided I had to get it through on my next try. But I looked at his ear and saw that he probably had one of the thickest earlobes a guy could have and that it was not going to be easy driving it through. "Hold the ice, this'll be the last time," I said. He held it tight against his bleeding ear, letting it get as cold as he could stand, and then yelled, "Ready! Go!" Again I took the needle and aimed, but this time I held it with my fist, pulled it way back, and hit him with as much force as I could put behind it. I felt his ear smashing against the block and the needle going all the way through. Blood was gushing out, covering everything, but I got a wet washcloth and cleaned his ear, poured peroxide on the hole, and put Bacitracin on the gold earring post before pushing it in.

"Done," I said.

Baby Huey stood up, looked around, and smiled. "A fucking bloodbath, huh?"

"I guess." And I laughed, because I had actually gone through with it, but I also had to sit down, because I felt faint.

He went to the big mirror over the bureau and looked at his ear. "You did a beautiful job."

"Thanks."

I stood up carefully and picked up the bloody towel and the needle but Baby Huey took them from me and put them on the chair. He reached for my hands and said softly, "Go lie down and wait for me. Think nice things, sweet things. I'll clean up."

When he was done, he lay down on his side next to me and started kissing my face. "I'm starting to fall for you," he said.

"Uh-huh," I said.

"What about you? Are you falling for me?"

"I guess."

"You guess? You're not sure?"

"Well, I think about you all the time. But we don't really know each other yet."

"What do you think about?"

"I think about your smile, how tall you are, your dark wavy hair."

"I think about your breasts."

"Baby Hu—"

"What did you call me?"

"I . . ." I looked at his face and he looked either sad or mad, I couldn't tell which. "Nothing."

"No, tell me, what were you going to call me?" I didn't answer so he said, "You were going to call me Baby Huey, right? My name is Ernesto, and that's what I want you to say from now on, okay? Not this Baby Huey shit. Now, let me hear you say it."

"Okay. Ernesto."

"That's better." He was quiet and we both lay there looking up at the ceiling until he said, "Let me explain some things to you. Baby Huey was my name in Nam and somehow the guys at HomeMade heard of it and tagged it on me here. But it's got bad memories. You see, one guy over there was like a brother to me. His name was Carlos, a little punk from Bay Ridge. I loved the guy. Me and him had been together from the very beginning. We did everything together. The other guys called us the Spanish Mafia, 'cause we were both Cuban, but they didn't mean no harm by it. It was Carlos that made up my name, Baby Huey, from the Baby Huey cartoon. Remember when I was mad about Wally smelling so bad? I was telling you and Jimmy how we were stuck down those trenches for days. Well, that was the first time me and Carlos got separated, the first time in three years. And all those days when we were stuck down that hole, all I could think about was getting out and finding Carlos and the others.''

His voice went on like he was telling a story, and my eyes started to close even though I was wide awake. ''One morning when the gunfire seemed a long way off, we made a run for it. We moved out, heading back towards where we last saw the rest of our troop. Me and the three other guys walked west for a few miles and come to this place with trees, like a little forest. And we found Carlos and four other guys hanging there, tied up by their arms, their chests cut open by machetes down to the bone, gashed out. But, you know, he recognized me. I mean, through all that he kept screaming 'Ernesto,' he knew it was me. And while he was calling me he asked me to kill him. I couldn't stand it. I mean he was almost dead already so I did. I killed him fast and walked away. I don't know what happened with the others hanging there or if they were alive at all. But the guys caught up with me and we kept heading back.''

I was lying there holding my breath, feeling slightly nauseous as he told it all in an even voice and when I looked over, there was almost no expression on his face.

''I was sent home after that,'' he continued. ''They had me checked out and couldn't find anything wrong. But I couldn't sleep at night and went down to about a hundred and sixty pounds—and you see me now, I'm at least two-twenty. Anyway, I came home and the service arranged a job for me with HomeMade, and I been working for them ever since.

"So you see, the name Baby Huey's got bad memories for me, not only of Carlos but all of Nam."

I thought he was done but he kept talking in that same low even tone. "And the bad times stayed with me for a long time. I got married a few months after I got back. I'd been writing this girl Connie the whole time. She threw a big party for me and invited my family, her family, the whole neighborhood. Crepe paper everywhere, welcome-home signs, wall-to-wall people. But I'll tell ya, it was lousy." He lay there looking up at the ceiling, not saying a word, grinding his teeth. " 'How many did ya kill? Did ya shoot women and babies too? How were the girls over there?' Now what the hell kind of questions are those to ask? I walked out. Didn't say nothing to nobody, just walked the hell out of that big happy welcome-home party. Me and Connie got divorced a few years later. She was a nice girl, a pretty little China doll, but I guess I wasn't ready for a commitment."

There was a long pause and then he said, "I only been with one other girl since I was married. Me and a girl named Louise. We were engaged but that didn't work out either."

"What? I thought you went out almost every week."

"Nah, just once in a while, and never like that."

"Do you mean the only ones you ever slept with are your wife and this girl Louise?"

"No, I got syphilis in Vietnam. And after that I promised myself I wouldn't ever mess around again. So the last time was with Louise."

"How long ago was that?"

"Four years."

"Four years? You mean you haven't touched a woman in four years?"

"Touched, yes. I've done things with girls like kissing and touching, I'm not a weirdo or nothing. But I haven't been to bed with someone since then."

"So what does that mean for us?"

"Well. I would like to go to bed with you, if you would like to with me. You're clean, aren't you?"

"Well, the only man that I've even kissed since I'm eighteen, other than Tom, is you. And after Tom left, I went to the doctor to make sure he hadn't given me anything."

Baby Huey suddenly started to laugh, and he just kept laughing. He stood up and stripped naked, then lifted me off the bed, and holding me under the arms, he spun round and round with me. He lowered me down and kissed me all over the face, then raised me high as he planted kisses on my breasts and belly, and between my thighs.

"Guess what?" he said.

"I don't know," I said, "but I know it's good, 'cause you're laughing."

"You're right. I'm laughing 'cause we got the whole night together. And we're going to make love all night long until one of us says we can't stand that much loving."

"I can't stand that much loving," I said. And then, "Just kidding."

He fell back on the bed with me on top of him, both of us bouncing up and down until we came to rest with my face lying on his chest, my lips near one of his nipples. I gently touched it with my tongue and knew by the noises he made that he liked it. He managed to lift my skirt and get his hand into my underwear. He was playing with me, rubbing and pinching me gently. "Oh my God," he moaned, "you're killing me already."

I couldn't help but laugh. I moved my face down farther, tickling his navel with my tongue as I took his penis in my hand, wrapping my fingers around it, moving my hand up and down very lightly. I kept doing it, watching his cock get bigger and harder and liking it this time. I looked down the length of his body, from his face to his toes, at his nipples and penis standing straight up and it made my body feel soft and wet. I didn't help him but just lay there laughing while he tried to lift my ass up high enough so he could get my skirt and underpants off. He gently rubbed one hand back and forth across my ass and along the crack as he took off my blouse and bra with the other.

When we were both naked, with his hands on my waist, he lifted me up high and then brought me down, sliding me onto his penis.

"No, stop," I screamed. "Please, stop, you're not ready, you've got to use something."

"It's okay," he said, "I won't come." He started moving slowly at first, then faster and faster, and he felt so big and so good, and he kept moving me up and down while he pushed harder and deeper inside me. I wanted to stop him but I was loving it too much.

"Ooh, ooh," he said, "this is so good. You feel so wet and warm and nice."

"Ernesto, it's crazy, come in my mouth instead. Please, Ernesto, you got to pull out," I begged.

"I can't," he moaned, "it has a mind of its own and it wants to come."

"Please, no."

"Anna, it's so good, oh my god, it's so good, so goood," he kind of crooned to me. "Oh, Anna, sweet baby! I'm gonna come now!" he yelled.

"Please, Ernesto, not in me, no," I said and I pulled away fast as he pressed me to him, his sperm shooting out and covering my side and belly and running down my thigh.

"I'm sorry," he said, reaching out to hold me, "I couldn't stop." He pressed his face in my hair and laid his hand across my breast. In minutes he was asleep and I went to wash off in the bathroom. I was still so keyed up that I touched myself until I came and came again, and then I went back and lay down beside him. It felt strange lying in bed next to someone I barely knew, but it didn't take long for me to fall asleep.

Someone was shaking me and I woke to find that it was morning and that Baby Huey was standing by the bed fully dressed. "We got to hurry, Anna. I got to get you home fast. I'm supposed to meet Jimmy and the guys at the baseball field at nine. We're getting a team together and today's our first day on the field."

I spent the morning cleaning, feeling how empty the apartment was without Nick and Joey, not knowing what to do with myself. I decided I would scrub the bathroom walls from top to bottom and spent a long time on a ladder using a scouring brush. Finally I called Lily and asked if she felt like going for a bike ride and a picnic down by the river. She said yes, but we never made it.

"Hello?" I had the radio on loud and was dancing and vacuuming at the same time when the telephone rang.

"One second," I yelled into the phone, "let me turn everything off."

"What are you doing, having a party?" It was Tom. His voice was loud, as if he still had to yell over the noise even though I'd turned everything off.

"Uh-huh."

"I have something to tell you," he said even louder and for some reason, maybe it was the flatness of his voice, I felt scared.

"I hear you," I said. "You don't have to yell."

"I wasn't yelling," he said more quietly.

"Well, what is it?"

"It's about Nick."

"What happened? Something happened! Tom, you're scaring me and I don't even know what happened yet."

"Well, something did happen. It was last night," he said and his voice was so low that I could barely hear him. I pressed my ear tight to the phone and tried not to make a sound. "We took Nick and Joey to a movie, my mom and me, that is. They liked it but we didn't get back till late and Joey fell asleep in the car. Actually, he fell asleep in the movie and then slept the whole way home in the car. Nick took a little nap in the car too. When we got home, we put Joey right to bed and Nick stayed up for milk and cookies. Only, my mother had coffee, and we don't know how it happened, but the pot of coffee spilled on his arm."

"What?"

"Yeah, it was bad and he kept screaming, so we wrapped it in gauze and took him to the hospital."

"You wrapped it in gauze?" I had that same sick feeling at the back of my throat that I had one time when Nicky had a very high fever. "You idiot! You wrapped it in gauze?"

"Yeah, well, that was a mistake, and they had a hard time getting it off."

"You stupid idiot!"

"Well, where the hell were you when your kid needed you? You're the one who knows what to do in emergencies, but you weren't there when we called last night."

"You're their father—and your mother had three kids. It's just too bad that one asshole raised another asshole."

"Shut up!" he yelled. "Shut up and listen, would you? Nick had second- and third-degree burns, and his arm will take weeks to heal. He wants to come home and the doctor said it's okay, so we're leaving as soon as I get us packed. My mother's in bed. The doctor put her on Valium, so it'll take a while for me to get everything together."

"One second." I was nauseous, so I turned the faucet on and took some long drinks of cold water before I got back on. "Okay, I'm here."

"So I figure we'll be there in about three hours. And another thing, just so you know before you see it. They left the arm exposed. They think it might heal better and not leave as big a scar this way. He has to take a lot of baths to wash away the old skin and the infection. I just wanted you to know before you see it."

"Okay."

"Bye. See you then." He hung up.

"Nick, I'm sorry, honey. I'm sorry you got hurt so bad." I went into Nick and Joey's room and washed the windows and wiped fingerprints off the walls. I changed their sheets and found multivitamins under Joey's pillow, and I thought about how he didn't like the multis, how he only ate the C's because they were orange flavored. I went from room to room, doing all the jobs I never could find time for. "It's not my fault, is it?" I asked myself, and I answered no over and over again but thought it had to be.

Then I started leaving messages on Tom's answering machine. My first one went like this: "Tom, you bastard, this is your fault! These things don't just happen. You and your mother are careless and stupid. At least now I know who you take after. Neither one of you knows how to care for kids."

By the second one I was yelling. "Tom, I fucking hate you. The only thing you've ever been good for is your medical insurance. You have a shitty personality and you're lousy in bed. I hope you rot in hell."

I followed that by calling him a self-centered momma's boy and his mother a cold-hearted bitch. All in all, I left about five of them, each one getting louder and nastier. On the last message I apologized, though I knew it was too late, since by then he would have already heard all the others.

By the time they got home, the house was spotless, and I felt crazy and scared.

Joey came in looking sleepy and Nick started sobbing when he saw me. I led him by his good hand to a chair and took him on my lap. He sat there crying, sitting stiffly like he was afraid to move. "Hi, you sweet guy you," I said softly. "Had a hard time, huh?" He nodded. I kept my left arm around him and with my right hand I patted his head, saying nothing, every once in a while bending to kiss his head or his face.

"It hurts," he said, "it still really hurts."

"I'm sorry."

"A lot," he added.

"I know, I'm really sorry," was all I could think to say. I looked down at it for the first time. The burn was bad, reaching from above the elbow all the way down to the wrist. It was hard to believe that hot coffee did all that. We sat there for a long time. Finally, he climbed off my lap and looked at me and smiled shyly. "Do I have any new toys?" he asked.

"Well, I think quite a few are coming real soon, but I don't think they're here just yet. Maybe if you wait here with Daddy the new toys will show up in fifteen, twenty minutes the most. What do you think?"

"I think I'll go with you to pick them out."

"I'm not sure it's a good idea for you to be running around so soon."

"It's okay," Nick said, "I can do whatever I want. The doctor said it was okay as long as I take lots of baths and keep medicine on it."

"Well, then, I think I better hurry and get lots of money so we can do the job right. What do you think?"

"I think you better," he said and laughed, looking like a little kid again.

The store was only three blocks away but we took our time walking there, and Nick spent almost an hour deciding what to buy. We filled two baskets by the time we reached the checkout line.

Joey and Nick had been asking for wrestlers for months, but I didn't like wrestling and the wrestlers looked so nasty to me that I hadn't wanted to buy them. This time I let Nick pick out four wrestlers and promised I'd buy the wrestling ring for his birthday.

"Joey's gonna love what we got," he kept saying as we walked along. He held one wrestler in his hand.

"Know what this one is called?" he asked me.

"No, what?"

"The Undertaker."

"The Undertaker? Yuk!"

"Yup. Know what Joey calls him?" I shrugged and he told me. "The Underpants Taker. He thinks that's his real name." We laughed and joked all the way home, saying things like, "Hold on to your belt, the Underpants Taker is coming."

Nick tore a larger and larger hole in one of the bags so he could keep checking what else we bought and I had to carry some of the toys in my hand when they slipped out.

The kids had no problem going to sleep that night. I told them a long wrestling story about the Undertaker stealing Hulk Hogan's underpants and what Hulk Hogan did to catch him. Nick fell asleep before Joey, who lay there for another twenty minutes singing some song he made up about wrestlers being very strong but you shouldn't worry because they didn't really hurt each other and so on, until he slipped off and his breathing got heavy.

Pudgy found me sitting in their room in the dark, crying, long after the boys were asleep. He took my hand and led me to the kitchen. We made some tea while I told him about the burn. All through the night I checked in on Nick, but he seemed to be sleeping okay. A few times, when he rolled toward the side with the burn, he called out in his sleep.

Tom never mentioned the calls I left on his answering machine. It took a long time for Nick's arm to heal, and in the end he was left with a dark brown mark that the doctor swore would fade as he got older.

Mrs. Mahoney, Adeline, and Joanie's Big Sister Dolores

IT WAS A FEW MONTHS after the boys' weekend in Rhinebeck that I had the problem with Rudy. I knew I was in big trouble this time. HomeMade was not gonna take lightly my dancing on the pies and I might be out of a job for good. But there wasn't much I could do about it now except wait and see what happened next. So I was glad when Mrs. Mahoney called right after dinner asking did I want to bring Nick and Joey out to play with Eddie and Adeline's kids. She was phoning from the street, where they were getting ready to turn the fire hydrant on. Even with all the windows open and the breeze coming off the river, the apartment was way too hot, and I hoped it would take my mind off the job. So I said sure, it'd take us about ten minutes to get ready. When I got downstairs, me and Mrs. Mahoney used garbage cans and ropes to block off the street while Adeline turned the fire hydrant on. The minute the water was on, Joey and Nick went charging through the spray. They loved the water.

Mrs. Mahoney was a big woman and was dressed in her usual housedress that was pulled too tight over her huge breasts and belly and came to just above her fleshy knees. Varicose veins ran from her ankles up along her calves, and I thought of the spider veins that spread across my thighs. I was too embarrassed to even wear a bathing suit anymore, just shorts that reached to my knees. Adeline

was short, pretty, and dark-skinned, and never wore anything but long print or flowered dresses. That was because
Adeline's husband, Julio, was Dominican and only allowed
her to show a bit of neck, ankle, and wrist. Even so, Julio
paid thousands of dollars to have Adeline's spider veins
removed, which she said left dark brown spots along her
thighs and calves.

Me and Adeline used to be best friends before Tom
left. We did everything together, her and me and our
kids—sleigh riding, food shopping, picnicking down by the
river. Late afternoons when the weather was nice, we'd sit
on parked cars out on the street talking and joking while
the kids played ball or Kick the Can. Pinehurst and 177th
wasn't exactly a pretty street, just six-story buildings facing each other, but there were a few big trees to sit under
when the sun was out. After me and Tom split up, I'd only
seen Adeline when I passed her on the street, except for
when she borrowed my vacuum when hers was broke.
Julio had two German shepherds and their oldest boy,
Junior, was allergic, so Adeline vacuumed three times a
day. It was Mrs. Mahoney who told me why Adeline and
the other women wouldn't hang around with me anymore.
"They're nervous having you near their husbands," she
said, "now that you're single and seeing that you still got
your looks."

"That's okay with me," I said, "'cause I'm too busy
with my job and the kids to be hanging out in the neighborhood. And about their husbands, you can tell them for me
that I'd never settle for leftovers."

Sean, Mrs. Mahoney's oldest son, came and played in
the water with his brother Eddie and the other little kids.
Sean had baby-sat all of them at one time or another and
they were crazy about him. He'd stand in front of the

hydrant, blocking the water with his body, and when Nick or Joey or Eddie or Adeline's kids tiptoed up to him, he'd move away and they'd squeal as the water blasted them in the face and across their chests.

"Look, even the waterbugs hate a hot apartment," Adeline said, pointing to three waterbugs crawling out from under the building. "Isn't that gross? The good news is, if they're out here, they're not upstairs in my apartment."

I thought the same thing. The first night of the heat wave, I walked down the hall to the kitchen after putting the boys to bed and found the floor covered with water-bugs. They were big ugly things and I was worried that Nick or Joey might wake in the night and see them on their way to the bathroom. So I killed as many as I could and the next day bought bug spray and became the exterminator for me and Mrs. Mahoney and two of the old ladies in the building.

To take our minds off the bugs, I told Mrs. Mahoney and Adeline about Joanie's wedding, which was finally happening at the end of the month. Adeline loved to sew, and when I described the cream-colored dress I was going to wear, Adeline said maybe she could find some rhine-stone buttons to fancy it up. I made sure to tell her about Baby Huey, mostly so she'd know I wasn't sitting at home waiting to get my hands on anybody else's husband.

I came out after tucking Nick and Joey in that night and found Pudgy sitting at the kitchen table, drawing in his journal. He kept this big book in which he wrote down his thoughts and drew all kinds of pictures. He wasn't shy about it and sometimes would read what he had written or show me his drawings. Tonight he held the book up and I laughed at a drawing of me, Nick, and Joey.

"Give me a break," I said. "I don't look like that."

He held it up and stared at it for a minute. "I think it looks just like you," he said.

"Obviously, 'cause you drew it. But I'm not that pretty. My nose is longer and my face is thinner."

"Sometimes that's true," Pudgy said. "When you're worried or unhappy. But other times you're soft and pretty and sweet-looking."

"Sure," I said, "sweet-looking. That'll be the day."

I was tired but all I could think of was that the broiler was dirty and I should clean it tonight in case we wanted to use it in the morning. It had started to smoke when I made grilled-cheese sandwiches for the boys' dinner before we went out. The crumbs needed to be emptied and the bottom scrubbed. "Are you going to keep writing in your journal?" I asked Pudgy. "I have some cleaning that I don't want to do, but it would be a lot easier if I had you here for company. I'm not saying you have to stay, I was just wondering if you were going to."

"I'm yours for as long as you want me."

"Thanks." I took out the broiler tray and started shaking it out and washing it down. "By the way, I'm sorry if I scared you last night," I told him. "I was just checking to make sure the waterbugs were gone and all the burners were off. I do that when I'm nervous."

"Yeah, it was dark and I heard someone in the kitchen," Pudgy said, "but I didn't get scared. I thought it was Nick or Joey getting up for milk or juice or walking around half asleep. My grandmother used to do that."

"Do what?"

"She napped most of the day and then roamed the house at night, going through the drawers and closets with a flashlight. And if you asked her, she'd say she was looking for her lost youth.''

''Oh, no. Well, I get up in the night to make sure the burners are off. I've done that since I was a kid. My mother was always starting fires in the house—leave a dish towel near the burner or drop her cigarette in the garbage. Sometimes the firemen came. They'd break in through a window on the fire escape. Half the bathroom burnt down once before they put it out. So I double-check everything when I get worried.''

Pudgy looked at me over his drawing, ''You know, there was something I wanted to talk to you about,'' he said. I was sure he was going to ask about my being fired but he started telling me about Joey. ''I have a small pair of scissors on my desk and Joey saw them the other day and was using them. But from the look on Nick's face I could see there was something wrong. So I stayed with Joey while he cut up an old newspaper. He must've sat there for an hour cutting that paper into little pieces.''

''I know. Joey likes to cut. Would you hide the scissors so he can't get hold of them when you're not home?''

''Sure. I already put them where he wouldn't find them. But why? Does he try to hurt himself with them?''

''What? Oh, no, nothing like that. He just loves to cut. You know the slipcover on the couch in the living room?'' I asked, and Pudgy nodded. ''Well, I hate slipcovers. But over a year ago we bought this new couch, our first and only new couch. We didn't know about Joey and scissors then. So one morning I came out to the living room and found that he had cut forty-seven little triangles out of our brand new couch, forty-seven, mind you. I

counted. Do you know how long that must have taken
him? He was probably up half the night. I dragged him out
of bed the next morning and asked if he did it and you
know what he said?" Pudgy was already laughing, so I
didn't wait for an answer. "He stood there smiling and
said, 'Isn't it pretty? Didn't I do a good job? I worked
really hard, Mommy, really hard.' Since then, we hide the
scissors, but he always manages to find a pair."

I was done cleaning, so I went to wash up and put on
my nightgown. When I came back to say goodnight to
Pudgy, I found him exactly the way I had left him, sitting
at the kitchen table, drawing. But he looked different
somehow. I couldn't tell if he was tired or sad or what. I
asked him if something was wrong and he shook his head
yes and then told me that he had to go into the hospital for
a week. It was a yearly checkup to see how his bones were
doing after that radiation leak on the sub.

"I should be used to it," he said, "but I'm always
scared." He looked much older when he wasn't smiling.
I stood next to him and kind of half-hugged him and said
I was sorry. Then he pushed me away and told me I should
get some sleep.

I woke suddenly because someone was touching my
hair. I looked over and the door to my room was closed
and Pudgy was lying next to me, running his hands through
my hair.

"What are you doing?" I asked groggily.

"Touching your hair."

"Pudge, what should I do with that?"

"Whatever you want."

"I don't want anything," I said.

"Then we won't for now."

"For now?"

"We will someday if you want to."

"I love you, Pudge, but I may never want to be with you, not in that way."

"That's okay too," he said. "I'm crazy about you and Nick and Joey. That's all."

"That's good," I said and started to drift off to sleep again. At any minute I expected him to get up and go to his room but instead he moved closer, so that he was pressed up close against my back. He was so thin that it felt like a young boy's body against mine, holding me tight, still running his hands through my hair, talking about how good it felt to have me and Nick and Joey in his life. Sometime in the early night I woke again and the place beside me was empty.

"Honey, you better have a real good reason," Teddy the Greek Junior, head of the Bakery Drivers' Local of the Teamsters, said on the phone the next morning.

I didn't know what to say. I felt the bad taste in my mouth again when I remembered Rudy but I didn't want to talk about it, so I just said, "I got nothing to say about the pies. I don't even know why. But one of my storekeepers got nasty with me and I think I went crazy."

"You danced on the pies 'cause some storekeeper got fresh with you? And you think HomeMade is going to believe that? No way, sweetheart. You weren't suspended, you know, you were fired. That's no joke. We got to come up with something better than that."

"He wasn't just fresh. It was worse than that. He got dirty with me."

"How worse? You going to have to be more specific or they won't listen to you. Did he rape ya? What did he do? Did he touch ya? If he did, can you prove it?"

"Do you know what it feels like to have someone do disgusting things to you? It makes your skin crawl, that's what."

"You think just 'cause you say something happened, they're gonna believe it? You think the storekeeper is gonna say, 'Sure, everything she says is true'?"

"Shut up!" I screamed. "I don't care what that filthy bastard says. What if it was your wife that he put his hands on? How would that feel, Mister Organizer? Or wouldn't that bother you either?"

"Anna, calm down, calm down now, it's okay," Teddy Junior said softly. "I'm not trying to give you a hard time. I'm on your side. I just wanted to show you what management is going to say, so we can decide how our side will respond. I'm with you. Can you understand that? But I need your help to show that there were extenuating circumstances. Okay?"

"Yeah. I'm sorry," I said. "And, yes, I understand." I felt awful. I wasn't crying but I was close to it. Mostly I felt exhausted and had a hard time thinking. "I can't go back to Rudy's," was all I could think to say. "I don't care if I lose my job." I stopped to catch my breath.

"Okay, honey, take it slow and tell me what happened," Teddy said. "Start from the beginning." So I did and told him exactly what happened.

I finished with, "So you see, even if HomeMade lets me keep the job, I could never go back. I *wanted* Jed to suspend me, fire me, anything. I needed time to think."

He repeated some of what I said back to me and asked

if he got it right. Then he hung up, saying he was going to try to reach Jed at his home.

Teddy Junior called me back around noon. "You're a piece of work, Anna, you know that?" he said. He said he'd been talking to Jed for over an hour and that Jed agreed to rehire me. That Jed said he never wanted to hear about the pies again and that I wouldn't have to serve Rudy. He'd figure something out and I should show up tomorrow for work as usual. "It was tough, but it's water under the bridge now," Teddy said.

"I don't know how to thank you," I told Teddy.

"I'll think of a way," he said.

I finished out the week without any more problems. I did all the stores on the route except for Rudy's. The heat let up a bit, going down to the low nineties. I never even saw Jed until Friday.

On Friday when I drove in, I was feeling better and Ramon told me that Jed wanted to see me in his office after I finished emptying my truck. I met Baby Huey on my way to the office. He tried to give me a hug but I pulled away.

"I got to talk to Jed," I told him.

"I know. They say you had trouble out there this week," Baby Huey said, "and I heard that Jed is taking it serious and doing something about it for a change. But when you talk to Jed, take it slow, be nice, and I think he'll do all right by you."

"I will, thanks."

Jed asked me to sit down and did everything business-like this time, talking in a straightforward way, no nasty remarks or digs. He said there was nothing he could do about Rudy, seeing as I had no proof. But he was taking me off the route. Temporarily I would work like a route rider again, pulling vacations or routes for guys that were sick, and Wally, the regular route rider, would pull my route. A route was coming up soon that Jed thought I might get, because nobody else wanted it. Since I was newer than most of the other drivers, if someone bid against me, he'd have first dibs. But he hadn't heard of anyone else wanting off their route. It wouldn't be for a few weeks, and until then I'd be moving around again. That was fine with me. I went home smiling.

It was a week before the wedding. Joanie's mom and dad were going out for the evening with Joanie's sister, Dolores, so Joanie invited Little Dominic over for dinner. For days, it was all she could talk about. She asked me what I would cook if it was my fiancé and would I wear a skirt or summer slacks? And if Dominic offered to help clean up, should she let him? She decided on white wine with the meal but then worried that Dominic might think she was a boozer.

After the weekend, when I asked Joanie how the dinner went, she said she didn't want to talk about it. But she looked so down that I said maybe if she talked about it she'd feel better.

"Well, it wasn't that we didn't have a good time," Joanie said, "it's just that dinner didn't work out the way I hoped it would. And Dominic says that that doesn't mean I'm not a good cook. You lose some, you win some, is what Dominic said."

"What exactly *did* go wrong?" I asked.

"You might find it funny and tell everyone about it," Joanie said.

"I promise I won't, and I never break a promise."

"Well, you know that I take eating and health very serious." I knew it, because Joanie ate an apple, two carrots, and a yogurt every day for lunch. Three food groups in one shot is how she put it. "When my grandmother lived with us," Joanie continued, "I spent as much time as I could in the kitchen watching her cook. I planned to be a great cook when I got married. And my grandmother always talked to me while she worked, mostly about her life on the farm in Germany, before Grandpa died. Once she told me how when the hens were laying eggs without shells, she crunched up eggshells from some good eggs and mixed it in with the chicken feed. Eggshells have a lot of calcium, she said, made the chickens and their eggs a lot stronger. And Grandma was right, the chicken and eggs were fine after that. No more eggs without shells."

"Well? So what about your dinner?"

"Well, when I was planning this dinner, I thought about Dominic and how he needed strong bones to do the kind of hard work he did. Do you know that half the guys in the depot wear back braces? The loads are so heavy that their backs can't take it."

"I know, I'm afraid that's going to happen to me."

"So I wanted to cook a beautiful dinner and make Dominic strong as well. I took three eggshells and put them in the food processor that Dominic gave me for an engagement present. Then I added the eggshells to the meatloaf I was making. They were so crunched up you couldn't even see them. I was so thrilled about making something tasty and healthy at the same time that I served the meal standing over him while he tried everything. Dominic loved the soup and the homemade bread and the vegetable soufflé, so that part was perfect. And then he bit into the meatloaf. He chewed it slowly and took a second bite. But the food must have got stuck in his throat or something, 'cause he gagged and coughed and spit everything all over his plate. Dominic was so embarrassed. He kept apologizing for spitting. 'Sand,' is what he said. He thought some sand had gotten mixed in with the breadcrumbs and that maybe we could sue the breadcrumb company. So I explained about the chicken and the eggshells and all. He kept saying, 'Eggshells in the meatloaf?' like he couldn't believe it. Instead of the meatloaf, he ate lots of the dessert, which was peaches and cream. Then I couldn't stop crying but he told me that the meatloaf would have been delicious except for the eggshells and that he was looking forward to my next meal.''

I leaned over and gave Joanie a hug, trying to hold back the laughter that was bubbling up inside. I told her not to worry, at least the wedding was catered and neither of us great cooks would be expected to lend a hand.

When Baby Huey picked me up at the house to go to Joanie and Little Dominic's wedding, he gave a long wolf whistle and said I was a knockout. The night before, Pudgy had given me a rhinestone necklace and earrings to match the buttons Adeline sewed on my dress. I gasped when I opened the box. "It's an I-love-you present with no strings attached,'' Pudgy explained. Mrs. Mahoney helped me with my makeup and fixed my hair while Sean looked on and gave advice. My hair was piled high in a French twist with long curls falling down the sides and the back. I brushed on peach blush to match the Crazy Coral lipstick Mrs. Mahoney lent me.

I was so nervous I couldn't wait to get there, but we kept taking the wrong turns. The actual ceremony had been in the morning at Joanie's parents' house and included only the immediate family. But Joanie told me that there were wonderful things planned for the reception. I hadn't been to a wedding or a reception in a long time. Mostly I didn't find them fun anymore and made excuses to get out of going. But I was looking forward to this one. Joanie and Little Dominic would be good for each other.

"An ice sculpture carved by a real artist," I told Baby Huey. "Joanie said that was going to be the centerpiece." I was trying to change the subject, because somehow in the last hour our conversation had gone from bad to worse. We had gotten into talking about love and marriage and promises and everything that can go wrong. Baby Huey had started it by saying that even though his father had left when he was a baby, most marriages in the old days were what they should be, rock-solid commitments for a long, wonderful life together. So I told him how my mother and father had been married for forty years and when my father died, my mother wouldn't pay the twenty-six dollars to get rid of my dad's ashes because she was "sick and tired of putting out for the old bastard." He told me that his wife confessed on their wedding day that she lied about being a virgin, and then I described how I found pubic lice in my underwear on my honeymoon, Tom's wedding gift to me.

"Watch the road," I screamed. Baby Huey was laughing so hard about the lice that he almost hit another car and then swerved the other way so that our car jumped the curb.

"What is it with these people in New Jersey?" Baby Huey asked. "All this pollution makes them so crazy they can't drive straight or give the right directions?"

Finally we passed what looked like a motel with low buildings all in a circle. A big flashing sign out front said CATERING FOR ENGAGEMENTS, WEDDINGS, ALL OCCASIONS, so I made him stop and I got out and asked at the office. It was the right place. "Yeah, but if we had so much trouble finding it," he complained, "maybe the other guests won't get here on time either." Of course, nobody else had lost the little map that came inside the invitation and the only two empty seats had placards with our names, Ernesto Salazar and Anna Ferrara, surrounded by daisies and violets.

"The damn place ain't air conditioned," Baby Huey whispered, but loud enough that everybody looked our way. There were huge floor fans standing between the tables and at each door.

"The air conditioning went down an hour ago," Jimmy explained as we took our seats. Jimmy and his wife, Mimi, sat across from us, Baby Huey was next to Jed and his wife, and Mario the Mole was on my right with his wife, Sophie. I glanced around and saw Wally, Ramon, Roger, and a whole lot of others at tables around the hall. I'd never met any of the wives but most of them looked exactly the way I pictured them. Mario's wife, Sophie, was thin and mousy-looking; Jimmy's Mimi had her hair in a Cleopatra cut, wore way too much makeup, and looked like a fierce little ballbuster. The only surprise was Jed's wife, Cindy. I was feeling beautiful until I saw Cindy. It wasn't that Cindy was gorgeous like a magazine model, but somehow Cindy made everyone else look dull. She was only an inch shorter than Jed, but she sat high and looked a foot taller. She had long, almost black hair and everything she had on was real. Real gold, real diamonds, real silk.

People were sweating like crazy from the heat, but Cindy sat there looking perfectly cool and collected.

"A fucking queen, that's what Jed married," Baby Huey said in my ear, "a true American princess." Jed sat there acting even more bad-mannered than usual, belching and making passes at Jimmy's wife, dropping crumbs in a pile on top of his round beer belly. "Round number three," Baby Huey mumbled in my ear.

"Why'd such a classy bitch marry a guy like Jed?" I wanted to know.

"Obviously not for love. I think she did it to stick it to her parents. Jed said her sister came close to marrying an Arab."

The lights dimmed and the band started playing a waltz. From a little balcony on the side wall came a spotlight that followed Little Dominic and Joanie as he led her down the center of the hall. Little Dominic walked proud and Joanie looked lovely and shy. She wore a simple long white gown with an empire waist that did very little to hide the fact that she was extremely pregnant. The song ended to the sound of spoons clinking against glasses and Little Dominic stopped and pulled Joanie's head down to give her a kiss. She blushed, and I blushed, and I thought half the people there were probably blushing like crazy too. It was that kind of thing. Joanie was so much taller than Little Dominic that the kiss landed on her chin. But some guy who looked like Little Dominic's cousin or uncle stood up and clapped, yelling, "Bravo! Bravissimo!" and everyone joined in.

Joanie's family took up three tables. They were fair-haired, neatly though not fashionably dressed, and very quiet. By contrast, there were ten tables of Dominic's relatives, brightly dressed women with low-cut dresses and mostly short men in fancy tuxes.

Before dinner was served, Baby Huey went to the men's room to wash his hands. When he returned, he sat at the table, a napkin tucked under his chin, his wrists limp and dangling, trying not to touch anything until his food came. The food was great, beginning with a huge antipasto, which was followed by a lemon ice. Jed kept asking for more lemon ice until Mario explained that the ice was to clean your palate, not to keep you cooled off. The main meal took hours, dish after dish of pasta, chicken cacciatore, spaghetti and meatballs, or plain meat and potatoes for those who wanted American food. After the meal, the waiters brought out bowls of flaming cherries jubilee and then acted out a little ceremony with their napkins, twirling and bowing and presenting the cherries to the bride and groom. A few minutes later, five of Dominic's uncles, brothers, and cousins got up and imitated the waiters, doing exactly the same little dance with the napkins. At the end of it, they all faced the bride and groom and dropped their pants. All five had on huge boxer shorts decorated with big red hearts. Joanie hid her face behind Little Dominic while everybody clapped and cheered.

Everyone around me was sniffling when Little Dominic covered Joanie's hand with his and together they cut the wedding cake. And then the hall was quiet, and we watched as they gently fed each other their first forkfuls. At our table, Mimi did the same thing with Jimmy, only she shoved the cake so far down his throat that it all came right back up. After that, our table got more and more rowdy.

As the evening wore on, the gorgeous ice sculpture of flowers and wedding bells melted and the room was filled with the smell of sweat mixed with cologne, perfume, and underarm deodorant. The band played mostly Italian songs but it was too hot to dance and only when a song was sung in English—"I don't want her, you can have her, she's too fat for me"—did two very fat women in emerald-green dresses get up and do the polka.

I wasn't having a very good time. Mimi watched Jimmy like a hawk to make sure he wasn't looking at any woman but her. Jed sat by Cindy's side drinking champagne out of a bottle, getting drunker and louder by the minute. Every time he put the bottle down, the waiters took it away and Jed would disappear for a few minutes, coming back with another bottle of champagne in his hand. I was bored with the jokes and all the talk about houses, cars, and dogs, so when I saw Joanie get up to make the rounds, I ran over to join her and got introduced to her family.

"Two of my favorite people," Joanie said as she saw me coming toward her and a friendly-looking woman at her side stood up and held out her hand. "This is my best friend, Anna, from the depot," she said, "and this is my sister, Dolores." Joanie had told me a lot about her big sister Dolores, saying how Dolores had practically raised her after their mother took sick. Dolores smiled, saying that other than Little Dominic all Joanie talked about was me, and that she was glad to finally meet me. Dolores held my hand in both of hers and then patted the empty seat next to her, asking me to sit for a while.

Dolores asked where I was from and when I said Washington Heights she laughed. "I'm on West Eighty-third. Not exactly neighbors, but at least we're in the same borough." Dolores wasn't quiet and shy like Joanie. She was a smart woman with a lot of confidence who smiled or laughed at the littlest thing. I figured she was forty, forty-five years old because she was older than Joanie, but she could have been anywhere between thirty and fifty. Her blond hair was chopped short and she whispered to me that she cut it herself at night when she couldn't sleep. "I'm a dangerous woman with a pair of scissors," she said and loved it when I told her about Joey and all the cutting he did. It was the first time that evening that I started to relax.

I didn't know why, but very soon I was telling her all about Joey and Nick and about my marriage. "I was seventeen when I met Tom," I said to Dolores. "I only knew him a few months before we got married. But by then I'd been on my own for almost a year and thought I was in love. When I got married, the guests at my wedding thought I must be pregnant to get married so young and kept telling me that I was lucky I made such a good catch. To Tom they said I was a wild one but at least he wouldn't get bored."

"I've never been married," Dolores said. "I always seem to have boyfriends, but I prefer them asexual. The other kind is so demanding." I laughed out loud but she went on talking seriously about it. "I guess I'm devoted to my job and not too interested in men. My parents don't understand it. Thank God Joanie is getting married and they'll finally have a grandchild. I couldn't do it. My job is my life and I love it." She told me a little about computer graphics and how she started in the field and that it took years for her to get to the top. "I love computers and designing. I love managing people and making decisions. My job is all stress, I never get a break, but it's a perfect life for me."

When I told her about driving for HomeMade, she

said she admired my courage. "It's not courage," I told her, "it's what I do to get by." I found myself telling her about what happened with Rudy and some of the problems with Jed. "You've been so nice listening to all this boring stuff," I finally said. "I don't usually talk so much about it."

She took my hand and said, "Hey, if you're my sister's best friend, then you and I must be related too. You're part of the family." We both smiled. "Look!" Dolores was pointing to two groups of people gathered in the middle of the dance floor. A young boy got the garter and an old lady caught the bouquet. Neither of us could watch when the band played slow sexy music and a long drum roll as he pulled the garter up her wrinkled, varicosed leg. We kept our eyes closed until the music stopped.

No one was dancing and the guests were leaving early on account of the heat. But I wanted to dance at least once before I went home. Earlier I had asked Baby Huey but he turned me down, saying, "I never dance." So I asked Dolores if she knew how to dance the tarantella and she shook her head no but said she'd love for me to show her. I took her out to the dance floor and Little Dominic joined us. The music started slowly and then went faster and faster. We held hands and raised them high, taking Dolores carefully through the steps until she caught on. Round and round we went, our feet lightly tapping on the floor. The music speeded up and we went whirling through the room, our clothes soaked through with sweat, our hair dripping wet, each of us laughing louder and louder as we circled across the floor until more and more people came out to join us.

When the music finally stopped, Baby Huey tapped

me on the arm and said he was ready to leave, he'd meet me at the door.

"Time for me to go," I told Little Dominic and Dolores.

Dolores gave me a big hug and and we stood holding each other while we caught our breaths. Then she reached into her pocket and came out with something and put it in my hand. I looked down and it was her business card. "Someday," she said in that same serious way, "if you get tired of your way of life, give me a call. I'll have a job for you."

"What?" I looked down at her card, which had her name engraved on top, and that she was vice president of a company called Creative Computer Graphics. "You must be kidding," I said to her. "I have no skills. I'm a housewife and a trucker. That's all I've ever been."

She shrugged. "I didn't think anything else," she said, "but it's not necessarily all you'll ever be."

I held up the card. "I could never do something like this. I wouldn't even try. I don't even have secretarial skills, no college, a degree, nothing."

"You don't know what you have," she said. "You're a survivor, that's what counts. The rest you can learn."

I laughed. "You're a dreamer," I said. I didn't want to leave, but we said our goodbyes and I went to find Baby Huey.

I didn't think much of Dolores's offer, knowing that when they're feeling nice, people say things that they never expect you to follow up on. But I taped that card to the dashboard of my truck, and whenever I felt really down, I looked at the card and thought—maybe.

Angel and Diego

"I DON'T LIKE THE IDEA of leaving you out here," Richie, the guy who ran the route before me, said. "On other routes," he explained, "drivers get held up once every few months, but on this route it's the daily news. They got the Pepsi man before the holidays. And last week they shot the Key Food store manager in the leg, then looted all the cash from the registers. We carry a lot of money and the guys on the streets all know it. Take care of yourself, sweetie," he warned. "Be real careful, you being a woman and all. Remember to keep looking over your shoulder."

I envied Richie his going over to Stella D'Oro, to a nice, easy route out on the Island. Bethpage, I think. Stella D'Oro was like working for a family business. It wasn't big bucks, but the money was steady and you could finish the route by noon. A person could retire on a nice salary with very little agita from that job. A lot of the guys even had a second business on the side. I don't mean an illegal one, like drivers who sold drugs or hot stereos right off the truck, but a real business, like contractors or carpenters. Richie was a lucky guy. Our company, HomeMade, was near the bottom on the cake-route scale. Crusty Bake and those generic-type cookies and cakes were the lowest, and Hearthland and HomeMade were the next level up. Hearthland and HomeMade competed for second-worst in terms of salaries, the condition of the trucks and depots, and how bad the managers were. Entenmann's, Hostess, Drake's, and Stella D'Oro were in a class of their own.

But I was glad when they gave me Richie's route down by the docks in Brooklyn. On my old route on Flatbush Avenue, the German, Jewish, and Italian store-keepers were always on my case, yelling at me for not getting there on time, complaining when HomeMade raised its prices, calling the depot if I didn't show up on a holiday or in a snowstorm. Rudy was the worst of the lot, but some of them weren't much better. I'd miss those pretty streets, with trees and flowers and all, but I figured it was a reasonable tradeoff, since I'd get half the hassle from the storekeepers.

The only thing I was worried about was how danger-ous this new route was. Richie swore that it was a good route and the "tips" were high, though that didn't matter to me, since I wasn't into stealing from my customers. "But you have to be careful," Richie kept repeating, "those streets aren't safe for a woman walking around with her pockets filled with money."

Half the route, the area they called Bush Terminal, was down by the docks on dark streets under the El and there was a lot of drugs and bookie joints and drinking down there. But since it was the kind of neighborhood where everybody was out on the street, I figured it would provide a sort of natural protection for me. In some ways it felt less dangerous than routes in neighborhoods where the people stayed in their little one- and two-family houses, not opening their shades even when there was trouble.

After a few weeks, I found that I wasn't worried about those streets anymore. I got used to the neighborhood, and I think the neighborhood got used to me. And the fact that there were a lot of people out there did prove to be a big help. Along the docks there were hundreds of longshoremen lined up each day, waiting to sign in and collect their money or to see if a boat was going out. And there were always card tables set up on the streets, with maybe four or five guys sitting around in shirtsleeves, gambling and smoking, looking over their cards and tossing in chips. They concentrated hard on their game, but you knew they had one eye on everything that went on in the neighborhood.

And then there were bars like Millie's. Sometimes as many as ten of Millie's regulars stood smoking and talking outside the door, it didn't matter how early in the day it was. The bar itself was one long, narrow, dark room. It was always packed, and even in winter her customers spilled out onto the street. She ran it herself, no bouncer or anything, just the old bartender, Raul. It wasn't that Millie wasn't afraid. You'd be crazy not to be scared, what with all the drugged or drunk crazies roaming those streets, bothering people, holding them up. Millie, like all the storekeepers, had a gun—maybe a whole arsenal— under the counter. But in Millie's case, the fact that most of her customers were regulars was her best defense.

Millie herself was a well-dressed, well-spoken woman somewhere in her mid- to late thirties. She had a full head of dyed blond curly hair and deep olive skin, which set off her almond-shaped hazel eyes. She was powerful-looking and tall, taller than half her customers, but she was pretty too, and had a quick, easy smile. I stopped at Millie's once a week, because she always bought a few boxes of cupcakes and Chocos off my truck to bring home to her kids.

A short way down the block from the bar, on one of

those aluminum and nylon beach chairs, sat Millie's Tia Vieja, or Old Auntie, as the rest of us called her. Except for when it snowed, she sat there, under a huge beach umbrella, stitching and knitting from noon till dusk. I figured she was about seventy-five years old, but Millie once said that Tia Vieja was much older than anyone would think. Millie came out regularly to chat with the old lady, but more often than not, they'd end up going at each other.

Like when I drove up one day at the end of the summer. It was eighty-five degrees out there, at least. Millie was unbuttoning the collar of Old Auntie's dress, swearing that she wasn't about to be embarrassed by a relative of hers suffocating to death in a dress made of polyester. Tia Vieja was muttering back in Spanish something about not throwing out half her clothes just because polyester wasn't fancy enough for "la familia." As I stepped down from my truck, Millie turned to me for help. "You be the judge," she said. "Like you don't know either one of us." She stood there, hands on hips, in front of the old lady. "Look at my Old Auntie. Would you want your mama or auntie to wear a dress made of that? Why not wear a plastic bag, no? Same difference. Que caliente!" She moved closer to Tia Vieja. "Que caliente!" she repeated, even louder than before, in case the old lady was hard of hearing that day. Some days Auntie's hearing was worse than others.

Millie and Tia Vieja waited for me to answer. But what could I say? I would've agreed with Millie except that I was wearing my usual cheap polyester uniform.

"You can't bring me into this," I said. "Look who you're talking to—your fucking HomeMade polyester special, excuse the English." I pointed to my black shirt, which was pulled so tight across my breasts that the buttons were ready to pop, and opened the top button so they could see the heat rash that covered my chest. My pants were made for a man and bulged around the fly, stretched out by my hips and ass. I turned in a circle so Millie and Old Auntie could get a good look at me. "I'm sweating like a pig and spraying deodorant all day long with these clothes."

I think that was the first time that either Millie or Tia Vieja noticed what I was wearing. Millie stood there eyeing me from top to bottom and then burst into a series of short laughs that got louder and louder until she was almost howling. "Pardoname, I'm sorry," she mumbled between laughs as she walked away, "I'm sorry." Old Auntie joined in, rocking back and forth in her chair, giggling behind her hands.

The next week a whole wardrobe of polyester dresses, skirts, and blouses hung from nails in the bricks on the side of Millie's bar. They were mostly turquoise, lavender, and orange, but my favorite was a long shiny pink dress with bows on the sleeves, a wide sash, and ruffles along the hem. The hand-painted sign above the clothes said, CAMISAS FALDAS Y TRAJES: 50 CENTAVOS, $1, $2.

Of the forty to fifty stores that I visited each week on my new route, Nueva Vista quickly became one of my favorites. It was run by Angel and his sons and his sons' friends, any of at least ten different boys between the ages of seven and fifteen. It was rare that I saw any of the boys two times in a row—except for the littlest, who everyone called Angelito, though his real name was Francisco. Apart from Angel and Angelito, they became a blur of smiling faces to me as I rushed in and out with my order. There were always some little girls poking around too, looking through the shelves or holding on to Angel's leg or shirttail while he worked. Nueva Vista was no bigger or prettier, or even cleaner, than my other stores, not that it was uglier or dirtier either. But something to do with Angel and those kids made me feel good no matter what my day had been like.

I could bring three, even four trays of cake to Nueva Vista, and that's a lot for a small bodega, but they would always sell out. On a Friday, when I had maybe a hundred dollars' worth of cake left over and didn't want to waste time visiting five more little stores to get rid of it, I'd drive over to Nueva Vista, dump it all in there, and by Monday it'd be gone.

"Hey, mala puertorriqueña, qué pasa?" Angel always called out the same greeting to me as long as one of his girlfriends wasn't around. Rita, his regular girlfriend, was a heavy, fierce-looking woman with a long, slightly hooked nose that gave her something of an Indian look. I got the feeling that she was nicer when she was alone with Angel, but whenever I saw her in the store, she was slapping and snapping at the kids for no reason that I could make out, and complaining that they were no help and only made the place dirtier. I'd also met Carla on some of my visits to the store. Carla was a spaced-out nineteen-year-old and the mother of Angel's three-month-old baby girl. Carla had black eyes framed by bleached white hair and light brown skin. Carla and Rita were friendly enough to each other, but jealous and short-tempered toward everyone else. Angel hinted that he had many more girlfriends, but only Rita and Carla showed up at the store.

If Rita or Carla weren't around, after I brought in the

fresh cake and packed it out onto the shelves, Angel would start his teasing. "Hey, mala puertorriqueña," he'd say, "where's my kiss? Besame, mi amiga dulce. Ven aquí and plant a big kiss on my cheek to say hello to your friend Angel."

"Give me a break, feo," I would call back, "you're too ugly to kiss." Angel was about thirty years old, well-built, and very good looking. Mostly, he had one of the nicest smiles I'd ever seen. "I got better things to do than kiss somebody as ugly as you," I'd tell him.

Then he'd always bring some wide-eyed little girl into it. "Hey, chica, you hear that," he'd say, pinching her lightly to get her attention, "you hear what la señora said to me?" He'd bend down, sticking his face close to hers and ask, "You think I'm feo, huh? You think I'm feo like la señora says, huh, mamacita?" And if she weren't too little or too shy, she'd usually examine his face seriously, smile a big smile, and say, "Si, muy feo," and look at me and laugh. Angel would throw his hands up in the air, turn his back on her, and head toward me.

"See," I'd tell him, "all the girls agree, you're feo, so don't go planting any kisses on me." And he'd come around the counter, rest his hand on my shoulder, and give me a big kiss on the cheek. "Yuk, now I got to go home and wash," I'd say. I'd rub hard where he kissed me and he'd gently give me a second longer kiss, making a lip-smacking sound as he did it. Then he'd mess up my hair and send me on my way. But he always checked the window to make sure neither of his girlfriends was coming down the street. If they were anywhere in sight, he'd barely look at me or say goodbye.

.   .   .

In between Millie's bar and Angel's was a store called
Bodega Nueva, run by a mean little man named Diego. I
hated Diego, the Seven-Up man hated him, as many people
as knew him hated him. Diego was the kind of guy who got
a kick out of getting you to hate him. The very first time
I walked into the store, my second day out on my new
route, I knew Diego's place would only be trouble for me.

That first day in his store I checked out my cake,
which was stuffed into three shelves on top of Uncle Ben's
and Minute Rice, and went over to introduce myself.
Diego was about five foot two and extremely wide. He was
wearing a white T-shirt rolled up over his arms, and the
bottom of the shirt was cut off so that his naked stomach,
which was as large as a basketball, stuck out. To add to the
picture, his belly button and arms were covered with tufts
of black hair. I had a hard time looking at him, he was so
ugly. Not ugly because his features weren't regular, but
because he was nasty-looking. He had angry black eyes and
a turned-up nose, with these wide-open nostrils. I couldn't
help thinking of a wild pig I had seen at the Bronx Zoo
when I took the kids there for Joey's birthday. It charged
at anything that moved.

"Hi," I said, hoping I sounded a lot friendlier than I
felt, "I'm your new route person."

Diego looked at me, then turned his head away and
spat on the wood floor. "La mujer belongs in la casa," he
said in a deep, low voice, banging a can down hard on the
counter. I jumped but didn't answer, simply wrote down
what was needed, which wasn't much, as the store obviously did very little business, and went out to my truck.

Take care of business, I told myself. Don't look him
in the eye or answer unless you're taking care of business.
Think of Angel or Millie or Baby Huey, but don't let him

get to you. I remembered how the other HomeMade drivers used to say the same kind of thing to me when I first started. They'd rather I was home on welfare than out doing "a man's job."

This time when I went back in, I kept my eyes down.

"El lugar de la mujer es en la casa," he repeated when I returned.

I concentrated on looking at the rows and rows of Goya chickpeas and red beans on the top shelf near the register. I had never seen so many cans of beans. I figured he used the beans to fill his empty shelves because beans were a safe bet. I wanted to tell him that I was working to feed my kids, like every other fucking driver on the route, but instead I raised my tray and counted out the cake I brought in. "Five, ten, fifteen Honeybelles, two Bonzos," I said. I kept my eyes on anything but his face. I noticed that at least he kept the place clean. "Five, ten Chocos and three apple pies. That's it," I said when I finished.

"Yeah?" Diego put out his hand to stop me. "You count too fast," he said coming right up into my face and bringing back his arm as if he was getting ready to swing. "How do I know you're not cheating me?" I turned away quickly, sure that he was going to smack me across the face, already feeling the sting. Instead he swung at the tray and knocked it out of my hands so that the cake went flying.

I had to admit, the guy scared me. After all my years of fighting on the streets and getting kicked around by my father, you'd think I wouldn't be afraid of a guy like that, but I was.

"Look, if you don't want service, that's okay with me," I said softly, trying to sound businesslike to hide the fact that I was shaking. "Call Hearthland, they'll serve you. I don't have to put up with this." I stopped myself from cursing, I didn't want to rile him up any more than he already was.

"HomeMade serves me," he answered. "Pick up that cake and start serving."

"No thanks," I told him, thinking maybe I could make a run for it. "I got enough business on this route, I don't need your store." This time I kept my eyes on him as I moved toward the door.

"Start serving, blanca," Diego snarled like a dog and kicked the cake out of his way. He grabbed a long pole that was leaning on the wall by the window and did a kind of fast shuffle toward me. "Now!" he yelled as he smacked the stick against the wall nearest me. I went back, picked up the cake, and carefully put it on the shelves, watching the stick out of the corner of my eye in case he waved it in my direction. "Arrange it nice," he directed me. When I was done I gave him the bill, which was $19.86, and he handed me a twenty. I put the change in his hand and he threw it across the room. It hit the wall, then clattered as it rolled across the floor. "Come earlier next time," he said.

When I left, he didn't look up. He stood there staring down at his belly, his finger poking around his navel.

That afternoon I went to see Jed to talk about Diego. I made sure not to raise my voice. "I'm not going back to the Bodega Nueva," I told him. "The guy's crazy and probably dangerous."

Jed rubbed his hand along the smooth skin of his forehead to the back of his neck. "Is that so? Well, the owner of Bodega Nueva just called, knowing you would make trouble," Jed answered, smiling. He had a way of smiling that came off as an insult even when it was a simple smile. "Anna, I've told you a million times," Jed went on, "you wanted a man's job, now you got it. But every time there's a little trouble, you act like a helpless lady and come whining back to me. If you could just do your job like a man and go back and serve the store, everyone would be happy."

"It's not my job to take shit from customers," I said to him. "None of the other guys do."

Jed didn't bother answering. He turned his back on me, walked into his office, and closed the door. I stood outside and yelled, "Jed, what is this shit? You didn't even ask what happened." There was no answer. I kicked at his door a few times and called him a redneck sicko, but I knew that that was the end of it in Jed's book. I wouldn't be able to get out of serving Diego.

The next morning, I was still angry about what happened with Diego. That's all I could think about as I loaded the trays on my truck. I was slamming them around and must've been careless, because one of the trays scratched me along the wrist. I stood there cursing at everything and everybody as Jimmy and Baby Huey came over to say hello. I was surprised 'cause it was only 5:00 A.M. and they usually didn't get in for another twenty minutes. They'd been doing this job for a long time and they were fast. They could stroll in at five-thirty and have their trucks loaded by the time we rolled out at a quarter to six. You rarely saw them a minute before their usual time. As the two of them walked over, tears came pouring out and Baby Huey took me in his arms.

"Come here," he said, pulling me to the side, in between mine and Wally's truck. "Yeah, go ahead, baby," he said, "cry if you want." He wrapped his arms around me and I put my head on his shoulder. He always smelled so clean and it mixed with the scent of his cologne, which he'd told me was Armani. Sometimes when I was on the street or in a store and some guy was wearing Armani, I'd get a rush thinking of Baby Huey.

"We heard one of your store owners gave you a really bad time yesterday. If only he had put his hands on you or hit you," Baby Huey said.

"What?" I said. "Are you nuts?" Sometimes Baby Huey came out with the strangest things.

"No, no, not like that," he said. "I mean if he had touched you or hit you, you wouldn't have to serve the store anymore. But if he's just mean, you can't do nothing."

"That don't mean we can't do nothing about it," Jimmy spoke up. Jimmy rarely said a thing. Actually, Baby Huey rarely said anything either, except sometimes when everything came pouring out at once. "We don't have to let him treat you like that," Jimmy went on, "we can pay him a visit on your personal behalf if the company won't do nothing." Jimmy was a head shorter than Baby Huey and not as broad, but powerful-looking in a different way. Both men wore short-sleeved shirts all year long and when they loaded their trucks you could see their muscles flex and veins pop while they worked. Baby Huey's arms were massive, while Jimmy's looked like steel wires ran through them. I never understood, with Jimmy being that strong, how Baby Huey had managed to crush the air out of Jimmy's lungs when he came back from vacation one summer and bear-hugged him. But he did. It put Jimmy in the hospital for a day.

"Thanks, but no thanks," I said in response to Jimmy's offer. Baby Huey still had his arms around me, so I moved away and stood facing them. "Look," I said seriously, "I don't want you guys to get into a fight with this guy over me. He's crazy but he'll leave me alone after a while. I'll be okay. I just have to do my job and not let him get to me, right? Treat it like nothing happened."

Baby Huey took me in his arms again and hugged me to him. Then he kissed me lightly on the lips and put something in my hand, folding my fingers over what felt like a small box. "From the boys," he said.

"A present for me? What is it?" I asked, but they walked away without answering. A few moments later I heard the sound of their trucks pulling out. I wished they had waited while I opened it.

The box was beautifully wrapped in white and gold paper, no bow or ribbon. I couldn't imagine what it could be. From the boys? Which ones? And why would they buy me a present? I tore off the paper and inside was a small gray velvet box, rounded like a jewelry box, but different somehow. Jewelry? A gold star for being their favorite Choco? I couldn't guess. I opened the box and sitting in a nest of gray velvet was a very small pearl-handled gun. It took my breath away. "Uh-uh," I said softly, shaking my head back and forth. "Uh-uh, I couldn't. Not me." I didn't even want to think that I might *want* to shoot somebody. I closed the box and looked for someplace to hide it. Everything on the truck was open and the box would be too easily seen. Finally I slid my stale tray out and stuck it behind all the old and smashed cakes. I put it there temporarily until I could figure out what to do with it. The stale tray was on the highest rack and I kept my eyes on the bottom of the gray box as I pushed the tray back in.

I knew that almost all the guys carried guns. Baby Huey had explained it to me a few months after I started there. "You need to on a job like this," he said. "We carry too much cash, and every little shit out there knows it. We got to protect ourselves, there's no other way. Even if you use it just to threaten them, to show them you're not someone to mess with, it's worth carrying just for that. The bread driver on my route was held up four times. One more time and he's quitting, he told me. He figures five is his lucky number, after that he's dead. The guy carries one gun stuffed in a loaf of bread and another strapped to his calf.''

At the first traffic light out of the depot, Baby Huey's truck was parked by the corner, waiting for me. He signaled me to pull up in front of his truck. I came to a stop and waited on my steps while he walked over and stepped up into the cab.

''What's up?'' I asked.

''Anna, you're my girl,'' he said, taking my chin in his hand, ''you know that, don't you, honey?'' I nodded. ''So if that greaseball touches you, I'll kill him. In fact, if he keeps giving you trouble, me and Jimmy are going to visit him and give him a little warning. Remember that! No matter what, we're going to look after you, so don't spend your day worrying about that animal.'' He put his hands on both sides of my face and drew me toward him until our lips were touching. His lips felt full and soft on mine. Then he put his hand around my waist and pulled me to him hard, but only for a moment, and then he let me go. ''Now get out of here,'' he said, ''or we'll waste the whole day fooling around.'' He jumped off the truck, blew me a kiss, and waved me to drive out first. So I took off with him following, and after a few blocks we parted to go our separate ways.

Later that day, when I pulled down the stale tray to clean it out, the box with the gun lay there among all the old cake. I had no idea what to do with it. The guys would be hurt if I gave it back. But I couldn't bring it home on account of my kids, and there was no place for it on my truck. The truck didn't have a glove compartment, and if I left it on one of the trays, I was sure someone would eventually find it. Finally I decided to hide it at the bottom of my safe under the driver's seat. It was a good place for the gun, even though it wasn't smart to leave money there. If a driver depended on the safe to protect his money, he wouldn't have a penny left. There were signs painted on our trucks saying that we carried no cash, but every criminal and junkie on the street knew that was a lie. Still, there wasn't a driver that'd risk leaving money in those useless safes. They didn't even have proper locks. Instead, our pants and shirt pockets bulged with the hundreds of dollars that we received from the storekeepers every day. We should have worn signs around our necks saying ROB ME, it was that obvious. The safe was good only as a place to store the payments from large stores that didn't pay cash. So I hid the gun in the bottom of the safe under the checks.

I did feel more secure having the gun on the truck with me. Sometimes I'd just hold it in my hand, curling my fingers around the pearl handle to get the feel of it. Other times I'd take it out and practice aiming. I loved that the guys got it for me and that it was so pretty. I never threw the gold and white paper away either, and instead used it to wrap around the gray velvet box. Eventually the paper turned dark brown and yellow, but I still kept it.

I didn't go back to Bodega Nueva for a week. I knew it would make it worse if I didn't show, but I couldn't seem to get myself to go there. Diego called the depot again to report me and Jed said if I didn't visit the store that day, he'd take my not going as my resignation. I'd already gone through being fired and rehired and didn't want to go through it all again. Even though the Teamsters said there was no easy way he could get rid of me, since I was the only woman to last this long on the job, it was always a big hassle.

That was a Tuesday, and I pulled up to the Bodega Nueva about noon, glad to find a woman and two kids behind the counter, with no sign of Diego. The woman, who I figured was his wife, was stick thin, but the kids were short and square like Diego. I smiled at the kids but they never looked up. Actually there was no expression on any of their faces. Just one happy family, I thought to myself. Then I heard the sound of glass breaking somewhere in the back and Diego appeared. He looked no different than the first time I'd seen him except for the fact that this time he was chewing on an unlit cigar.

Diego talked without removing the cigar from his mouth. It was hard to understand his words but I think we all got the meaning. First there was a mixture of Spanish and English cursing, and then, "A bottle broke. Clean it up, ahora." He spoke without looking at anyone in particular. The woman disappeared into the back. He took out the cigar and pointed it at me. "Where were you last week?" he asked. "You another driver that don't show, huh? Don't try it with me!" I didn't answer or look at him, just went about my work checking the cake. The shelves looked almost exactly as I had left them, maybe two or three pieces less, probably eaten by Diego or his family. This stop was bad news. No customers or very few at the most. The Seven-Up guy had told me that no one shopped there except by accident, that people would walk the extra block to Angel's rather than shop at Diego's. Diego was nasty to everybody, drivers and customers alike, he said.

I think Diego did book from the store, because sometimes there'd be sleazy-looking guys slipping in and out. They'd stand there counting money but they never bought anything. How else could Diego support the store with no real business to speak of?

Once again, when I handed him the change, a moment later it went flying across the room. None of the family flinched or raised an eyebrow, and this time I didn't look back. But as I walked away, I had the feeling he was following me. So I jumped on the truck, slammed the door, and started the motor. When I checked my sideview mirror, I saw him standing outside the store, his arms crossed on his chest, the cigar still dangling from his mouth as he watched me drive away. He had the same look my dad used to have, like a stocky wrestler, with his face looking like someone had marked it with a few good punches and he was looking to get even.

Even though I never sold more than a few dollars out of that store, the next time I made a stop there, Diego demanded that I bring in some of the bigger cake. I added a variety pack of doughnuts and a box of coffee cakes to his order, and at the end of each week, I took them back unsold. One time Diego found a box of doughnuts with a piece of the plastic wrapper slightly torn. He picked it up, grabbed a knife from the counter, and sliced it all the way open, dumping the rest of the crumbling doughnuts into my tray. "Don't bring me no used merchandise," he snarled with the raised knife inches from my face. I thought, Go ahead, motherfucker, but if I'm still alive when you're done, I'm going to come back and blow your fat head off.

Every time I served Diego's store, I left feeling edgy. Even at home with Nick and Joey, I'd find myself worrying and getting short-tempered with them. It got worse and worse with Diego, and after a while I dreaded going out on the route. I felt like I was waiting for something bad to happen. Over and over I'd picture what I'd do if Diego came at me. I'd jump on his back and dig my fingers into his eyes or grab that long stick that he kept near the window and jab it into his crotch. Don't show him you're scared, I'd tell myself, or one day he'll sense it, and that's the day he'll kick the shit out of you.

A few weeks later, he insisted I bring in a stand for the cakes. "All the other stores have stands," he told me, "fancy ones. I want one tambien. Makes the store look good." So I brought in a small aluminum stand and put it near the register so the customers would see it when they were ready to pay. But it did nothing for business since he had no customers. Thank God he filled it with every kind of cake that they sell on the route. It was against company policy to put any cake but HomeMade on our stands, but I was glad that I didn't have to waste my stock trying to fill it up.

The next time I was there, I found him standing on milk crates cleaning the huge window in the front of the store. He had a bottle of Windex and was spraying and then wiping with a dirty rag that left streaks every place it touched. His wife stood silently at his side as he cursed and swore at her and the window. At one point he spit on the rag then leaned down and swiped it across her face, calling her "Puta." I froze when he turned and looked at me, "Coño, la blanca esta aquí," he said and threw the rag at me.

Enough is enough, I thought. My job was hard enough without having to put up with this bastard. I worked carefully, keeping one eye on him as I checked out the new rack and went out to stock my tray.

Back in the truck, I emptied my pockets, hiding my money in a brown paper bag on the stale shelf and instead slipped the little gun from the box in the safe into my pocket. When I returned, Diego accused me of doing a sloppy job putting the cake up. "You think you can throw your cake on the stand any way you want?" he yelled. "Like my store is garbage? What do you think I am? You think I'm some stupid pendejo?" he shouted and grabbed for my arm. I raised the metal tray between us before he could get his hands on me, intending to ram it in his face if he came at me. He was almost foaming at the mouth, he was that mad. I thought about the gun in my pocket but Diego must've known I was ready to fight because all of a sudden he turned and walked to the back.

My dad was like Diego. Swearing at me and my brothers and accusing us of some crime that we knew nothing about. From when I was really young, my dad had a special way of getting me to agree with anything he said. He'd hold me from behind, grab a handful of hair from the back of my head, and drag me over to a wall. Then he'd ask a question, and if he didn't like the answer, he'd rap my face against the wall. It was stupid stuff like, "Did you steal the pencil from my desk?" Or, "Are you the little shithead that left a cup in the sink? Do you think we have slaves to clean up after you?" I wouldn't know who left the cup and if I did, I wouldn't tell. But whatever answer I gave, he'd say I was lying anyway. And if he didn't like what I said, whack.

"No."

"No what?" Whack.

"No I don't know who left the cup."

"Someone has to know." Whack.

"Did you ask Mommy? Mommy uses that kind of cup."

"Your mother wouldn't leave her cup in the sink." Whack. Which was a lie, because my mother was a slob, especially in the kitchen. "And even if she did, that's none of your business." Whack.

I always got a bloody nose from his whackings and it would make a mess on the wall. At the end of the whacking, he'd make me get a sponge and clean off the blood. When I was little, I was scared of him and his whackings, and he'd have to pull me out from wherever I was hiding to get to me. But by the time I was seven or eight, I didn't care about his cursing and stupid whackings anymore. I wouldn't answer when he called, and I'd laugh when he hit me. One time I threatened to kill him when I got big enough. For some reason that stopped him for the moment, maybe because it surprised him, I don't know.

"Some stupid pendejo that you can fuck over, huh, blanca?" Diego repeated. "Well, don't even try." Most of the cake on the stand wasn't even mine, but he cursed me out telling me that me and my cake were shit. Then he tipped the whole stand forward so all the cake landed on the floor. "See," Diego said, "you put it on so bad, it all falls off." He headed toward me, I guess to make me put the cake back. But I ran out before he could grab me again. No way was I going to let him force me into picking it up another time. If it turned into a fight, one of us would probably get hurt bad and I wasn't sure which one.

I went right to Angel's even though I had already served his store an hour ago. I guess I must've looked wild or angry or something because Angel asked what was wrong but I wouldn't tell him. I didn't want to involve him in it. I just stayed next to him while I caught my breath. "It's okay, niña," he said softly, "it's okay." He didn't question me again and went about his business as if I was always with him when he served his customers. I didn't leave his side for almost an hour. When I felt better, I went in the back and washed up. On my way out I whispered, "I love you, mi amigo," to Angel and left.

I saw Old Auntie sitting out there with her knitting as I headed for the highway. I stopped my truck but kept the motor running. Grabbing a cherry pie from the back, I ran out and put it in Old Auntie's lap. Old Auntie loved cherry pies. She smiled a big smile and waved as I drove away.

Some days Diego would say he couldn't pay me my money. I'd pay for it out of my pocket then, because the company didn't give credit and it would be more trouble than it was worth to take out all the new cake and bring it back another day. I never knew if one day he would just decide not to give me what he owed me. I didn't know what to expect from him at all. He liked keeping me on edge, knowing I was afraid of him. Angel told me that years ago when Diego's wife was planning to leave him, Diego deliberately dropped a can of paint on her foot, breaking or fracturing half the bones in her toes and foot.

Some nights I would lie in bed thinking of my pearl-handled little gun and what I'd do to Diego if we got into a real fight. Maybe I'd give him a limp to remember me by for the rest of his life. I decided never to go into Bodega Nueva again without the gun.

For months I complained to Jed that the store not only didn't make money, it lost money, and that Diego was not only nasty, he was dangerous. Jed would smile and repeat the same old bullshit to me. That there was no trouble on that route until I came along. That he had never heard a peep out of Richie when Richie ran the route. If I wanted to keep my job, I had to serve Bodega Nueva.

But in all that time I never mentioned the store again to any of the other guys in the depot. If Baby Huey or Jimmy asked me if I was ever bothered by Diego anymore, I always told them no, that Diego left me alone after that first time. "He must have found someone better to give a hard time to," I told them and smiled so they wouldn't know I was lying.

One Friday morning early, I got to the store, checked it out, and went back to my truck to bring in fresh cake. All the cake had been outdated so I took it out and came back with a full tray of cake. As I got to the store, balancing the tray with one hand, trying to open the door with the other, the bill in my mouth, Diego came out. He looked at me and laughed, slammed the door in my face, and locked it. I startled and dropped everything. "Got to bring my kid to school," he laughed again. "Come back in la tarde when I'm open." I never went back that day even though I knew he'd be nastier the longer I waited to serve him.

But that afternoon, I sprained my ankle at the depot. I tripped carrying a heavy load of cake over a kind of half pipe that marked the space for each truck in the garage. The doctor said it was a bad sprain and that I would be out for a few weeks. They gave me Worker's Compensation and I was thrilled. I badly needed a vacation.

A month later, when I returned to work, I looked in my route book and found that Bodega Nueva was crossed off my list of stores. When I asked Jed what had happened, he told me to see Karl, the new supervisor. It seemed that Karl ran my route when I was out. Jed made sure to mention that Karl did a great job reorganizing my route for me while I was away. But Joanie took me aside and explained that Karl didn't like to work in the office, so he'd stay out on the route as long as he could. Stores that I might go to once a week, he'd visit two or three times a week just to shoot the shit. That was bad news for me, because the storekeepers might expect the same treatment from me when I took back the route. I usually finished by one and had no intention of spending my afternoons doubling up on the route.

I went to find this new supervisor, Karl. He was out talking with Ramon the packer while Ramon loaded some racks. Karl looked like a clean-cut college guy. I introduced myself, asked how he found the route, and then said straight out, "What happened to Bodega Nueva?"

"Which one is that?" he asked, and I described the store and Diego. "Oh, that one," he said, "the little bulldog. Well, I'll tell you, that guy was something else. The first day I'm out on the route, I show up in the afternoon and he says I'm too late, come back tomorrow. We have some words and I tell him I'm never coming back. But when I go to leave, he takes out a gun, lays it on the counter, and orders me to pack out the order. I do it, no problem. But when I get back to the office, I tell Jed

I'm crossing him out of the book. They'd be crazy to think I'd serve a nut like that. Besides which, the place was a total waste of time. We never made a penny in there. HomeMade should never have served a store like that in the first place.''

I went by Jed's office. He was on the phone, so I stood by his door waiting for him to get off. ''I'll get to the lawn Sunday,'' he was saying. ''If ya don't think it can wait, pay Mikey to do it.'' It didn't matter that Jed married a high-class WASP from a wealthy family, he still sounded like white trash from out West, especially when he was talking to Cindy. ''How much can it cost? Ten dollars? Ten dollars is nothin'. Ask him to do the hedge too. No I ain't lazy, I'm tired.'' He slammed down the phone and looked up. ''What can I do for ya?''

''I heard you took Bodega Nueva off the route? Why now, Jed? Didn't I come in here every week asking you not to make me serve him? And then some college kid comes along, takes over my route, and within a day you get rid of Diego's store, no questions asked? What am I, chopped meat?''

''Look, Anna, if you come in here to fight with me, don't bother.'' Jed looked down at his desk and shuffled through his papers. ''Take your personal problems somewhere else.''

''These aren't personal problems,'' I told him, ''they have to do with work.''

''I have no time to listen to complaining women.'' Jed pointed to the phone. ''I would've stayed home if I wanted to hear that all day. I got real things to deal with in managing this here depot.''

I put my hands on his desk and looked him in the eye. ''I'm not real enough for you?'' I asked.

He threw up his hands. "I guess not," he drawled, "though you're certainly real good to look at." And he smirked as he carefully checked me out, spending a long time eyeing my breasts, then letting his eyes travel down to my waist and below my hips as he fingered the zipper on his fly.

"Uh-huh, I understand," I said. "Well, maybe this is real enough for you," and I leaned forward and grabbed his desk from underneath. It wasn't a big desk but it was covered with stacks of paper, a cup with pens, a stapler, all the stuff you have around the office. I gave one big heave and turned the desk over onto him. He tried to get out from under but it pinned his legs as everything on the top slid into his lap and on the floor. "Tell your little pussy at home that you'll be a little late, you got some extra cleaning up to do around the office," I said and walked out.

I figured I'd get a call that night or the next day to tell me that I was fired or suspended again, but it never came.

So that was that. On Tuesday, when I drove past the docks and down the narrow, treeless streets on my way to Angel's, I stopped in front of the Bodega Nueva. I couldn't believe my eyes. It was burnt to the ground.

"Happened in the night," Angel explained. "Nobody around. Some say Diego burnt it himself, for the insurance. But others that know say he was mean one time too many. Either way, the whole neighborhood celebrated, todos, mujeres y muchachos tambien." Angel looked at me closely as he brushed the hair out of my eyes. "Good for you too, niña, no?" he asked softly.

Back on my truck, I took the little gun from its new hiding place under a pillow on the seat and tucked it back in the bottom of the safe, covering it with the old wrapping paper. With Diego gone, I was hoping that I'd never need that kind of protection again.

Baby Huey's
Sister Lena

I WAS LOVING THIS new route of mine. I felt like I had been given a second chance. It didn't matter to me that it wasn't as pretty or as safe as the Flatbush one. It felt more like me. I had had no friends on the Flatbush route, though not all the store owners were as bad as Rudy. But on the Bay Ridge route, especially down by Bush Terminal, I had Angel, Millie, Tia Vieja, and more. And every store and street was different. I had a lot of bodegas like Angel's and little drop-off spots like Millie's bar, but there were also the usual delicatessens and large modern supermarkets on the streets farther from the water, away from the docks.

For a long time I had put off going to one stop on my route because it looked so down-and-out and seedy that I was nervous about even parking there. It was a few blocks nearer the water than Angel's and was called "the Shack." That's how it read in my route book and that's what it was. Four pieces of board with a roof, not even painted. I circled it for weeks before I finally got the nerve to pull up in front one day. And, as with Angel's and Millie's, it wasn't long before it was one of the places where I knew I was always welcome.

Hernando, the owner, was a fast-talking hustler who sold greasy sandwiches and hot plates of chicken with rice and beans to the factory workers. But he made his real money selling loose joints and whiskey by the shot. His wife cooked the food in their house next door, and his daughters, four of them ranging from five to ten years old, were the busboys. Hernando opened the Shack at about eleven, did an outrageous lunch business, and by three in the afternoon, the place was boarded up, closed for the day.

Against one of the side walls of the Shack, Hernando kept an eight-by-ten picture in a gold painted wood frame that he balanced on some empty boxes of Raisinettes and Goobers. When he first put it there, I could just make out the trees and some yellow-looking grass or weeds. But Hernando would say proudly that it was a picture of the land he bought in Florida, the land on which he was building a home. Every three or four months, the Shack would be closed for two weeks while Hernando and his family were down in Florida. Each time they came back, he put a new picture in the frame. First there was what looked like a roof on some poles, then walls were added, and eventually a door appeared.

"Mamita mia," he said to me, "I'm leaving you soon, me and mis niñas. You won't see me no more, 'cause I'm never coming back, that's for sure. I won't have nothing to come back to this dirty city for. Everything I love will be there. A year and a half more and I'm free. By then the windows will be in and the walls painted. I'll have the garden planted and my girls will be in school." He smiled an almost shy smile when he added, "And maybe it will be time to start another bambino, for the last time."

Whatever cake I gave him he sold, even if it sat there for three weeks turning color. Eventually someone bought it. Maybe someone too stoned and hungry to notice that it didn't look exactly right. The only pieces he returned were the rat-bitten ones.

Every once in a while I'd take a short break and have lunch with Hernando. It was cheap—chicken with rice and beans or a pastrami sandwich for ninety-five cents. He'd pull up a wooden crate for me in the back and we'd chat while he served up food or whatever else he was pushing. We'd talk about his kids or mine, about how hard life was, or what life was going to be like for them down in Florida. He never broke pace while he chatted away. He served up food, drugs, cigarettes, or alcohol, added numbers, and made change quickly and accurately, while naming the flowers he was going to plant or taking bets on whether the next baby would be a boy or girl. Whenever I had lunch with him, no matter how many napkins I used, food leaked down my shirt and onto my pants and the smell of grease and smoke hung over me for hours.

If I took the street that ran in front of the Shack straight down for about three miles, I ended up in a more central part of Bay Ridge with a lot of small houses and six-story buildings crowded together, one short block after another. And right in the middle of one of these streets was my favorite S&R Supermarket, which was run by a manager named Chris. I had a bit of a crush on Chris, but nothing big since he was married. He had sandy hair and big blue eyes, and even though he was sort of heavyset, he was strong and good-looking. There was also a cashier there, MaryJo, a short, thin, red-haired black woman who I liked to goof around with, and sometimes we'd talk about our boyfriends and our kids. I usually started my route every morning at the S&R, because they opened real early and I liked having my first cup of coffee with Chris and MaryJo. Next I'd do all the stores in that area and then head for the water, toward what the other drivers thought of as the rougher side of the route. But now that Diego was gone there was nothing there that made me feel edgy or that I didn't belong.

One Friday afternoon in September we were working late because HomeMade Cakes decided to run another week-long special on chocolate cupcakes. By the end of the day, the vanilla stripe on the cupcake blended with the chocolate and the cupcakes were mashed and runny-looking. I gave Angel's, the Shack, and S&R way more cupcakes than they could handle, sprinkled the rest throughout my route, and still almost half the cupcakes ended up in the thrift store, which is where they should have been in the first place.

I was tired and pissed—all the drivers were—and it took a long time to empty out my truck. Baby Huey was the only one moving fast. He had a ticket for the Mets and was hurrying to make it home in time to shower and shave before the game. Baby Huey had already cleaned out his truck, and Jimmy had agreed to do his bookkeeping. He was on his way out when Jed waved him into his office, saying there was a long-distance call for him.

"Well, she's done it, stupid kid. I'm glad, 'cause once the funeral is over we can wash our hands of her for good." That was how Baby Huey told us that his sister Lena had died. It had been his mother calling from Chicago.

Jimmy was counting his money and never liked to be bothered until he was finished tallying. "What the fuck are you talking about?" he asked, not looking up from the table where he had spread out piles of singles, fives, tens, twenties, and checks—"Pardon my French, Anna." I cursed a hundred times a day but the guys always apologized if they cursed in front of me.

"My sister Lena," Baby Huey explained, "she overdosed on methadone last night. Saved up all the drugs the clinic gave her over the past few weeks and took them all at once. Same month as her cousin Silvia died last year, just when the weather is picking up again and days are starting to feel cool and nice. Now my sister Gloria's stuck with the arrangements. After all the trouble they had last year at Silvia's funeral, when they forgot to invite the second cousins, Mom said she's putting her foot down and sticking to weddings. The funerals she leaves to us. But it shouldn't be too bad, 'cause we're putting Lena in the same plot with Silvia. I just wish the kid had picked another time, especially with the game tonight."

No one knew what to say until Jimmy bowed his head and mumbled softly, "I'm sorry." On the way out, Baby Huey asked Jimmy if he would buy the Mets ticket off him. Jimmy said sure, but I knew from talking to him in the morning that his in-laws were coming for dinner and he was making marinated beef, fish, and rice while Mimi cleaned up the house.

Over the past two years, me and Jimmy and sometimes Little Dominic or Mario the Mole had been hearing a lot about Baby Huey's sister Lena. "The black sheep" is how Baby Huey described her. "Even my father, who makes every excuse for her, admits she's different." Baby Huey would tell us how when the others were in the kitchen making dinner, baking, and cleaning, Lena would be out on the street getting high with her friends.

Baby Huey didn't talk much about his personal life except for when he'd go on and on about Lena. "She's beginning to look like a cow. Wastes all her money on junk food, soda, and chocolate bars. Eats that crap for breakfast, lunch, and dinner, like there's nothing to eat in the house. My mother moos when Lena hits the fridge. Someone's got to tell her what they think instead of letting her get away with that crap.''

The first summer I worked out of Knickerbocker Avenue was the only time I actually met Lena and the other two sisters, Cookie and Gloria. They came to New York to spend the summer with Baby Huey in that ranch-style house that he'd built for himself and his future wife on Long Island. The three girls stopped by the depot to talk to Jed about being clerks in the thrift store while they were in New York. The thrift store, where day-old or extra cake was put when it hadn't been sold on the routes, was down the block from the depot. During the summer they hired extra help to do inventory, and this summer they gave all three girls a job. But even though they worked only a block away, we never saw them after that day, because Jed didn't want ''ladies'' in the depot. Company policy, he said. Even when wives came to pick up their husbands, Jed wanted them to wait in their cars instead of them ''coming in and bothering the men.''

But from just that one day when I saw them there, it was easy to see what they were like. Cookie and Gloria were friendly girls, talking and laughing nonstop. They dressed in tight V-necks, miniskirts, and spiked heels and were thin, really thin, and leggy. The guys on my route had nicknamed me Flaca, skinny one, but these two girls were a lot thinner than me. Cookie and Gloria stood outside the cashier's booth telling Joanie about their boyfriends, describing every movie they'd seen in the last year, and flirting with every driver as they turned in their cash and receipts. Even the nerdy accountant who came by once a month to balance the books got special attention.

Lena stood at her sisters' side, not saying a word, looking shy, angry shy. Unlike Baby Huey and the other two sisters, who had jet-black hair and dark eyes, she was fair, with blond hair and big blue eyes. And she was taller than her sisters, but overweight and kind of sloppy-looking in a loose T-shirt and baggy blue jeans. I could see how Baby Huey, who was the only guy in our depot who pressed his own shirts and wore creases in his pants and polished his work boots, wouldn't like having a sister that he thought wasn't classy-looking.

"You let her go out looking like that?" Baby Huey asked Gloria, the older sister, nodding his head toward Lena—"and looking for a job, no less?"

"She can take care of herself," Gloria answered, taking a compact from a white, shiny purse and reapplying lipstick to already red lips. "I'm not responsible for how she looks."

"But she don't take care of herself," Baby Huey continued, "she don't even wear makeup. Look at her, she looks like a zombie."

"I got makeup on," Lena said real quietly, almost to herself.

"She's hopeless," Gloria said, "she don't listen to nothing nobody says." Baby Huey threw up his hands and walked out to the garage.

The three girls worked only a week and a half in the thrift store when a call came from their father saying their mother got the flu and needed them home. He and their Uncle Louie couldn't find their way around the kitchen, much less handle a broom. So that, and the fact that Cookie and Gloria missed their boyfriends, made them decide to pack up and go back to Chicago. Baby Huey was relieved. "I'm tired of their yapping and I'm sick of looking at Lena's sour puss."

Again, after they were gone, Baby Huey continued to

come to us with all the family news about Lena. When she finally got a boyfriend, he called the guy a loser. "She picked a loser 'cause *she's* a loser," he said. "Lena never fit in," he explained. "She shoulda gone and lived with Aunt Mary's family, would've done better there. They're all nuts over there, take after Uncle Oscar. Aunt Mary's the only one in that family who makes any sense."

"Lena was always closer to her cousin Silvia than to her own sisters," he told us. "Both named after their grandmother, Magdalena Silvia Salazar. They were like two black sheep following each other, since they were babies. Silvia," he continued, "killed herself last year driving the old Chevy they gave her for graduation into a tree. Some thank you, huh? Aunt Mary hasn't been the same since. I wouldn't be surprised if Lena does the same."

The only thing we heard after that was when Lena signed herself into a drug addiction center and Baby Huey's mom asked the family not to talk to her or speak about her anymore.

It was only a few days before Baby Huey called, asking me to go with him to Chicago, that me and Lily were sitting around the table having hot chocolate and Lily started telling me how proud her brother was about his new baby. The little girl was premature, only two pounds at birth, but now, a month later, she'd grown to almost four pounds.

"The world's upside down," I said. "Here you got a dad in love with a two-by-nothing little baby that barely stands a chance, and then you got other parents that hate their kid from the day it was born." I mentioned Lena and told her about my mom too. How my mom wanted to sell me when I was a few days old. "To a Mrs. Hurley who lived down the block and couldn't have kids. But the doctors at the hospital told my mom to take me home and give it a try. If she didn't like it, she could give me up later. She didn't even look at me in the hospital nursery but she took me home and for the next three months she did just enough to keep me alive. She never grew to like me any better, but by then she felt it was too late and that she was stuck with me. And she wasn't even embarrassed when she repeated the story to me and my brothers when we were growing up." I laughed when I told Lily, "No one called me a black sheep when I was a kid 'cause that would've been crazy. I came from a whole family of black sheep."

I was almost asleep when Baby Huey called that night and asked would I go with him to Lena's funeral. He told me he had bought his ticket that afternoon and now there was no room on his flight, but he could get me a spot on an earlier one. He said he couldn't afford to pay for my ticket, what with the monthly payments for his new car and the house and all, but he would cover the hotel, could I please come? I hung up, telling him I'd think about it.

The fact was, I had a week's vacation coming to me, and even though I was happy on the new route, I needed a break. And Tom had called a few days before, saying he wanted to take the boys fishing with Peter to his brother's cabin upstate. Nick's burn was healing okay, and the boys loved to fish, so I thought it'd be a great idea. So when I got the call from Baby Huey asking me to go to Chicago, it felt like everything was already in place.

I'd never been to Chicago. I thought Chicago was

nothing but another big, dirty city like New York, even worse than New York. But it wasn't New York, and that would be different. Then I started thinking about spending every night with Baby Huey, four nights in a row, making love in a hotel room in Chicago. I pictured how we'd come into the room and put our bags down and start kissing and getting so worked up that we couldn't keep our hands off each other. And I thought, four days away from the kids and the route was four days away. Whatever happened, it wouldn't be the same old same old. So I called him back at one in the morning and I said yes. Yes! As soon as I told him yes, I couldn't wait to go.

A nice thing about Baby Huey was that he was almost always on time. A bad thing about him was that he often treated me like he barely knew me. His plane came in an hour after mine and it took him another half-hour to collect his luggage and find me. After a quick hug and a kiss on the cheek, he grabbed two of my bags and hurried out to the cab waiting at the curb. No hi, how are you, I'm so glad to see you, how was your trip. He threw my bags into the trunk, then stood there holding the door of the cab, moving it back and forth, like that would hurry me in. Glad to see you too, I said to myself.

Baby Huey looked good. I rarely saw him out of his HomeMade uniform except for our one big date at the old hotel in Brooklyn and some summer days when he wore his own neatly pressed short-sleeved shirts. Today he was wearing a brown and orange plaid shirt, khaki pants, and brown loafers. He looked relaxed but classy. I was wearing purple silk shorts and a white low-cut blouse but I don't think he noticed.

I got in the cab, he got in, neither of us said anything. "Hi, it's me, your little HomeMade Choco," I kind of shouted in his face.

"What's that supposed to mean?" he asked and I decided to relax, give us both a break.

"I'm just saying hi. How was your trip?"

"Fine, but they didn't serve lunch. I'm starving."

"Are we going to your family's or do you want to eat dinner at the hotel?" I asked him.

"My family don't know we're here until tomorrow. I wanted to have a night on my own first. I smelled pizza at the airport, now all I can think of is pizza. Chicago has the best pizza. Wait'll you taste it."

When I was packing my clothes for the trip, I'd taken one of my onyx stud earrings, put it in a tiny box, and wrapped it in pretty paper. Now I handed the box to Baby Huey. He opened it and gave me a big smile, removed the gold stud he was wearing, and replaced it with the new black one. Then he gave me a quick kiss on the lips and I think we both felt better.

I don't know where I got the idea of Chicago being exactly like New York, only smaller and dirtier. It wasn't. As we drove from the airport, I realized that it was one pretty city, clean and easygoing. The people weren't hustling and pushing and rushing. We headed for the middle of the city and I was dying to be out on my own, walking the streets, seeing firsthand what it was like. I felt lucky to be there. Some people never got to leave their neighborhoods. When I was a kid I only went off my block in the summer, when my mother got scared that the city was full of diseases and shipped us off to fancy relatives in Queens and Long Island.

At the hotel, Baby Huey and I unpacked and picked

drawers and corners and which side of the bed we were sleeping on and were out the door in half an hour. Remembering how I kept thinking what it would be like when we got to the hotel, I gave him a nice long kiss before we left the room.

"I keep smelling pizza," he told me. "I can't think of nothing else."

We took a long walk and found a pizza place where we each got a small round pizza. We'd walked in silence, now we ate in silence. Baby Huey said he was trying to get used to being home again and wasn't into talking. But the pizza was good and it was a pretty city and a great night for walking, with a cool breeze coming off the water. When we got back to the hotel, he would've brushed his teeth and gone right to bed, but after my shower, I put on a pretty almost see-through pink nightgown that Adeline had made me borrow and I started bothering him. Kissing him and touching him and blowing raspberries across his chest and then farther down past his belly. I was getting into it and was loving the smell of his Armani as I nuzzled his pubic hair. He laughed and liked it, but once he got excited, he turned me over and took me from behind. One two three and he was done and that was that. I went to sleep trying not to be mad, thinking that his sister had just died and that that was on his mind, whether he knew it or not, and I had to take all that into consideration. But I couldn't remember when he was any different.

Baby Huey rented a car, a Plymouth convertible, and the next morning we drove about fifteen minutes out of the city to what was definitely a Cuban neighborhood. There were all kinds of flowers around every house and little gardens on the sides with tomatoes and peppers. We pulled up in front of a big old blue and gray three-story house.

I reached for the door handle but Baby Huey put out his hand to stop me, so I sat back. "I wanna say something to you before we go in," he said. He stretched his arm across my chest and played with the locket around my neck while he talked. "I know you think I hated Lena, the way I talk bad about her to everyone back at the depot. And I got to admit that it's true, she got on my nerves." With his other hand he began to drum on the steering wheel as he talked. "But when she was little, I didn't walk around hating her. I was good to her then, and she was a sweet kid. She'd bring me funny presents too, like a twig with berries on it, or a flower made out of tissue paper that smelled from perfume. She wouldn't have done that if she didn't think I was nice to her, right? But somehow things got worse and worse in the family. My mom would get so mad at Lena for every little thing, and as we got older, we joined in. After a while, we gave her nothing to be good for. She didn't stand a chance." A few seconds later he was out of the car and heading toward the house.

I caught up with Baby Huey as the door was about to slam. It took a minute for my eyes to adjust, the house was so dark inside. I grabbed hold of his hand and he kept walking. Straight ahead was the kitchen, which was brightly lit and filled with people, but everywhere else was dark. We took a right and he guided me up some stairs, then down a long hall past three closed doors to a bedroom in the back. It was very warm in the house, the air felt like it wasn't moving at all, and the smell of arroz con pollo followed us everywhere. The room we came to was large, painted blue with dark maroon drapes. Three single beds lined the walls and three bureaus with large mirrors stood at the side of each bed. The three bears, I said softly to myself. A lace lampshade on a tall standing lamp was the only sign that it was not a man's room. Gloria hadn't heard us come in and was sitting on a bed staring at maybe nine or ten dresses spread across every bed and chair in the room.

"This used to be my room," Baby Huey said. Gloria looked up when she heard his voice and came over to hug him. "The girls got it when I left," he explained. "It's bigger than their old room." He turned to face Gloria. "So what's going on here, Glori, huh? We doing a fashion show or what?"

"You gotta help me," she said. "I been trying all morning to pick out a pretty dress for Lena." She looked both nervous and tired as her eyes flitted around the room, looking over the choice of dresses for what must have seemed like the hundredth time. She reached down and held up a dress with layer after layer of light blue material. She pressed it up against herself and ran her hands through the skirt. "This one would look perfect, right?" she asked. "'Cause of Lena's blue eyes?"

"I think it's really nice," I told her.

As we were talking, Cookie came into the room and stood watching us. She looked different from the last time I'd seen her. The tips of her dark hair had been frosted blond and it made her look older and harsher somehow. Cookie's eye makeup was smeared and she kept blinking her eyes quickly, as if trying not to cry. She grabbed the dress out of Gloria's hands. "It doesn't fit her," she said. "It's my dress and it doesn't fit her."

Gloria turned on her. "Selfish, you always been selfish and you'll stay selfish your whole life. So what if it's your stupid prom dress. You're not going to any more proms. And it fits your sister fine, if we left it open in the back.''

"I don't want her wearing it," Cookie protested. "If she has to wear blue, what about the blue one with the lace, the one you wore to the wedding? How come that one's not out here, huh?'' Cookie went over to the one closet in the room and after a few minutes of searching, pulled out a royal blue silk dress with white lace around the neck and sleeves. By this time, Cookie's face was red and her hands were shaking as she said, "Here it is." She held the blue lace dress over her blue prom dress and walked back and forth as if modeling it. "Perfect! Now I won't have to be the one that always gives in, no thank you." She threw both dresses down and faced Gloria, her chin out, hands on hips.

Baby Huey went over to the bed and picked up a plain but pretty peach dress draped over the back of a tall chair. It was a bigger dress than the others. "Was this hers?" he asked, and when Cookie and Gloria both nodded, he said, "This is the one. She's wearing this one." He stood in front of Cookie and took her face in his hands, then quickly kissed her on the lips. "Wash up, little one, you look like a baby owl." He gently brushed at the black makeup around her eyes. Then he gave Gloria a whack on the butt and left the room.

I followed him back down the stairs and into the kitchen. A small, frail-looking woman, her dark hair short and permed, sat alone at the table, talking to a canary that was sitting on her finger. The canary fluttered as we entered the room, so she pushed it through the door of the cage that hung over the kitchen table. "There you go, honey, thata girl."

"Ma, what happened?" Baby Huey asked. "Where'd everybody go?" He waited until she locked the cage, then grabbed her under her arms and lifted her up high so they were face to face. Baby Huey was close to six feet and his mother looked like she barely made four feet ten. He kissed her on both cheeks before putting her down.

"I needed a break, so I sent them out. How are ya, Ernestico? Ya look tired, muy cansado. I got a pot on, ya want coffee?"

"I'm not tired, Ma. No thanks, we just ate. Ma, this is my friend Anna."

I went over to shake her hand but she didn't take my hand. Instead she picked up a cup of coffee and took a sip.

"Glad to meet ya, lady," she said, not looking at me.

"Anna. Her name is Anna, Ma. She's a good friend of mine and I respect and care for her. You want me to come here and visit all of you, you be nice and respect her too, Mom. Comprende?"

"Anna," his mother repeated slowly, "glad to meet you, Anna." She wiped her hands on a badly stained apron and held out her hand. I was glad Baby Huey got her to say hello, but I wished he'd said I was his girlfriend instead of just a good friend.

We shook hands. "Glad to meet you, Mrs. Salazar."

"You can call me Nettie," she said. "Sit over there, Annie, next to Gigi." She pointed to a seat by the table. I looked around but there was no one else in the room but me and Baby Huey.

"Gigi's the bird," Baby Huey explained.

"Sit down, sit down." Nettie half-pushed me with

the back of her hand into the chair, then used a dish towel to brush birdseed shells off the table.

Baby Huey sat in a chair on the other side. "How many times I have to tell you, it's not healthy to keep this bird where ya eat?"

"My Gigi's so sloppy," she said, her face pressed against the cage. "Yeth, yeth, you're a sloppy bird." She jabbed her finger through the bars, wiggling it until the bird came over and nipped it. She teased it, moving her finger in and out, as the bird hopped around, biting at her.

"Ma, get us some coffee, Ma."

She brought three cups to the table, placing them down carefully while keeping her eye on the bird. "Gigi's my third one," she told me. "I had two others, all of them singers, but Gigi number three is the best. Isn't that right, Gigi? Didn't Uncle Louie say he was gonna get you a job singing at the Met? Ernestico got me the first one, didn't you, big boy? How old were you then?"

"Ten, Ma, I was ten years old."

"Ten years old, God bless him, and he got the birdie without no one asking." She stuck her finger through the bars again, poking at the bird until it came over. "This here Gigi number three is the best of the lot."

"Ma, has anyone stopped by the funeral home to check it out, to make sure everything's okay? Did Dad go over?"

His mother shook her head no. "What's to do? We're not havin' no wake, she killed herself, just the service and the burial."

"I know, I know," he said, "but someone should still make sure. Anna, we'll head over, okay?" He kept his eyes on me, so I shook my head yes.

"But Ernestico, honey, ya just got here," his

mother's voice pleaded as she undid the tie on her apron and stood up.

"Ma, we'll see you later. After the funeral home, we'll stop at the hotel and change and be back here in an hour or two." He gave her a kiss and walked quickly toward the door.

"Nice to meet you, Mrs. Salazar. See you when we get back," I said as we headed down the hall.

"Nettie," she yelled out, correcting me.

"Nice to meet you, Nettie," I called back.

"Why are we going to the funeral parlor?" I wanted to know. "Isn't it all arranged? Can't you just call?" I wished we were back in the hotel already.

"No, I want to make sure that Mom and Dad ride in a limo, not Uncle Louie's Chevy. And it's too hot for me to stay in that house, even in winter that place is an oven. I don't know how they can stand it. She won't use a fan, 'cause Gigi usually has the run of the house and she's afraid Gigi will get pneumonia or caught in the blades."

Baby Huey zipped the rental Plymouth down side streets until we stopped in front of a large gray awning with ORTIZ BROTHERS—WE HANDLE WITH CARE engraved in gold. We were greeted inside by two men in their mid-fifties. Their dark hair was sculpted into high front waves and parted perfectly down the sides.

I left Baby Huey and the two guys to discuss the coffin and went to the ladies' room for a break. I took my hair down, combed it all out, and put it back up in a clip, then redid my makeup. When I went back in, Baby Huey was nowhere in sight, but I found the funeral director sitting in his office counting a pile of money. "For the new coffin," he explained. "Your husband preferred something more elegant for his sister. I told him the coffin was still open, so he went down the hall to say goodbye."

I didn't correct him and say that we weren't married. What difference did it make? I stood in front of the director's desk not knowing whether to look for Baby Huey or wait for him. "No, no," the director said, seeing me hesitate, "your husband asked that you find him as soon as you return. He's in the first room on the right."

I tiptoed into the room the director had pointed to. Baby Huey was seated on a chair near the head of the coffin and I took a place by the door. It was air conditioned, nice and cool in there. Lena's head was raised and I could see the outline of her hair and the profile of her face. Baby Huey was touching her hair, combing it with his fingers away from her face. He sat petting her, then bent toward her and kissed her face, her nose, her cheeks, her chin. Then he took her hand in his and sat there talking softly. I couldn't hear the words, just a quiet murmuring. Finally he stood up, leaned over, and kissed her forehead once again and this time I heard him say, "Goodbye, sweet baby."

Back at the hotel, Baby Huey stayed in the shower for a long time, and I was glad for the break. I wanted the chance to call home—in this case, Lily, who I knew might be off in the afternoon and hanging around her house.

"Chica, is that you? Is that my sweet amiga loca?" she asked breathlessly. I laughed and she said, "Sí, that's definitely you. Where you calling from? You're still on vacation, aren't ya? Nothing bad happened, did it?"

"No, Lily, I'm fine," I told her. "Yeah, I'm still on

vacation. No, nothing happened, I wasn't calling for no special reason. I just wanted to hear your loud mouth.''

''Perdoname, chica, I wish that was true. Usually everyone says I'm too quiet. But what's up? You're not fighting with Baby Huey or getting lonely or nothing your first big time away?''

''No, nothing like that,'' I told her. ''Baby Huey is just what he is, is all and I just wish he was more.''

''Honey,'' she said, ''oye, listen carefully. Shit runs downhill, so if you put someone on a pedestal, that's what you get, comprende? Just take him as he is, baby, and you'll get as much as he has to give.''

''I know, I just get lonely sometimes. You know what it is, Lily? It's not just Baby Huey this time. It's that no one here except Baby Huey seems to care that this kid Lena is dead. It's their own daughter, their sister. And his family's not much different from mine. The black sheep, they call her, but black sheep is just a name for someone you don't want.''

''I know, baby,'' Lily said, ''but you got your kids and your friends, and sometimes that's more than family, right? And ya know what? Ya just been gone a day and already I miss ya. Me and Pudgy had dinner together last night, but your apartment was so quiet, it was like a church without you and the boys running around. I kept listening for that big mouth of yours. Now don't go worrying and trying to figure out your whole life in one day. It's your vacation, so have a good time.''

The sound of water running in the bathroom stopped, so I knew Baby Huey was done. ''I gotta go, he's getting out of the shower. I feel better. Love ya, Lily.''

''Adios, chica. Bye.''

. . .

Neither of us are drinkers, not even wine with dinner. But for the occasion, Baby Huey went into the little mini-bar in our room and made us gin and tonics, which he put in plastic cups so we could drink them on the way to the church. In the car Baby Huey turned to me and kind of matter-of-factly said, "You know that Lena and Cookie were twins, don't you?"

I was surprised. No one had mentioned it and they looked so different. "No, no, I didn't know that."

"Well, they were. I mean, it's no secret, twins are twins and there's nothing wrong with that, but they were."

"Uh-huh."

Our Lady of Good Faith was small and pretty, a lot like the church I used to go to when I was a kid. The Salazar family and friends took up almost eight rows on both sides. After Baby Huey shook hands or kissed just about everybody, we took a seat slightly behind them all, in direct line with his parents.

"Don't you want to sit up front with your family?" I whispered.

"I don't want to be part of no sideshow," he answered.

We were sitting behind a tall blonde with black roots and a guy whose hair was so thick with gel that you could see more of his scalp than his hair. "He should have left some mousse in Canada," Baby Huey whispered. "Moose, get it?" Baby Huey was still laughing when the priest started his sermon, so I put my hand over his mouth and shushed him. He bit the palm of my hand gently until I was laughing with him and I had to cover my mouth with my other hand.

It wasn't particularly warm in the small chapel but the priest kept wiping at his face and neck with his handkerchief. He was young. This was probably one of his first sermons, and he talked for a long time without a break. I didn't follow what he was saying and instead looked around at the rows of people. Suprisingly few were dressed in black, only Baby Huey's mom, his Aunt Mary, and two or three old ladies. They were also the only ones crying. I noticed Cookie and Gloria standing off to the right of the priest, candles in their hands, waiting for him to finish so they could light them. Meanwhile, they were talking non-stop to each other. Finally the priest was done and he tried to get Cookie and Gloria's attention, but they were so busy talking, they didn't notice. The priest cleared his throat a few times. "Young ladies, the candles. Young ladies, please." Gloria turned Cookie around to fix her collar while continuing to talk to her over her shoulder.

People started to smile and then laugh or giggle, until Baby Huey's mom finally stood up. She had a tiny black hat on with a veil that caught in her mouth as she shouted, "Dummies! Those girls are dummies, always been dummies, and they'll be dummies for the rest of their lives. Give 'em one little job to do and they can't even do that right. Locas y stupidas, Papa," she turned to her husband, "they got no brains." Cookie and Gloria covered their faces with their hands and peeked out at the congregation, then at each other, and smiled kind of embarrassed-like.

When the service ended, the church emptied out fast. On the street, Baby Huey and Uncle Louie directed cars into place in the procession, and when everyone was in line, they moved out. The long black hearse was first, followed by the family limo, then Baby Huey and me in the rented convertible with the top down, and about eight other cars bringing up the rear. Slowly we made our way through the streets, headlights on, beeping through traffic and red lights. At one point Baby Huey told me to stand up, and I did, facing backwards, my legs spread in a wide V, while he drove slowly through the streets. I signaled to traffic, making sure that friends and relatives stayed in line in the procession while other cars passed us. It was tough when we came to a crowded intersection, and at one point a city bus joined us when Uncle Oscar left too much room in the line.

On a small highway, halfway between the church and the cemetery, the hearse broke down with an overheated radiator and pulled into a gas station. We waved the other cars on but some stopped anyway. Some others thought they were supposed to get off at the next exit, but the rest continued behind us to the cemetery. Somewhere along the line, the limo with Baby Huey's family disappeared. They were taking directions from Ernesto Senior, who drove a limo on weekends. It took another fifteen minutes to reach the cemetery, and when we finally parked in front of the cemetery office, the limo was already there but we'd lost all but two of the cars behind us.

"C'mon, let's get it over," Baby Huey's mom said, so we took some flowers and followed a blue-suited man to a newly dug hole. The man recited a short prayer and then, "May she rest in peace." Flowers were tossed on the coffin and we got in our cars and left.

We regathered at Baby Huey's mom's house long enough to have a nine-course meal, which ended with homemade flan, wedding cake, and *café Cubano,* which I followed with a pony glass full of brandy. There must have been a hundred people spread out between the dining room and kitchen. I barely recognized anybody but Cookie, who sat at my side telling me the story of her last boyfriend, who she met when he came to her beauty salon for a haircut. It seemed that she only found out he was married after she sent him a birthday card and his wife showed up at the salon looking for her. Cookie never mentioned to him that she met his wife, but the next haircut she gave him, she left the sides long and shaved a six-inch path down the center of his head.

Baby Huey, who'd disappeared a few hours before, finally showed up, declaring he was "sweating bullets."

"I gotta get outta here," he said, so we went back to our hotel to relax and cool off. I found out later from Cookie that Baby Huey, Uncle Louie, Ernesto Senior, and a few other men took their food to the back porch, where Baby Huey whipped them all in a few rounds of poker.

Baby Huey was back in the shower, his third shower of the day. I'd already taken my bath and was watching a movie on the pay TV channel. Baby Huey came in, a towel around his waist, and switched channels. "You don't watch TV at home, I don't see why ya got to spend good money on it here," he said. He changed channels until a baseball game came on. "The Cardinals'll kill 'em," he told me as he put on his underwear and climbed in beside me.

"I'd give them five hundred dollars to kill you," I mumbled under my breath.

"What'd ya say?" he asked.

"I said it's been a long day," I told him. I put the blanket over my head and lay there chewing my nails while he fell asleep watching the game. I started feeling lonelier and lonelier. I thought about Lena and the funeral and the Salazar family. I remembered how a few weeks ago, when I asked Baby Huey to come home with me to meet Joey and Nick, telling him I would make a nice dinner for him and the kids, he said no. "I want my own kids, I don't want two reminders that somebody was there before me."

About eleven o'clock I got up and noisily packed my bags, feeling alone and sad and angry even though I knew I wasn't being fair since today had been his sister's funeral. I was hoping that he'd wake and ask me what I was doing, but he didn't even turn over. Then I sat on my suitcase and cried, but he slept though it, so finally I knelt by the side of the bed and gently shook his shoulder.

"Ernesto, Ernesto, wake up and say goodbye, I'm going home."

He tried to sit up but didn't make it and settled for leaning against the pillows. "Are you crazy? Can you give me one good reason why you'd wanna go home?" He kept blinking. He'd been so sound asleep that he had a hard time keeping his eyes open. "Did I do something? Did I sleepwalk and beat ya with a pipe or molest ya in my dreams? What did I do?" He covered his mouth between each question to hide his yawns.

"Nothing."

"Nothing?" he said. "Then there's no reason to go home. Were ya gonna just walk outta here and that's that, see ya in New York."

"I was lonely," I told him. "I was mad and I was lonely."

"Lonely for what?" he asked. "I'm here, aren't I?"

"Yeah, but I feel like sometimes you don't even know I exist. You want me around for company in case you need me, but then you never really need me or want me.''

"You crazy?" he asked. "You're my girl. You know that.'' He put his arm around my shoulders and gave me a kiss on the cheek.

"Yeah, I guess." It's not that I changed my mind about being lonely, but I wasn't mad anymore and didn't want to leave. It was late and I was getting tired and wished he'd tell me to unpack my bags and stay. "I don't want to leave anymore. Do you want me to leave?" I asked.

"I didn't want ya to leave in the first place," he said.

"Would you kiss me and say sweet things and make real nice love to me?"

"You must be kidding," he protested. "I'm tired, what with the funeral and all the drinking."

"I know, but that doesn't mean you can't be sweet. C'mon, please." I kissed him on the mouth but he pulled away and jumped up.

"I got sleepy breath," he said. "Just lemme use some mouthwash." When he was done in the bathroom I went in, washed up, and came out in a long T-shirt. He'd turned out the lamp and the room was pitch-black except for some light that slipped through the shades from the street.

"Are you in bed?" I called out but he didn't answer, and when I looked at the bed, there didn't seem to be a bump where his body should be. "Ernesto, where are you?" I asked but there was no sight or sound of him. "If you're hiding on me, don't 'cause I get scared." I walked slowly toward the bed. I thought I saw the long window curtain move and I screamed. "C'mon, Ernesto, I'm scared, c'mon out." There was no noise, nothing. "Ooooh, ooooh," I made noises and banged the night table but he didn't answer. "Well, I'm going to bed," I

said and jumped under the covers on my side of the bed.
Still nothing. Then he grabbed my foot and I started to
scream.

"I hate you," I told him when he climbed in bed on
top of me and started kissing me all over, on my face and
neck and on my belly. He was such a big guy and he made
me feel small, almost petite as he bent his head down and
ran his tongue around my navel and along the inside of my
thighs. "I hate this," I said giggling.

"You hate it?" he asked. "Well, then, I might as well
give up now, not waste all this great loving I been saving
up for you." He rolled over, lay on his back, and pre-
tended to snore. He looked dark and handsome in the dim
light and for a few minutes I just lay there looking at him.
Then I sat straight up, reached over, and grabbed his penis,
pulling it softly a few times, yelling, "Wake up, wake up,
time for the whole town to wake up."

He rolled over on top of me again and we started
making love seriously, kissing and touching our tongues
together and petting.

"I want you," he said, "you been so bad but I want
you so much," he said and he spanked me softly on the
butt as he slid inside me, gliding in smoothly, moving in
and out almost gently, until with an extra thrust, he exploded inside me. It felt so sweet as he came that I came
too and I was glad that I had woken him up. I fell asleep
loving him.

"Anna, you awake? Anna, honey, you awake? I wanna tell
you something."

It must've been at least two hours since we had fallen

asleep together. I'd been dreaming—a nice dream, I could tell, 'cause I felt nice. "I'm awake," I told him.

"Are you full awake? I want you to be awake. I wanna tell you something important."

"I'm awake, Ernesto. I'm listening to you."

"You remember I told ya that Lena and Cookie are twins?" he whispered.

"Uh-huh."

"Well," he went on, "there's something I want to tell you that I never told anyone." I waited and he cleared his throat a few times and then went on. "For a long time when I was a kid, I knew something in my heart and I thought about it but I didn't know it could be true. Then in high school, in my science class, they said it could be true."

I had no idea what he was talking about but I just waited and let him go on.

"Well, it's about my mom, and it happened a long time ago. I been laying here a while, wanting to tell you, so I'm just going to." He took in a big breath and began. "My mother was a kid when she had me, just turned seventeen, and her and my father did good together back then, they were crazy about each other. And then they had Gloria, and they were still doing good together. For years they did really good. But when I was about eight, they started doing bad. I mean it wasn't *bad* bad, but it was bad. My father got laid off and he had no work for a few months, and I guess he got mean, 'cause they started fighting and he would get drunk and hit her and even hit me and Gloria once in a while. He wasn't really a bad guy, it was just hard times for him and he took it out on her and us.

"But then he started working for my Uncle Louie, which was good. He stopped hitting us and everything felt better, but the problem was that he was working nights— like the rats, he would say. Anyway, things didn't calm down all the way, 'cause they still fought some of the time. He would come home in the morning and start pawing her and ask her for nookie all the time. You know what I mean?"

"Uh-huh," I nodded my head in the dark.

"And she didn't like it. 'I got two kids around my ankles and a house to get straight by noon,' she'd tell him. But every morning, it felt like, he'd be busting her chops to give him some nookie."

Baby Huey stopped and I could hear him breathing hard, but he didn't say anything for a few minutes. "So down the block from us, there was a guy who fixed shoes, maybe he was Czech or Yugoslav, something like that. I just knew he wasn't like us, he wasn't Cuban or any kind of Latino. He was light-skinned and had these deep blue eyes. And he wasn't one of those old guys that had been fixing shoes all their life, he was young, you know? He was young and he liked my mom, treated her like a princess. Once he called her 'a shining light.' "

Baby Huey stopped again and cleared his throat. "And my mom liked him. She was always going in there to fix our shoes or the broken strap on her pocketbook or the zipper on my winter jacket. And he made her things, little presents, a small leather bag for her makeup and a real bag, a pocketbook, and even a leather bookmark, though she don't read. And he gave her extra shoelaces and fixed our shoes for nothing."

We lay there in the dark for a while with neither of

us saying anything. I was afraid to even move, I didn't want to interrupt.

"Then he started coming by, not for dinner or nothing like that, nothing formal. He came by at night, when Gloria was asleep and my dad was at work. But I was older than Gloria and would stay up reading comics or watching TV if my mom was feeling nice and didn't mind me sitting in the living room. And they used to go into the bedroom like Mom and Dad did. And I knew they were doing it. We used to talk about stuff like that on the street and I could tell by the noises they were making and the way my mother looked when they came out that they were doing it. Gloria was little, so I don't know if she ever knew a thing, but my mom knew I knew and she told me if my father ever found out, that he would kill her. I never told no one about it. I was afraid my dad would really kill her if he found out, like those times when he was drunk. I never told no one until now. Luke, that was the shoemaker's name, Luke stopped coming after she got pregnant with the twins."

He leaned close and whispered in my ear. "I could never be sure until high school. Until they told us that fraternal twins come from two different eggs. And I asked the teacher could it happen from two different guys. I mean could a woman have fraternal twins in her from two different dads, and he said sure.

"No one in the family ever says anything, but you seen the twins. Cookie looks like every other Salazar that's ever been born and Lena was the spitting image of Luke, his eyes exactly. I always thought that maybe my dad knew but that somehow he forgave them both, her and Lena, I mean."

When Baby Huey finished, he lay on his back, not

moving at all, and I could see in the faint light that his eyes were open, staring up at the ceiling. I started rubbing his shoulders and arms, along his chest and down his legs. Sometimes I reached up and ran my hands through his hair. I kept this up for a long time before he started to relax. I kept rubbing, it felt like hours, before he closed his eyes and I knew he was asleep. Usually Baby Huey fell asleep facing away from me, his head stuffed into the pillows. Tonight his head rested on my shoulder, his hand on my breast as he slept.

Chris and MaryJo
and the Robbery

"ANNA, ANNA HONEY, you hear me?" Chris's voice came over the PA and it made me smile, and then I started to laugh. I'd been moving down the aisle carrying three trays of doughnuts, Chocos, and coffee cakes. I had two more trays of snack cake on the truck but it was too heavy for me to carry in one trip.

"Anna, what are you doing with those Chocos? Want me to help you with them?"

I laughed aloud, I couldn't believe he was doing that, the whole store could hear him. "I'll be right there," he said. I bent down and took a look at myself in the mirror over the fruit stand. Not too bad, a little pale, I thought, combing my hair with my fingers. My shirt, which was black with HOMEMADE CAKES across the pocket, was buttoned all the way up, so I undid two buttons. The shirt was new and the heavy polyester had rubbed my neck raw. I look like a man in this lousy uniform, I thought, and almost popped a button hurrying to roll the sleeves up before Chris got there. But my hands were black to the wrists from carrying the metal trays, with cuts and bruises that ran to my elbows, so I rolled the sleeves back down again.

"You look fine, you always look fine. I love the way you look." Chris had come down from his office, which was on a platform overlooking the store, and was heading toward me, the fruits on one side, the mustard and salad dressing on the other. His shirt was slightly dirty, a thin line of grease across his chest, which was unusual for him. In this business, managers worked hands-on and their clothes were usually grimy, but not Chris. Somehow he always managed to look clean and businesslike in neatly pressed suits or sports jackets and matching ties.

When he reached me he smiled and gave me a quick flick under the chin. "What'd you bring me today?" he asked, tipping my trays slightly to look over the cake.

"Careful, they're heavy." I rebalanced the trays and moved toward the bread-and-cake aisle and he followed.

I loved that Chris always said something funny or told me how pretty I looked.

MaryJo worked the register but did most of the book-keeping and some of the ordering too. MaryJo would've made a great assistant manager if S&R Supermarket would've considered making a black woman an assistant manager, which they didn't. We joked around a lot and had fun ganging up on Chris. She'd been busy doing bottle return when I came in—with a customer who had two shopping bags overflowing with bottles—so she didn't see me wave to her as I went by.

The HomeMade Cakes stand was an old aluminum one with a spinning picture of a spaceship perched on top. I put my trays on the floor and removed the old cake first. Chris was right behind me and reached over to pick up one of my trays. He stood at my side and held it out so I could work standing up.

"Thanks." I was glad he'd come down to say hello, because I was dreading the day's work ahead of me. October thirtieth—not only late in the month, when people had no money and welfare checks weren't out yet, but also the day before Halloween. Everyone was buying candy, not cake, which meant a lot of stale cake and extra work.

"What's that frown for?" Chris asked. "Smile. You've got such pretty white teeth, you should smile and show them off."

I emptied all my trays, filling the lower shelves with the long boxes of sugar doughnuts, and went out to the truck to get the last two trays of snack cake. When I got back, MaryJo finally noticed me and yelled hello. Chris hadn't moved from where I left him. The HomeMade stand was high, so I stood on tiptoes to put the lines of apple, cherry, and blueberry pies up on top.

"Let me help you," Chris said to me. He wasn't that tall, maybe five-nine, but that was four inches taller than me. His arms came around me and he took the pies, pressing against me as he reached up to put them on the top shelf. I leaned back against his chest, and felt his face bury in my curls and his lips touch the sore spot on my neck. "You're pretty, you are. And sexy too," he whispered, "though sometimes it's hard to tell in your uniform."

"Chris, don't pull that stuff with me," I told him. "I'm filthy and messy-looking."

"I'm serious, I think you're beautiful," and his breath was heavy on my neck as he slid his hands along my hips and up toward my breasts until he saw a customer coming down the aisle toward us. I got embarrassed and pushed hard against his chest with my elbows, accidentally knocking his arms to the sides.

"Careful," he warned as his arms flew out and his hand crashed against the cake stand. He tried to catch a box of chocolate doughnuts that went flying, but it landed on the floor. The box looked fine but the doughnuts inside were fractured.

"Not a total waste," he said. He took the broken box and cracked it open wide, taking a doughnut from the box. "Want one?" he offered, holding the box out. "At least we're sure they're fresh." Chris held the box carefully while he took a big bite of the doughnut.

"No thanks, I eat that stuff all day long." When the woman disappeared up toward the frozen food, Chris put the box down and reached around my waist, pulling me to him. This time I didn't resist but rested against him while he finished the doughnut, neither of us saying a word.

"Chris, you leave that girl alone," MaryJo's voice drifted across the aisles from the front of the store. "Let her do her work. She got better things to do than have you bothering her."

"I've got to go," I said, my voice sounding heavy, almost husky. I pulled away, still feeling his hands moving toward my breasts, and I grabbed my trays and the broken box of doughnuts. I couldn't look at him as I walked to the front of the store. "I've got a lot of work to do."

"You do your work, all right," he said as he passed me to go through the swinging doors into the meat department, "at least on me. Hey, Marty," he called, "come out here! What are these cartons doing blocking the doorway and the aisle? Do something with them. One of my customers will trip and I'll have a suit on my hands." He stood planted in front of three huge meat cartons, shaking his head at the blood leaking onto the black tile floor. As I turned the corner, I looked back and Chris waved.

I passed MaryJo's register on the way out. "MaryJo, I'm going to get a new box of these doughnuts," I said and held up the crushed box.

"Shouldn't let that man crush your doughnuts, honey."

"Don't be funny. See you in a minute." I rolled up the bill for the cake, took aim, and shot it into the brown bag that MaryJo had just packed. "Yes!" I shouted.

"Watch it, girl!" MaryJo said smiling.

"Be right back."

I climbed on the truck, threw the broken box on the stale tray, and pulled out a fresh one. Leaning against the racks, I started thinking about what just happened with Chris. What was I doing letting him put his hands on me when I was going with Baby Huey? But Baby Huey never felt like a real boyfriend, and something about Chris made me feel alive and good inside.

But Chris is such a baby, I almost said aloud. Last week he told me he was twenty-five and that he was already tired of it all. "I'm getting out of this business soon," he said, taking out a picture of his four-month-old baby. "I'm staying just long enough to get Jesse into a good private school and that's it. I'm not dying in this lousy job. My wife thinks I'm staying till Jesse's through with college, but she better think again. And she wants us to try for a girl in a year or two. But I warned her, I won't be a lifer, not like Henry. Henry wasn't even fifty when he died." Henry, the S&R manager before Chris, died of a heart attack while arranging the frozen food in the walk-in at the back of the store.

Chris had left his wallet open and I'd looked at the wedding picture across from the one of the baby. Chris's wife looked like the girls I grew up with in the Bronx. Dark-haired, with big eyes, pretty, and very young, probably not even twenty.

Standing there in the truck, I made up my mind to

stay away from him, even though it felt nice. I couldn't let myself fool around like that again. He was married and I'd end up losing my job for nothing. When I returned from my truck, I held up the new box of doughnuts as I passed MaryJo's register but MaryJo barely looked up. Chris trusted me completely and he and MaryJo never checked what I brought in and out, knowing that I wouldn't cheat them.

On the way out again, I stopped at MaryJo's register. Chris was only a few feet away, helping Alex, his new assistant manager, stack Perrier boxes to make a huge display for the front of the store. Chris climbed up, balancing himself on two of the boxes, while Alex passed him some empty cartons to place on top to make a pyramid. From time to time Chris turned and winked at me and I smiled back.

"You think if I take a picture I'll make the supermarket magazine for display of the month?" he called out to me and MaryJo.

"Take your clothes off and you'll make the front cover," MaryJo yelled back. Then she turned back to me and her eyes carefully searched my face. "What's doing?" she asked me quietly. "You look worried today."

"Nothing, I'm fine. At least I think I am. How's Andy doing in his new school?" MaryJo was right, but I wasn't sure why I was feeling so nervous. I felt like that as soon as I pulled out of the garage that morning. "Is he getting used to the teacher and the kids?" Andy, MaryJo's nine-year-old, had just switched from Catholic to public school because MaryJo and her boyfriend, Greg, were trying to have a baby and were cutting costs to get ready.

"Andy's not doing good. He's scared. Says the kids are too rough."

"It'll probably take some getting used to. It's not easy going to a new school, starting all over again with new teachers and kids. Give it time. It must seem like a whole new world to him."

MaryJo closed her eyes and sighed. "I guess. It's just that he's a good kid and I don't want him to have such a hard time."

I told MaryJo how Joey's teacher had sent a note home saying that he had scissors hidden somewhere and was cutting things up again.

"But he hasn't done that for a long time, right?" MaryJo asked.

"Yeah, but he started doing it again. Thursday he cut the knees out of his brown corduroy pants while everyone was listening to story hour. The teacher's afraid that the other kids might try to imitate him. And he won't tell anybody where the scissors are."

"He's got his own idea of what's beautiful," MaryJo said. "If cutting holes in everything is his biggest problem," she added, "you're pretty lucky."

I didn't want to leave but it was getting late, so I said goodbye to MaryJo and waved to Chris. When I was almost at the door, Chris called after me, "Bye, Anna. Stop by later if you have time."

Back on the truck, I slid the door closed behind me and would've run up to my seat, only the door hadn't shut right. I turned and hit the handle again, this time with more force, until I heard a click. To make the door close all the way, I had to slam it hard. But if I did that, it would often be stuck when I tried to open it again.

My truck was the usual kind of HomeMade truck, built like a UPS van, with small sliding doors in the front and a large roll-up door in the back, which is how we loaded the cake in the morning. Rows of cake racks lined each side, leaving only a narrow aisle down the middle. The only difference between my truck and the rest of the trucks in the depot was that mine was one of the oldest and so was slightly smaller and more broken-down than the others. Just this morning I had had another talk with Gus, the mechanic, about everything that needed to be fixed.

"Gus, what have I done to make you hate me, to wish me dead?" I asked him. "Three weeks ago, my battery went dead and you replaced it with one that was so corroded it exploded the same day and my truck went off the road." Gus nodded, he couldn't deny it. I went on. "My tires got no tread, my gears slip, my front door don't open or close right, and I can't lock my back door 'cause of the way you fixed it." While I was complaining, Gus walked around my truck and tested each tire his usual way, by hitting it with his wrench. I followed him and kept talking. "Putting a screw and bolt through a tiny hole is not what I would call fixing the lock on my back door. If robbers came through the front and I have to run out the back, how long you think it would take me to stand there and unscrew that fucking little bolt, huh? By that time they'd have mugged the shit out of me." I stopped, waiting for an answer but Gus said nothing. "Just put a sliding bolt or a real lock like other trucks have, okay? Is that asking too much? I got kids at home. Please, Gus." I held my hands up like in prayer and tried to smile at him but he wouldn't look my way.

"When the locks come in, I could put one on," he said and went up the steps of my truck. Gus was small and thin, always dressed in a dark jumpsuit covered with grease. He pulled out a rag that was as dirty as his jumpsuit and stuffed it into an opening in the floor near the steering wheel. The fumes had been so bad the last few weeks that I was getting nauseous whenever I drove more than a short distance. Gus's solution was to try different rags to stop the fumes from coming up into the cab from the engine. "But I don't think we're gettin' any locks in for a while," Gus mumbled. "Jed didn't order none." He stood up and bent over, then turned from one side to the other, his hands on his waist, stretching out his back.

"Can't you tell him you got a special problem, a truck that needs one bad?"

"Too many special problems on this job," he said. He moved in front of me and faced me, looking directly into my eyes. "Why do ya want a job with so many problems, lady? Why didn't ya stay married, let a guy take care of ya? It woulda been a lot easier."

"What good does that do me now? Just fix my locks so I won't get killed on this goddamn job, okay?"

Throughout the morning, I didn't feel right. I was jittery. MaryJo was right when she asked me about being worried, but I still couldn't put my finger on why. Later I marked it up to premonition. Partly it was because it was the holiday season, the worst time of the year for drivers. Halloween, followed by Thanksgiving and Christmas. 'Tis the season to be jolly! For us drivers it's a time when people are desperate because they don't have money for food, much less for Christmas presents for their kids. Muggers and robbers are out there trying to support the Christmas habit. Every driver spends November and December watching his back, jumping at every sound.

"Nineteen dollars and eighty-eight cents going out." "Fifteen fifty-six going out." "Twenty-seven fourteen out," I heard myself saying all day long. Jed was going to get on our case about how poor the routes were doing, but it wasn't our fault, it was the season. Stores had too much cake and there wasn't room for the cake I was bringing in. Chocos and cupcakes were still sitting there from my last visit. I chomped on a honey bun and two coffee cakes when I felt like I was slowing down, but after a while the sugar just made me jumpy and then tired.

One o'clock. Three more stops. Not too bad for a lousy day. I pulled up in front of Bodega del Oro on Fifty-third Street off Fourth Avenue. Bodega del Oro was small, cluttered, and not very clean, the counter crammed with cans of beans, jars of peppers, Italian bread, penny candy, and cake. It was hard for me to get through the narrow aisles, past the three or four guys milling around, and make my way to the counter. I served the store once a week, giving it the same fifty-dollar order each time, two huge trays of snack cake and lots of doughnuts. It took extra time to move everything around to make room for my cake.

Miguel, or Big Mike as everyone called the owner, was a huge fat guy. He always wore a white T-shirt, but you couldn't tell what else because he never got up from his seat at the long desk way behind the counter. Two other men, different ones all the time but always red-faced and smelling of alcohol, took care of business. Big Mike took care of the numbers and whatever else he was dealing.

Bodega del Oro did a pretty good business, and the few pieces I took out were usually squashed and hard as rocks, having been left sometimes for weeks, hidden under everything else on the counter. "Four going out," I said holding up the stale cake.

Back on the truck, I slammed the door and took my time loading the tray. I felt like I needed a break. If it wasn't so late, I would've loved to stop back and see Chris, like he said. After what happened this morning, I knew I was going to spend a lot of time thinking about him, and a lot of time trying not to. I remembered the feel of his chest against my back when I leaned against him while he ate the doughnut. I stood there resting against the racks, thinking about Chris when something outside caught my attention. I kept still, listening carefully. Everything was quiet except for a man shouting. He was somewhere down the block, near the corner. "La señora, ¡la Gringa!" the voice cried out. Another person answered him and then the first one called again, "Si, la señora está adentro." The urgency in his voice reminded me of two guys I'd seen a few weeks ago, yelling to each other as they hit and robbed an old lady on the street. They were gone by the time I got there.

I waited and listened. Again I heard it. "La señora, vamanos, rapido." This time it was closer. I figured it didn't have anything to do with me, but I moved to the steps to make sure the front door was closed tight. It was quiet out there again and I stood waiting for another sound, some regular street noise to signal me that everything was all right, that I was just edgy today. But there was nothing, no sound at all. I was sure I heard the faint sound of someone running. Why? What was happening? And then I got scared. Just as I decided to drive away and come back later, the sound of the back door rolling up pounded in my ears.

There were four of them and they were moving fast, single file, because the truck was narrow. It was too late to get the gun from the safe. Four of them, and the motherfuckers were all smiling as they headed toward me, the first one with a big grin as he turned to the others. "Sí, la señora."

I knew him, that first one, I recognized him from the neighborhood. Slim, dark, good-looking, and well-built. The others were shorter, stockier. I couldn't see the faces of the two in the back, but the second guy had scars, slashes across the left side of his face. They moved closer, one after another, heading toward the front of the truck, heading toward me.

"Wait," I pleaded, looking at the one with the beautiful face. He was watching me carefully, smiling. He knows me, I thought, the son of a bitch knows me and he's going to hurt me anyway.

"Señora," the first one held out his hand, rubbing his fingers together, "el dinero. Where is the money, lady?" He came at me and I turned, thinking to run out the front door. But it might be hard to open and I'd be trapped there. When I looked back, he was even closer, with the others right behind. "Ahora," he said, moving more quickly and signaling by a nod of his head for them to follow.

He shot forward and I screamed and picked up one of the empty metal trays, holding it in front of me. "You got me, pretty boy. That's what you want, isn't it?" I said. "You get your choice, to rape, rob, or beat me." I could feel the tears rolling down my cheeks but I stood my ground, there was no place to go. Then I threw the metal tray at him as hard as I could and yelled, "But it's not over yet." He lunged at me again and I grabbed another tray and swung at him, missing, and the tray banged against the racks with a loud crashing sound. His other hand came up holding a knife and I screamed and screamed. We moved slowly, facing each other, watching each other carefully. He was still smiling, a big smile with a lot of teeth. His hand shot out and he stabbed at me with the knife as I took another tray in both hands and came down with all my might on his hand, slamming his fingers between the metal tray and the racks. I did it again and could feel his fingers being crushed under the tray. He let out a kind of high-pitched cry while the others stood behind him, unable to do anything but watch because the aisle was too narrow for them to pass.

An old aluminum stand had broken a few weeks ago and I'd put part of it behind my seat, a long pipe bent like a claw at one end. I pulled the metal claw out and held it up. "Mira, muchacho. See this?" and I swiped at his face. "You got a real pretty face, qué bonito, but no more," I swung at his face again. "Oye, you hear me?" I yelled at him. "Yours will be the ugliest face you ever seen. Qué feo, they'll say." He rushed at me and grabbed on to the end of the claw. "No," I shrieked and tugged, but he held on. Then I pulled hard and the claw ripped into his palm and he screamed, throwing himself back against the racks. I moved fast, running straight at him like a crazy woman, yelling, "You'll never look in the mirror again," and went for his face. I reached out and struck his cheek, drawing the claw like a rake across the skin. Blood ran down his neck onto his shirt. I went at him again but somehow I tripped and landed on all fours, the claw on the floor beside me. I felt his hand in my hair. He pulled hard, jerking my head back. My scalp hurt and my neck made a cracking sound. I could feel blood in my mouth where my teeth clamped down on my tongue. My hand balled into a fist and I punched him as hard as I could in the groin. A small growling sound came from his throat, and as I stood up, I punched him again in the crotch. He staggered and fell to his knees. Then I grabbed the claw and charged at him, screaming, ripping at his neck and slicing his arm. He got to his feet and started to back off, and the other guys moved back to give him room. I dropped the claw and picked up one tray after another and threw them as hard as I could at him and the guys behind him. "Fucking bastards! Fucking, fucking bastards!" I yelled.

He pushed backwards against the second guy, trying to get away from me, calling out to the others, "No mas! No mas! Pronto! Pronto!" He wasn't smiling anymore. I never stopped screaming and swinging, and I think I cracked his wrist with one of the trays as they backed out. They kept pushing toward the rear. There was yelling, I couldn't tell whose, and I heard one jump down, then another. They landed in a pile on the street. In a minute the truck was empty. They ran down the block, not fast, but away.

I ran yelling onto the street, into Bodega del Oro, trying to catch my breath as I called out to Fat Mike to phone the police, to get help fast. Fat Mike was sitting at his desk. I told him that some guys had jumped my truck and pulled a knife on me, if he got the cops there fast they might still be able to catch them. Fat Mike didn't move a muscle. He sat still, not answering, then opened a drawer and took out a small adding machine and punched in a few numbers. He never looked up.

"Mike, please call the cops," I asked again. He didn't answer. "I hope they come back and blow your fat ugly brains out!" I shouted at him and left. I closed my truck and drove off, looking for a cop, a phone, any kind of help. When I finally found a phone, I called the depot. Joanie, anyone, please answer. The phone kept ringing. Then I remembered that Joanie was sick and Jed was out on the route with Mario the Mole. I called 911. "Is this an emergency?" the woman asked. "Your name and number, please.'' I hung up and did the only thing that made sense to me at the moment. I drove to my next stop.

"How come you don't give me as good service as Hearth-land?" Sam, the owner of the next store, asked, wiping his wet hands on his white apron. Sam always had a wet rag in his hand, he was forever cleaning. "I never know when you're coming. If you don't do a better job, I'm calling the company to complain.''

"I come every Thursday on the dot," I said quietly, trying not to think of the pain that was pounding through my head. "Look," I said, pointing my finger at his chest and staring down at him since he was almost a head shorter than I was, "I gave you twenty dollars' worth of cake last week and I'm taking out almost sixteen dollars today. For four dollars you want me to come twice a week? Just what I want to do with my time!" I knew I was losing control but I couldn't stop myself. "Half the time when I get here, the store is closed 'cause you're next door playing cards with your wife, Rosie, who I usually send a box of Chocos to 'cause I know she loves them. And I never forget to come back the next day, do I? Do I?" I screamed at him. Sam shook his head no. "But if I'm a half-hour late, you're on that damn phone calling my boss, complaining, aren't you? Aren't you?" I grabbed him by the strap of his apron, pulling him to a black wall phone near the counter. "Well, call, damn you," I yelled. I picked up the phone and put it to his mouth, "Call my fucking company. And fuck you and your damn Rosie.''

·   ·   ·

I drove another few blocks, then stopped and dialed the S&R Supermarket, hoping that Chris and MaryJo weren't on lunch break. Chris answered the phone, and through my tears I told him about the four guys and the robbery. He spoke softly to me, saying, "I'm sorry, baby. At least they didn't hurt you. You're okay, that's what counts."

"I had almost nine hundred dollars on me, Chris. If they took it, I would've had to pay it out of my pocket, and the company would've never made it up to me. Where would I get that kind of money?"

"I know, sweetie, but look, next time, if you have to give it to them, do it and don't worry about it. The money doesn't matter if you're dead, right?"

"Uh-huh."

"Look, why don't you head back to the depot?" he suggested. "MaryJo and I are taking half a day, but MaryJo's boyfriend can't pick her up like he was supposed to, so I'm dropping her off at the train. We'll come by and get you. Isn't that a good idea? By the time you're done settling up, we'll be there and I'll drive you into the city, okay?" I kept crying as he talked. "It'll be okay, baby, it's going to be okay. Talk to your boss. Tell him what happened. At least get him to fix the lock on the back door. We'll see you in about an hour."

I got lost on my way back to the depot and ended up circling around Brooklyn College, so the ride took fifteen minutes longer than usual. When I rolled the extra rack of stale cake over to Ramon the packer, he gave me a dirty look. "Look," I explained, "it was a lousy day for everybody."

Most of the guys had already left and Jed was in the office talking to Mario, who always took his time settling up, because he dreaded going home to his sick wife. Jed was tacking up an announcement on the cork board outside the cashier's booth.

"Here comes trouble," Jed announced as I walked in. "That's all she gives me is trouble."

"That's a lie," I said. "I give you a lot more than trouble. I work my ass off for you and bring in more money than that route's ever done."

"You're not lazy," he said, "you're just trouble. Just like a lady, right, Mario?" Mario rarely answered Jed, just stood there shaking his head back and forth.

"Get off my back," I told him, "I had a hard day, I don't need this."

"If I was on your back," Jed said, "it wouldn't be that easy to get me off," he said, slapping his knee and chuckling stupidly.

I thought of how bitchy his wife had been at Joanie's wedding and how Jed acted when he was with her, and I said to him, "If Cindy gave you enough, you wouldn't be begging it off me all the time."

Jed's head snapped back. He looked so much like an eagle with his pinched face and bald head as he shook his finger at me. "I'm sick and tired of listening to your bad mouth. You're suspended. We're pulling your route till further notified. You can't talk about family that way and get away with it."

"Gimme a break," I said, and now I was begging. "I was just running my mouth. I got held up today."

"Go home," he told me. "Sam called up on ya just ten minutes ago. That's the third call we got on ya in two months. Three strikes and you're out." His face had turned bright red and he tucked his shirt in carefully around his belly. He was thin, almost gangly, but his big beer belly hung way out over his pants.

"Please, Jed."

"Tell it at your hearing," he said and walked into his office, slamming the door.

When I came out of the garage, I found Chris and MaryJo parked by the fire hydrant in a shiny black Maxima. When MaryJo spotted me she jumped out and put her arms around me and I started to cry again. MaryJo pulled me into the front with her. Chris drove away with the two of us squashed together, sharing the front seat. "It got worse, can you imagine, it even got worse. Now I'm suspended until I get a call from the Teamsters asking what happened and setting up a meeting. HomeMade can't suspend me with everything that happened. Anyway, I hope not. But it's all such a mess."

I tried to relax but my hands were shaking and I felt like my eyes were bugging out of my head. The tears came again, and Chris reached over and took one of my hands in his. "Let's stop for coffee," he said.

But MaryJo wanted to get home in time to put a roast in. "I promised Greg I'd cook dinner tonight," she said. At the next light, Chris pulled over and ran into a small delicatessen. He returned with three containers of coffee to drink in the car.

"So tell us what happened," MaryJo said, ripping a triangle out of her lid and taking a sip of the steaming coffee. I nodded and began to speak quietly and told them about the robbery, my visit to Sam's, and the fight with Jed. I tried to tell it simply, like I might tell them about a movie or book, but every once in a while I'd stop because I'd lost my place or felt like crying again.

MaryJo said she was glad I could hold my own.

"I learned to fight like that from looking after my brother Danny," I told her. "Danny was a year and a half older but somehow *I* was the one who took care of *him*. Danny was always getting beat up. One time he ended up with eleven stitches from having his head smashed into the sidewalk. On my way home from school, kids would come screaming after me, 'They got your brother Danny,' and there'd usually be five or six boys holding him down. I'd jump into the pile and go crazy, yelling and swinging, kicking and punching the nearest one to me."

"Well, I'm glad you messed up the guy with the pretty face," MaryJo said. "Make him think twice before he tries that again. I'm just sorry you had to go through it at all." She gave me a hug. "Anyway, you guys, it's late and I better hurry, the roast will take a few hours." She climbed out of the car, saying, "Bye, honey, and Chris, you better treat this girl nice. I'd stay to keep an eye on you but I don't want to have to listen to my old man complaining again."

"Some way to talk to your boss!"

"Some boss!" MaryJo leaned over and kissed him on the cheek and then kissed me and gave me another hug. "You'll be all right, baby, once you get home. You're that kind of woman. Take good care of her, Chris!" she called and then ran down the steps to the train.

Me and Chris didn't talk on the drive into the city except for when I gave him directions, which were pretty simple since I lived right near the George Washington Bridge. He put his arm around the back of my seat, sometimes ruffling the curls that were gathered in a clip at the top of my head. More than halfway there, I closed my eyes and he lightly massaged my neck and shoulders. I was glad I still had a few more hours before Joey and Nick got home from the after-school center. And Pudgy was working late this whole month. I rested my head on Chris's shoulder and he leaned over and kissed me on the head again and again as we drove along.

He found a spot right down the block from my house, but after he parked, neither of us moved. I could almost feel the tightness in my head and body ease up as I rested against him. Finally, Chris's legs were starting to cramp, so we shifted our weights and ended up facing each other. We looked at each other and smiled. He put his hand under my chin and gently pulled me toward him. Our mouths came together intensely, but tenderly. His tongue searched my lips and pushed forward into my mouth. My tongue played with his, and I moved it in and out, teasing, tasting the sweetness of his mouth. He pulled away and then bent his head, placing his lips against my breast, kissing and nuzzling until I felt like I couldn't get enough of him.

Then I thought how crazy it was. How this morning I'd decided I wasn't going to let it go any further, and now things were out of control again. I stopped, pushing him away gently, and leaned my head on his shoulder. When he tried to turn me toward him for another kiss, I shook my head, not looking at him.

"What?" he asked.

"You're married."

"Yeah, but I'm crazy about you, you can see that. And me and my wife haven't made love since she got pregnant over a year ago. Before that, it was never more than once every three, four months anyway. That's the truth. She just stopped wanting me. I been falling for you for a long time, I can't help it."

My thoughts went to Tom, how he'd never been in love with me, not even in the beginning. I'd always been after him. And I couldn't picture Baby Huey ever being crazy about me.

"I love your smile, the way your hair falls in your eyes. I'm nuts about you," he said softly and he laughed and kissed me on the tip of my nose. "At night, sometimes I fall asleep thinking about you."

"Then you must be nuts, all right." We kissed again and I giggled at how nice it felt. I couldn't remember Tom ever kissing me. I couldn't picture Baby Huey saying he was nuts about me. Chris kissed my face, my neck, my chest where the buttons were open. He opened two more buttons and reached inside my shirt for my breast, sighing, saying how soft my skin was. Then he kneaded my breast, lightly squeezing the nipple between his fingers.

"Someone might see us," I whispered, nervously checking up and down the street for my neighbors or the super. "Please, we've got to stop." Chris took his hand away and leaned back against the seat. He closed his eyes and his breathing got more regular.

"I want to make love with you. Will you take me home with you?" For just a moment I thought about Baby Huey and knew I should say no. Why was I starting with Chris, a married man, when I already had a guy? But in just a few moments Chris had made me feel that I meant more to him than I had to any man I'd ever been with. That he liked me, really liked me. And that made all the difference.

I nodded yes.

In the apartment, we stood just inside the doorway, kissing and letting our hands travel over each other lightly. I felt dizzy and tired and a big yawn escaped in the middle of our kiss. Chris laughed. I pulled away, holding out my hands, which were still covered with grease. "I need a bath," I told him and slowly walked toward the bathroom, undressing as I went. He caught up to me and took me in his arms again. He looked down at my unbuttoned shirt and moaned, pressing himself against me. "Please," he begged.

"Not yet, I'm too dirty."

I didn't hurry my bath, and fifteen minutes later I came out in my terrycloth robe, still tired but at least clean. Chris was stretched across my bed, his eyes closed, his hands under his head. His jacket and tie were neatly folded on the chair.

I knelt and whispered softly in his ear, "Are you asleep?"

"Maybe," he shook himself and sat up. "Yeah, I guess I dozed off."

"Smell me!" I put my arm under his nose, hoping he could still smell the scent of the bubble bath. Mrs. Mahoney had given it to me last Christmas and this was the first time I'd tried it.

"Mmmmm. Smells good enough to eat!" He bit my arm gently and tried to pull me down next to him, but I wasn't ready. "Not yet," I pleaded. "I need a few minutes to get comfortable. I want to feel like I know you, that I'm not jumping in the sack with some strange guy."

"We've been friends for a while," he said, "and now we're going to be lovers. That's a big jump."

"I know. And it's okay, but I've got to feel good about it. I don't want to wake up tomorrow thinking I'm a tramp." I sat down at the side of the bed, my feet touching the floor.

"I want you so much," Chris said, "but I want you to take your time, to be sure it's what you want too." I moved closer to him and took his hand in mine, raising it to my lips. "I'd like for it not to be a one-time thing," he added. "I want to love you for a long time." He gently lifted one after another of the stray strands of hair that hung over my eyes.

"Can we lie down next to each other and hold each other tight and not make love just yet? Would that be all right?" I asked.

"That would be great." Chris laughed again and fell back on the pillows. I climbed on top of him and his round belly softly pressed against mine. He petted me as I lay in his arms. "Anna banna bobana," he began to sing, "banana banna bobana, fe fi fofana, Anna." Chris sang heartily and we both laughed, because he couldn't carry a tune at all.

"You're about the worst singer I ever heard," I said.

"Thank you. I've always been the worst singer, from grade school to high school. And I'm proud to say that I've never improved." He sang the verse again and again and we both laughed until we had tears in our eyes.

"You're the best bad singer I've ever heard."

"I joined the glee club in high school to see if I could get better at it, but they asked me to leave. It made it too hard for everybody else to concentrate."

"I can't believe you had the nerve to join a glee club. They didn't have a glee club in my high school. Actually, they didn't have much of anything. You know, when I was with you and MaryJo, I wanted to tell you about my high school, but I didn't want to bore you. Could I tell you now?"

"I don't mind. I want to know about you," he said, and while I talked he stroked me from the top of my head down to my waist, sometimes lightly and other times harder, digging deep into my muscles.

"I grew up in a rough part of the Bronx." I began like I was telling a story. "And when I was eleven, my mom moved us to a better neighborhood, where the kids dressed nice and didn't curse. When it was time for me to go to high school, the only public school in the area was Franklin K. Lane, so that's where I went. Nowhere in the city was there another school like Franklin K. Lane. The school had riots and knifings every week. I was twelve when I started there, a skinny, scared-shitless little twelve-year-old. It took only a week before some girls jumped me down in the locker room. There were three of them, all almost a head taller than me. Later, I couldn't even remember their faces. They came at me while all the other girls looked on. I wasn't big like they were, but I was crazy. I started screaming and took the head of the first one in my hands and smashed it against the lockers. I climbed onto the back of the second girl and reached around and kept poking her in the eyes. I never stopped yelling and slamming which- ever one was near me. The third one I punched hard in the breasts. And then it was over. They disappeared and the locker room was empty. I could barely walk, but I wasn't badly hurt. I got a reputation from that fight and no one ever gave me a hard time after that.''

When I was done, Chris gently cradled me back down into the pillows, whispering softly, ''Everyone's crazy in different ways. But it's not crazy to take care of yourself. The world is crazy, is what.''

He started to kiss me and his kisses got more and more passionate and little by little I felt myself responding, wanting him to touch me, and I was glad. He raised himself above me and looked at me, his Saint Anthony medal swinging from his neck and gently bumping my chin. He put his tongue in my mouth, moving it across my teeth, one by one, as if counting them. I smiled and he smiled back.

Chris moved onto his elbow, and with his other hand he opened my bathrobe and lay there looking at me. I held my stomach tight, hoping it didn't look flabby and tried to push my breasts together with my arms. I pulled at my robe to close it but he stopped me by leaning down and kissing my breasts, catching my nipple in his mouth, sucking and pulling on it until I moaned aloud. "Don't worry so much about how you look," he whispered. "Looking at you makes me feel good."

He got off the bed and quickly took off his shirt and unzipped his pants. He tugged at his belt and then changed his mind, pushing out his stomach toward me. "You undo it, please." I got on my knees near the edge of the bed, opened his belt buckle, and helped him out of his pants. He took off his underwear, and when he was naked, he stood by the side of the bed while I touched him. "Do you like it?" he asked.

"You're sweet," I answered and gently slid my hand along his cock and under his balls. He started to moan and I pulled lightly on his cock, bending over to gently kiss the crown, then taking it all the way in my mouth. He called out my name as I pressed my tongue along the shaft, kissing and sucking, moving my mouth slowly up and down as he held tight to my head.

"Not yet," he groaned and pulled himself out, "it's too soon. I'm so excited, I'll come right away."

I lay down and pulled him on top of me. "I can't wait," he moaned. He slid inside me, moving in and out slowly, then harder until he stopped for a moment, holding me tight.

"Do you like it?'

"Mmmmm."

"Is it okay for you?"

"It's okay, but not so fast."

"Do you want more?"

"More."

"Now do you like it?"

"Yes." He stopped again and stayed still except for his hand moving gently along my ass and back. Then he slipped his hand in front and played with my clit. It felt so good I could barely stand it. He stroked it while he sank deeper and deeper inside me. This time when he started moving again, he went faster and faster, still stroking while he plunged, and each time it felt like it went farther and farther in.

"Ooooh, I want to come. Anna, baby, I want to come." He moved faster and harder, moving his hand from my clit up to my nipple, pulling on it as he called out, "I don't know if I can stop, I'm going to come."

"Go ahead, sweet baby. It's okay, let it go."

He called out again and pulled me to him, holding me tight. Then he opened his eyes and stared at me and smiled as he gave one last push. And I could feel him pulsing inside me as his sperm shot through me.

"I want to come too," I said almost to myself and he laughed and started moving again. "Not too fast," I whispered in his ear. He moved in and out more slowly, thrusting with a gentle force until he was all the way in. Over and over I thought I was going to come but didn't until I pictured him taking me on the floor of his supermarket, my legs spread open, my breasts exposed, and then finally I came.

I woke with a start to a phone ringing and wasn't sure at first where I was. Then I remembered, grabbed my robe, and ran to answer it.

"Hello?"

"Anna Ferrara?"

"Yeah?"

"Mike Dupree from Merrick."

"I remember you. I met you last year at the union meeting with Teddy, Teddy the Greek."

"Yeah, that's right. I'm calling because I'm acting as shop steward for your depot since it doesn't have one of its own. The union just got a call from your boss saying you were suspended. He said you'd know what it was about."

"Yeah."

"It's only for a day, because they're having a meeting on you the day after tomorrow. We'll let you know where and what time."

"Oh, great." I'd been hoping that it would take a few days to set up a meeting and that I'd get a few days off while I waited.

"It's not a joke. This is your second suspension."

"Sorry, I'm just tired. Anyway, thanks for calling."

"See you at the meeting."

"Bye."

"Was that the call you were waiting for?" Chris asked. He had gotten up and was dressed by the time I finished the call. His hair was wet and he stood in front of the mirror, running a comb through his thick, wavy hair.

"Uh-huh."

"It's late, I'd better go." He reached out to hug me but I moved away, bending down to pick up a piece of lint from the rug.

"I know," I said.

"I had a wonderful time."

"Uh-huh. Me too."

"Will you walk me to the door?" Chris held out his hand and I said yes, so he led me down the hall. He took me in his arms but I was looking back so he kissed my cheek and said goodbye.

I watched from the window while he started up his car and pulled out. I followed his car as he drove down the block toward the West Side Highway.

The room needed straightening before Joey and Nick came home. I started with the bed, pulling the covers tight, and the smell of Chris's cologne rose up as I fluffed the crumpled pillows. I didn't know the name of the cologne but I knew it wasn't Armani. I wished Chris could've stayed. I felt so lonely. But the truth was, with Baby Huey somehow I always felt a bit lonely, while with Chris it was only when he was gone.

Mike Dupree and
Teddy the Greek Junior

THE ALARM RANG at seven o'clock. I must've been dreaming, because I woke up scared, thinking I had lost my job. I knew I wasn't going to work today but couldn't remember why. Then everything that happened yesterday came back to me, the robbery, the fight with Jed, Chris coming home with me. The kids weren't up yet, so I took a shower and washed my hair. I had scabs near my hairline that I got from scratching out of nervousness and they burned when I poured on the shampoo. But I felt more relaxed after the shower. I toweled dry, and with my hair still wet, gathered it back tight with a rubber band, then twirled it into a bun.

"I want pancakes and waffles," Joey said, "and some orange juice." Nick was still in the bathroom and Pudgy had left a note saying not to wake him, he was going in late this morning.

"One or the other," I told Joey. "Either pancakes or waffles. If I made them both, it'd be too much and you'd end up eating only one of them anyway. So choose."

"Okay, I'll do eeny meeny," Joey said.

I poured two cups of orange juice and put up hot water while Joey sat there doing eeny meeny on his fingers. Only he didn't do it exactly right and kept saying "eeny

meeny miny mo'' a lot and skipped most of the rest of it.
He must've been doing it at least five minutes before he
looked up and said excitedly, ''Mommy, guess what?''

''What?''

''I did eeny meeny and it came out both, pancakes and
waffles.''

''Joey, I guess you're just one lucky guy.'' I measured
the milk and started mixing batter for the pancakes and
waffles. That was one of the only things I missed about
Tom. He was a great pancake and waffle maker.

By the time I fed the kids, got them off to school, and
did some shopping, it was still only nine in the morning
and I had a whole day ahead of me and no idea what to do.

Lily made her own hours on her job so I called and
asked if she'd like to play some handball this afternoon.
''Sure, what time should I come over?'' For months I'd
been promising to teach Lily how to play but we'd never
gotten around to it. We decided that we'd meet in the park
after lunch.

Pudgy came into the kitchen wearing a T-shirt and a
pair of gym shorts. His hair was sticking up on one side and
flat on the other. ''Don't get all dolled up on my account,''
I told him, but he didn't seem to think it was funny. Pudgy
looked tired. There were dark rings under his eyes and his
skin was pale but splotchy in spots. I poured him a cup of
coffee.

''Were you out late drinking last night?'' I asked.

''Nah, they had us in meetings from five to ten. I
came straight home, but it was a long day. I think I'll call
in sick, spend the day in bed.''

''I could make you some breakfast. There's pancake
batter left, or I could make some eggs. Whatever you
want.''

"I'd love some pancakes," Pudgy said, rubbing his eyes. I took down the big pan and started heating the oil. "I heard you were suspended again," he said, so quietly that I almost didn't hear him.

"Yeah, but just for a day, I think."

"I didn't believe it," he said. "I thought it was a mistake." I couldn't tell if he was angry or disgusted or what.

"No, it's no mistake. I got under Jed's skin again."

"Sometimes I wonder if it wasn't a bad idea, my getting you the job. You have such a hard time and it never seems to get better."

"How else could I earn that much money? I was making less than half that before. Look, I don't want to talk about it."

Pudgy came behind me and put his arms around my waist while I poured the batter into the sizzling pan. "I heard you were robbed and it was pretty ugly. Is that true too?"

I nodded.

"I love you," he said softly. "I'd die if something happened to you because of this lousy job. It's not worth it. Even with how much money you make."

"I know. But I don't have a choice. I'll be all right, I promise. Please, let's talk about something else, okay?"

"Okay."

I didn't want to tell him that I was scared. That I was afraid to drive down those same streets again. Afraid that the guy with the pretty face, that was not so pretty anymore, was going to come back for me, maybe not this week but someday soon. From now on, I decided right then and there, I would keep the gun on me at all times.

Neither of us said anything after that. I sat quietly,

sipping my coffee while Pudgy gobbled down his breakfast. After he finished he went back to bed.

I was fifteen minutes early and started hitting the ball against the wall while I waited. It felt good to be playing handball again. I tried not to think about anything but the ball, placing it and taking it off the wall on one bounce. I hit it softly at first, then harder and harder. I found myself sweating, my teeth clenched, punching it as hard as I could. Lily came ten minutes later, like I knew she would. Two things I knew for sure about Lily. That she just took a shower and that she wouldn't be late. We had that in common, me and Lily—being on time and showering two and three times a day.

Lily gave me a big smile and as usual I was struck by how beautiful she .was. No matter that she never wore makeup or that she always dressed in the same white shirts and dungarees, the woman was breathtaking and either didn't know it or didn't care. And when she smiled that smile, looking half shy and half glad, I was happy just to be near her.

She told me that a friend had started giving her hand-ball lessons and that she'd been practicing on her own for the last few weeks. So I asked her to show me what she could do. She served the ball slowly and it came smoothly down the center of the court. I returned it and she swung nicely but carefully, like a good beginning player. We volleyed for a little while, and she was a lot better after she got warmed up. It was fun, because even though she was still learning, she missed very few shots and we didn't have to spend all our time chasing after the ball. An hour later, it was hard to tell that she was new at the game. She was fast on her feet and had a powerful arm. We took a break, sharing some lemonade I'd brought in a thermos, and when I asked her if she had had enough for one day, she said no. I felt the same way.

Lily wanted to get the feel of a real game, so we played for eleven points with me using only my left hand. But that didn't work because she was too good. Then we played other variations, like a twenty-one-point game in which I spotted her a ten-point lead. We tried with me playing lefty for ten points and then with both hands for the rest of the game. That was better.

I told her how my father put weights on my ankles and wrists when I practiced so that when I played in a game, my hands and feet would fly when the extra weight was taken off. I showed her how to flip her wrist and shoot the ball off the tip of her fingers for a quick, sneaky side shot. And I explained how if I was tired and wanted a sure winning serve, I aimed the ball dead center at the other player, real fast and real hard, so he couldn't get it with either hand. She laughed and began calling me "Coach." "Okay, Coach, I understand, Coach," she kept saying.

A white-suited deeply tanned old man stood behind the court and watched us play for almost half an hour. Then he disappeared, but he returned ten minutes later with six or seven other old men. "Oye, misses," the man in the suit called out but we kept playing, not realizing he was talking to us.

"Oye, misses, señora y muchacha," he repeated, and when we stopped and looked up, he continued in a mixture of Spanish and English that I couldn't understand very well, his hands gesturing wildly as he talked.

I looked at Lily. "He wants us to play again," she said, "a serious game. The usual, for twenty-one points.

They want to see who will win." The old man stood there smiling and nodding, his head bobbing up and down as Lily translated.

"Why? What's the point?" I asked. "You and me are having fun. We're not competing really. Tell him no, whatever he wants, we're not interested." I shook my head no at the old men. "Tell them all to go back to their checkerboards or card games, whatever they were doing before, and leave us alone. What do they think this is?" I waved my arms at the old men. "Scram, vamanos, get out of here." I threw the ball hard against the wall and caught it, waiting for them to leave.

The old guy started talking again. "He asks what's wrong?" Lily translated. "Is la señora afraid of being beaten by a young girl? Afraid to look bad in front of a group of old men who just want a little fun?"

"Don't answer him," I said. "I don't care what he thinks, I'm not getting into it."

"Why not?" Lily asked.

"What?" I couldn't believe she was saying that. "'Cause it's ridiculous. We're practicing, that's all. You've played maybe ten, twenty times in your life and I've played hundreds of games, probably more."

"But I'm willing to have a go at it. What are you afraid of? That I might beat you?"

"You're joking. Of course not, no way."

"Then c'mon, what do you got to lose?" Lily smiled at me and I gave in.

"All right. This is stupid, but if you want to, I'll do it."

The game began and I let Lily serve first. Out of the corner of my eye I saw some ten- and twenty-dollar bills passing between the old man and the others. They just wanted to see who would win. Right! What bullshit, I thought to myself. He worked out some stupid scam and was setting up bets, not small ones either. I assumed they'd probably gamble some small change on the game, for fun, but not like this. I didn't like it one bit and wanted to end the game as fast as possible. I decided to play hard, but I didn't want to make Lily look too bad. Lily was playing to win. Somewhere in her mixed-up head I guess she thought she had a chance and was playing for real. I didn't hit any killers but I didn't miss a shot either. Steadily I racked up points while Lily made only an occasional point off me when I got sloppy. Lily got madder and madder. She cursed and spit and twice, after she missed a shot, picked up a soda can, bent it in half, and bit into it.

"Let's stop," I finally said, but she wouldn't answer me, just stood in position until I served. The game ended twenty-one to four, and Lily walked off, furious, while the old man in the white suit collected his money.

I called to Lily as I retied my sneaker but she was quick, and before I finished she was up the ramp and out of the park. I ran after her and grabbed her by the shoulder. "Listen, you little princess," I said, "who do you think you are?" She turned and I thought she was going to hit me. I went on talking. "You wanted to prove that you were a hot shot, that's fine, but that's later, after you've practiced a few more months." She started to pull away but I held tight. "Look, I haven't played in a long time, but when I was younger I trained, really trained, for years. My father entered me in every tournament in the city. And I told you all that before we started. But you thought that maybe you were such a good athlete and I was so rusty that you could wipe the court with me anyway. Well, not yet you can't! And the old guy knew it. He set us up. The bastard got everybody to bet on la muchacha while he bet on la señora. He watched us earlier, so he knew." I smiled at her and took a chance touching her hair, but she wouldn't look up. "You look like an eighteen-year-old athlete, and look at these." I pointed to my thin calves. "I look more like a dancer, not a handball player." I thought she almost smiled. "Lily, you were the sure thing." Lily kept her head down, but I knew she was listening. "And who gives a shit, anyway? I'll teach you to play, and with practice you'll be a lot better than me soon. Big deal."

Something I said must've got through, because all the air seemed to go out of her and then she smiled that outrageous smile of hers. "So you're going to teach me to be better than the best, huh, Coach?" she asked.

"It won't take long."

Lily mumbled something I couldn't understand except for the word *sucre*. "What'd you say?" I asked.

"I said you're a piece of sugar," she said softly and took my hand.

"What a surprise!" a voice called out. "I was looking for one pretty woman and I found two." Lily and I both turned to see Pudgy heading down the street toward us, grinning and whistling. He gave first Lily and then me a kiss on the cheek and then told me that I'd gotten a phone call and that it sounded important, so he came to tell me.

"Someone named Chris. Said to call as soon as possible, and that you had the number." I asked Lily to come up to the house but she said no, some other time, she was going home to take a long cold shower. Pudgy seemed happier, whistling and humming the whole way home.

. . .

"S&R Supermarket."

"Chris, it's Anna. My friend Pudgy said you called."

"How are you?" Chris asked.

"Fine."

"I miss you, Anna."

"What?"

"I miss you. I can't stop thinking about you."

"Oh. Oh, thanks. Me too."

"I thought I could stop by after work."

"Pudgy said you sounded like there was an emergency."

"I guess it is to me."

"Chris, I can't see you. Pudgy is here and Nick and Joey are coming home soon."

"So?"

"So that's all."

"I'd like to meet them."

"But who should I say you are?"

"Your friend Chris."

"Oh, I guess. Okay, sure."

"I'll pick up a pizza for dinner. How does that sound? Does everybody like pizza?"

"Of course."

Chris showed up with two pizzas, flowers for me, and two Matchbox trucks for the boys. For just a second I thought about Baby Huey and how he never wanted to meet Nick and Joey.

"Chris, these two wild boys are Nick and Joey. Nick is the big guy dressed in blue and the smaller one in the Mets T-shirt is Joey."

Before Chris could give us the presents or say anything, Joey was pulling on my hand asking, "Am I always going to be smaller than Nick?"

"Nick is older, Joey, that's why he's bigger," I said. "But you're both going to grow and grow until you're big men. And when you're men, you might be the same size as Nick, or you might even be bigger." I helped Chris with the pizzas.

"Or *I* might be bigger," Nick added.

"That's right," I said. "We won't know who'll be bigger until you both stop growing. But, Joey, you're four years old and Nick is six. You're both tall, handsome boys."

"When we were in your stomach, did you know we would be tall, handsome boys?" Joey asked.

I laughed. "Yes, I guess so. Yes, I knew you'd be two of the handsomest boys in the world."

Chris held out the flowers to me and handed the trucks to the boys. I put the flowers in water and set out napkins and drinks.

"Thanks," Nick said shyly to Chris. "And this is Pudgy," he said as he climbed into Pudgy's lap. Chris leaned over and he and Pudgy shook hands.

Joey asked Chris did he know I drove a truck and Chris said yes and took a seat near Joey. He told the boys he was a manager of a supermarket and that I drove up to his store every day in my truck. Then Chris told us about a friend of his named Wayne, from when he was a kid, who drove one of those big trucks with lots of wheels on each side. "When I was just like you guys, maybe five or six years old . . ."

"I'm four," Joey said, holding up five fingers.

"Yeah, well, I was probably a bit older. Anyway, my friend Wayne would drive up to our house, open the back door of the truck, and I'd be so glad to see him I'd run from one end of the truck to the other, laughing, and then go flying out the back door into Wayne's arms.''

Joey stuck one of his feet in the air. ''I have fast sneakers too. Pudgy bought them for me. I could run fast in the truck just like you.'' Pudgy bent over and kissed the top of Joey's head.

Chris told us how in the summer, Wayne would come and take him cross-country in that big truck for weeks on end.

''Without your mom?'' Nick asked, his eyes opening wide.

Chris nodded. ''Yup, just me and Wayne. And if it was night and I'd fallen asleep, when we came to a big hill Wayne would wake me up. Then I'd sit there holding my eyes open with my fingers as the truck climbed up, up, up to the top of the hill and then went speeding down to the bottom. My stomach went up and down with those big hills and I loved it. At the bottom of the hill I'd fall back to sleep again.''

''Me too. That's what I would do,'' Joey said, shaking his head up and down as he pulled all the cheese off the pizza. He mostly liked the crust.

After dinner, Pudgy put the boys in the bath and I walked Chris to his car. He was parked down on 177th Street near the highway. I wanted to get back to help Pudgy with Nick and Joey, but Chris kept asking me to sit for a while, so I slid in next to him. ''Nick and Joey are great boys,'' he said, ''and Pudgy's nice too.''

''I'm glad. They liked you, I could tell.''

''I can't believe that Jesse will be as big as Nick and Joey one day. I hope he'll be as nice.''

''Of course he will, he's your son. He'll be especially nice like his dad.''

"I feel like I'm still getting used to the idea of being a dad. You know, I always wanted a son and sometimes I can't believe I'm that lucky and that he's really mine. But everybody says he looks just like me. Anna—'' Chris stopped and took my face between his hands and kissed me softly for a long time. Then he sat there touching my face as he talked. "I don't know what to do about us. It's only been one day since we were together but it feels like months. I drove home last night, played with Jesse in the morning, worked all day and the whole time, in the back of my mind, I'm thinking about you. Wanting to see you, to touch you, to love you. I keep picturing your face, how sweet you smell, your breasts."

"Me too. Only I'm not thinking about your breasts."

"Very funny." He kissed me hard and I ran my tongue around his lips and into his nostrils. He laughed and pulled up my T-shirt and kissed each of my breasts. Then I climbed on top of him, facing him and pulled back to look at him. I liked his face. It was round with bright eyes, and when he smiled he had a slightly crooked tooth in front that made him look mischievous.

"Your face makes me laugh," I told him.

"Good. I'm glad it doesn't make you cry."

"You've got a nice face, a sweet, open face." I stopped because he planted his lips around my lips and I couldn't talk. He pulled my shirt up again.

"I'm all dirty and smelly."

"That's the best." He pushed his hand into my pants, under the underwear, and played with me, rubbing, pinching softly until I found myself making noises and asking for more. He tried to pull my pants off but I laughed and wouldn't let him. "No way am I going to do this in a car," I said.

"But we're almost at the highway. No one will see us."

"No!" I yelled, but I was laughing so hard that he almost got my pants off. Then I said seriously, "I can't do it here." But I didn't want to stop, so I unzipped his zipper and took it out. He must've been really excited, because it was huge, standing straight up, pushing to come out. Chris sighed as I started to rub gently and I didn't stop until he came. Before he left, he told me he loved me. Nobody ever told me that except for Nick and Joey.

"Mike Dupree from Merrick," the voice said. "I spoke to you yesterday." It was nine o'clock and I'd fallen asleep with the radio on. "I'm calling because I just spoke to Teddy the Greek Junior and Teddy told me to make sure I had your side of the story before I set up the meeting between your manager and you and your union rep, which is me for now. Teddy Junior said there had to be a reason for you going off the handle like that. He said for me to find out. So that's why I'm calling."

So I told him about the broken lock and the four guys and the robbery. Mike listened and then hung up and called back fifteen minutes later. He said for me to report to work tomorrow as usual, I was reinstated and the meeting was off. He reminded me that there was a union meeting in the afternoon and said that Teddy Junior would be there, I should be sure to attend.

"But why didn't you tell me about the robbery last night, when I first called?" Mike asked.

" 'Cause I needed a day off and I wanted the meeting with Jed and a union rep," I said. "Without a meeting, Jed will never bother to have my lock fixed and I'll be back where I started, with nothing to prevent them from breaking in a second time.''

''Anna, c'mere. Look at this and tell me if I'm crazy?'' Baby Huey took my hand and dragged me over to his truck. I had just come in off the route, my first day back since the robbery. It hadn't been bad. Work as usual, nothing eventful except for a problem with my truck, which was scary when it happened, but it was being fixed now. Baby Huey and Jimmy were going to drive me to the union meeting, and they'd probably been hanging around, waiting, for the last hour or so. ''Look,'' Baby Huey said, ''stand back a little. That's it, stay right there. Now, does she tip to one side?''

I was about fifteen feet from the back of his truck, dead center. I closed one eye, then the other. I moved off to the side and looked from there. Then I bent down and looked underneath. ''What is it? The shock? You're right, it slants to one side.''

''Nah, it's the tires. That son of a crazy man Gus gave me new tires.''

''Well, that's good, all your tires should've been trashed months ago.''

''Yeah, that's the truth. But something's wrong here. I don't get it. Can't trust Gus for nothing.''

Jimmy came out of the office stuffing a pile of bills into his back pocket. ''Jimmy, come over here and take a look,'' Baby Huey yelled. ''Tell me what you think. Gus put on new tires but I'd swear that now she's lower on one side.''

''Gus does great work on cars,'' Jimmy said as he walked around Baby Huey's truck. ''Did a great job fixing my brakes and charged less than my regular mechanic. But he hates working on the trucks." Jimmy kicked each tire with the heel of his boot. "Yup," he said when he was finished. "He gave you new tires, but only two, and he put them both on the same side. They're smaller. That's why the truck tilts to the left."

"I'm gonna make that cheap bastard give me another two or I'll take them off his Corvette."

"It's not Gus, it's Jed that's cheap. Jed's the one that decides how money is spent around here," Jimmy said, "and HomeMade set it up. HomeMade gives the managers extra vacation days when they cut the depot's budget. They're the ones giving us these pieces of junk in the first place." Jimmy gave the tires one more kick and then turned to me. "By the way, Anna," Jimmy asked, "why was Jed driving the spare yesterday? He pulled your route when you were out but he wasn't driving your truck."

"What? This is the first I heard about it." I wondered if it had anything to do with what happened with my truck today.

"That was 'cause of her gears," Baby Huey said. "Jed went out in Anna's truck in the morning, but her gears were slipping, so he brought the truck back in the late morning and used the spare for the rest of the day. That's what Gus told me when he gave me the new tires yesterday."

I must've been standing there with my mouth open, because Jimmy ran over and put his arm around my shoulders asking, "What is it? You look like you're going to choke or cry or something. Are you sick?"

"They let me drive it today and it wasn't fixed," I said. I could hardly get the words out.

"What're you talking about?" Baby Huey said, but

then he must've understood. "They didn't! Jed *had* to report it. Gus would've fixed it last night. Anna, they wouldn't have let you drive it out today without it being fixed."

I shook my head. "This afternoon I was parked on a hill. My emergency brake barely works, so I put the truck in second, knowing that would hold it. It was a steep hill. I went in to check the store, and when I came out, my truck was going down the hill at about ten miles an hour and picking up speed as it went. I'd been double-parked, so no cars were in the way, but it was heading down a busy street. I started to scream, really scream, 'Please, somebody help, stop my truck. There's no driver. Please, somebody stop my truck.' A man getting into his car heard me and chased the truck. Luckily it was a nice day and I'd left my door open. He jumped in, got hold of the wheel, and put on the brake. Nobody was hurt and nothing damaged. I drove straight back."

"Jed probably forgot to write it up and Gus didn't remember to fix it since there was no report on it," Jimmy said.

I went in to wash up and change for the meeting. I made sure to write up the problem with the gears, and I gave the report to Gus and left a copy on Jed's desk.

"Are these meetings always in the same place?" I asked. Baby Huey was driving, and I was squeezed between him and Jimmy in the front seat.

Jimmy slapped my hand because I was biting my nails. "How can someone get all dolled up like this," he said to Baby Huey, "and then sit there biting her nails like a baby?" I'd put my black HomeMade shirt and pants and work boots in an overnight bag and had changed into a short black skirt with a wide belt, a tight pink turtleneck, and heels. Usually these meetings consisted of fifty to a hundred men and me. So I liked to wear something nice and have them fuss over me when I walked in. "And the answer is yes," Jimmy said, "the union meetings are always in O'Reilly's, the neighborhood dive."

"It's such a nasty little place, so dark and dirty, and it stinks of beer."

"O'Reilly's is used to handling a hundred drunk Teamsters, it's cheap, and no one has ever suggested another place. That's not nothing."

"It's not something either. What's this meeting about?" I asked.

"All the meetings are the same. If there's an issue, we don't usually know about it until later. The men come in, say hi, gab and drink a while, and by the time anything serious comes up, the men are too wrecked to think straight."

"Then why do we go?"

"I'm not sure. 'Cause it's where we get together with the other drivers, maybe in case something does happen. 'Cause it's better than not going. I don't know."

"You two are giving me a headache," Baby Huey complained.

Mario and Little Dominic were standing outside, under the O'REILLY's sign, which was white lettering on a dark-green background with a shamrock on either side.

"Why'd Mario come back to work so soon?" I asked. "I figured he'd be out another few days at least." The last I heard, Mario had been in the hospital for the second time in two months. Something to do with his eyes and being dizzy. I think they said it was vertigo.

"His wife's mental," Baby Huey said and touched his head. "Easier coming to work than having to stay home with that all day."

"Everybody inside, old man?" Jimmy asked Mario, waving hi to Little Dominic as we headed for the door. "Junior here yet?" Teddy the Greek Senior was also in the Teamsters, so the Teddy we knew was called Junior.

Little Dominic started giggling but it was Mario who answered. "Are you kidding? When was Junior ever less than an hour late? Waits till we've had at least three beers before he shows his face." Mario and Little Dominic followed us into O'Reilly's.

I took off my sunglasses the minute I stepped through the door, the place was so dark. Men in HomeMade uniforms lined the bar, surrounded the pool table, and stood around talking and drinking in small groups. I wanted to drop off my bag, so I headed for the big room in the back where the meetings were held. A group of guys from Douglaston were straddling some chairs, listening to a big-mouthed guy they called Bobo. Bobo was describing a girl on his route named Ruth who gave him blowjobs instead of cash for the cake he delivered. Two or three wolf whistles came blasting my way and Bobo came running over and put his arm across my shoulders as I dropped my bag under a seat. "Look what just blew in from Knickerbocker Avenue," he said, "our favorite Home-Made Choco." I slipped out from under his arm, told them I'd see them all later, and joined Mario at the pinball machine.

"Play you a game, mister?" I asked. Mario smiled, his cigarette dangling from his lips and said, "Sure." I put my quarters in and we started to play. Two teenage girls in tight jeans had gotten Jimmy and Baby Huey to play pool with them and they were cueing up.

Mike Dupree from Merrick showed up fifteen minutes later. "Hi, folks, everybody here?" Mike Dupree was the kind of guy you never noticed. Fair-haired and pale, nothing to look at, nothing to remember. The only reason he had the job as union rep was because he wanted it and because he made no trouble for the union or management.

"We've been waiting," Mario said, "but you're the only union rep so far."

"Yeah," Mike Dupree said, "we'll be getting started as soon as Teddy Junior gets in. He was at a meeting in Buffalo. Didn't think he'd make it this time, had such a tight schedule. But he wouldn't stand you up. Always gets here for you guys. How're you doing, Wally?" he called out to the route rider from Knickerbocker Avenue. "What happened to the beard? Wife get tired of sleeping with a broom? Baby Huey! Jimmy! Robbing the cradle again? Don't you guys ever give it a break?"

Mario looked up from the pinball machine. "How late's Junior gonna be?" he said over his shoulder to Mike.

"Soon. Very soon. Give him another half hour. That should do it."

"Waiter," Mario called out, taking out some singles, "two beers, that what you drinking, Anna?" I nodded. The waiter brought over the two beers but put his hand up when Mario went to pay.

"On the house," the waiter said and Mario thanked him. It was happy hour, and Mario had this round coming to him.

After one more beer, Teddy Junior showed up and all of us stopped what we were doing and followed him into the meeting room. I sat between Baby Huey and Mario. The rest of the guys from Knickerbocker Avenue were spread out on both sides.

Mike Dupree from Merrick started the meeting by reminding us that elections were coming up. "You'll get information and ballots in the mail. Put a mark in the box and send them back. Don't forget how to spell my name when you see the box for Treasurer. We never gave you any trouble, so you should think about keeping us again for another term." He asked if there was anything anyone wanted to bring up that wasn't on the agenda. If not, they would begin with the first item.

Jimmy raised his hand and asked when they were going to do something about the trucks. Then Mario, who was sitting next to me, yelled out, "That's right, when is something going to be done about the death traps we drive around in?" I was glad we were finally saying something. I still felt nervous about what had happened that afternoon with my truck. I knew that if my truck had hit someone, it wouldn't have been my fault, but I might've been blamed for it. And I know I would've blamed myself, thinking that there must've been something I could've done to prevent it.

Mike Dupree answered. "Now, fellas, I don't think we want to waste our time complaining about trucks again. This has been going on for as long as I've been in the Teamsters, and that's at least eight years. It's not the way to go unless you have something new to add."

Mario stood up. "Look, you're right, we complain and nobody does nothing about it. It goes on year after year. So maybe we shouldn't bore you with it again to-night. But I got a suggestion this time. I suggest that tonight each depot should write up a list of complaints and make copies of it. Then we send one to the union, one to the company, and I'll keep one, so we have a record of it.''

Jimmy stood up and clapped and Baby Huey and Little Dominic and the rest of the Knickerbocker Avenue drivers joined in.

"But—" Mike Dupree just got the one word out before Mario stopped him.

"I'm not done," Mario said. "I think this is a good idea. And I'll appoint myself official tracker. Every time management fixes something on the list, I cross it off. Maybe we can even have Andrea, the union secretary, write up a letter that we send out after three months enquiring into how come they haven't fixed such-and-such like they promised they would." Again, all of Knickerbocker Avenue stood up and whistled and clapped and hooted. The fact was, it was Knickerbocker Avenue that had the worst trucks. Almost all the trucks at Merrick, HomeMade's "country club," were brand new, and half of them were diesel. Douglaston got most of the hand-me-downs, still in good condition, from Merrick and the suburban depots. It was only at Knickerbocker Avenue that they dumped all the trucks that no other depot wanted. The next stop for our trucks was the junkyard.

When Teddy Junior got up to talk, everybody quieted down. Teddy the Greek Senior was supposedly the head of the Teamsters, but he was never seen at any of the union meetings anymore, and everyone knew that Teddy Junior was the real power in the union these days. Teddy Junior was nothing like Mike Dupree. Teddy Junior was noticed wherever he went. I'd seen his father, Teddy Senior, a short, dark, ugly runt of a man, only once. But he must've married a beautiful Scandinavian type, because his son, Teddy Junior, was a tall, lean, blond, kind of rough-cut college type. He was more than attractive, and a great dresser—the Italian silk ties he wore to meetings must have cost over a hundred bucks.

"I know you mean well, Martin."

"Mario, not Martin."

"Well, then, Mario it is," and he gave him a big smile. "And I want you to know that I personally look at every complaint that comes to my office. So please don't feel that I don't think this is a good idea. It is, it's a great idea. It's just not practical. You know that Andrea, my secretary, is swamped with work. Now if you start sending in these lists, she'll probably quit on me the next day. Then where would we be? And why? Because it's not the solution. The real problem is lack of communication. Talk to your shop steward. He's not hard to talk to. If we have better communication, we'll have better trucks."

"We don't have a shop steward," Mario said. "And even if we did, the shop steward can't do nothing if he doesn't get backed up."

"But we always back up our stewards." Junior stopped and rubbed his eyes and sighed, probably to make sure we knew how tired he was. "When have any of you come to me, or to my father for that matter, and not been listened to? The problem is not one of backing up, and I'm not referring to trucks backing up"—he laughed a little at his own joke—"that's not an area of concern. The place that I see there being a—"

"Wait a second." Mario had just sat down but now he was out of his seat again.

"Martin—excuse me, I mean Mario—let me go on. I'll give you time to respond later. I'm trying to clear something up. Now it's true that over the years the problem with the trucks has come up again and again. But the fact is that every moment the trucks are aging, so as time goes on, the trucks break down . . .''

Jimmy got up and smashed his fist on the back of the empty seat in front of him. "Shut up for a second," he yelled, "we know all that. We're trying now to figure a new way to end this problem with the trucks."

"I know," Teddy Junior said, that same understanding smile plastered across his face, "we're together in that. We're all working on solutions. But there's not just one solution or answer. Because the problem itself is multifaceted. Consider the problem of parts. Now, parts come from all over the world, so it's not just America we're dealing with. I remember one driver had to wait eight weeks for a part to be shipped—"

"Excuse me," I called out and stood up. "Excuse me, you, Mister Teamsters Representative for the men and women in this room." I was pointing at Teddy Junior. "I'm not sure you heard Mario or Jimmy. And look at me when I'm talking to you, 'cause I don't think you hear or see anybody in this room. To you we're all just one big group of HomeMade drivers to practice your smooth talk on. You walk all over us, you don't walk with us, and we don't like that."

Teddy Junior laughed. "Anna, how can you think that any man in this room doesn't see you? The fact that you're here in that appealing little sweater, and not in your HomeMade uniform, makes it impossible for any man, who calls himself a man, to ignore you." Guys hooted and laughed.

I waited for them to quiet down and then I went on speaking. "Do you have any idea what it's like to drive a truck that may either kill you or make you a killer at any time, simply because it needs to be fixed?" I asked.

"Yes, I think I do," he said, "but I'm not sure I see your point. And now, even though I find it hard to take my eyes off you, I must, in order to get on with this meeting. Wally, is that your hand I see raised. Yes?"

I covered my breasts. "You bastard," I said softly, but I sat down.

Wally stood up but then slid back into his seat when Teddy started talking again. "Before Wally starts," Teddy Junior said, "I just want to make clear that I'm not ignoring anyone. I'm trying to present the many sides of the dilemma that I have to come to grips with. It's not just a problem-and-answer situation. If it was, we would have solved it years ago, in my father's day."

"But *I'm* suggesting that we take some practical steps toward change," Mario said.

"I don't agree with you," Teddy interrupted. "I consider your idea unreasonable. It's the practicalities that tie us up."

"What can you do for us *now*?" someone yelled from the back. "Say nothing if that's what you're leading up to."

"But the answer's never nothing. The answer depends on how much you want and how soon, and that's where the discrepancy is. Now I have to work with you guys and with management, and that's no picnic."

"Get to the point—any point," another voice yelled from the back.

"I would prefer you to raise your hand when you want to say something so I can see who I have to respond to. This is a bar but it's supposed to be a meeting of the Bakery Drivers Local of the Teamsters, not a free-for-all."

Teddy Junior paused and then went on, "Now that we've cleared the air—"

"I've been listening to this shit for years," Mario said. "I need another drink," and he walked out. I left right after him with Baby Huey following.

Mario ordered beers all around but I told him I had enough and asked for a glass of water. "You should've been around when his father was running the show," Mario said, shaking his head back and forth. "Teddy Senior was just as smooth but even meaner. You, me, and Jimmy would've been out of our jobs tomorrow if we'd said even that much to him. We should count ourselves lucky."

"And what about the new contract coming up?" I said, "I always heard that Hearthland and HomeMade stick together, and if things can't be worked out they go out together. But this time Hearthland drivers are getting what they asked for and HomeMade drivers are getting nothing. And the union is saying to split, let only HomeMade go out on strike. I thought Hearthland and HomeMade never split."

"Yeah, well, Mike Dupree's kid works for Hearthland and so do half the Greeks. They don't want their family out on the street. The union sides with management whenever it benefits them or their family. If they have to split us to take care of family, you know they will."

Just then Teddy the Greek Junior came out. His shirt was open an extra button, his tie unknotted and hanging down, and two medals hanging from a gold chain were half-hidden in the curls of his chest hair. "When she was good she was very very good, and when she was bad she was horrid," Teddy Junior recited softly in my ear.

"Meeting over?" I asked.

"No, just beginning. Dupree's running it, I have to go to the john. What's the matter, Anna? Why did you get angry with me? You know I have your interest at heart."

I didn't look up. "What heart?"

"Anna, honey, don't be like that. You should be nice to me. In a few years I'm going to be mayor of this city, and then what will you do if you need a favor? Besides which, I think you owe me a little something already. It's twice now that I got you out of trouble, but who's counting?"

I turned to Teddy Junior. "You got it wrong. I owe you nothing, not now, not ever. That time I had trouble with the storeowner that was nasty with me and I danced on those pies, if you weren't around, they still would've reinstated me once they knew the facts." I wanted to get everything straight between me and Teddy. "And now with the robbery. You've done nothing really. I'm still out there every day listening for the sound of the back door rolling up, knowing that at any time they can come back for me. My life is as much in danger as it was before, maybe more. You can help me in the simplest way, by making sure Jed has my locks fixed. It's as easy as that. But it's not a big enough issue for you, so you don't bother."

Teddy Junior held his arms out. "C'mon, Anna, don't act like this. Let bygones be bygones."

"No, Teddy, 'cause if you don't do for us, then your words are meaningless, they're nothing. These meetings are bullshit. I don't know how many I've been to, 'cause I don't remember one from the next, they're all the same and nothing ever gets resolved. The men get drunk, you put in an appearance and roll right over us with your smart talk, and the end result is, nothing ever changes. I've had enough," I said, turning my back on him, "why don't you go zip down your fly and take care of the important business in your life?"

He walked toward the men's room without answering.

I picked up my glass of water and threw it against the wall. The owner of the bar came over with a broom and dustpan and started sweeping up the broken glass. "I'm sorry," I mumbled. Baby Huey put a ten-dollar bill in the owner's hand. Then he said he was going back to get my bag and told me to wait outside, he would meet me by the car.

I was waiting by the entrance to the parking lot when Baby Huey came out. He took my hand and led me to his car.

"Mario sure had a fire under his tail tonight," Baby Huey said. "Didn't he? Probably never talked that much in his life."

"I guess."

"That's 'cause the rumor is they're messing with his route. But let's not talk about work anymore, Anna. Let's you and me take a drive over to the bridge and fool around, so we can forget all this bullshit. We can come back later to pick up Jimmy."

"Uh-uh."

"C'mon, we need to get this union bullshit out of our systems."

For the last two days, I'd been thinking of talking to Baby Huey but I kept putting it off, not knowing how to do it. I guess now it was time, time for me to say what I had to say. "It's over, Ernesto. It's over for me and you."

"What are you talking about? Don't talk silly. You're just upset now. Me and you do good together. We been pals for almost a year. And you and me turn each other on. We got a lot going for us." He was smiling at me, trying to get me to smile back.

"That's not enough anymore," I said. "I want things to be different, I don't know, sweeter, more exciting, something. I want someone who's crazy about me, who thinks I'm wonderful and funny and pretty. Someone who can't get enough of me. We know each other for over a year, but in all that time did you ever feel like you were crazy about me? Did you ever think that maybe you loved me, even a little?"

"Not like that, no, but that's not the point. What you and me have is good. Maybe I'm not in love with you, but I look out for you."

"I need more than that. I'm tired of settling for nice and nothing more."

"What's this serious stuff all of a sudden? I never said I was that kind of guy. I never promised you nothing like that. You're not the type I get serious with. I go for girls that are small, kind of petite and feminine-looking."

"I remember."

"Why now? What happened? 'Cause of this stupid meeting? 'Cause of your truck today, or 'cause I won't meet your kids? What is it?"

I looked straight at him. "You don't care about me. I don't know if you care about anyone and I don't think you ever will. There's nothing under your shirt where your heart should be."

He started backing away, shaking his head no. "Shut up, Anna. You don't know anything about me. How do you know what I care about?"

"Oh, I know. I know that the only thing you care about is yourself, Ernesto Salazar." He came closer, his jaw out, his eye twitching slightly.

"Shut up, Anna."

"Yeah, Ernesto Salazar and a big empty house with

clean sheets and nobody to mess them up. That's what you want out of life.''

"You stop talking like that, you hear me?''

"No one to make you feel anything, to mess up your spotless little home.'' Baby Huey raised his hand and I could almost feel the sting of the slap across my cheek, but he thought better of it and put his hand down and squeezed it between his thighs.

I kept going at him, yelling, "No come on the sheets, no dog shit, no dirty diapers.'' He put his hand over my mouth and my words came out jumbled. I pushed his hand away, laughing. "You can't stop me. Yeah, no one to ever tell you no. You just want to fuck me and leave me, like a prostitute, only I don't get any money for it, or nothing much else for that matter.''

"No, Anna, no,'' he tried to clamp his hand over my mouth again and somehow his fingernail tore at my lip and ripped a chunk of skin off near the top. It hung there, the blood running down onto my chin, over my shirt.

Baby Huey stepped away and stood there shaking, saying, "I'm sorry. I never hurt a woman before. I never even hit one. I'm not that kind of man. I'm sorry. I don't know what came over me. I'm not like that. I didn't mean to hurt you. Please, I'm sorry.''

"It's okay,'' I said, moving against the car and taking him in my arms. I was surprised he even let me hold him. "It's okay, it's not your fault.'' I wrapped my arms around him tightly and rocked him gently back and forth. "It's okay,'' I said over and over again. "I pushed you into it. I guess I'm that kind of woman.''

Jimmy and the Arabs

MY MOTHER KEPT HER MONEY rolled in flowered handkerchiefs pinned into the bosom of her blouses and housedresses. She hid at least three of these money rolls in different pieces of clothing. When she went shopping, she'd reach between her breasts, unpin the handkerchief, and pull out as many bills as she needed, then tie it up and repin it. The blouses and dresses with the rolls of bills hung in the closet when my mother wasn't wearing them. Somehow we all knew that she never kept track of how much money she had in each roll.

My allowance was nothing, a dollar a week. And if my friend Carmela showed up on allowance day, my father gave her a dollar too and she'd say he was a great guy. A dollar a week wasn't enough for a nine- or ten-year-old and lasted only a day or two. So without much thought, I'd go to one of my mother's money rolls, secured by a large safety pin to the bosom of the dress she wore the day before, and take as much as I needed. I usually took singles, but if I found four or five tens, I'd take one of those too if I thought she wouldn't miss it. Only once or twice that I can remember did she pull me and my brothers into her room, look carefully at each of our faces, and ask whether we took any of her money. We'd silently shrug and shake our heads no. I wasn't really scared of getting caught, because it didn't feel wrong to take it. It was only much later, as an adult, that I gave a name to what I did, that I knew that I had stolen from my mother and that others would call it a crime.

One day around the holidays, Jimmy didn't come back to the depot until late. I had a dentist's appointment at four and decided to wait the two hours in the depot rather than sit in the dentist's office, which was only one stop away on the train. Baby Huey had been pacing up and down the office for the last few hours, waiting for Jimmy to get off the route so they could go home together. When Jimmy finally came in he was a mess. One side of his face was covered with blood and it looked like part of his eye was hanging out. His clothes were ripped and muddy and he had a hard time standing. Baby Huey and Jed supported him under the arms, put him in a company van, and took him to the hospital.

"Don't tell Mimi," Jimmy cried. "Make up anything but don't tell her what really happened." Baby Huey had me call Mimi and tell her that Jimmy wasn't feeling well and was staying at his mother's house in Brooklyn. Then I called Jimmy's mother and told her what to say if Mimi called. To his mother I told the truth. Jimmy's mother had five boys, and Jimmy always said you could tell her anything, since she always expected the worst anyway. And it was true. She took it like a trooper, asked me to give him a kiss for her and to tell him she'd say a prayer to Buddha for him.

I didn't know how Jimmy got hurt, if he got mugged or if it was one of his girlfriends' husbands paying him back. But Baby Huey called me that night and gave me the details. He said Jimmy was going to be okay, and that even though he had stitches halfway around his eye, the eye wasn't seriously damaged. Jimmy also had three broken ribs and a fractured ankle, and the doctors were checking for possible brain damage. What happened was that the owners of a Foodcity had been watching him for months. When they found he'd been ripping them off for at least fifty bucks a week, they hired someone to do a job on him. I remember once watching Jimmy pocket a pile of bills at the end of a day. It wasn't a payday so I figured he must be taking good tips and asked him why he cheated when it was so risky. He said, "How can you not steal from somebody that holds your bill upside down and counts 'five, ten, fifty, twenty-five, forty'?"

HomeMade Cakes fired Jimmy while he was still in the hospital. Foodcity was such a big account, it was either fire Jimmy or lose the store. But for a driver like Jimmy, who'd been with the company for years, we all figured it wasn't really the end. They'd keep him out of work without pay just long enough to make good on his loss of salary and to scare him into thinking that maybe this time he'd be out of work for good. Then they'd hire him back when things calmed down and put him on a route in a neighborhood far away from the one where he had the trouble.

Baby Huey, Mario, and Little Dominic were driving to the hospital the next day to visit Jimmy and asked did I want to come along. I looked at Baby Huey to see if it was okay with him and he nodded yes, so I went. They went in separate cars and I rode with Little Dominic.

We found Jimmy in great spirits. "Hey, this is like having all my brothers show up, only better."

"Do I look like one of your brothers?" I asked.

"Not a bit, but I don't have a sister."

"How are those crazy brothers of yours?" Baby Huey asked. "Any of them been to visit yet?"

"Nah. When I spoke to my mom I asked her not to tell any of the family. None of them live nearby anyway."

"Everyone in Jimmy's family is nuts, even the cousins," Baby Huey said, then slapped his knee and smiled. "I'll never forget what you told me about your brothers and the tennis ball, remember?" Jimmy nodded. "Tell these guys about that time, Jimmy, go ahead." Baby Huey sat there grinning.

"That was such a dumb prank," Jimmy said. "I was maybe nine or ten, but my brothers, they were older. It was a hot summer day and they had nothing to do and were looking for some fun. Everybody else was at the beach, or at a pool, but they were being punished and I had a cold. We made peanut butter and jelly sandwiches for lunch and were sitting in the sun eating them when one of my brothers, I don't remember which one, came up with this idea. I was just finishing my sandwich and I watched as my brothers poured gasoline over a tennis ball and then put a match to it. They played a game of king queen with the burning ball, hitting it against the garage wall and shaking their hands in between shots to cool them off. Then somehow an old mattress caught fire, and before we could put it out, the whole garage went up in flames. One of the neighbors called the fire department. My father was alive back then, and when he came home and saw the garage all black and soaked with water, he took a stick and beat them hard."

Baby Huey laughed out loud. He obviously loved Jimmy's stories about his brothers, and he begged Jimmy to tell us more. So then Jimmy told us about how they farted on each other's pillow at night. How in the winter they built a wall out of snow across their whole street, a barricade, so cars couldn't go by. Then they'd pelt the cars with snowballs and run when the drivers got out of their cars. Mario joined in, and him and Jimmy took turns telling us about when they were kids. Me, Baby Huey, and Little Dominic mostly listened and laughed. I found myself watching Baby Huey, noticing things about him that I'd never seen before and thinking about what he was really like. He never took his eyes from Jimmy's face, and seeing Baby Huey laugh so hard at every story about Jimmy and his brothers made me think about Baby Huey being the only boy in his family. It was funny how in such a short time Baby Huey was starting to look different to me, kind of dull and not so good-looking. This was the first time I'd noticed that he was heavier than I thought, and not only was his neck thick but he also had a double chin.

We left Baby Huey at the hospital with Jimmy. He wanted to stay until visiting hours were over. Jimmy's wife, Mimi, wasn't coming, because she still didn't know the truth. "I'll wait another day or two until some of the swelling goes down before I let her see me," Jimmy said. "Otherwise I'm afraid she'll get so mad, she'll knock out my other eye."

As we were leaving, Little Dominic shook Jimmy's hand and said he hoped Jimmy learned his lesson and wouldn't take chances anymore for a few extra bucks. Mario answered for Jimmy. "Stealing's part of the job," Mario said. "Ain't nobody, except you and maybe some of the new guys, that don't take tips. But the idea is to find the way that works best on the route so you don't get caught."

Baby Huey shook his head. "Maybe you were getting

sloppy, Jimmy,'' he said, ''thinking 'cause you'd been doing it for so long that nobody would catch you. You can never think like that, 'cause that's when you mess up.''

Mario drove me to the train. In the car Mario turned to me and said, ''Baby Huey was wrong. Jimmy wasn't getting sloppy, he was taking bigger chances, is why it happened. Remember about a month ago, we thought Jimmy had ulcers? He had those pains in his stomach and was losing weight and all? Ulcers, bullshit! He'd been rewriting bills in a big way and he knew what was coming before those guys from Foodcity caught him. He was a nervous wreck was what.''

Before I went to sleep that night, I thought about my fight with Baby Huey. There was still a bandage over my lip to hold it together. Maybe someday after things settled down again, when it was easier between us, I'd tell him I was sorry. He was what he was, and what he said was true. He'd never promised me more.

There was a store in Bay Ridge, behind BestMart, that was run by three brothers and did great business. It was like a minimarket and was a few blocks off my route. Originally the Douglaston depot served it, not Knickerbocker Avenue. But the owners, who were Arabs, didn't get along with their HomeMade driver and had thrown him out of their store. So one afternoon, Teddy Junior, who lived in that neighborhood, visited me on my truck and asked would I do him a favor and serve the store, the owners were friends of his. He promised that if it didn't work out, he wouldn't hold me to it. So I said sure.

The brothers were all dark and well-dressed and sleek. Not my type. And with their fast, easy smiles and sharp eyes, they weren't the kind of people I normally trust. But they treated me like most of the other storekeepers on my route, and I usually had no problem with them. All of them called me "pretty lady," that was their name for me. "Hey, pretty lady, are those trays too heavy? Want me to hold them for you? Pretty lady, you got a nice boyfriend like me that can show you a good time on the weekend? What do you do with all the money you make, pretty lady?" I'd smile and check the cake, count out what I brought in, and then wait to get paid, shaking my head yes or no to their questions but never really answering them. Once in a while one of them would come too close, whispering sexy words in my ear, resting their arm on my shoulder, or pressing against me from behind. Those times I'd move quickly, saying, "Please, don't make me bash in your skull with my tray" or "Don't make me break your wrist." Things like that.

The trouble I had with them came on a Thursday. Not big trouble exactly, but nasty enough. Thursday is payday, the one day that drivers, or salespersons, whatever they want to call us, don't take checks. We get paid that day and use the money we collect from the stores to cash our own paychecks. Most stores accept checks from their customers since it encourages them to shop there. But many store owners don't want to bother taking them to the bank, so they pass them on in payment to their drivers. Now, our company policy is not to accept checks, but no driver follows that rule. We all take checks, except on payday.

That Thursday morning, I passed the Thomas's English Muffin man as he was leaving the minimarket. He pulled me aside to talk for a minute. "They're gonna try to pass some checks off on you," he said. "They already tried it with me but I turned them down. They know it's payday. Don't let them push you around.''

''I won't,'' I said and went inside.

As I passed the first register, the oldest brother waved a handful of checks at me, saying, ''Got some checks for you, pretty lady. We need you to help us out with them today.''

''Sorry,'' I said, smiling as friendly as I could, ''it's payday. I can't take checks on Thursdays. Any other day, I'd be glad to.''

''We'll see,'' he said.

''No, look, I just can't,'' I said, ''not today.'' The night before, I'd promised Nick and Joey that I'd pick them up after school today and take them to buy new shoes, so I needed my cash. I smiled again, and went to work on the order. This store took a lot of cake, two loads, which was seven trays in all, and it was more than twenty minutes later that I finished packing everything out. I put it all on the first counter for the oldest brother to tally up. Five, ten, fifteen, twenty Chocos; five, ten chocolate cupcakes; five, ten, fifteen, twenty, twenty-five pies; four variety doughnuts; and so on. I picked up half the trays and headed down the cake aisle, and when I returned for the rest, he said, ''I have a nice fat check to pay you with.'' He stood there grinning, pulling on the ends of it to smooth out the wrinkles.

''No checks,'' I said again.

This time as I walked toward the HomeMade Cakes stand he followed me, and when I turned to face him, he said, very calmly, ''Look, bitch, you will take checks any day I tell you to. You will finish your business here and put away the cake or I will slap your pretty face. Is that clear?

I'm the boss, and you,'' he stuck his finger in my face, "you will do what I say.'' He stood there watching me, waiting to see what I'd do. I felt my face go red, and very carefully I set the trays down and packed out the cake, very slowly, watching him out of the corner of my eye. He stood there doing nothing, simply watching, and when I was done he accompanied me to the first counter, where I waited for him to pay me. He smiled as he handed me two checks, saying, "Now you are a good girl.'' I checked that they were the right amount and put them in my pocket.

I started to leave, but just as the magnetic doors slid open in front of me, I dropped all but two trays, and those two I threw like Frisbees straight at his register. The first one crashed into the register and the other smashed into four or five bottles standing on the counter. Without looking back, I ran to my truck, started the motor, and pulled out as fast as I could. But not fast enough, because the brother leaped onto the side of the truck, one foot on the step, holding on to my big sideview mirror. The youngest brother came racing out right after him and chased me from the other side. I hit the gas and the truck shot forward, then I slammed down hard on the brakes. The older brother fell to the street, but the younger one continued to run forward, a carton of eggs in his hand, and landed three or four of them on my windshield.

I drove miles away, to a tree-lined street by the water. By then the eggs had dried and it was a mess to clean up. It took me a half an hour to scrape and wash off the eggs, and another fifteen minutes to calm down.

I never mentioned the incident to anyone, because I knew they'd just say, "Oh, another one of your fights,'' and that I'd only be making more trouble for myself. But

I never went back to the minimarket either. Then one day as I was driving through the neighborhood, I was stopped at a light when my door slid open and Teddy Junior stepped onto my truck.

"He wants you back," Teddy Junior said. "My Arab friend wants you back in his store."

"Are you crazy? What is this? Is *he* crazy? Do you know what happened back there? Did he tell you? If he did, you know my answer's no."

"Anna, he wants you back. He didn't call your depot, but he said he wants you back or he'll call and make trouble. Big trouble. And I believe him. He's that kind of guy. He said if you come back and serve his store, he'll wipe the slate clean. You'll start again as if nothing ever happened."

"But you said I wasn't tied to that store. I was just doing you a favor."

"Yeah, but that was before. Now he wants you back."

"To hell with you and your Arabs," I said. "I just won't do it." But I didn't need any more trouble, and Teddy knew that, and he knew that I'd go back. I put it off for a few days, and went back on a Friday, around noon, when I hoped it would be crowded with people buying food for lunch. As usual, the older brother was on the first register.

"Good morning, pretty lady," he called out. I didn't answer. I served him as I always had, saying nothing, looking from side to side, and checking behind me as I worked. When I was done, after I pocketed the checks that he gave me, I turned and asked him, "How come? How come you want me back in your store? You don't need

HomeMade in here. You can have Hearthland, Crusty Bake, any of the others. How come you told Teddy to get me back?''

"You're right, pretty lady. I don't need HomeMade. Half of it is stolen anyway, by the guys who work here as much as by the customers. But I like you, pretty lady, I like having you in my store. That fight we had? So what? I fight with you the way I fight with my wife. It makes for the excitement.''

Well, I thought, it was fine with me as long as it didn't happen again. But I left there with a bad feeling, and I knew I was going to find a way to pay the Arabs back.

I visited Jimmy once more, a few weeks later when he was home recuperating. This time only me, Mario, and Baby Huey went. Joanie's time to have the baby was getting close, and Little Dominic went straight home every day after work.

Jimmy looked different. He'd lost weight and didn't talk much except to say that he was trying to get Home-Made to take him back. "Sooner rather than later," he said. "I can't stand it anymore." He said he was sick of listening to Mimi's mouth going at him all day long, was tired of the kids fighting when they were home, and was getting ready to shoot the dog, a white, furry little terrier named Rocky.

Baby Huey told Jimmy he should give Roger over at Douglaston a call. Said Roger ran a sprinkler-system installation business on the side and might need an extra hand for a few weeks. "No harm in trying," Baby Huey finished. "Roger's driving a new white Mercedes these days. Sprinkler systems must be making him a bundle.''

"Roger Thompson and his forty thieves," Mario said.
"What?"

"That's what everyone calls Roger and the guys who work for him. Wheeling and dealing every way they can."

"Roger from Douglaston?" I asked. "He was one of my trainers. He was the cheapest son of a bitch. Got me to buy him lunch."

"The guy makes a ton of money. Coulda taken you to the Rainbow Room," Mario said. "He keeps the Douglaston depot in a state of chaos, enough so you can't track what him and his compadres are doing. From what I understand, he makes sure the guy who checks the stale at the end of the day gets a lot of overtime every week. The drivers overstate their stale and the stale guy writes down that he has such-and-such returns that were smashed and thrown into the big Dumpster out back. That stuff gets turned into animal feed, and nobody can check how much goes in. Roger fixes up the figures from his end. Takes care of most of it over the phone, calling in the cuts and plusses, overcharges, unpaid balances, whatever he has to do. That way everybody gets a piece of the pie. Over there you can get away with anything short of murder."

"Yeah," Baby Huey added, "that's true in any depot. What they see and whether they decide to make trouble depends on if they want to pick on you or not. Always the case."

Jimmy's stomach growled real loud and we all laughed. "Is that all you have to say for yourself?" Mario asked.

"Nah." Jimmy looked embarrassed. "Mimi's on a new diet, so all she has in the fridge is cottage cheese and fruit and vegetables. That's not what a grown man eats. I need real food, rice, beef, fish, anything. But she doesn't want it in the house."

Baby Huey's face lit up. "Let's get some pizza. She won't get mad if we get it for you, will she?"

Jimmy laughed. "Nothing she can do about you bringing me a present. That would be great. There's a pizza place two blocks down, but they don't deliver."

"I'd love to take a walk," I said. "I'll get it. What do you want? Everything on it?"

"No anchovies," Baby Huey said.

"And no mushrooms," Mario added.

"Two pizzas with everything except mushrooms and anchovies, is that right? Any soda?"

"Yeah, get some soda, and a six-pack if you want. Mimi only keeps diet soda in the house."

"That'll be too much to carry. I'll go with you," Baby Huey said.

The first block, me and Baby Huey didn't say anything to each other. Then he started talking about the depot and Mario. "Did you see Mario the Mole bawling yesterday," he asked, "right in front of everybody? He looked so sad, I was afraid I was gonna start crying along with him." Baby Huey glanced over at me but I shook my head no. I hadn't heard anything about it. I figured it probably had something to do with his wife.

"Jed finally gave him the news about his route. It's been up in the air for weeks."

"I don't know anything about it."

"Well, they're getting rid of Mario's route. Consolidating routes is what they're calling it. Mario's being transferred to Douglaston to a route that's just opened up. He has only one more month at Knickerbocker Avenue."

"What? He's been on that route for twenty years, hasn't he?"

"At least. But the route don't do good figures, just average, I think. That's why they're taking him out and splitting his stores between me and Little Dominic. Mario's sales have never been nothing to talk about, but he clips his stores good with those boxes of his. Been robbing them for years and never a complaint. The switch is gonna kill him. Stores on his new route will never go for him using those big old boxes of his. He'll have to do something else or stop."

I didn't want to hear about Mario or the depot anymore. I was trying to think how to apologize for what happened after the meeting, for me getting so mean that day. But it was Baby Huey that started talking about it by saying, "You know, I've been wanting to tell you something, just to get things straight."

"I'm sorry," I said, "for what I said to you that time after the meeting."

"Thanks," he said, "I figured you'd be sorry later. But it's about me I been thinking. Whatever you said about me might be true, I don't know." He pounded his chest over his heart and laughed. "I don't know how much or how little I got in there, that's a fact. But it don't stop me from wanting to be with you, liking you a lot more than I knew, actually." He looked down at his shoes when he said, almost shyly, "Sex was nice, but that was only a part of it. Mostly, I liked spending time with you. I'm not saying I would've ever made room for you in my life, but I'm gonna miss you, miss having you for my girl."

"Me too. I miss you already." We were quiet again, but when we got to the door, I held his arm to stop him from going in. "I want something from you," I said.

304 / SUSAN JEDREN

"Anything," he said, but then he thought about it and smiled a funny little smile and added, "I guess."

"It's not something you'd think I'd ask."

"I'm not thinking anything, so ask."

"I want you to teach me to steal. Please, would you do that for me?"

"Are you crazy?" He stopped and faced me.

"No, I'm serious. I have no idea how to start. I do the same work that every guy in the depot does. More, even, than most. I work faster and harder than a lot of the guys, but I make half what any of you make. You were saying yourself, even the managers steal. Why is it different for me?"

"Look, you may not be my girl anymore but that doesn't mean I want you dead. Jimmy should be a lesson to you. No, the answer's no."

"You mean it's okay that everyone else in that lousy depot steals except me? Is that it?" I found myself yelling. "Fifty men can do it, but me being a woman is different? A fucking boys' club, and I'm still the outsider, that's what it is. Well, the hell with you. I'll do it my own way."

Baby Huey grabbed me by the arms and shook me, not too hard, but enough to make his point. "For the last time, I'm saying no. I don't want you asking nobody else either, you hear me? You think it's a breeze? That stealing comes easy to me, to anybody? It don't. Most nights I go to sleep feeling sick over it, scared of what might happen to me. As if life ain't hard enough. Get it out of your head. You hear me?"

Fine with me, I thought. I'll go someplace else for my answers. I shook my head yes and he took my hand and pulled me into the pizza parlor.

The place was crowded, filled mostly with kids in

blue parochial-school uniforms and a few tough-looking motorcycle types in black leather jackets. The noise of teenagers laughing, yelling, teasing, filled the room. "Relax," I said to Baby Huey, who was waving his hand back and forth, trying to get the waiter's attention, "it might take a while, especially with this many kids for them to wait on." Baby Huey pulled out two stools for me and him. We sat down, and for a moment he closed his eyes, letting his head fall onto his chest. I put my hands on his shoulders and kneaded the muscles, rubbing hard wherever they felt tight beneath my fingers.

"Hey, Wop Wop," one of the boys called out, "we want some Cokes over here." Baby Huey opened his eyes and followed the sound of the voice to the booth behind us. The boy had light brown hair and very blue eyes and was talking to a short, thin, dark-haired waiter with nervous flitting eyes. The waiter mumbled something in Italian and took out his pad.

"No Coke for me," a girl with curly blond hair said to the waiter as she lit up a cigarette. "I want an orange soda." The waiter wrote down their order.

"No, never mind, make it a diet orange," she said, pointing to a poster with diet orange soda on the wall. There were two girls and two guys in that booth, and the other girl also changed her order to a diet orange.

"Wop Wop, change mine to a root beer," the same blue-eyed boy said, and the waiter left. Meanwhile, a guy who looked more like a cook than a waiter came over and took our order and a few minutes later, the waiter for the booth behind us came back with a tray of sodas.

The blue-eyed boy took a sip of his soda and then grabbed hold of the waiter's sleeve as he was about to leave. "What's this? This isn't Coke," he said. "We ordered two diet orange and two Cokes. This isn't right, you dumb Wop Wop." The boy's eyes narrowed and he sucked in his cheeks as he threw back his head, tossing his hair out of his face. He glanced toward the boy sitting across from him. "Aren't I right, Paul? Taste this. This idiot gave us the wrong drinks." He pushed his glass toward his friend but the other boy looked away. The waiter nervously stood wiping his hands along the sides of his black vest.

Beside me Baby Huey started to get up, his fists clenched. I gently pushed him back down.

"No, is right," the waiter said, taking his pad out to show them where he wrote it down. "See here," he pointed to the bill, "is right what I have on the paper."

The boy grabbed the pad from the waiter. "Look at this." He held it up for the others to see, spelling it out, "R-O-T B-E-E-R. Wop Wop, they may have rot beer in Italy, but we don't have sodas like that in this country, not in America. We ordered two diet orange sodas and two Cokes and that is what we'll get." Baby Huey was out of his seat again just as the boy yelled "Now!" at the waiter.

"Is right," the waiter said again but took the drink away murmuring, "but is okay, I will bring Coke. Is okay."

" 'Is okay, is okay,' " the boy mimicked. "What kind of English is that?" Then he pushed a stool over with his foot, jumping aside as it fell.

Baby Huey headed for their booth. I saw him standing over the kid, pulling him up by his collar as the kid went to sit down. He was almost a head taller than the boy. "Is right," Baby Huey said. "And I'll tell you something else, little American boy. You better give my buddy here an extra big tip for having to be your baby-sitter as well as your waiter." He shook the kid a few times and then stood him up again. "I hope you understand. Am I speaking good enough English for you?" The kid didn't answer. "Am I?" Baby Huey yelled.

"Yeah."

"Good." He pushed the kid's face with a hand that was bigger than the boy's entire head and the boy sat back down.

Two young men in black leather jackets, barely older than the teenagers in the booth, were standing face-to-face with Baby Huey as he turned to walk away. Baby Huey was a lot bigger and broader than the other two, but across the knuckles of the two guys in leather was a lot of metal.

"We don't like some shithead coming in here and threatening the nice kids in our neighborhood," one of them said.

"I don't care what you like," Baby Huey said, moving slightly back and looking from one to the other.

"I think you should. Two against one, with a little extra help," the same guy said, raising his hand with the thick silver band across it in front of Baby Huey's face, "is something worth thinking about." Baby Huey grabbed the guy's wrist and forced his hand down as the second guy was about to jump him. I had a stool up and rammed it against the second guy's face before he got a chance to tackle Baby Huey.

"Two against two," I said and jammed the stool legs almost into his eye. He pulled away fast and then came back at me with his fist raised. I couldn't see what was happening with Baby Huey as I stepped forward and swung the stool again, this time clipping the guy across his forehead. He fell back, and I turned to find Baby Huey watching me while he continued to twist the wrist of the first guy, who was squirming on the floor. Out of the corner of my eye I saw two more guys in black leather jackets getting out of their seats and walking toward us. In fact, one teenager after another stood up until I was sure the entire pizza parlor was headed our way.

"You ready to take on this whole place, honey?" Baby Huey asked with a kind of half-smile.

"I don't think we have a choice." I grabbed another stool and stood at his side. Baby Huey faced the crowd of kids straight on and yawned.

"I'm going to need a smoke after this," he said. But none of the kids came nearer to us than about five feet, and after a minute or two, Baby Huey said, "Let's get out of here, I want some fresh air." Our pizzas, sodas, and a six-pack were waiting on the counter. I threw down two twenties and we left.

On the way back to Jimmy's house, Baby Huey walked with his head down, kicking every rock that was on the ground. Without looking up, he said, "It makes me crazy thinking you might be out there stealing. Promise you won't ever think about it again."

"Okay."

Two weeks later it happened that me and Mario were the last ones in on a Friday afternoon. I usually left earlier than he did. On my way to the train, I passed Mario as he was getting into his car and he called out to me, "Hey, Anna, I'm heading out to Jersey by way of the George Washington Bridge. You're near the bridge, aren't you? I could drop you off on the way." I never let on that I knew about Mario having to spend every night in a New Jersey jail for the next few months. The Jersey cops caught him driving with a suspended license and somehow HomeMade arranged that he get his license back, but Mario had to make it up by spending the nights in jail. Jimmy was sure Mario did it to get a vacation from taking care of his old lady, that he was glad to leave her with the hired nurse while he got a good night's sleep in jail.

It had been a long week. I missed having Joanie to talk to, and Baby Huey and me hardly saw each other anymore. I was glad for Mario's company and said sure.

I knew that Mario didn't want to talk about his transfer to Douglaston. HomeMade never gave parties, so in two weeks, after twenty years at Knickerbocker Avenue, Mario's truck just wouldn't be in that spot anymore. Instead we talked about the weather and stuff like that, but finally I asked him something that had been on my mind ever since we had been at Jimmy's together. "Was what you said to Little Dominic true that day, that everybody takes tips?"

He nodded and mumbled, "Yeah."

"Why is that? Is it just 'cause we can?"

"I don't know. The way I see it, the company rips the store owners and us drivers off every way they can. The storekeepers do the same in reverse. As a driver, I got to feeling so ripped off that the only way to make myself feel better was to get back at them by ripping *them* off."

"Do you remember when you first decided to steal?" I asked, following the line of his thick, brown hair from his neck down to his fingers on the steering wheel. "What happened? Were you scared?" He really did look like a mole or a hamster to me. I wondered if his wife minded him being so furry or if she was used to it.

"Well, my first time was an accident. I was only at HomeMade for a few months when it happened. I made a mistake and got away with it. Then I thought about doing it seriously, and I came up with the idea of using the boxes. Nobody ever questioned me. I seen the same thing happen with Baby Huey. He always rung his bills up on a calculator, was never without it. The first time he punched in the numbers wrong, he was off maybe twenty dollars. The manager said his total was way too high, it was impossible. So Baby Huey held up the calculator for the manager to see. The guy looked at it, said fine, and paid him. That afternoon I found Baby Huey sitting in his truck, trying to figure it out. I took the calculator from him, punched in the numbers again, and it came out right. Baby Huey saw where he made his mistake. He's been clipping stores that way ever since.''

The rest of the way we talked about the usual things, his family, my family, how much longer before Joanie had her baby. Mario did most of the talking and it was a nice, easy ride. ''I like to take the lower level of the GW Bridge,'' he said as we pulled up in front of my house, ''but when the traffic gets stuck, I can feel the bridge shake. Then I say my Hail Mary's until I get to the other side.''

''Well, I hope there's no traffic on the bridge,'' I said, trying not to laugh, and leaned over and gave him a kiss on the cheek. ''Goodbye, and thanks.''

I went to sleep that night thinking about the three Arab brothers and their minimarket, about how they treated me like shit and thought they could get away with it. I was finally going to get back at them. I knew those brothers were careful businessmen and that I had to be careful in planning how I was going to steal from them. I spent hours

thinking of different ways to do it and finally decided on
changing their bill. I knew if I'd told Mario what I was
thinking, he'd have said that all those Arabs were sneaky
and that they deserved it. But it just happened that it was
the Arabs that I was going to steal from first, it could've
been anybody. Hating the Arabs was just an excuse. I was
ready.

There was a loud crash in the night and I went flying out
of bed. I must have been sweating a lot, because my
pajamas were soaked through. The clock showed 2:00 A.M.
I grabbed an empty vase and went tiptoeing toward the
living room, hoping that Pudgy had heard the noise too and
would be there to help. There was another loud bang and
then nothing. Then I heard Pudgy's voice, so I followed it
in the dark. There was enough light coming through the
window to see that it was Pudgy and Nick. Nick hadn't
sleepwalked since he was about four years old, but I guess
he'd started up again.

"Nick, this isn't the toilet," Pudgy was saying.
"Come with me to the bathroom, big guy, and we'll pee
in the toilet." He had Nick by one hand and with the other
was trying to keep Nick from pulling down his pajamas.
"That a boy," he said like he was talking to a baby. "This
way, follow Pudgy, good boy." As they passed me, Pudgy
whispered in my ear, "I think you got some cleaning up
to do." When I heard the flush of the toilet, I turned on
the living room light. A lamp had fallen over. The bulb was
broken but the lamp looked in good shape. It was the big
comfortable chair that Nick had mistaken for a toilet. Half
the back and the entire seat were dripping wet.

Pudgy came out laughing. "He drank two huge

glasses of lemonade before going to bed tonight," I explained.

"Just like his mom," Pudgy said.

"What're you talking about? I don't wet anything." Pudgy pointed to my pajamas. He was right, I was a mess. "It's not pee, I must've been sweating." I went and changed into a dry nightgown and came back out. He had straightened the lamp and gotten up the broken glass. I cleaned the chair. We decided to pour vinegar over it like you do with cat pee, so it wouldn't smell. But after that, we had to leave the room, the vinegar smelled so bad.

We sat down in the kitchen and I offered him some of the lemonade that I'd made for the kids earlier that night. "Not on your life. Not after what it did to your son." We looked at each other and started laughing and then neither of us could stop. When we began to calm down, Pudgy started us up again by saying some really stupid things like, "Would you like a liquid lunch?" and "Lemonade, five cents a glass." Then we were off laughing again until tears were coming down and my stomach hurt.

"Why were your pajamas soaked with sweat tonight?" he asked when we finally quieted down. "Did something happen? Are you worried about something?"

"No, just the usual. The job, the kids, men."

"Chris seemed like a nice guy. What happened with you and Baby Huey? Is he history?"

"Yeah, that's over. There was a poem my English teacher made us learn in high school. I thought of it after my fight with Baby Huey. It goes something like: 'This is the way the world ends, not with a bang but a whimper.' In my head, I always turn it around so that it goes 'not with a whimper but a bang.' "

"That was why you were wearing that bandage, isn't

it?'' Pudgy asked. ''There's a scar across your lip.'' I
started to cry. I didn't know why. Not just because of me
and Baby Huey, but because of everything. How mixed up
I was. Nothing felt right anymore. Pudgy came over and
took me in his arms.

''It wasn't his fault,'' I said, and I found myself
repeating Baby Huey's words, ''he's not that kind of guy.''

''I'm not blaming anybody, I'm just thinking. Anna,
I never want to put you on the spot, but one thing I always
wonder is, why not me? What's wrong with me?''

''What?''

Pudgy sat there tearing a paper towel into tiny pieces
as he talked and I found myself carefully watching his
fingers while I tried to listen to his words. ''What about
giving me a shot? What do Baby Huey and Chris have that
I don't have? Is it that you aren't attracted to me? I ask
myself questions like that all the time.''

The words came spilling out. ''No. Nothing. I don't
know. I can say lots of things but none of them are exactly
right. You're my friend, Pudgy. I love you, and I think you
love me, that's true. And it might be nice sleeping together, maybe wonderfully sweet, who knows? But I can't
see myself feeling sexy and sensuous and trying all kind of
crazy things with you. 'Cause I don't think you want me
like that. 'Cause you see my breasts hanging out in flannel
and T-shirts every day. I can't see you dying for a glimpse
of my left nipple. And that's what I want.''

Pudgy started laughing again but when I asked him
what was so funny, he wouldn't answer. I waited but he
wouldn't stop laughing and after a few minutes I found
myself getting mad. ''What is it?'' I asked and then after
another minute or two I got even angrier. ''Pudgy, what
is it?'' I was almost yelling at him but he kept giggling.

"Please, please," he said, though I could barely understand him, "just one left nipple or I'll die."

"What?" I screamed and threw the roll of paper towels at him.

I started laughing as he came crawling along the floor, yelling, "Please, I'll do anything for a nipple." I tried to run past him but he grabbed my ankle, yelling, "A nickel for a nipple, lady, please." He held on tight while I dragged him across the floor. Then he took hold of the hem of my nightgown and wouldn't let go, tugging at it until he pulled me down on the floor with him. He held me there, pawing at me like a puppy, pulling on me and then tearing at the top of my nightgown. A tiny white button came flying off. "Please, be kind enough to give a poor dying man a glimpse of your one and only left nipple," he said.

"You're crazy, you're crazy," was all I could get out, I was laughing so hard, trying to keep my nightgown together.

"That's all I ask for in life." He pinned my arms down and grabbed the top of my nightgown in his teeth and pulled. The nightgown tore right down the middle, and, still using his teeth, he drew it back so that my nipple was exposed.

"At last," he called out. I tried to get him off, pushing and shoving against his face and chest, but he clung to me and I finally gave up. Then he gently rested his face against my breast, kissing it softly. We lay there, Pudgy nestled in my breasts while I stroked his head. We stayed on the floor for a long time, with me patting him and him playing with my breasts, sometimes sucking hard like a nursing baby, until he dozed off.

"What a jerk," I whispered softly to his sleeping face.

. . .

It was the older brother, like I knew it would be. "Hey, pretty lady, what a beautiful day it is, no?" I smiled and nodded and did everything exactly the way I always did. I checked the stock, went back to the truck to fill up my trays, piled the trays on the counter, counted the cake, gave him the bill, and packed out the cake. On the way out he gave me a check and the rest in cash. I looked it over quickly. It was exactly right. I said goodbye and left. I drove several miles, ending up at the same place I was a few weeks ago, where I went to clean off the eggs. I sat there looking at my copy of the bill. It had no date on it. I'd left it off so that if they checked I could say they'd mixed up their bills and that they were showing me a bill from another day. On the copy that I had in my hand I had written down *11* boxes of doughnuts. But I put a tip on the second *1* so it could be either a *1* or a *7*. Then, even though I had counted out eleven boxes of doughnuts in front of him, I charged them for seventeen. If he caught me, I was ready to say that I had accidentally mistaken the *1* for a *7* when I multiplied the price times the quantity. Since they hadn't caught me earlier, they would assume it was seventeen when they did their accounting, and it would add up correctly. I did it. No problem. But I had a horrible pain behind my eyes that wouldn't go away the whole day.

The next day I gave myself a break and did everything legal, but the following day I tried it again. This time I used a slight variation of what I pulled in the minimarket, changing a *5* to *15* on a bill for BestMart. BestMart was easy, because they used one of the stockboys to check me in while one of the bosses took the bill. In BestMart, one hand never knew what the other hand was doing. I was in and out of there as fast as it took me to load out the cake.

Big Mike's store, Bodega del Oro was pretty much the same. A different red-faced man smelling of alcohol checked me in each time. I could've held the bill upside down and backwards and I don't think they would've noticed. Big Mike's store I ripped off slowly, raising the bill by a dollar or two each week, so he wouldn't suspect. In a month I was making an extra ten dollars a week off him. He was one of the few storekeepers I was glad I was ripping off.

Some of the smaller mom-and-pop stores I clipped by bringing out stale and "forgetting" to subtract it from their total. Or I'd take one Choco out of every large box of Chocos and sell them to the smaller stores as singles.

It was a funny thing about stealing. A part of it made me sick, and I found that there was nothing I could do to feel good about myself as long as I was stealing. Store owners and managers and cashiers who had grown fond of me, calling me Sunshine and Smiley, gave me their trust and allowed me to do what I wanted in their store. And I repaid them by ripping them off. I would try to tell myself that in their souls they knew what I was doing. That every owner or manager takes stealing into account when he figures out his losses, and that I was just getting some of the benefits for a change. But I couldn't look them in the face anymore. I stopped smiling and calling out greetings and tried to slide in and out each day without being noticed.

And once I started, it got worse and worse. I'd think of something new I needed each week that the extra money could buy. I didn't know the exact figures of how much money I took from each store, but I knew for sure that it made life a lot easier. These days I never had to think twice about whether or not I could afford something. Most everything I wanted now was within my means. It seemed impossible to stop once I got rolling. And I was always on the lookout for new schemes. When we got a new packer, named Sam, I worked out all kinds of deals with him. The most reliable way involved his cousin. His cousin worked at the plant and regularly shipped him racks of extra cake. Sam would put some of the trays on my truck each morning, I'd sell them off, and we'd split the money at the end of the day.

I don't know why it was that I started getting careless. It wasn't that I wasn't smart enough, but somehow I just didn't care anymore. I think the first guy that caught me could hardly believe it. He was an older Puerto Rican store owner who used a fishing tackle box as his register. I wrote down that I'd taken out two dollars' worth of stale when it was really closer to five. He figured it out and asked me for the money I owed him. I didn't argue. "I'm your friend, no?" he said. "Su amigo. Then keep your hands out of my pockets."

Chris took to stopping by after work on Fridays. He told his wife he'd joined a regular Friday-night poker game and sometimes stayed as late as ten or eleven o'clock. Sometimes he brought dinner—pizza, pasta, heros—and other times me or Pudgy cooked. Chris always had a present for Nick and Joey.

One Friday night Chris had to stay late at work but showed up just in time for Nick and Joey's bath. The problem was, the boys were trying to prove to me that they weren't dirty and didn't need a bath. But this time Chris had bought two toy racing boats for the tub, and without another word, Nick and Joey threw off their clothes and jumped in. Chris rolled up his sleeves, handed me his watch, which I put on the sink, and practically dived in with the boys. Up to his elbows, anyway. I could hear the three of them laughing and splashing and making motorboat sounds while I sat on my bed, balancing my checkbook. Chris never even came to get me when the bath was over. He tucked them in himself and came tiptoeing out.

"I told them a story about a great speedboat race and I think they're settled down for the night."

"Thanks," I said. He sat next to me on the bed, took my pen and checkbook out of my hands, and laid them on the dresser, then began kissing my shoulder.

"By the way," he said, "what did you do with my watch?"

"It's on the bathroom sink."

"No, it's not. I just looked and it's not there. I looked on the floor and the windowsill too, but I couldn't find it."

"That's where I left it."

"Yeah, I thought I saw it on the sink before the bath, but it's not there now. Joey and Nick said they hadn't seen it, so I don't know where it could've gotten to."

"I'm sure it's in the bathroom somewhere. Maybe one of you racing-boat drivers knocked it down and it fell behind something." I got up and searched the bathroom but couldn't find it anywhere.

Chris was sitting on my bed looking through a magazine. "I don't see it either," I told him. "It's got to be around here somewhere. Do you mind if I look some more later and maybe bring it to you on Monday? Will your wife notice if it's gone?"

"Nah, that's fine. If she sees I'm not wearing it, I'll

say I took it off when I was doing dirty work in the store and probably left it in the office."

Later that night, after Chris went home, I began a search for the watch. I pulled the bathroom apart but there was no sign of it. I thought maybe Joey might've picked it up without thinking and carried it to another room. I went from room to room, looking under every piece of furniture, every cushion, but I couldn't find it anywhere. I started to get more and more nervous, I didn't even know why. I lay in bed and listened to the radio for a while to calm down and think about what could've happened to it. By the time I got up, I guess I knew.

I went into Nick and Joey's room and pulled out each of their drawers, running my hands through all their shirts and pj's and underwear. I didn't think they'd put it in with their toys, since it might get broken there. I did look through their books, thinking they might've hidden it between the pages. I ran my hand under Joey's pillow and then Nick's, but it wasn't there either. There was no light in their closet so I searched through it blindly with my hands. Finally I found it at the bottom of the closet, in Nick's sneaker. I left the watch there because I didn't want to scare him into thinking he'd lost it. I'd have to think of some way to talk to him about it when he woke up in the morning, to tell him I found it and see what he said.

That night I went to bed wondering why. I wasn't stupid enough to think it was in the genes. But it couldn't be just an accident that we both were stealing. Maybe he was feeling cheated or something, or that he didn't get enough from me, from life. I hoped that there was a good reason in Nicky's case, like that he was fond of Chris and wanted to hold on to something of his. But that didn't make it okay that he stole. I felt bad to think that maybe Nicky went to sleep feeling scared like I did every time I stole, afraid what would happen if he was caught.

I woke up the next morning not able to shake the heavy feeling I had from a dream. In it a disheveled woman with brown hair had a baby that she fried with food on the griddle. She moved the food from pan to pan, cooking the baby along with the scrambled eggs. The baby's arms were hot, so I told the woman to stop, but the woman wouldn't look up or listen to me. Another kid was standing by the woman's side, tugging on her skirt. The woman was so overworked and worn out that she didn't realize that she was burning her baby. The other boy screamed, "Mama, stop! Please, mama, stop!" I started to scream too, to warn her, but it was as if she was deaf.

The kids were still asleep, so I decided to do some cleaning while I had the time. I scrubbed out the tub and washed the floor, but even so, the bathroom still looked dirty to me. There was a stain in the tub from a dripping faucet that would never come out, the shower curtain was grimy at the bottom, and the windowsill was covered with a thin layer of soot. As I worked I noticed that the whole house looked faded and not very neat and clean anymore. What was happening here? I was working so hard to keep it all together—the house, the kids, myself—but it wasn't good enough, everything was going wrong. I started thinking about Nicky again until I couldn't think of anything but Nicky. Was I such a bad mother? Adeline's kids didn't steal. Mrs. Mahoney's kids didn't steal. Why was my kid stealing? I was assuming this was the first time, but maybe it was just the first time I caught him. Was I going to get a call from his teacher saying he took something from her or one of the kids at school?

I heard noises coming from Nick and Joey's room, and before they were even out of bed, I was standing by Nicky's side, telling him that I'd found the watch hidden in his sneaker. He tucked his head in his arms and I almost cried to see the ragged skin of the scar still there from the burn. But I wanted to get it over with and said he should think about it for a few minutes and then meet me in the living room so we could talk about it. I paced back and forth while I waited, until he slowly dragged himself in to see me, Joey trailing after him.

I walked over and stood in front of him. "Why?" I asked him. "Nicky, honey, what happened? Why did you take Chris's watch?"

He wouldn't look at me. He held his head high but he was looking over my shoulder at something on the wall, maybe at nothing, I couldn't tell. I grabbed him by the shoulders and shook him softly. "Nicky, look at me, tell me what happened." We stood there, me shaking him, but he wouldn't say a thing. "Tell me why. Did you want a watch? You know I would get you one for your birthday if you wanted. Was that it? Or did you want something of Chris's? What was it?" He kept looking over my shoulder, his eyes blinking fast but not crying, and not saying anything. I grabbed him by the side of his arms and raised him in the air, shaking him. I shook him hard as I yelled, "You got to tell me why. I got to know what's happening to you, don't you understand? You're my kid and if something bad is happening, it's my fault." Joey was grabbing on to my legs and screaming at me to stop, not to hurt his brother, but Nicky wouldn't say anything at all. "Tell me! Say something, anything!'' I shook him again and again and finally I lifted and flung him away, out of my arms, just away. He went flying through the air until he hit the wall, not hard, but not soft either, and landed like a rag doll on the floor. I was crying and Joey was crying, and finally Nicky was crying too. I held them both, saying I was sorry, not knowing what to do.

A Little One
Named Francesca

IT WAS ONLY TEN to seven on Friday morning, but I knew Chris and MaryJo got in early and I wanted to return Chris's watch so he'd have it before his workday started. I usually parked right in front of the store but today I drove around back to the lot reserved for employees because I thought I might stay a little while. Every time I delivered to Chris's supermarket, he slipped a note in with my bill scribbled on lined paper from an S&R scratch pad. I collected them in a drawer at home under my panties. They were all like these four:

*Every morning when I wake up I remember that you love me
and I laugh.*

I feel like I've died and gone to heaven because I have you.

At night I fall asleep thinking about you.

*I like to touch myself while picturing your breasts and
imagining I'm inside you.*

I felt like the luckiest woman in the world to have a man like Chris so crazy about me.

Only Chris, MaryJo, and Alex, the assistant manager, were in the store this early. I knocked and Alex had to unlock the door for me, since the store didn't officially open until eight o'clock. MaryJo and Chris waved to me as I went in to check the cake but they were standing outside Chris's office arguing. It was the first time I'd seen either one of them even slightly angry. I overheard MaryJo say something about the weekend schedule as I passed the office. Alex went back to fixing the tape on one of the registers. There was no stale so I marked down what was needed and came back with two trays of cake, knocking each time and getting Alex to let me in. Chris and MaryJo were still going at it, so I had Alex check me in and went straight back to the cake aisle.

I wasn't in a hurry today and had intended to stay and talk to MaryJo about the trouble with Nick and maybe spend some time saying sweet things to Chris, but now I wasn't sure. Maybe I'd hose down my truck in the back lot instead. Someone had written EAT MY CHOCO in red, and I knew Gus would never get around to cleaning it. I went behind the deli counter to look for paper, thinking I'd leave Chris a note and come back later in the day to say hi to him and MaryJo. I found the roll of paper that they wrapped cheese in and tore off a piece.

CHRIS—

WHAT'S ALL THE FIGHTING ABOUT? EVEN WITH YOUR BIG MOUTH GOING, YOU'RE STILL THE SWEETEST GUY THIS SIDE OF THE BROOKLYN BRIDGE. I LOVE YOU. CATCH YOU LATER WHEN THINGS HAVE CALMED DOWN. YOU'RE MY FA-VORITE MONKEY.

XXOO

I wrote another quick one to MaryJo, saying I'd stop by sometime after ten this morning, could she take her coffee break with me.

From the front of the store I heard what sounded like a small explosion followed by loud banging and a big crash. Then a scream rang out but it was cut short in the middle. After that, nothing. I knew whatever was happening up front was bad and unexpected. That Chris, MaryJo, and Alex were as surprised as I was. A bomb or fire is what I imagined.

I ran toward the front of the store, but for some reason I stopped just before I reached the end of the aisle. Instead of charging out, I carefully peeked around a wall of salad dressing and saw men dressed in S&R smocks holding serious guns on Chris, MaryJo, and Alex. A tall guy with red hair and a beard was talking and pointing. He looked relaxed, almost easygoing, while a short, husky guy went behind Chris, MaryJo, and Alex and tied their hands and feet together. The others were busy trashing the office, moving fast, like soldiers at work.

A huge part of the ceiling was ripped open and it looked like they had blown up the safe. Two of the men took sledgehammers to the desk and filing cabinet, which were in pieces within seconds. The red-haired man waved toward the back of the store and one of the men broke from the group and started walking in that direction. I was far away, on the other side from where he was heading, but I ran for cover as quickly and quietly as I could, toward the deli counter. I didn't want to abandon my friends, but I didn't know what else to do. Behind a curtain in the back, there were piles of boxes filled with paper cups, aluminum foil, and other supplies for the deli. I often went back there to use the restroom and I thought it would be the safest place for me to hide. There were shelves on one side with enough room under the lowest one for me to slip in and cover myself up with the boxes. That's what I did.

It was hard to tell what was happening, but it felt like the banging went on for a long time. I stayed there, crouched down and shaking, my eyes closed, hoping they wouldn't bother to search this small storeroom. I thought of what they might do to Chris and MaryJo and Alex and found myself crying, saying prayers that they wouldn't hurt them, promising that I would be a better mother and that I'd stop stealing, anything if they'd let them go. There was yelling, and the sound of breaking glass. Then a few more shouts. I counted to a hundred over and over again while I waited. It was some time before I realized that there hadn't been another sound since the glass and the shouting. I looked at my watch and decided to time myself. Five more minutes, and if I didn't hear any more noises, I'd sneak out and check what was happening. The five minutes seemed like hours, so I changed it to three.

It took longer than usual for the cops to get there because a call had come in a few minutes before and they were sent five blocks away to a car that had been set on fire. "It's the fourth robbery of this sort in four weeks," the sergeant said, "and the same pattern each time. Very professional, dressed in supermarket uniforms and carrying automatic weapons. They come in through the ceiling, blow up the safe, and smash the office to bits. They always stage a diversion nearby to keep the police busy while the robbery is taking place. One time the red-haired guy, who we think is the leader, waved to the officers as they drove by Best-Mart heading for a bar where a neat little fight had started. Too cool and confident, if you ask me. One time they'll be just a bit too cocky and that's when they'll slip up. It's just a question of when."

Chris and MaryJo never went to the hospital. They didn't even leave the store until lunchtime. The S&R head office sent word that there were no replacements available and that they were to answer all the questions from the police and then open the store as usual.

It didn't matter that there was a gash over Chris's eye and that his forehead was badly bruised, turning black and red where the short, husky guy had hit him with a gun. It didn't matter that after I untied her, MaryJo didn't stop sobbing until the police finally showed up. Or that she stood quietly trembling while they took notes on what happened.

After I fixed up a bag of ice for Chris's lump and talked with MaryJo until she seemed calmer, there was nothing much for me to do there, so I left, saying I'd stop back later in the morning.

It was ten-thirty when I dropped by again and by then Chris's left eye was swollen shut and the lump had grown to the size of an apple. MaryJo was still walking around in a daze, making all kinds of mistakes on the register. It made me crazy. What kind of life was this? I couldn't believe Chris hadn't called the office and made them bring in replacements for the day, for the next few days for that matter. Any of the deli or meat managers who rode around in their company cars, chatting and checking on S&R personnel, could've filled in for them. I found myself getting so mad that I had to leave. That night, when I took off my HomeMade pants, I found Chris's watch and the two notes I'd written to Chris and MaryJo in my pocket. I added the notes to the pile in the drawer and put the watch near my wallet so I wouldn't forget to give it to Chris the next time I saw him.

.   .   .

Sunday morning I made my best breakfast, fancy omelets and popovers that came out almost perfect. The kids and me were having a great time and I was hoping things were going to get better. I had had another long talk with Nick, and unless it happened again, I was going to assume that taking Chris's watch was a one-time thing. I decided to ignore the fact that the new pajamas Mrs. Mahoney bought Joey for his birthday had holes cut out front and back. No more worrying. At least Joey wasn't chopping at his hair anymore. I knocked on Pudgy's door and yelled, "Breakfast, come and get it!" but he said he needed to sleep and would be up around noon. I went to the boys' room to bring them in to eat and found Nick sitting in the middle of the floor next to the large kitchen garbage can.

"What's that doing in here?" I asked. "Who took it out of the kitchen?"

"I think Oscar the Grouch moved into our house last night," he said.

"Oh, really."

I knocked on the garbage can and a deep, growly voice hollered back, "What d'ya want?"

"Oscar, time for breakfast."

The lid flew off and Joey's head popped out. But when he tried to stand up, his foot had fallen asleep and he fell back in the can. "Hit it," Joey said, "hit my foot. There's sand in there."

I reached down to lift him out but it was so smelly that I backed away. He hadn't emptied the can and he was sitting in last night's garbage. We had had fish and sweet potatoes and broccoli for dinner and I could smell all of it when I got close enough. But breakfast was waiting, so I grabbed him out as fast as I could, then stripped off his pajamas, wrapped him in a bathrobe, and carried him into the kitchen. It was hard for me to enjoy the popovers and omelet with that smell at the table, but the boys didn't seem to notice.

By one o'clock I started to worry about Pudgy, and when he didn't answer my knock, I opened the door to his room and went inside. He was hidden under a pile of pillows with one leg sticking out of the sheets. I sat down and softly rubbed his leg, trying to wake him without startling him. Slowly he raised himself up from the pillows, sat back, and looked at me. He swallowed hard and spoke quietly. "I'm sick. I can tell it's bad this time. I think I've got to go to the hospital."

"I'm sorry. I'll help you get your things together and go over there with you. I'm sorry, sweet guy."

"You know," he said, "the facts are right in front of me but I try not to believe them. I've been nuked, my bones are getting worse, the pain's not going away. But I collect my little stipend from the government, go in each year for observation, let them see how far it's progressed, and pretend it's not happening, that it won't catch up with me. I'm scared it's catching up."

He sat there nervously scratching at his head, and when I saw his scalp beginning to bleed, I took his hand and brought it to my lips. I couldn't think of anything to say. After a few minutes I left so he could shower and dress. I started making calls to see who could take the boys. No one was home at the Mahoneys', and Adeline's husband said she was out shopping, but Lily said she'd come right over.

Nick and Joey went flying out of the house when Lily walked in and asked them if they were interested in going to the movies and dinner at McDonald's.

"Can we have popcorn and soda and ice cream? Mommy lets us have everything," Nick said as they ran out the door.

"What about candy?" Lily asked. "Does your mom let you eat candy?"

"Yes, if you say yes. Can we have candy too?"

"Yes, yes, yes to everything," Lily said as the elevator doors closed, and I could hear them laughing and jumping up and down in the elevator as it went down.

I called the emergency number Pudgy gave me for his doctor and made arrangements. While Pudgy was eating some eggs and a muffin, I packed his things in a large suitcase. Everything he thought he'd need was laid out in neat piles on his bed. It was obvious he didn't expect to be back for awhile. After he finished his breakfast, we left.

For the first few days, the hospital had him in a private room. That was all that was available. I helped him settle in, arranged for a TV, and fixed his room up pretty with some things I'd brought from home—a caterpillar that Joey made at school, a drawing by Nick of a baseball game, and a picture Pudgy had taken of me and the boys sticking our tongues out at him. While they were giving him tests, I snuck out and bought some chocolate and flowers. For the rest of the afternoon we read magazines and watched TV. Toward evening, when Pudgy started looking tired, I sat at his side, telling him stories that I made up about him and me being little kids together. I left a few hours later, only after the nurses asked me a second time to leave.

· · ·

In the middle of the week I got a telephone call from Joanie asking if I'd come to Staten Island for a visit. She'd been going through early labor for a few days but it'd finally settled down. "Dolores calls it the calm before the storm," Joanie said. "But I'm so bored and lonely lying around waiting for this baby, and I realized there wasn't any reason I couldn't have company. Is there someone you could borrow a car from and drive out here Saturday afternoon?"

"My next-door neighbor Mrs. Mahoney has an old car that I use sometimes," I said, "but I don't know what I'd do with the kids. Pudgy's not here and it's hard to get someone on the weekend to watch them."

"Bring them. And bring a friend if you want. We'll have a barbecue and I'll invite my sister Dolores. She always asks about you."

I always think all pregnant women are crazy and I don't think anybody can prove otherwise. They laugh and cry for all the wrong reasons, they're in such a daze they can't cross the street by themselves, and you can talk right in their face and find they haven't heard a thing. And Joanie was no different than every other pregnant woman I'd ever known.

We saw her sitting in a rocker by the window as we drove up, and when I pulled into the driveway, she came flying out the door, ran right in front of our car, and slipped on her behind. I screeched to a stop and when I went to see if she was okay, she wouldn't say a word, just sat in the gravel and cried. Thank God for Joey. He walked up to her and pointed to her belly. "Is that Zachary in there?" he asked her. Joanie looked at him like he was crazy as I helped her to her feet.

"Zachary's his friend Caroline's new baby brother," I explained. "No, Joey, there's a different baby in there. This is Joanie's baby, and a man named Dominic is the daddy."

"Is Joanie's baby named Zachary too?" Joey asked me.

"Well, right now, nobody knows if it's a boy or a girl, but I don't think its name will be Zachary."

"Francesca—what do you think of that name?" Joanie asked, brushing off her bottom and smiling down at Joey. Joanie hadn't gained much weight, except for her belly, which was huge.

"I like Zachary," Joey said and went up and put both hands on Joanie's belly. He laughed and jumped away when it moved.

"I think Francesca is a beautiful name," I said.

"Or Frank, Frankie, what do you think about that?"

"Frankie's okay, but I love Francesca," I said.

"I hope it's Francesca," Joanie said dreamily. I waited for Joey to say he hoped it was Zachary, but he was busy ducking under the bushes in front of the house, smelling flowers. Nick was sitting on a rock by the side of the driveway, blowing at a long blade of grass between his fingers, trying to make it whistle.

Chris got there about ten minutes later and parked on the street. He'd been planning to visit his grandmother in a nursing home on Staten Island anyway today, so I invited him to the barbecue. Joey came running out of the bushes the minute he saw Chris walking up the driveway. "Dressed kind of fancy, aren't you, young man?" Chris said, tussling Joey's hair. Joey was wearing his favorite blue and yellow jungle-print shirt. His pants were Nick's old green and black striped ones, and they barely reached Joey's ankles. Joey thought he looked cool. He checked himself out in the mirror and said so before we left our house. I wasn't going to argue.

Joanie had mentioned that Dolores was bringing her dog, and I was glad, because Nick and Joey loved dogs. Tom was allergic to everything, so we could never have a cat or dog when he was with us, and now I didn't want the extra trouble. When Tom first left, I bought the boys a guinea pig, but it died within a few months, mostly, I think, because I wanted it to. He was just a big, fat, dirty lump to me and I was sure he knew what I thought of him. I felt bad about it, but not bad enough, I guess, or I would've treated him better.

Before we saw Dolores, we heard her dog barking on the street. "Sounds like Joanie's sister Dolores and her dog," I said to Nick, who was standing at my side. Nick went running down the path and came back with a black and white and brown mutt barking at his heels.

"Isn't he great?" Nick asked and got down on his knees and faced the dog, who licked him right across the mouth. "His name's Norman and he's one year old, the lady said."

"The lady's name is Dolores," I told him, as Dolores kind of half-skipped up the driveway toward us. Me and Dolores hugged and laughed and pointed at each other because we looked like twins in our dungarees and white long-sleeved T-shirts.

When I'd asked Joanie how we should dress she had said to wear blue jeans. "We'll get nice and dirty in the backyard," she said. So I wore my favorite faded dungarees. But I must've gained weight in the last few months, because I had to lie down on my bed to zip them up. A few minutes before Dolores arrived, when I needed to use the bathroom, Joanie showed me to a small one off the kitchen. I felt ridiculous when I was done, lying on the cold tile floor, my feet on the wall, zipping the dungarees back up. Next time I was going to use the master bathroom.

Joey suddenly appeared out of nowhere, probably following the sound of the barking. "Its name's not Zachary," Nick said to Joey, "it's Norman."

"I knew that," Joey said. "Zachary's a baby's name."

"How'd he get the name Norman?" Nick asked after I introduced Dolores to the boys.

Dolores was looking from one to the other of us and smiling. "I guess I named him Norman because it was such an awful name," she said. "I thought it would teach him to stand up for himself when the other dogs made fun of him in school."

"I go to school too, like Norman," Joey said proudly.

Nick was rolling in the grass, holding his stomach and laughing. "Norman doesn't go to school," Nick said. "Dolores was joking, weren't you, Dolores?"

"I don't know, was I?"

Nick stopped laughing and asked seriously, "Weren't you? Dogs don't go to school, do they?"

Dolores grabbed him and threw him in the grass, tickling him as she explained, "Well, they can go to obedience school, but yes, I was joking, you smart boy, you," and Nick started laughing again.

"I think Norman's a great name," Nick said and rolled partway down the hill with Norman yelping and jumping around after him.

The last ones to arrive were Joanie's mom and dad, who I'd met at the wedding. They were friendly but quiet people. They didn't say much, but they smiled a lot, especially when Nick and Joey were around. Later in the afternoon, when we ran out of milk for coffee, it was Joanie's dad who took Nick and Norman on a walk to the nearest store to buy some more.

If I had a favorite kind of day, this was it. A sunny, easygoing, beautiful day with nice people. The only thing I missed was Pudgy, to make the feeling of family complete. Chris and Joey hunted for caterpillars and poured mustard in the dirt under the tree, trying to catch worms. Dolores and her dad, who loved to fish, goaded them on, trying to get them to fill a whole coffee can with worms. Norman and Nick became inseparable, and even though I saw very little of them, I knew they were okay by the sound of Nick's laughter and Norman's barking. Mostly all I did was sit under the trees in the backyard with Joanie and whoever else joined us, while Little Dominic barbecued. At one point I fell asleep in the hammock. There were so many things I wanted to say to Joanie and Dolores, but I knew it would have to be some other day when we had time to ourselves. And I was just as glad to spend the afternoon relaxing and cooling out, not talking except for some idle chitchat from time to time. I did tell everyone the story of how Chris got the huge bump on his head, because they all asked. And at one point, when Chris wanted to know if Dolores was the same Dolores whose card he had seen taped to the dashboard of my truck, I got embarrassed. Dolores looked at me and grinned. "Really?" she said. "Well, just so you know, the offer still holds."

The smell of food brought Nick to the backyard. He sat waiting for the hamburgers to cook with a shoebox filled with his baseball-card collection on his lap. He sat there arranging them alphabetically, then changed his mind and put them into teams and later redid them again by favorite players. Everybody else joined us out back when the food was ready. Joey pulled the skin off three hot dogs and then rubbed them in a mixture of ketchup and mustard before he gobbled them down. Nick shared his food with Norman, saying, ''A bite for me, a bite for you.'' After three pieces of blueberry pie, I told Nicky no more, realizing that so far Norman had eaten two of them.

Joey had been begging all day for us to play sardines, so after we cleaned off the table, everyone except Joanie, who went upstairs to rest, joined us in the game. Even Joanie's parents and Norman played. In sardines, one person hides and when someone finds him, they silently join the first person in the hiding place. In the end, everyone is hiding together and the last person has to find them. When it was Joanie's mother's turn to hide, I had to stop myself from laughing out loud when I found her giggling in the bushes.

I picked a big walk-in closet off the master bedroom as my spot, and Chris was the first one to find me. He tucked himself behind me and started nuzzling my hair. ''Am I lucky or what?'' he whispered in my ear.

''How did you find me so fast?'' I asked.

''Your perfume.'' He fit himself snugly against me and reached around to hold my breasts. ''This is a great sardine can,'' he said and pressed the front of his pants against my butt. He was already hard and was pressing himself between my cheeks. ''I swear, woman, you kill me,'' he said. I heard his zipper open and knew he was touching himself while he rubbed his hand over my butt. ''My God,'' he moaned.

''Put it away,'' I whispered, ''or I'll break it off. Someone'll be coming soon.'' I was glad I'd heard him zipping himself up because Little Dominic found us a minute later.

The last one to hide was Joey, and nobody could find him anywhere. Twenty minutes later I was getting really nervous, because it was late and the sky was starting to look nasty. I wanted to head out before it rained, but he was nowhere in the house or on the grounds as far as we could tell. I was almost frantic by the time Little Dominic took me to the back of the house and opened the door to the small room that was to be the new baby's. Joey was snuggled up, sound asleep, next to Joanie on a single bed, his arms wrapped around her belly. I left Joey there while I went to find Nicky and put all our things in the car.

Nick was trying to choose one of his favorite baseball cards to give to Norman. He wanted Dolores to attach it to Norman's bed when they got home so Norman would never forget him. Meanwhile, Chris helped me collect our belongings and pack up the car.

"Anna, something happened last night that's going to change things between us," Chris said as I opened the trunk and threw in balls, pails, and two bats. "I've been trying all day to find a way to tell you." Chris wouldn't look at me and instead kept staring down at his feet.

"What is it?" I asked. He looked so sad that I added, "Don't worry, I won't be mad. Whatever it is, we'll figure it out. We won't let something silly come between us." I thought he was going to confess that he slept with his wife.

"My wife found out about us," he said, swallowing hard.

"What? How? You didn't tell her, did you?"

"No, of course not. But last Friday night she called

over to where I'm supposed to be playing cards every week. My friend Brian would've covered for me but his mother-in-law answered the phone while he was in the shower and said there was no card game there that night, there never was. My wife says she smells your perfume on my clothes. She swore that if she even suspects me of seeing you again she's taking Jesse and never coming back. She'll change their names and start over someplace where I'll never find him. So this is it. We can't ever be together again.''

''What? Let me get this straight,'' I said. ''You came here and joined me and Nick and Joey for this great family day, one we'll never forget. You played with the boys and made them laugh, and they hugged your legs and held tight to your hands. You pressed up against me and told me what a sexy, desirable woman I was, how you could never have enough of my loving. You did one affectionate, caring thing after another, knowing the whole time that at the end of the day you were going to dump me?'' I could barely see. It felt like my eyes were coated and cloudy, and I almost lost my balance. ''I hope you rot in hell, you lousy two-faced bastard.''

''Now, Anna, listen to me. I'm trying to do this as nicely as possible, without us getting mad about it.''

I bent down and picked up one of the rocks that lined the sides of the driveway. This one was the size of a small cantaloupe. ''Do not stop,'' I said to Chris, ''do not pass GO, do not say goodbye to my kids or my friends. Leave now, without any more trouble, or I will break your head open with this rock and tell everyone that it was an accident, that you tripped.''

''Anna, honey, don't be stupid.'' The rock landed on his thigh with a thud. ''Ow, that hurt. Cut it out.'' Without another word, I picked up an even bigger rock and threw it to the left of his head. "The next time I won't miss."

"Stop, I'm going," he said. He was mad, his jaw jutting out, his teeth clenched as he walked backwards down the driveway to his car.

I told everyone that Chris got beeped for an emergency and had to leave immediately, that he asked me to say goodbye for him. It wasn't a very well-thought-out lie, but no one questioned it. After a lot of hugs and goodbyes and waving, me and the kids left too.

And then it started to rain. I was sure this beautiful sunny day took its cue from my life and turned dark and stormy. I hated driving in the rain.

As we passed over the Brooklyn Bridge, I cried quietly to myself, hoping Nick and Joey were too busy in the back with their coloring books to notice my body shaking. Thoughts came pounding through my head, one after another. I hate you, Chris. Why didn't you just call last night and say it was over? Why all this bullshit to remember you by? I missed him already. All the tenderness and goofing around, having someone I was so crazy about that was in love with me. Everything about him was perfect, his broad nose, his deep eyes, his shy smile and easy laugh, the mole over his eyebrow. Why'd he let it go this far?

I kept my eyes glued to the road, driving with extra care since I knew how mixed up and mad I was. As I drove onto the FDR Drive, the rain came down harder, so I turned the wipers to the fastest speed. I wished we were home already. The only good thing was that there were very few cars on the road, so I could drive at my own pace.

I found myself thinking about Chris again, and, of all things, what I started remembering was one of the stupidest times that we had had together. Even now, I couldn't help but laugh. It was a night a few weeks ago when Chris had stayed at my house later than he ever did before. Nick and Joey had been asleep for hours, and for some reason, Chris found it especially hard to leave this time. And I was making it even worse by teasing and begging, kissing and sucking on every part of his body and saying, "Please don't go. Just this one time, spend the whole night. Let the loving and sweetness last more than a few hours. Please stay, we'll make it the best night ever."

He didn't spend the night, but sometime about two or three in the morning, the radio was playing softly and Chris kind of drifted out of bed and stood in the middle of the room and began dancing. He was naked, and Chris was a pretty husky guy, with a wide chest and a big, full belly. He started to glide across the floor, his chest and belly weaving in and out like waves that started at his feet and rolled up across his body to his head. Chris said to watch carefully, that this was the way Marty, who was a head taller and half again as wide as Chris, danced with a mop in the back of the S&R. Softly, Chris hummed along, his feet taking small steps while the rest of his body gyrated in a rippling, jellylike mass. His left hand he held poised in the air, and his right rested lightly on his belly as his hips swayed forward and back to sound of the beat. Chris kept it up while I rolled around on the bed in stitches, laughing harder than I think I had ever laughed before. Even then I knew I'd never in my life forget Chris doing what we named The Dance of the Fatman.

Nick and Joey were very quiet in the backseat. I checked in my rearview mirror to see Joey asleep on

Nick's shoulder and Nick with a comic book in his hand, his eyes closed tight. Relax, I told myself, it doesn't matter if you get home a half-hour later. They're fine, it won't make a difference to them. But I hated the idea of coming home after dark and trying to find a parking space, especially on a Saturday night, when everyone had guests and all the spots were filled. And the thought of carrying Joey and dragging Nick a block or two in the pouring rain disturbed me more and more as we got closer to home. I picked up speed, but I was a good driver and I drove carefully, slowing down slightly to take each of those winding curves. That's why it was so surprising when it happened.

Later, the men at the garage said I must've hit an oil slick on one of those curves. I had no control of the car when we started to spin. The car just slipped out from under my hands and slid across the highway as if on ice. My scream must've pierced through Nick and Joey's drowsiness, because they were screaming with me as the car went flying across the highway. I stretched out my arm trying to reach for them in the back. "Nick! Joey!" I yelled. "It'll be okay, it'll be okay." The car turned and spun and smashed hard against a wall, then skidded to the other side of the highway and smacked into the divider. A second later we were bouncing off in the other direction again. It was one thud after another and I wasn't quite sure what we were hitting each time. Nothing I did helped, but I clung tight to the wheel and kept my head back so I wouldn't crash into the windshield. And I kept screaming at the kids that it was going to be okay and that I was sorry. After a while the car lost speed and came to a stop. I climbed over the seat to Nick and Joey, who were still screaming and crying, though they looked fine. One or two cars passed us but no one slowed down. Even later, when I got the kids out and tried to flag down a car, not one would stop for us. It took a long time for us to get across the highway. Cars were coming in both directions and I was afraid they wouldn't see us in all that rain. I crossed only when I was sure it was safe. When we got to the other side, we had to walk for two blocks to find a public telephone. On the way, I stopped at an apartment building and rang a few buzzers asking for help, but people were too afraid to let us in. Finally, I telephoned Tom and told him to come get the kids, that we'd just had a car accident and they needed him, they needed to stay at his place for the night. He started to protest that he didn't have room for them but I told him he had no choice, they couldn't come home with me. I gave him the cross streets and hung up.

After Tom left with the boys, I waited an hour for the tow truck. The garage I called said that if I didn't stay with the car, it would be stripped by morning. I sat on a low wall at the side of the highway in the pouring rain, watching cars almost crash into Mrs. Mahoney's car, still amazed that we came out alive. It never dawned on me that the car was totaled and there was nothing to save.

The house was emptier than it had ever been before. I thought of Chris and Baby Huey and Pudgy, and that there was no one for me to call. I hung up my wet clothes and took a hot shower, thinking I would make sure that Tom gave Nick and Joey a nice warm bath before they went to bed. But then I thought no, let him figure out what they need. It'd be a lot better for all three of them for Tom to make the decisions and for me to step back for a change.

It was late, almost ten o'clock, when I thought of Lily and decided to tell her what happened and ask her to spend the night. Like when I needed her for the kids, fifteen minutes after I called she was on my doorstep with an overnight bag in her hand.

In the middle of the night, I was sitting upright and screaming over and over again, "I don't want to die! I don't want to die!" Lily took me in her arms and tried to gently pull me back down into the pillows, but I couldn't lie down, so she rocked me back and forth, cradling me like a baby and murmuring in Spanish, words I couldn't understand. I don't know when I fell asleep again, but in the morning I was exhausted.

I remembered only the dream I had right before I woke, in which a young woman, who was not fully formed at birth, came out with a monster face. Her face was all smooth where her eyes and nose should be, and there was just a point, like a beak, for her mouth. I walked through the neighborhood that I lived in as a child, down all the familiar streets, with my brothers and some friends. So many of us were taking this walk, but it was only me that the young woman with the monster face didn't like. She followed after me, never letting me get too far away, and came up behind me and attacked me again and again, pecking at my shoulders, neck, and head whenever she had the urge. I kept running from her but I couldn't shake her. I knew I deserved whatever she was doing, that I was all the awful things she thought I was.

Neither Lily nor I had gotten around to closing the curtains the night before. In the morning light the blue walls looked dull, almost gray, the bedspread and curtains worn and faded. Lily lay on her back, snoring softly—

sawing wood for winter, is what Pudgy would say. I lay beside her, looking up at the ceiling, trying not to think of yesterday, or today, or tomorrow.

Instead, I thought of something that happened when I was ten years old. I'd gone to the bathroom and when I looked down I saw little worms wiggling around in the toilet bowl. I kept waiting for them to go away, month after month, not knowing who to go to for help. I couldn't think of someone to tell, so I just kept waiting, and it felt like it went on for years. One day, two young mothers who lived in my building were standing outside watching their kids play tag in the courtyard. I was waiting for Carmela to come down. One of the mothers said her little girl, Maggie, had been itching her butt and that she took her to the doctor last week. "Pinworms, that's what the doctor called them," she said. "They're awful to look at, tiny little white worms squirming around, but the doctor gave Maggie medicine and I think they're gone. One two three, just like that."

I walked over and stood between the two young mothers and looked hard into Maggie's mother's face. "Me too," I said.

"What?" she asked. "Me too *what*?"

"I have worms too."

"Well, what is your mom doing about it? Did you get medicine from the doctor?" I looked down at my sneakers but didn't say anything.

She took my face in her hands. "She doesn't know, is that it?" I didn't answer. She touched my hair and said, "Don't worry anymore, sweetie, I'll take care of it." The next day I was in the doctor's office and he gave me the same medicine Maggie took. This was what I thought of as

I lay there that morning after the accident, I have no idea why.

Lily stuck around all day, and I was glad for the company. She came with me while I shopped for food. We went for a bike ride after lunch, and at night she sat around listening to music while I cleaned. We didn't talk much. I couldn't.

Sunday night she asked did I want her to stay another night and I said yes.

"Do you know what you're going to do?" Lily asked.

"About what?"

"About everything."

"I don't know. I guess things were starting to get to me, huh?" And then I began talking like I'd never stop. But it felt like I was talking about someone else. I told her about the fight with Baby Huey and about Chris breaking up with me. "We would have had so many good years together, I'm sure of it," I said. "And I would never have asked him to leave his wife, to leave Jesse." I told her about my stealing, and about Nicky and the watch. I described how scared I was during the robbery at Chris's store and how it seemed that none of them, not Home-Made, S&R, the Arabs, or the union gave a shit about the people who worked for them. And I told her how tired I was of it all, and yet I was becoming worse than any of them. And I knew I didn't have the answers, but I also knew I couldn't go on the way things were.

Lily told me a story about her grandfather, and how when he was thirty and married with three kids he was unhappy with his life but didn't know how to change it. Then one day, he was taking his wife and three kids on a ride to town when he decided to race a train. The race was over quickly and he lost, their car ending up right smack in the middle of the track when the train hit. His wife died and the three children, one of whom was Lily's mother, were badly bruised. The only reason the court didn't charge him with manslaughter was because the children would've been made wards of the state.

"Different strokes for different folks." I said.

"Yeah, great! Well, he could've tried something else."

"If in trouble or in doubt, run in circles scream and shout."

"What's that?" Lily asked.

"My brother used to walk around the house saying that when he was upset," I answered.

I called my job and told them there was a death in the family and took a week off.

"Tom? Hi, it's Anna."

"Well, at least this time I don't have to ask you if anything's wrong with the kids 'cause the kids are here with me. They're in the bath."

"I was calling to say goodnight to Nick and Joey. It's kind of late for a bath, isn't it?"

"No. Bedtime here is later than when they're living with you."

"Well, I'll try again later, but if I don't get a chance to talk to them, would you say goodnight for me?"

"Sure, and you and I need to talk real soon. Anything else?" It was quiet while I tried to decide if now was a good time to ask him the question that had been on my mind for days. Then the phone slipped out of my hand and banged along the floor. The mouthpiece was cracked from the last time I dropped it, when I called Lily after the accident. Now I saw a small piece of plastic go flying under the fridge. I got down on the floor and pushed my fingers under the fridge until I caught hold of the broken piece. It was almost a minute before I picked up the phone again. "Sorry, the phone dropped." And then, finally, I got it out. "Tom, I actually wanted to talk about me, which I guess is about Nick and Joey too. Can I call you after they go to sleep?"

"Well, everybody goes to sleep the same time in this house. What about now? I just put them in the bath, so we have fifteen minutes. Shoot."

There's never going to be a good time to ask, I thought, so it might as well be now. "Hold on a second, okay?" I poured a glass of apple juice, took a sip, and began. "Well, I keep trying to make sense out of what happened, but all I know for sure is that that was a real bad accident that me and the kids had."

"Obviously. The car was totaled. But the kids are okay, and that's what matters. So there's no reason to keep worrying about it."

"Tom, I was going nearly seventy miles an hour on a narrow curvy highway in the pouring rain. I could barely see out the front window. The fact that we all weren't killed is amazing."

"Don't be so hard on yourself," Tom said cheerfully, "everyone deserves a second chance."

"I don't want a second chance to do something like that again."

"Aren't you being a little dramatic? Anyone can have an accident."

"I don't know, I hope so. But the fact is, I almost killed me and Nick and Joey. And it wasn't just an accident. I was at fault. I don't seem to be holding it together anymore, I'm just not making it." I took another drink of juice and swallowed hard before I went on. "I been thinking about Nick and Joey, that's all I been thinking about the last few days, and what I keep ending up with is that they shouldn't come back to me right now. I need a few months to get my life in order before I can be a decent mother again."

"What?" he yelled, and my hand flew out and knocked over the glass of juice. It crashed into the sink as he went on. "Anna, those boys are four and six years old. They're not much more than babies, and they need their mother."

"That's not true," I said, "they don't need me in the state I'm in. I'm their mother but I'm no good to them if I'm feeling trapped by it all, and I don't how to make it different right now." I cut my hand picking up the glass and wrapped a paper towel around it to stop the bleeding. "You got to help me. You got to help them, is what it really is, 'cause they shouldn't have to go through this with me right now. I got to stand on my feet again and then I'll be ready to take them back."

"I think you're crazy, is what."

"That's what I'm trying to tell you," I said.

"I can't believe you're asking this. I never intended to be a father *and* mother."

"Look, do you think for one second that I want to hand my kids over to someone like you? I'm desperate!" I heard myself screaming.

"I'm going to hang up if you keep yelling at me. I don't have to take that from you anymore."

"I'm sorry. See, I've stopped. I'm sorry."

"Okay. Okay, let me think about it. The idea is insane, but let me think about it." He hung up.

Tom called a week later. "Three months, that's what I'm giving you. You better get your act together by then, missy, 'cause that's all you're getting. My lease here is up in two weeks, so me and the boys will be moving in after that. That means I'll want you out a few days before. Is that clear?"

"Uh-huh."

I had to sit down. I never expected him to say yes. I had no idea where I'd move to. We'd been in that apartment for over five years. Before Washington Heights we'd lived in a housing project on 125th Street. I couldn't go back there. But it didn't matter now. He said yes. And the second he said yes, I felt Nick and Joey being torn from me, I felt the loss deep in my gut.

There's a hole in the bucket, dear Liza, dear Liza.
Theres a hole in the bucket, dear Liza, a hole.
With what shall I fix it, dear Henry, dear Henry?
With what shall I fix it, dear Henry, with what?

That song kept running through my head all day long while I cleaned and cleaned.

"What will I do now?" I asked Lily.

"Get back in your truck and drive, 'cause that's what you do well and you need the money. Get yourself packed and out of the neighborhood, maybe move downtown. Start again. Think about what you want for you."

I went back to HomeMade and started delivering

again. Things were worse than bad. I was stealing everywhere and stole as much as I could from Chris's S&R,
almost wishing he would catch me so we could have it out
again. Right now me and Chris were cold toward each
other, acting like we'd never met. I don't think I was very
nice to MaryJo either, because I couldn't bear being in the
store anymore. I was losing all the friends I had at Home-
Made and on the route. Mostly I was just passing time, not
knowing what to do next but knowing that I had to get out.

The same day that Joanie had her baby—a girl, Francesca—I moved downtown, to a temporary furnished
apartment at Ninety-fifth and Broadway. I called Joanie at
the hospital and sent flowers. I also bought the stroller
they'd picked out and had it sent while I was fixing up my
new place, trying to make it look like my own.

A few weeks before, I ripped Dolores's business card
off my dashboard. But after I was settled in my new home
for a few days, I found myself wanting to talk to her again.
It took me a week to get up the nerve to phone her, but
I was glad when I finally did, because Dolores was nice, as
always. First thing she said was to tell Nicky that Norman
slept with the baseball card taped to the pillow in his
doggie bed. Then she told me all about Francesca. That she
was long and lean and had beautiful blue eyes and a single
tuft of dark hair sticking out from the top of her head. That
she was alert and sweet and had a nice, strong yell when
she wasn't getting what she wanted.

We laughed together when she described how Joanie
and Dominic were so nervous that their hands shook when
they diapered the baby. Dolores said she loved the luxury
of being crazy about a baby without having to have one of

her own. And then she asked me a lot of questions about how I was doing. It wasn't long before I was telling her how bad I was doing on the route and about giving up Nick and Joey.

"So does this mean you'll be coming to me for a job soon?" she asked.

"Are you serious?"

"Look, Anna, I'm very serious about my work. And I take pride in the fact that I have good judgment, especially where people are concerned. I'm telling you that if you want to, I'd be glad to take you on. I'd have to work my butt off teaching you about the kind of work I do, tutoring you on how to work on a PC and all the ways of an office, everything I think you'd need to know to get through an interview with my bosses. But I'd be happy to do it if you want to give it a try."

"I've never even been in an office," I said. "I know that seems lame, but I never had a reason to be."

"I don't care. I'm up for working with you, if you are."

"But why?" I asked. "Why would you do that for me?"

"Why not?"

The first evening, when I met her in front of her office building, I warned her again that she was getting the bottom of the barrel if she took me on. But she said the bottom of the barrel was no different from what was on top. And she thought I was the kind that was going to kick my feet and swim to the top no matter what. That woman knew how to make me feel good.

Every evening after work I met her in front of her

office building. It wasn't easy, what she took on for herself, being my coach, my tutor, my mentor, all those things she was doing for me, because when I started, I didn't understand the simplest things. I couldn't even find my way back from the ladies' room through the rows of cubicles to her office. I stood in one of the aisles and called her name until she found me. And that was only the beginning.

Dolores made a book for me, which she divided into sections with titles like Computer Graphics, PC, Office Terms, Buzz Words, and others. She made sure I kept it with me all the time. Then she took me over every inch of the office, from the floor plan to the supply closet to the drawing board to my computer. I wrote down everything I learned and needed to remember. She made me practice over and over again—turning the computer on, logging on and off, using the mouse, naming and describing everything I did as I went along. We also worked on weekends, and when we weren't working together, I was studying my notes, even memorizing them because I'd always been good at memorizing.

I was amazed that someone thought I could be something more than I ever dreamed I would be.

I only saw Nick and Joey twice during those weeks. Both times they were dirty and their hair looked like it hadn't been combed in days. They showed up in ripped sneakers and wrinkled clothes that barely fit. But I had to admit, they were smiling. Both of them talked a mile a minute as they filled me in on everything that I'd missed in the time I hadn't seen them. Tom had found a tiny broken-down two-wheeler on the street and he fixed it and was teaching Joey to ride. Grandma Vera was thinking about getting a dog and had promised Nick he could name it Little Norman. They bought a bowl of fish but Tom had dropped it and both boys were sure the fish had slipped through the cracks in the floor and were living downstairs with the neighbors. For the most part, it was clear that the boys were doing fine with Tom. Much better with him than with a mom who just wasn't making it. And I kept saying to myself that I was doing what I had to do for me, and hopefully for them too. The truth was, I felt lost without them.

"Know something funny?" Pudgy asked, almost a month after he'd been admitted to the hospital. I shook my head no, so he went on. "With everything that's happening to my body, I got this huge hole in my tooth, and the thing I'm afraid of most isn't the cancer but the dentist. Whenever I'm in the dentist's chair, I flex my feet and tense my muscles so tight that by the time he's done, all my muscles hurt. They're bringing a dentist in tomorrow, and I've been having nightmares about it for days."

"I'm sorry," I said, covering my mouth and faking a yawn to keep from laughing. "Do you want me to be here when he works on your tooth? I'd be glad to come and hold your hand."

"No, I don't want him to think I'm a baby."

Dolores went shopping with me to pick out two sets of clothes for the interviews. I had three interviews for the job as administrative assistant to the vice president in charge of marketing and design—in other words, Dolores's right-hand person. The first interview was with her, the other two were with her bosses. Afterwards, Dolores told me that when both her bosses said I was very light in my knowledge of computer graphics, she'd looked them right in the face and said, "Anna's not light, she's a total novice." They said that as long as she took into account that I still had a lot to learn, they thought I would do fine.

"With a lot of hard work, I think she'll be one of the best," she told them.

Everyone treated me nice when Dolores introduced me around, saying I was going to be starting in two weeks as her assistant. I hoped no one noticed me checking them out to see what they were wearing and how they walked and talked. I thought of when I was a kid and I used to watch the neighborhood women through the window, trying to figure out how I wanted to look when I grew up.

I quit HomeMade a week before I started my new job. No one but Little Dominic was around my last day to say goodbye. Joanie was still out on leave, and it wasn't clear if she'd ever come back. Jimmy was on a route again, but more silent than ever, barely nodding when he passed me in the garage. Mario was working out of Douglaston, and I'm sure Jed purposely stayed away, knowing it was written all over him that he wasn't sorry I was going. Only Baby Huey, who was on vacation, had taken me out to lunch the week before. He held my hand and said that all the guys were definitely going to miss me. And Sam, the new packer, made a point of leaving me a box of doughnuts with a note telling me it had been nice working with me.

By the time I left, there were very few people on the route that I cared about or who would notice I was gone.

In S&R Supermarket, MaryJo gave me a hug and a pink rose as Chris looked on. He mumbled something about how glad he was that I was getting out of this life and that new opportunities were opening up for me. But that's not what I wanted to hear from him. I wanted him to follow me out of the store and say how he was going to miss me terribly, that he already did, and that there was an emptiness in his life without me. That he'd never forget me or stop loving me and that he didn't want to let me go. Instead, he just stood by the register, head down, not even looking up when I passed by for the last time.

Tia Vieja was dead, but I stopped by the bar to say goodbye to Millie and to tell her that I wouldn't be coming by with boxes of Chocos anymore. "No importa!" Millie laughed. "Los niños no quieren mas. We don't eat that kind of cake anymore. I was still buying them just to make sure I got to see you every week. Now that you're going, we'll stop for good." Then she yelled over her shoulder to Raul, "Raul, ven aqui with two glasses of wine for me and the missus!" Raul showed up, wiping his hands on his apron, and handed each of us a glass of red wine. "The best to the best," Millie said, pressing her glass against mine.

"To the future," I answered, and we emptied our glasses.

Hernando and his wife and the girls had finally made the move to their little house in Florida. A few months ago Hernando had sent me a postcard telling me that the last baby was another girl, and that she was the sweetest one of all. They called her Sucre.

My last stop on the route was to Nueva Vista to say goodbye to Angel. Angel was standing behind the counter, laughing as usual, his arm around a pretty little pouting girl in a flowered sundress. Angelito was older now and was more often out playing on the streets than trailing after Angel in the store. But there were always lots of other niños around. Angel came toward me smiling and I cried when he took me in his arms and held me tight. "So this is it, huh, mala puertorricaña? It is time now for you to leave us, no?" he asked quietly, softly kissing my cheek and rubbing his face in my hair. "It was a good life for you for a while, but now it's time to move on." He held me away from him and looked carefully at my face. "I will always save a place for you in my heart," he said. He placed his hands along the sides of my face and kissed me long and hard on the lips and then pushed me away. "Adios, mi amor."

Maybe there were a few others on the route that I would think about over the years. But it was clear that it was time for me to go, and no one was surprised I was leaving.

Driving the truck into my spot for the last time, cleaning it out, and hanging up my keys by the side of the cashier's booth seemed to take such a long time. I left my route book in Jed's office and threw out most everything else. It was only when I was walking out of the garage that I remembered the little pearl-handled gun hidden in the bottom of the safe. I went back and dug it out and put it in my pocket. Then I went looking for Little Dominic.

"Give it to Baby Huey for me when he comes back, will you?" I asked. "I have no use for it anymore. Baby Huey will know what to do with it."

It was a sunny, cool day in September. I was dressed in a black suit, black pumps, and a trenchcoat and was walking down Gold Street in the Wall Street area. I glanced around and no one was looking my way except for a cute Federal Express guy delivering a package. At first I was sure he thought I was weird because I was smiling to myself, but then he winked at me.

A few blocks later I stopped on the corner of Gold and Maiden Lane and faced all those big buildings on Wall Street that I had heard so much about. I clenched my fists tight and found myself yelling at the top of my lungs, but silently, so no one on the street could hear me. Mama, I screamed inside, look at me. Take a good look, will you? I am one fucking lady dressed in business shoes walking down Wall Street. Can you believe it? Not a housewife, not a trucker, nothing like what you'd expect of me. I am a fucking working woman going to her job at a desk like every other fucking person I see. And no one's looking at me like I'm any different than anybody else.

And I called out to Nick and Joey too. Hey you guys, I cried, hold on, you sweet guys you, and keep holding on for just a while more. I'm coming back to get you, so don't you worry. Soon, I'm not sure when, but know inside that I'm coming back. And just remember I love you.